Dive

Dive

LISA TEASLEY

BLOOMSBURY

Published by Bloomsbury, New York and London
Distributed to the trade by Holtzbrinck Publishers

All papers used by Bloomsbury are natural, recyclable products made from
wood grown in sustainable, well-managed forests. The manufacturing
processes conform to the environmental regulations of the country of origin.

Library of Congress Cataloging-in-Publication Data

Teasley, Lisa, 1962–
   Dive / by Lisa Teasley.—1st U.S. ed.
      p. cm.
ISBN 1-58234-398-5
   1. Crime scenes—Fiction. 2. Alaska—Fiction. I. Title.
PS3620.E43D58 2004
813'.6—dc22
                                          2003015293

First U.S. Edition 2004

1 3 5 7 9 10 8 6 4 2

Typeset by Palimpsest Book Production Limited,
Polmont, Stirlingshire, Scotland
Printed in the United States of America
by R. R. Donnelley & Sons, Crawfordsville, Indiana

for Daniel

Chapter 1

The Farmer in the Deli

Ray

Ray didn't know that the South Florida property on Indian River Drive was willed to him by a wily old man who had opened the phone book, closed his eyes, and put a manicured fingernail on any name just to avoid leaving it to the sister he despised, or worse yet to charity. The old man happened to be pleased with his choice. His finger hadn't landed on any initials—which would have meant a woman—and luckier still, the first and last names were monosyllabic. Ray Rose. The old man then died as he wanted, peacefully and alone of throat cancer.

Legal papers arrived exactly one week after Ray had killed a man as young as himself. It was a murder of principle. Ray hadn't slept more than two hours that entire week, and when he'd opened the mail he was devastated. How is it, he wondered, that he was anonymously rewarded for his crime? But one thing had nothing whatsoever to do with the other. It was a freakish concurrence. He didn't know yet either that not only had this property and a little money just fallen into his lap after his hideous deed, but he would also find the kind of love he'd tried three times for and failed. All he'd have to do was leave Florida for Alaska to claim it.

Before Ray moved into the house on Indian River in Port St. Lucie, he lived in a Jensen Beach shack that was a two-bedroom apartment split off into the bachelor he occupied. On the other side in the one-bedroom was Gary, who insisted he was living with his brother. Ray knew it was his lover and wished he'd say so. Gary was the cook at Conchy Joe's where Ray used to bartend when he was working two jobs besides construction. The locals were welcome there barefoot and shirtless until the arrival of high-rise condos and hotel-fancy old folks. By the time Ray left with the management change, even tank tops weren't allowed. And this was a shame since locals were the better tippers. In those fonder Conchy Joe's times well before they were neighbors, he gave Gary rides home on his motorcycle. Ray was still living in Fort Pierce with his treacherous second wife and her kid.

Born and raised in Union City, Michigan, population eighteen hundred, Ray had no one to play with but his two older sisters and the girls on the neighboring farm. There had been no boys born for miles, way past the five hundred acres of Ray's family farm. He ran around most with his middle sister, Sadie, who would take their father's truck to the nudist colony, sit smoking cigarettes or joints, and watch various textures of flesh on the landscape. Because of his oldest sister, Sonya, Ray could expertly massage feet, braid hair, buff and paint fingernails in intricate, gaudy designs. His father took a picture of Ray playing with dolls, and said that later he would use it against him. Since the dolls were then attached to a threat, he turned his focus to the animals. Black-and-white dairy cows, spoiled cats, and ravishing, stubborn horses gave Ray his first few lessons on the nature of love.

Ray was always the tallest boy in class. Strong, quick, and deft with his limbs, he learned early on how to hide his feminine side in the crucial moments. And just as important in the face of a bully's challenge, he found how to bare the raw, naked nerve. Few dared to mess with him in grade school.

Hard physical work came naturally to him on the farm, so when he moved to Florida at eighteen for the community college in Fort Pierce, carpentry led him to construction, which he'd always preferred over restaurant service. He found soon, as well, that he preferred women to girls. Days before his nineteenth birthday, he married the apartment complex's most rakish beauty fourteen years his senior. That's when he really learned how to fight.

On the construction site they called Ray "Goldilocks." While in Michigan his hair was naturally corkscrewed and the color of oak veneer, the Florida sun bleached his strong curls a soft and lank platinum. He'd grown his hair long to avoid a red neck. Standing six foot five, he caught driveby whistles from the girls ogling his sinewy, tan legs in cutoff shorts, and so he also caught endless shit from the guys. Gary from Conchy's was a foil to all the locker room swagger. The two would play poker with neighbors, or go sailing in the manager's boat much like the one Ray later bought to dock across the street from his inherited home. That this house stood under power lines with a view across the river of the nuclear power plant was the booby prize Ray thought he deserved. There were the pilings to avoid when swimming. Just as menacing was the dock's leading edge—the mounds of fire ants, whose sting felt like someone put a cigarette out on his flesh.

During his precious few free hours, he made a splendid master butterfly garden just beneath his bedroom balcony. He did this without removing all of the native sea grapes in front and the palmetto field in back that had taken over most of the lot. He also aimed for subsistence, the herbs and vegetables whose seasons he knew intimately. He drew up plans for a greenhouse.

Gardening, like farming, was calming to him. Speed too. He found comfort in adrenaline, whether it was handgliding, a roller-coaster ride, or driving his long beloved Hemi-Cuda, which he sold for eleven thousand dollars just weeks after he'd put a dead man's body in the trunk.

With his mild dyslexia, it was mostly a frustrating experience trying to read the books Gary lent him. Still, he would push on through to prove his grade school teachers wrong. As a friend, Gary was a good transition for Ray. Gary could play a good game of poker, but he didn't down beers, hound strippers, drop acid, or pick fights with rednecks in bars. All of these things Ray's college friends aced, and with exception of the strippers, he had gone along in moderation with the rest.

Ray never forgot his macho initiation the first day on construction. A guy named Fran hit his thumb so hard with a hammer that he turned the instrument around while yelling to his thumb, "Throb, you bitch," and proceeded to cut the thumb off. It tumbled off the roof, blood spurting. Ray struggled not to throw up. Fran was rushed to the hospital where they sewed it back on. He returned to work two days later. Ray soon found that Fran had always been on steroids, consistently amped. Every day Fran brought his coffeemaker in, and rather than using a mug, he drank from the pot.

Compassionately, the guys didn't make Fran pay for the beer that day, though it was a site rule that whoever bled had to treat. They would circle the drops of blood for the number of cans. For three years Ray avoided springing for the crew until the day he'd had his fill of an asshole who beat his own dog and pestered the guys daily. He told one prowess joke too many, and Ray pushed him straight off the roof. Miraculously he was fairly unharmed, save two broken ribs. But at the same time this was happening, a few guys were shooting nail guns for sport. Ray was hit on the forearm, and instead of cans they all figured he should spring for six-packs. This was a small price compared to the guy who months later caught a nail between the eyes. Still, Fran's thumb remained the epitome of hardcore site brutality, except for the one fatality Ray missed witnessing, having been two scaffoldings above.

Ray eventually left that company for another owned by a contractor named Kirk, whose son was the lazy crew leader. Wasn't long before Ray got the son's job, and not once on Ray's watch did anyone ever overturn a Plop John to reveal the maggots. This happened everywhere else in order to get the day off. They knew the health inspector would come shut down the site. Ray kept his sites clean and orderly, and was always fair. He worked twice as hard to cover any other's slack or hangover, just as Kirk gave every lagging drunk the benefit of doubt. Even when Kirk, fat and sweet, fell on the roof and slid off with the ladder, landing one story down to a broken foot, he took it in stride. He suffered Ray's raucous laughter over the event as well. Like all the other guys at times he flaunted ignorance, but Kirk also had innocence, and he recognized the loving nature in Ray, and vice versa.

"Heard you're divorced again, Goldilocks," Kirk says as Ray enters the trailer door to get his check.

"And what of it?" Ray's diving scar moves in a crooked arc between his brows.

"At thirty-two, you're battin' a thousand, kid," he laughs.

"Fuck you, Kirk."

"Oh. Well, excuse me if you're in pain." His pampered, pencil-pushing hands go up in surrender; he bares his large stained-tooth grin. "How long did you know her? All of six months?"

"Just give me my check."

"She wasn't worth it, kid. You're better off."

"Suck my dick, Kirk."

"Hey, watch your lip. I could fire you tomorrow."

"Wish you would."

"Ah, come on, boy. Why don't we go squeeze in nine holes? Might get eighteen before dark. It's been at least two months since our last game, and it's a gorgeous spring day. Damn hot too, but maybe I can get you to crack a smile. Lighten up on yourself."

"Think I'll pass, man. Just want to take a ride on the bike, then go lay down for two days."

"Whatever you say, boy," he says, slapping the check down on the desk. Kirk winks at him. "Listen, you're a good kid. I was happy to see you get that house—how long ago was that now, a year?"

"A little better."

"Then right away you go and get married. And what was it for, really? A green card? You can't marry a Brazilian, kid. And how did you ever understand a fuckin' word she said?"

"Fuck you, Kirk. I'm outta here."

"Go on, then. Get on out there on your crotch rocket. Why don't you run by that hot dog stand, pick up that good-looking heifer wearing the dental floss up her ass, and give her a roll in your hay!" he calls after him.

Straddling the bike, revving up, Ray is relieved that Kirk was so late on the news. It had already been two months since his third wife moved out of the house. A month before that, Ray was already over it.

His helmet still strapped to the back, gaining momentum, Ray moans with the cooling of his sweat and the breeze through his hair as he heads for the corner orange stand, fresh from the grove. He could take an orange by to his friend with the hot dog cart.

She wears only a thong bikini, but it's not her rollerblader legs and amazingly smooth-looking bronze peach ass that Ray likes most, or so he thinks. Rather it is her politeness. Her respectful chitchat with him in the midst of rude hardhats and farm dogs. He would never fuck her, not only because he already knew he could never fall in love with her, but because fucking is what she would expect. Ray always told himself he avoided the predictable.

The corner orange stand is already closed. He makes a U-turn, has to jerk to a full stop for a wild peacock crossing the road. Since he can already taste the juice, anticipate the pleasure of licking what escapes from the corner of his mouth, he heads for the new deli he's never been in. Responsibly, Ray returns an empty crate blocking the walkway to the stack at the entrance. The air conditioner drools a thick drop on his head, making his scalp feel all the more oily and filthy with sawdust, dirt, and sweat. Bells jingle like Christmas as he pulls open the heavy glass door. The blast of cold air is so stifling he sneezes. They have oranges, all right; he grabs three, but there's a line of two ahead of him. He holds up the three oranges in one big, blistered, red hand and some money in the other, so the surly old cretin behind the counter can see. Ray nods at him and starts to peel one, cradling the others in his arm. The clerk squints, counts out the change to the customer in front of him, while resuming conversation with the farmhand behind.

"I know, I heard about that. We were still living in Delray, but my daughter was going to Fort Pierce College at the time. She knew your cousin, not well, but I remember her talking about it," the clerk says, sucks his teeth, now bagging the goods for the farmhand.

"I went to Fort Pierce too," Ray jumps in, fancying himself never dealing with assholes, but attempting to warm them on occasion.

"She's well after your time," the clerk says flatly.

"Never know," Ray says, popping a juicy peg in his mouth.

"Anyway, it's a shame about your cousin. Thing about a grown man disappearing is what can the cops do when they find nothing? It's not like Florida isn't full of no-counts arriving here to hide out after pulling God-knows-what. The Right-to-work state is a hoodlum's Right-to-reinvent. No offense to your cousin, of course. They should have never gotten rid of Old Sparky."

"'Old Sparky'?" the farmhand asks, stretching his neck forward, screwing his brows together.

"The electric chair, boy. Fry the shit out of 'em, like they deserve," the clerk answers, shoots a look back at Ray.

"Yeah, well, whatever. My aunt's sure suffering. She *always* knew where her son was." The farmhand gently pats his back pocket where the chew can is highlighted in worn denim and bare threads. Without looking at the clerk or Ray, he picks up his bag, and walks out.

Ray, with a sudden tic in his cheek, walks up to the counter, puts the two oranges down.

"Trash is over here," the clerk says, looking at the peels in Ray's front pocket. Though it seems uncharacteristic, the clerk smiles. "Did anybody ever tell you you look like Jesus? That beard and your eyes, and everything?"

Like a kid, Ray chuckles bashfully, then looks straight at him. "I have heard that a few times but if you think about where Jesus actually came from, then why would he look anything like me?"

The clerk shrugs. "What do I know. Your type ain't that uncommon. So how was the orange?"

Ray smiles in almost the same manner he uses for pretty girls. "It was righteous." Ray winks, gathers up his change.

Feeling as drained as he was before he'd picked up his check, Ray did not expect the energy and joviality now taking over. The terror of hearing about a guy who disappeared in the same sentence as the college in Fort Pierce put his guilt in overdrive, but then his charm and defenses came winging in faster than that. If one is to live with the fact of single-handedly seeing to it that one particular vermin lost his space on earth, then one also, at times, has to be almost merry about it. When Ray wasn't letting the bigger, soft, sensitive part of his nature take over, he knew intimately how it is that anger can justifiably reign.

Chapter 2

The Dog and the Doll

Ruby

Leave now the Atlantic for the Pacific, and Ray's future—Ruby—who is his opposite in every obvious way, except that now she too will have her brush with murder.

The ivy, rose, and tree-lined path to Ruby's place snakes around from the front gate, then scales the hill of the canyon a good distance from the main house. As she makes the long way down to her door, her big hair bounces, her small but athletic, voluptuous yet compact body ripples. It's Saturday morning, April. No fog. There is an unusually brilliant and stark sun, but Ruby still doesn't notice the drops of blood down the first tier of the backyard forest maze near her entrance.

She drops her yellow duffel on the welcome mat. While searching for her keys, her phone falls out of her baggy skate pants pocket. "Shit," she hisses. She picks it up. It drops from her hand. She bites down on her full bottom lip, lets it go hard. "Fuck," she says emphatically under her breath. She yanks open the duffel bag, aggressively rifles through it.

"Caspar!" she calls. No sound.

Caspar should have come running from anywhere on the eight-acre lot in Laurel Canyon. Unless her landlord Jeannie had kept him inside, which she did from time to time when irked with Ruby. Jeannie parks both the Corvette and Range Rover in the garage—Jeannie's boyfriend, Al, could very well be there, though Ruby didn't see his Trans Am in the drive.

"Agh, fi-nal-*ly*." She finds the keys in the duffel. She won't know how much she talks to herself until Ray points this out much later. Feeling frightened, Ruby opens the door. When she closes it, her skateboard falls over. She jumps, her wild puff of kinky hair flops back down in slow motion. The large bouquet of purple calla lilies, tulips, pink roses, and freesias are dead.

"What is *your* problem?" she asks, looking into the kitchen mirror. Nothing strange anywhere at all, her shoulders smooth. One more survey of the room and she shakes her head, irritated to find she'd left the coffeemaker on since Thursday morning. And what a hellish thirty-sixth birthday Thursday had been.

Jeannie's party the week before had been something of a celebration for Ruby, since she refused to let Jeannie throw her a surprise the day of. That would have been a disaster. A cold and stale mix of Ruby's younger, uptight sister, clingy boss, natural-high friends, politically intense and now ex-boyfriend Pej along with Jeannie's porn buddies, coke fiends, and tarot card readers. When Ruby refused a gathering of her own friends, Jeannie threw a party anyway, excluding them. She rarely socialized with her landlord, but they were fond of each other. Ruby had been there long enough to see Jeannie become a widow, fight her dead husband's kids protesting the will, then fall in love with the every-now-and-then Al. Her affection for Jeannie's fifth and youngest Rhodesian Ridgeback, Caspar, and his for her, made Jeannie especially trusting. Jeanette Susan Bravern's fame name was Rochelle Rosewood. Years ago the dogs were more about fitting her favorite alliteration, later they truly grew on her.

Last Saturday night's party touched Ruby. She knew no one in that house save Jeannie, Al, and the dogs, but it was perfect that way. Lying back on the plush olive couch, she was eating only the broken pieces of cashews from a crystal dish, when a warm, mildly reassuring stranger sat down next to her. He brushed the salt from her small, dark brown hand and cushioned it in his large beige one. As he read her palm, he told her she had a remarkably long, deep lifeline. Right then, Jeannie approached with the tall, crooked pistachio cake she made—her big, childlike, gold eyes flashing. The ash blonde hair fluffed her preserved but mischievously animated fifty-two-year-old face. Her body, as always, was hot and taut in

9

a tastelessly expensive, tight, and tawny leather jumpsuit. She stopped in front of Ruby, purposely kicking her toe with her favorite two-toned cowboy boot. She loudly sang "Happy Birthday" over the tired eighties music thumping the wood floors. Two beats behind her, the rest of the room joined in with the song. Ruby blew out the candles, closed her eyes, and wished for an adolescent's adrenaline. Better yet, a white boy's freedom. The room's applause startled her, and Jeannie's hair tickled her nose as she bent over to kiss Ruby's forehead.

Rare as it was, she got a little high that night. So when the palm reader asked if he could escort her past the pool and back to her house through the dark of the forest's graveled dirt labyrinth, Ruby called for Caspar in a tense, paranoid voice. Caspar galloped out from the kitchen, stood between Ruby and the palm reader, stared him down. Caspar never growled or barked. He was coolishly intimidating with his kinked tail and imperfect bite. The palm reader backed up, then awkwardly but boldly dashed forward for a hug. He squeezed Ruby tightly enough to smash her large C-cup saline breasts into his chest. With a yawning kind of sound, Caspar stepped on his toe, then led Ruby to her house.

Always, as Ruby fiddled for her keys, Caspar would make a fast gallop all the way around the house. By the time her key was in the lock, he was back at her side, and he would enter before her as she turned on the light. The house has three rooms with a red claw bathtub in the kitchen, and a water closet—much like a New York apartment. Only the skylights, opening to tall eucalyptus, birch, pine, and Japanese maple, give the feel of the country. The front window lends a more to-the-point view of the Hollywood Hills celebrity palatial spread.

Ruby lay down on the bed with the phone, Caspar on the floor just beneath her. She called Pej's cell, got his voicemail. Not wanting him to hear the toasted paranoia in her voice, she hung up and called her skate pal, Joop—short for Jupiter. She had been seeing Pejman Shahpour for almost a year and a half. He was forty-one, handsome, compulsively clean, almost feline. He'd taken her on banking trips—New York, London, Tokyo, Zurich—but never to Paris where his parents were. By a year's time, Ruby had met every good friend or lover's parents, listing their phone numbers next to the notation "(p)." Because this wasn't yet the case with Pej, she felt she couldn't quite believe in him. Even Joop—tall, muscular, twenty-three, funny, daring, and glaringly indecisive—gave her more to trust in. And too much lately she had been comparing the two in her mind.

When Joop heard she was taking Thursday off for her birthday, he wanted to take her to Magic Mountain. She told him Pej was taking her to Palm Springs for a long weekend. Come Thursday, they never got there. First the flowers arrived with a card saying simply, "For the Beauty on her Birthday." An hour later, Pej stood at her door. His dark, flawless hair was combed back with a slightly different side part. Their hello kiss hurried and nervous. Whenever they led with his shy, vulnerable tension, the excitement would build. This time, however, the faint and sweetly sad scent of his cologne filled the room, and Ruby wanted swiftly out of the house. With too much effort to his right shoulder, he picked up her lightly packed duffel bag. She wanted to grab it from him, but knew that would start a fight. In the car, they talked about her work at the animation house, and how tired she was of the show. Pej wasn't necessarily preoccupied, he usually gave her his full attention, particularly when she was leaning toward the combative. This gave him the chance to pull her through polemics, a semantics dance of fundamentalists, socialists, globalists, environmentalists. Still, neither of them was there, so quiet became them. She sighed as they pulled up to the valet, it would be too fancy a lunch. Once they were seated, he realized he'd forgotten to put his own bag in the car, so after eating, they had to double back to his place.

They ended up in bed. Often she felt like blindfolding him or doing a striptease, but she never seized the moment, and settled for one of their three usual routines. Afterward, she could have fallen asleep with him, but it was evening, near seven, and Ruby wanted dinner and birthday cake. She didn't really care about Palm Springs either, even though a mud bath would have been delicious. At lunch he'd given her three dresses she would probably wear only out with him, so she got up out of bed and tried on the gorgeous white embroidered slip, and over it the serious, constructed lady's black linen shift. In the mirror, she looked into her bright, open brown eyes without recognition, then at Pej who was curled up on his side, his lids fluttering, the perfect plum mouth closed. His breathing was barely audible. This gave her the opportunity to run to the storage room, and see if that huge crate was finally unlocked.

She felt tragic sneaking into the one room Pej insisted wasn't worthy of a visitor. Boxes and suitcases left unpacked, he wanted to sell everything in it. She didn't know it was really a third bedroom with a walk-in closet until the second to last time she'd snooped around. The crate was at least five feet long and two feet deep.

The combination lock was open this time. She held her breath, lifted it. The first glimpse of a woman's body elicited a grisly, piercing scream. Cold spread through Ruby's bowels and turned to liquid. She ran for the bathroom, knocking her kneecap at the doorway, her big toe at the basin cabinet, her thigh at the wall by the toilet and bidet. How Pej slept through that commotion was inconceivable to her. Crying, cleaning the awful stench and mess off the new slip, she gathered her courage. Returning to the open crate, she realized it wasn't a dead body. This was not a human being, but a horrifically real doll.

Auburn hair, tan skin, and vacant, gorgeous painterly eyes. Black eyeliner around them, rose-colored shadow brushed to the perfect brows. Rudely ample breasts, the nipples pinched in excitement. The pubic hair was shaved. The nails were bronze, the lipstick cinnamon. The body smelled like fruit. Ruby lifted it up by the shoulders. The black satin bra and panties were under the head. The body was cold. Ruby stuck her finger in the doll's mouth, felt her soft tongue and teeth. She knew it had to be made of silicone. The vaginal lips stretched apart. Curiosity overtook her. This doll looked nothing like either of her past female lovers. Equally foreign was the feeling the doll gave her. In another space and time maybe she could have felt desire. But the fact that the doll looked nothing like her returned the rage inside full tilt.

She picked up the doll in her arms—the spine so excellently articulated—and ran with it to Pej's bed. He must have felt the energy because he jerked up just as she threw the doll and hit him whole with it. She heard nothing he said. She was yelling. He was standing, his skin flushed, his legs thin, his balls hanging small, wrinkled, and lopsided. Ruby then remembered her own nakedness, and that of the doll's lying in an obscene position on the bed. Pej so helpless in front of her. She wanted to break all of the glass in his house. Now she heard something about the doll being a "twisted gift"—from a friend or business associate. Ruby slapped him on the side of his face, and he held his ear. Both of them were crying. She'd heard him say the word "love," but she was already on the phone. Now Pej was angry, stomping around the room. Clothes were flying, gracefully hitting the air like ballerinas. Joop was on the other end, gasping that as quickly as he could, he would pick her up.

Joop gave Ruby his bed and took the couch. She lay awake all night rolling her eyes at herself. None of this was such a big deal. When she put it into perspective, she couldn't understand why she'd felt so violated. She hated herself for thinking how she wanted to take revenge on Pej by having sex with Joop.

Friday morning, for two hours they sat in his filthy apartment at the breakfast table of half-eaten, stale bear claws, a box of Cheerios, espresso grinds at the bottom of their mugs. They went for a long skate. Upon returning, Joop collapsed for a nap in the bedroom, while Ruby showered. Listening to him snore as she dressed, she thought of calling a cab, but instead found herself sketching the characters that for months she'd been hounding her boss to bring to life.

Watching a movie, early evening, Joop sat at the opposite end of the couch, insisting she spread out her legs. Her toes touched his thigh. When she'd grabbed the remote to backtrack the DVD, Joop stared at her. He took her by the head, sucked and bit at her lips, devouring her mouth so that she couldn't breathe. She let him strip the clothes from her, but as he entered and began thrusting too fast, she gripped his hips and soulfully slowed him down. She almost came before he did, but the TV screen distracted her. So instead of encouraging him to finish her off, she made him lay there, his face on her chest as she watched the end of the movie.

In Joop's bed that night, they were slightly more successful. But as she'd expected, breakfast wasn't even an eighth as pleasant as the morning before. Their heads ran at two different speeds. He was giddy; she was removed, full of regret. He drove her home, talking excitedly the entire way. Though she made him drop her at the top of the drive, he got out of the car and followed her to the gate. She refused his escort, so he waved, watched her make her way down the path until she was out of his sight.

And this is when she misses the blood on the maze near her entrance, Saturday morning. She's inside of her house, having turned off the coffeemaker. It seems late not to hear any of the dogs barking or roaming the property. She picks up the phone.

"Hey Jeannie, I'm back early. No worries. If you're around, no need to call. Maybe you have the dogs with you? Or Chauncey's still at the park with them? Um. So, whatever. I'll be here. If you're gone for the weekend, give me a shout." She hangs up, opens the door.

"Cas-par!" Nothing but the buzz of bees and flies.

She puts her hands on her hips, steps off the welcome mat, and off to the maze. She walks up the path to the pool, hurrying now, as she imagines bees are chasing her, the buzzing sounds closer to her ears. Now at a dead run, she sees the pool gate is open, but stops at the post, and screams.

Below the nearest chaise longue is a large, furry heap. A small puddle of blood spreads, flies buzz around the body. Though she's wearing soft skate shoes, all she can hear are her footsteps on the patio cement. It's Ralph, the oldest Rhodesian Ridgeback. Her eyes, nostrils burn with the stench of new death. She leans over him to find he'd taken a bullet through the head.

"JEAN-NIE!" Ruby shrieks toward the sky, leaning backward. She turns to face the sliding glass door, but her eyes stop at the pool. There is a nude body floating face-up. The water is pink near the head, the long, dark hair flowing.

"HELP!" Ruby screams again. "Help me, God, HELP!"

The body in the pool is Chauncey, the dogwalker. Her large gray eyes are open, a single fly crawls on her nose. Ruby first staggers, then rushes from the shallow end to the deep, screams again to find that farther to her right by the poolhouse where the water bowls sit, is Tug, the third oldest.

"CAAAAS-PAR! CAAAS-PAR!" she calls, looking into the house. Her eyes revert back to Tug, who has a shot through his neck and breast. Screaming, Ruby runs to the sliding glass door, but because it's ajar, she doubles back, thinking better of going inside.

Missing the ghoulish sight of the other two dogs, Roddy and Rob, she sprints back down the path to her door, her hair flopping behind. She screams for help the entire way. This time she catches in her peripheral view that just around the side of her little house is Caspar's body. She runs to him, wailing his name, falls on the ground, grabs him to her, violently flicking away flies, kissing his muzzle. Her hand caresses his jaw and his jowls, his mouth open, catching her tears. His fur is stained with blood on his left hip and right breast.

Ruby knows she's got to get on the phone and call the police immediately. But she's frozen in position, holding Caspar, shaking him with her sobs, moaning in deep pain of imagining his last gallop around her house, making sure, as he always did, that she was safe.

Chapter 3

The Last Frontier

Ray

"It's your turn," Gary says, raking back his short brown hair with his fingers. The unruly strands return to their preferred place on his freckled forehead. He wriggles his nose, which is his frequent twitch.

"You got me running here," Ray says, leaning over the board, both elbows on his knees, one hand cracking the knuckles of the other.

"Shouldn't have you running. Feeling nothing but shame taking so long to close in on your pitiful king, so far from home with only a lousy rook and one lame knight."

"Ah, man. Douse me in it."

"Nah. You're doing good. Really." Gary smiles, leans back to stretch in the canvas fold-up chair. He is small, almost flimsy, but muscle-tight in a clean white T and army shorts. "Garden's looking good too." He folds his arms, nodding in approval to the yard.

"Could you take care of it for me?" Ray looks up, squints, rubs his bare chin. He sports a beard or goes clean-shaven, alternating the weeks with his moods.

"Wha' da ya mean?"

"While I'm gone, would you take care of the garden? Keep an eye on the boat."

"Where you going?"

"Alaska."

"Vacation? Finally got you some time off, man?"

"Nah. I'm quitting."

"What you going to Alaska for?"

"To fish."

"Hell, you can do that here. Why you gotta go all the way to Alaska to fish?"

"To make some money. I'm going to work on a rig for the summer."

"You already got a job?"

"No. But I'll get one."

"You're so damn impulsive. Why would you leave a spread like this, a job you like, to go work in some freezing ass place? You let these womens chase you around, man." Gary shakes his head, smirks.

"'Womens,'" Ray laughs. "I'm going for the summer, dude. To work. It's warm in the summer, don't you know anything?"

"I know they got *bears*." Gary opens his eyes wide, laughs.

"Yeah, yeah. So move in. Get outta that hellhole, bring Jason. Take care of the place while I'm gone. Make use of the big, fine kitchen. Who knows, I may not even come back."

"You've *got* to be kidding me. I'll watch your place, but I'm settled. Can't get Jason to move, the pack rat. I got a lease, anyhow."

"So what? Break it. Move out. Stop paying that scumbag," Ray says. "What's he gonna do?"

"Unlike you, I don't just pick up and leave."

"Ah, give me a break. Like you haven't gotten yourself into trouble before," Ray says, looking straight at him, his eyes narrowing, mean.

Gary breathes in deeply, looks Ray in the eye. Then he shakes his head, as if shaking him off. He doesn't know he has any part in Ray's crime. He does know, however, the extent of Ray's unshakable loyalty. And this is the part that always scares him.

"Are we gonna finish this game, or what?" Gary says, straightening up in his chair, reaching into his back pocket for a crushed cigarette. Ray holds out his hand for one; Gary obliges, leans over to light it. Ray takes a deep drag, moves his knight; Gary takes it with his queen. The smoke leaves through Ray's nose.

"Checkmate," Gary says. Ray points his finger like a gun at Gary, bends his thumb as the hammer. Gary cocks his head to the side. "I'll watch your place, Ray."

"Thank you."

"Hell, I'll be taking that boat out every day while you're working your ass off on some rig in Alaska, of all fucking places. Why don't you go on safari in Africa? That's more your style."

"What do you know about my fucking style?" Ray squints again, flicks the ash from his cigarette into the grass, then gets up and walks into the house.

Kirk is less incredulous that Ray should be quitting to leave behind a nice house and a string of ex-wives to forget. He gives him an extra fifty in the last paycheck, Ray nods in appreciation, and Kirk hits him squarely on both shoulders. They give each other a bear hug; Kirk shakes his head as Ray shuts the door behind him.

As he approaches home, he feels tempted just to keep on riding, but he knows if he did he would end up at the swamp. He has no business ever returning to the scene of nightmares again, so instead he heads for the hot dog cart. As he parks it, his cell phone rings. He takes off his helmet; Lula lights up at the sight of him. She grabs her long black hair, winds it around in back, tugs it tightly into a knot. Ray waves, looks at the number on his cell, hesitates, holds up the one-minute finger to Lula, then answers.

"Dad. Everything okay?"

"Of course. Sadie gave me your number." Ray puts two inches between the phone and his ear, now irritated at his sister. His father goes on, "Did you get my message?"

"Yes, Dad, but the home machine is messed up, so I only got it this morning before I left for work. Can I call you when I get home?" He looks up at Lula who is squeezing a thin line of mustard over the sauerkraut, just the way he likes it.

"What's all this about moving?" His father's voice still too loud, Ray puts another inch between the phone and his ear, then violently clamps it back.

"I'm not *moving*, Dad. Sadie got it wrong, as usual. Listen, can I call you back? I'm grabbing a little lunch, here." Ray turns his back to Lula.

"I'm leaving in a little while, son. Just checking in. Haven't heard from you since the last time you got married—"

"Dad, everything's fine," Ray interrupts. "I'll try and catch you later this evening. Will you be home then?"

"I hear you got divorced, son, and . . ." Ray walks a few yards away from Lula, who has pulled up a chair, put the two dogs and a root beer there waiting for him.

"The last time I got divorced, Dad, do you remember what you said to me? The *only* thing you said to me?" Ray asks with a thrash in his voice, his lower jaw tense and protruding.

"Call me tonight, Ray. I'll be home." His father hangs up.

"*God*," Ray says under his breath, wipes his brow, recovering composure, turns around.

"Hey," Lula says, a big smile spreading.

"How you doing?" He offers his hand instead of coming into her hug. She takes his right hand with her left and squeezes. As if there were crumbs there, she brushes off her bare, tan, flat belly. Her thong is orange, her bikini top white, all body hair meticulously waxed.

"Everything all right with you?" she asks. Her cruelly plucked brows touch, then she hits the back of the fold-up chair, for him to sit down. As he does, she hands him the soda and the dogs. She tiptoes and inches her gym-pumped ass back down on her bar-high stool. He takes a big bite and a swig, nods, smiles.

"That was my dad on the phone." Ray's smile now all-charm. "Sometimes he gets himself in a tizzy over nothing."

"Really? So you take after your mom, the cool-headed one?"

"What makes you think I'm so cool-headed?" He swallows hard, winks.

"Oh, you seem to have things under control, all right."

"Well, my mom's . . . dead. She wasn't so cool-headed. She could be downright frantic and nervous, especially over her kids. Really my father is normally calm, but they were so in love, he sorta took on some of her qualities since she's been gone. He has never re-married. Doesn't even date."

"I'm sorry."

He downs the rest of the first dog. "No, no. It was a while ago that she passed. I was twenty-six."

"Couldn't have been *that* long ago. How old are you now?"

"Thirty-three. Just had a birthday." He chomps half of the second dog.

"Ah, a May man. Taurus. Of course. I should have known."

He chews awhile before answering. "No, the last week of April. But Taurus, yes, whatever that means." He smiles, choking the rest of it down in a blink.

"Very stubborn, then, huh?"

"I don't know. I spose so." He delicately wipes the mustard and kraut from the corners of his mouth.

"So you'll refuse when I ask you to go to Bathtub Beach with me now." She puts her hand on her bare thigh, leaning toward him, her expression an intentional mock-tease.

"Correct. I'll have to refuse," he says, downing the rest of his soda. "Ah." He rubs his stomach. "I'm stuffed right full." With exaggerated discomfort, he leans forward to pull his wallet from his back pocket.

"Oh, come on, Ray. It would be nice. I promise to be a good girl." She pouts her thin lips, mock-teasing again.

"I've got so much laundry to do. And packing. I'm so behind," Ray says, standing up, shaking his head, now looking very stressed.

"You have a new place?"

"No, just leaving for the summer."

"You and your wife?"

"No, no. Don't have a wife anymore."

"Well, then, all the more reason to have a little fun before you leave! Come on, Ray. I'll help you pack after."

"I can't, Lula. Really."

"We'll go to the beach, then we'll go back to your place, you can pack while I make you something that will make you forget these hot dogs even exist, and after we eat, I can help you pack."

"No," Ray says, a touch more harshly than he meant. "Thank you, really. Lula, I can't. I have plans for dinner, and like I said, I have so much laundry to do, and packing." He pulls out the correct amount of bills and change, pays her. She hastily puts the money away, writes her phone number on a napkin.

"What's your last name, Ray?" she says, hands on hips, one clutching the napkin.

"Rose."

"Well, Ray Rose, before you leave for the summer, you'll call me, I'll pick you up, take you to dinner, then take you back home and"—she grabs his hand, forcefully brushes it up the length of her thigh—"I'll fuck your brains out." She puts the napkin in that hand that felt the smoothness of her thigh, and she folds his fingers into a fist around it. Without cracking a smile, he looks into her widely set, lemony brown eyes.

"Bye, Lula." He walks away, still holding a fist, grabs his helmet, and rides off without turning around.

Ray lands in Anchorage, early morning, mid-May, happy to find the extreme cold snap still in the air. The front windows down in the white rental Ford Taurus, he breathes in, thinking fondly of the tail end of Michigan winters. Slush. The sound of its soft crunching beneath his rubber boots. The smell of defrost, earth. Wet. Spring ready to burst. The house reopening to the buzz of outdoor chores. His mother uncovering the southern plants. Ray returning all the hoses, his father sharpening blades. The feel of fertilizer in his hands. His father always insisting Ray and the girls stay inside while he mowed the lawn. Ray didn't know until later how a distant neighbor had mowed over a stone that shot through the air and hit his only son. Square in the temple, killing him. Had he lived, that boy might have been Ray's only male playmate.

Disgusted by all of the Tony Romas, Outback Steakhouses, and Cal Worthington lots everywhere he looks, Ray drives through miles of pre-fabs and weekday morning traffic, seeking an old-fashioned country breakfast diner. He settles for a joint downtown next to a bar, trying to control his angst over the difficulty of finding a parking space on the numbered and lettered one-way streets. After five frustrating rounds, he makes a parallel-parking amateur of himself, then vaults out of the car into the glassy air to tinker with the clean, new meter. He takes long strides, decompressing with each block. He picks up an *Anchorage Daily News*, opens the cheap wood door to the diner, sits down in a cracked booth, and wrinkles his nose at the grease on the table.

"I'll be with you in one moment," the waitress calls gruffly from behind the counter. Ray's nose is still wrinkled as he wipes the table with two small napkins from the dispenser. He pulls out the classifieds and lays it down. His phone rings, and with much irritation he yanks it from the windbreaker pocket, bunched up on the seat. His expression changes to a kid's pout when he sees it's his sister Sadie's number. The waitress flings a menu on his table; he looks up sideways at her, shakes his head at the rudeness and anyone looking, then answers his phone.

"Hey, sis."

"Hey, little brother. So how's the Last Frontier?"

"I only got here an hour ago, so I really can't tell ya. I'm sitting down to a little breakfast here. Can I call you later?"

"Sorry I sicced Dad on you."

"I was gonna say."

"You know, he talked to Sonya, who I haven't spoken to in months, so . . ."

"Big Sis Sonya, or ex-Sonya?" Ray asks with alarm.

"Ray, I never even met your Sonya. Still can't believe they have the same name. So weird."

"Well knowing her, I thought maybe she somehow got to Dad. She's crazy. I'm glad it's over."

"So I called your place by accident this morning, and some guy answered."

"That was Gary."

"Who's Gary?"

"Gary's my friend from the restaurant, the cook."

"The gay one?"

"Yes. The *gay* one," Ray rolls his eyes. "So can I call you back? I'm grabbing a little breakfast here."

"I love you, little brother. Just remember that. Just remember who you are. Will you call me when you get settled?"

"Promise."

"Okay, then." She hesitates. "Bye."

22

"Bye." Ray drops the phone down on his jacket. He rocks his head from one side to the other to stretch his neck. He shakes his head again.

"Ready?" The waitress stands before him with the pad and pencil poised.

"I haven't had the chance to look it over," he says, the impatient tone growing with each word. "Can I get a rag or something to wipe up this table?"

The waitress walks away, returns with a rag, and roughly wipes down the table. Ray watches her in silence, holding his newspaper and menu up.

"Where are you from?" she asks, her voice raspy.

"Florida."

"You're a long way from home. Land of gators. What brings you here?"

"Gators, yes." Ray smiles, clears his throat, as if he were the one who needed to do so. He is unaware of all the buzzwords that split his chest with fear. "You been to Florida?"

"My ex-husband was from Florida, the Gulf. His folks are still there."

"Gulf is nice. I'm from the east coast. South Florida."

"So. You looking for a job here?"

"Not necessarily," Ray says, wondering why he'd lied, or whether he was in fact lying.

"You been here before?"

"No, first time. And I was hoping for a big plate of some righteous salmon and eggs."

"We don't have any salmon. We've got halibut." She opens up his menu, lays it flat on the table, and points. She poises her pad and pencil again, looking him over. She grins. "Fish 'n' chips are good here. The halibut's good."

"Fish 'n' chips in the morning?" Ray whines.

"Trust me on it." Her cheeks bulge, uncomfortable with the rarity of such a large smile. She scribbles, abruptly rips the check from her pad, and walks off.

Instead of looking in the classifieds, Ray turns every page of the paper, stopping on an ad for whitewater kayaking in Denali. Every single time Ray sets himself free from one responsibility, he drags his feet on approaching the next. This he never noticed about himself, but later when Ruby points this out, he'll truly consider taking a look at it. In the meantime, as the fish 'n' chips arrive, he promises himself to wash the blood from his hands and his mind, and set his sights on exploring Mt. McKinley.

Chapter 4

The Clean-Up

Ruby

Ruby and Jeannie sit together at the farthest corner of the long, black marble dining table. Both women have bloodshot eyes. Ruby, with a blue bandanna for a headband keeping her thick hair back from her face, occasionally waves from her nose the smoke from Jeannie's fourth cigarette. Just a holler away in the kitchen is Al, making waffles for himself. Ruby hasn't touched her cranberry juice or the plate of rice cakes, nut bread, and goat cheese in front of them. Jeannie's gin fizz is almost gone. Ruby has a perfect view of the magnificent black-and-white photograph of Jeannie standing poolside in a silver bikini, a phone at her ear, the other hand a blur of movement in conversation; near her are the four older dogs posed regally, on guard. This photograph was taken before Caspar arrived. Ruby stares at it blankly, then down at the annoyingly life-size and ugly, multicolored plaster of the angel that is scattered in multiples all over the city, as if to stand for civic pride.

"You want another drink, Munchie?" Al asks Jeannie. He lands his plate of waffles down hard on the table, gulps his coffee, one hand on his hip. Al looks like Giuliani, only taller, much beefier, with a thick mop of dyed dark brown hair. "Munchie, you hear me talking to ya? Do you want another drink?"

"No, baby." Jeannie puts her forehead in her hand, elbow on the table.

"How about you, doll? You must want something else."

"I'm fine, thanks Al," Ruby says, a smile lighting up half of her maple syrup brown cherubic face.

"You gals have to eat. You haven't touched a frickin' thing!"

Al roughly pulls out the chair across from Jeannie, plops down, and cuts his waffles, the knife loudly scraping the plate. Ruby, now with chin in hand at the head of the table, looks up with big eyes at Jeannie. Their heads, hands are all close enough to join in séance.

"Where's Marta this morning?" Al asks, waffles in his mouth.

"I told you I gave her the day off."

"You know I have that meeting at three, I can't cancel," Al says, chewing and pointing the fork of waffle at Jeannie. "What you got going today, kid?" He turns to Ruby. "Your boss give you the rest of the week off too?"

"I took a leave of absence," Ruby says, clearing her throat. Jeannie looks up at her as if she knows she is hiding something. She runs her fingers through her shoulder-length ash blonde hair, parts of it sticking up unnaturally at the back of her head. She lights another cigarette.

"So the show must go on without you, kid."

"I'm just a character designer."

"Yeah, well. And you," Al looks at Jeannie, sighs. "Don't know why you gave Marta the day off, Jean," Al gestures with both of his hands as if weighing two grapefruits, then lets them fall to his lap.

"I don't need a goddamn *baby*sitter, Al," Jeannie snaps.

Al gulps down the rest of his coffee, sits back in his chair, looks out past Ruby at the large potted palms outside on the patio. He overlooks the remnants of bloodstains the clean-up crew tried their best to get out. He inhales heavily and exhales so slowly it makes him cough. He pulls Jeannie's pack of cigarettes to his side of the table, lights up.

"You know that cocksucker doesn't believe nothing is missing from this house," Al says, pointing his cigarette at Ruby, blowing smoke to the side.

"I know, I got that feeling," Ruby says, clearing her throat again.

"Leave it to a pig to get grand ideas up his ass, only to find the truth staring him right in the fucking face, *every* time," Al says, now grabbing the ashtray from in front of Jeannie. "They didn't find *shit*. And that's 'cause the sick fuck, whoever he was, never

26

stepped foot in here." He flicks his ash, cocks his head, looks at Jeannie. "But it's about you, Munchie. He's thinking with his dick, and he's not gonna believe a gal like you if his mother's life depended on it."

"I keep thinking this all has to do with Henry," Jeannie says, staring out through the space between Ruby and Al.

"Probably has *everything* to do with him. Those bastard kids hate your guts, Munchie. And you didn't have to give them the money you did!"

"They're not bastards, Al. Henry was married to their mother."

"Whatever! You know what I'm saying."

Jeannie looks at Ruby who squeezes her hand. Jeannie squeezes back so hard that the large emerald and diamonds pierce Ruby's finger.

"You don't have to stay with me all day, Ruby baby," Jeannie almost whispers, her large gold eyes wide and wet like a baby leopard's.

"I know, Jeannie."

"You've been so good to me, all week. You've been so . . ." She sniffles.

"Munchie, don't get yourself all worked up again, come on," Al says, exhaling loudly, his nostrils flaring.

Jeannie is still holding Ruby's hand. She holds the tissue with the other, blows her nose.

"Let's just go back to the goddamn hotel tonight, Jean. Come on, already."

"I'm not letting *anybody* run me out of my house!" Jeannie yells from a delicate hoarse throat.

"Now, Ruby, have you stayed here *one* single night this entire week?" Al asks, nodding his head at her with exaggeration.

"No," Ruby says, looking at the table. She finally takes a sip of her cranberry juice. "I've been at my parents'." Still looking at the table, she swallows, getting mad at herself for putting off what should be the obvious, that she's moving out.

"*Why!*" Jeannie yells, letting go of Ruby's hand. "Why, why, WHY would someone KILL MY DOGS and *RAPE* and MURDER my dog WALKER! Who the *FUCK* could *DO* such a thing?" She

27

bares all of her teeth, bangs the table once with her fist, the plates buckle.

"Munchie, Munchie, settle down," Al says, getting up to sit next to her. Jeannie doesn't look at him. Ruby clears her throat. Al grabs Jeannie by the neck and shoulders for a short and awkward massage. He nibbles her ear, Jeannie still staring straight out in front of her.

"I'm gonna go," Ruby says, slowly getting up, picking up her juice glass.

"Where you going, honey?" Jeannie asks, looking up at her with desperate eyes.

"My friend Joop is coming by to—"

"Joop? Joop. What the hell kind of name is Joop?" Al asks.

Ruby smiles, glad that he interrupted. She cannot yet say she is packing, though she knows she should give notice.

"Don't you have some boyfriend, an Arab, Israeli or something, named Peg?"

"Pejjjj," she says, exaggerating the *j*.

"You sure go for the weird names, doll." Al smiles, the one fickle dimple appears.

"He's Iranian. And I'm sure Pejman is not such an uncommon name."

"Okay. Pej. Pejman. So this Joop is Iranian too?" Al asks, one arm still awkwardly around Jeannie.

"No. He's a WASP," Ruby says, standing, arms folded. "Pej is not my boyfriend anymore. I haven't spoken to him since my birthday."

"Wonder where the hell *he* was Saturday morning."

"Right, *Al*," Ruby says, her throat closing up on the back of her words as if to bounce them in echo. She takes her glass to the kitchen.

"Why don't you shut your big, dumb, fat, fucking mouth," Jeannie snaps, breaking away from his grasp. She gets up to follow Ruby to the kitchen.

"You okay, baby?" Jeannie grabs Ruby's wrist. "Listen. I know this has all been every bit as hard on you."

"Don't worry about me. Are *you* okay?" Ruby looks her in the

28

eye, Jeannie falls into her arms, they start crying. "*Caspar*," Ruby inaudibly whispers through her sobs.

Al stands on an invisible line between the kitchen and open space. He feels the scruff on his chin, licks his red lips, folds his arms, looks down at his feet.

"Ah, hell. Ruby, I'm sorry, doll," Al calls loudly into the kitchen as if the two women are a lot farther than they actually are. Ruby waves her hand like batting away a gnat. They now hold each other at the waist, looking into each other's faces.

"Call me if you need anything. I won't be far, probably will end up at my sister's, she's just over there, up off Outpost." Ruby holds Jeannie's pale, unmade face, squeezing Jeannie's cheeks, then lips into a pucker. They plant a loud smack upon each other's mouths. Ruby lets go of her, Jeannie pulls up the sleeves of her large, loose, white gauze shirt, the buttons revealing her freckled and barely wrinkled chest, her black satin bra, and the gold serpentine chain thinly pouring down her tight cleavage.

As Ruby makes her way down the maze, she sees Joop waiting for her at the entrance. His arms are folded around his knees, his thick wheat-colored hair in his face.

"You chopped it off!" Ruby says, speeding up for the last few yards. Joop pops up to hug her.

"I know, I know. Needed a change all of a sudden," Joop says as she lets go of him.

"Looks good."

"Thanks. So this is really a treehouse. I never realized it before," he says, following her in. "Have you been inside at all this week?"

"No, I've been at my parents' house. I'm probably going to my sister's tonight."

"Well, you're welcome at my place, Rube. You know," he says, looking at her then at the boxes on the floor.

"I'll be fine at my sister's. But thanks. You want something to drink? Think I've still got some coffee in here." She opens up the fridge, scratches her head under the bandanna.

"It was weird seeing you on the news like that, you know?" Joop says, pulling out the coffee pitcher, filling it with water. Ruby

29

stands behind him, irritated that he's in her way. She holds the bag of coffee near her thigh, lightly hitting herself there with it. "How come your landlord wouldn't go on camera?"

"Would you?"

"You did."

"I mean if you were *her?*"

"It's not like she's camera-shy or anything," Joop says with a smirk, backing away from the counter, carefully around the boxes, looking around for the closest chair.

"That's fucked." Ruby squints one eye at him, hands on hips.

"Well, come on. You know I rented one of her movies the other night. They weren't easy to find, dude said they'd been flying off the shelves, that I was lucky to find it."

"You watched one of her movies? That's weird of you."

"Wha' da ya mean, 'weird'? I was curious is all."

"I think it's disgusting. And why weren't you curious before all this?"

"Don't know. Didn't think of it, really. It's not like I'm into porn or anything."

"Yeah, right."

"And so are you so above watching a little porn?"

"No I'm not."

"Have you watched one of her movies?"

"Yeah. With her once."

"Now *that's* weird, Ruby. What a scene that must have been."

"It wasn't so weird. It was kinda bright orange. We were laughing, pointing, drinking, eating chips. Jeannie's really pretty together."

"What made her get into it?"

"Why are we talking about *porn?* I was close to that dog, Joop. I can hear the jingle of his collar tag right now," she says, stifling a tear. "I loved all of them. And someone was killed. Someone was raped and killed. Someone's daughter."

"Sorry, Ruby. I really am." He gets up to find coffee cups. Her mouth is still open, over-dramatically shuddering. He pours them both a cup, turns around to look for the milk. "I know you were close to Caspar, Rube. You talked about him all the time. I just thought you didn't want to think about it all right now. I know you couldn't return my calls with everyone coming after you, wanting to know you were all right."

"I know. It's okay."

Ruby sits on the floor near the red claw tub; she rubs her hands together. Joop hands her a cup of coffee, sits in the chair with his. They drink in silence, until Joop looks at her too warmly for her taste. Before this moment, she decided it wasn't so bad that they slept together, just a blip they could both forget. She puts her cup down on the floor, takes in a deep breath, and exhales like she's ready to wrap up the visit.

"So I'm starting another job next week," Joop says brightly.

"Yeah?"

"It's a video, so it won't be too many days. I got called on a movie this week but turned it down. Low budget, I couldn't stand all the overtime."

"Yeah."

"Can't be a PA all my life."

"I know."

"How much more time you taking off?"

"Don't know."

"That's really cool of your boss, leaving it open like that. He sure digs you."

"Maybe. He knows I'm unhappy anyway."

"What's to be so unhappy working for a hit show like that? You're gonna get your chance. Those characters you drew at my place the other day were *awesome*. I can totally see them coming to life. Don't dump such a good gig. It's the perfect place for your next move."

"I know. But I'm getting sick of L.A."

"What do you mean? Where else you gonna do what you do?" Joop says, jutting out his chin, raising his brow, shaking his head. "Come on, Rube."

"I'm just thinking of putting all my stuff in storage and getting out of town."

"Well then, get out of town! But come back and get to work. It's what you gotta do."

"Look who's talking."

"Come on. Once you get out of this house, you'll change your mind. You know I'm right. You gonna throw away your position just 'cause you moved into some coke hag's mess?"

"You sound like my dad." She rolls her eyes.

"Whatever. You'll wake up in your new place and forget it happened. This isn't about L.A."

"I've been here all my life."

"Santa Cruz . . ."

"Barely counts. It was just two years of school, so whatever. But I could sell my car, get quite a bit for it, and go move somewhere else for a while." Ruby gets up, stretches one arm at a time, like jazzercise.

"You're not gonna sell Dahlia, no way."

"You hear of anybody interested in a cherry Corvair, let me know."

"No way."

"I'm gonna take out an ad in the *Recycler* or sell it on eBay."

"Just wait on that, will ya?"

"I'm decided." She folds her arms over her breasts, butts him with her shoe.

"You wanna go for a skate?" His eyes plead.

"Got too much to do."

"Need help packing?"

"No thanks."

Joop gets up to hug her. She breaks away.

"Leave Dahlia with me, then. I'll take care of her. Go to Mexico or Hawaii for a week, then come on back." He holds her hand, kisses it. He blushes.

"Get on out of here, now. I'll be just fine." Ruby opens up the door, and with a purposefully big and goofy grin, Joop backs out.

Ruby's sister leaves the key on top of the highest brick just behind the security cage of the front door. Ruby tiptoes to get it, but she's too short. She finds an empty clay pot, carefully steps up to reach it.

With all the windows shut, the house still smells of last night's spinach and fish. Ruby slides open the back glass door, lets the cool breeze in. There are pictures of other people's babies all over the fridge. Ruby stares at them, then opens the door for leftovers. She sniffs a Chinese carton of rice and moo shu, takes it to the beige couch, clicks on the TV, kicks off her shoes, and sits cross-legged.

Although he hasn't yet called, she considers dialing Pej. She changes her mind, thinking how embarrassed her father would be by her, running from man to man. The slightest bit of distress she has never handled on her own. At thirty-six this strikes her as a troublesome point.

Ruby channel-surfs, fantasizing about rock-climbing, race car driving, living in a cave. Maybe Joop is right, she thinks. Maybe this is nothing Outward Bound can't fix. She spills a drop of moo shu juice on her nylon pants, dips her finger in, licks. The taste then brings sharply to mind the entire bloody scene.

She grabs her sister's phone, calls Pej.

"Hello?"

"It's me, Ruby." She clears her throat.

"*Azizam*," he says, hesitates. She melts.

"*Salaam*," she says, smiles.

"*Salaam*," he says. She can hear his smile. He hesitates again. "Are you okay?"

"You didn't call."

"I didn't think you wanted to hear from me."

"How could you think that?"

"I read your quote in the paper."

"So?"

"You just sounded so disillusioned by all men, as if any of us were capable of such heinous things."

"I had no idea I sounded like that."

"But it doesn't matter. You're right. I should have called. And so . . . can I come see you now? I'd love to talk to you."

"I'm at my sister's. I'm staying here tonight, but I just wanted to hear your voice."

"Me too," he hesitates. "I miss you." Long silence. "I'm sorry about . . . everything—"

"No, no," she interrupts. "I'm the one who messed up . . . now everything is just so . . . surreal." She loudly exhales.

"I should have been there for you."

"It's okay. I'm okay."

"Can I see you tomorrow?"

"I'm . . . I want to. I'm not sure yet if I can." Ruby clears her throat. "Can I call you in the morning?"

"Yes, of course." He clears his throat too. "Anytime, yes."

"Okay," she says, waiting for courage to say something tender.

"Bye, baby." He waits.

"Bye." She hangs up.

Even though it is Ray who will be her true love, and it won't take her too long after meeting him to realize this, just before her last breath she will think of how it feels in the moment to want to say something loving, something life-saving and romantic, and it will be the end of this conversation with Pej that pops in. The feeling of it, she will remember word-for-word, and this will make her angry that she isn't instead thinking of something terribly profound, an answer to any mystery in life—nor for that matter is there even a thought about Ray—but rather just of this simple shortcoming, that could have been with almost anybody, just a small regret at the moment of passing, a disappointing and long-forgotten zit in the scheme of all things.

By the end of the night, long after her younger, taller, stronger-in-a-pinch sister has come home, and they have eaten together, Ruby is surprised to find herself happily sketching at the dinner table, a blanket over her feet, which Caspar used to warm as he lay under her drafting desk. There seems to be less pain to squeeze out. Ruby's sister, Hannah, sits on the couch, laughing at the TV screen, calling for Ruby to look at bad outfits and bad hair, the smell now in the house of the chocolate chip cookies they baked from the ready-made mix. Hannah also spares her the chill of aggrandizing the fact that Ruby very well could have met the killer the night Jeannie threw her the party. Spares her the boredom of having to go over and over it again, as she did with the detectives. Hannah—usually so uptight and judgmental even as a kid—is right now so thoughtful and funny and warm and relaxed, the best gift Ruby ever had.

She can leave her tomorrow or the day after next. Why should she get too caught up and comfortable in anyone else's space?

Chapter 5

Abigail in Healy

Ray

Just above Denali National Park with a view of the Alaska Range's highest point, Mt. McKinley, Ray finds a small blond wood cabin to rent from an older couple who are slowly building on their alder and black spruce-thick land. Walking the grounds, fragrant with woodsy, fresh mold, he is struck with the feeling of an unending distance from civilization. Here nature rules, and its presence is overpowering, even to a farmboy like Ray.

From his bed, he stares at the knots in the raw wood, like hundreds of eyes on the sweat of his guilt. They watch the phantasmagoric beating of a man into slabs of pulpy, crimson flesh. They see the body's bludgeoned balls, the penis crushed into a cunt by Ray's boot. The midnight blue at the swamp. The weight and mess of the pulverized body as he lifted it like a baby to the grassy edge. The night alive with crickets, frogs, humming with the bubbling of waking gators. What they cannot see are the dead man's acts, or his victim who would feel he deserved it. Ray might want out of this room, but his special logic concludes that the cabin's audience picked him.

In its vast spread of surrounding, unspoiled earth, the small community of the coal-mining town, Healy, is comforting to him. The number of people he passes in any given day reminds Ray of his unfettered birthplace, Union City. In the older couple he adopts an aunt and uncle. Ethel, in her late sixties, with eyes as opaque as the glacial till, is a fellow Midwesterner. She is thin, wispy, teetering between sprightly and morose, one day game for mischief, entirely apathetic the next. She greets him with the latest of Fairbanks' front-page news, or she barely looks up at him. While making his way to the communal fridge, he sympathizes with her scoffing at the tedium of her chores. When he suggests they take a trip to the nursery together now that the soil may be sufficiently thawed, she grabs her cheeriest coat and his elbow, and off they go. Among the Alaskan throngs who rush to the nursery for the same reason, they chitchat with enthusiasts who boast of their robust seedlings that have been kept inside the house as starter plants. Ray picks native chocolate lilies, arctic daisies, pink pussy-toes, and darkthroat shooting stars. Following Ray's lead, Ethel also takes the indigenous geraniums, bluebells, lady's slippers, and forget-me-nots. Delighted, they unload her truck by armfuls of joy. During the course of the week, they get all of it planted around the main house. Then much to Ray's dismay, it's back to Ethel's usual every other day cold shoulder. Her Canadian husband, George, however—slightly younger and miraculously naïve—consistently brightens at the sight of Ray each morning, happy to talk carpenter shop.

Ray could easily talk his way into a job with George, helping him to realize a compound of lodging cabins and a breakfast café. But he avoids the commitment, even while using their address to receive the month's Florida bills from Gary. In two weeks, Ray has already hiked past the point in the park one can go without a guide, split open his shin in an idiotic fall across public boundaries, and become a regular at the town's only real restaurant and bar.

He is the sole patron who calls the gregarious part-time waitress by her given name. It is Abigail, rather than Abbie, who fancies herself easy. This in particular helps cushion his way in past her fun-but-tough-girl defenses. Since Ray imagines what the enraged face might look like of everyone he meets, he is relieved to find that he can't picture Abigail's. So she in turn jumps the hoop of his first test. He surprises himself by sharing pathetic tidbits of his third ex-wife's idiosyncratic jealousies and rages, and meandering tales of lonely adolescent stoner days. Abbie, who just turned twenty-seven but comes off much older than her years, will tell most anyone how she got to Alaska. Originally from Marin County—her mother Korean, her father half Korean and Jewish—she'd come with her naturalist lover. He had just gotten his degree in environmental science and was scouting the world for his best impact. Abbie left him and remained in Alaska, since he was younger and too keen on saving the planet. She'd wanted instead to be his damsel in distress. For years preceding the naturalist, Abbie had been going from coke to heroin and back again. Before she could commit to quitting, she became diabetic, steadily losing her sight. This is the detail she lets no one in on. Other than her thick glasses, Abbie keeps her bad vision to her ophthalmologist and herself. People are blurs, the printed word is art, and driving a dangerous instinct.

Abbie is often mistaken for an intelligent, attractive native who does not know or care what the Lower Forty-eight has to offer. Besides Ned who once brought his horse in to get drunk from his pitcher of beer, she has not fucked any of the locals. Ray is not the first tourist through these doors to impress her with warmth and compassion, but she lets him know, in no uncertain terms, that her clit stands at attention for him.

Ray has not touched a woman in the four months since it fell apart with his ex-wife Sonya. Most of it had been about sex, though he'd briefly tried convincing himself that he could love her. As much as his father's one-line advice—"Keep your dick in your pants"—angered him after his second divorce, at this point in time it seems like words to live by. The ache in his balls he relieves almost nightly to the room's voyeurs, those dreaded eyes in the wood paneling. And he resists and resists again, especially since he believes Abbie will make a much better friend. Still he does not realize that all the resisting is more because he believes he no longer deserves any more casual sex quickies. After all, he ended up marrying three of them.

Abbie invites Ray over for dinner, and with a bottle of red wine in hand, he enjoys the view up the walkway of yellow monkeyflowers, blue iris, arnica, and narcissus. Abbie opens the door, and he enters a soundtrack of thirties big band music, the house softly lit with brightly colored scarves thrown over thrift store lamps. He is overwhelmed with a feeling he could describe only as a deep turquoise blue, watching her move in a clingy black dress with small, fussy print from the kitchen to the living room. She maintains a confident speed of constant gabbing and theatrical gesturing that he realizes remind him of his mother. He smiles with warmth that smoothes the inside of his chest. Then it painfully converges, rises like helium in his esophagus. With her back to him, Abbie never notices the tears well up as he quickly wipes them away. Relieved by this, he doesn't know she could never have spotted them in the first place.

They sit down to a meal of mashed potatoes and green pepper caribou; they eat in silence until Ray notices a skull on top of the television cabinet.

"What's that over there?"

"What?" Her small pink mouth makes an O as she pushes back the ridge of her black-framed glasses.

"Is that a *dog's* skull?"

"Can you believe it? I found it hiking more than a year ago. Way on the other side of the Nenana River. Seemed like some kind of sign to me, but what, I've never figured." She flips her hand like an old lady, takes in a large forkful of gamy meat.

"Near the mine?"

"Sort of. I could show you where. It's gorgeous. Felt like I discovered this trail all on my own—which is impossible, of course—but I remembered saying to myself when I found it, this is why I moved to Alaska. It's the perfect time to go and check out the trail, before all the wretched mosquitoes come back for the kill."

"This is amazing," Ray says, having gotten up from the table to feel it in his hands. "Looks like a wolf's."

"A friend says it's more likely a malamute or husky."

"This is something, the shape it's in. Looks really old," he says, examining the skull with the earnestness of a fifties television hero.

"You should have it, then. Right?"

"No, I can't," Ray says, his hand up in a stop sign. He returns to the table, tosses his yellow tresses back like a girl.

"I insist." Abbie scoots her chair back. Her dainty nostrils flare. "Where's your coat?"

"On the couch," Ray says, turning around, alarmed that she might be kicking him out. Abbie gets the skull, wraps it up carefully in his jacket. Uncomfortable with gifts, Ray shovels in the last of his food. "This is delicious, by the way."

"I wanted to make you a roast pork, but . . ." She blushes, swallows hard, pushes her glasses back on her face. Ray interrupts before she can deliver one of her bad Jewish Korean jokes.

"Hmm. This is such a treat. I've never tasted caribou, and haven't had venison since the last time I went hunting. That was years ago. Roast pork is good too. When I first moved to Florida, I went with my friend where they had these wild boars near their property. We were stupid enough to try and catch one. This hog came charging, gashed open my friend's leg. That was a bloody time, I'd forgotten about that! You should see those hogs too." He crinkles up his nose as if smelling something stink. "They have really thick and long but sparse kind of hair." Ray shoots his finger from his joints in illustration.

"Sounds pretty gross."

"Good dinner conversation, heh?" He raises his thick dark brows. "I should tell you some construction site stories, more bloody and 'gross.'"

"You can say anything in front of me." She flips her hand at him, straightens up in her chair, and strokes her throat, exposing her bitten nails down to the quick. "So how long you planning on staying?"

"Long enough to go whitewater kayaking down the glacial river."

"This cold is hanging on a little longer than usual. But I thought you were planning on working. The first opener was called. And I hear from the guys that sockeye salmon gets going mid-June in Bristol Bay."

"Yeah." He heavily breathes in. "At first I was even thinking about doing the Bering Sea king crab thing—"

"Now that's really dangerous," Abbie cuts in. "People die all the time out there. I hear like six or seven boats go down a season."

"That doesn't scare me none. If anything, it sounds all the more worth it. You can make good money. But just as I was going to say"—he raises his brows, irritated that he had been interrupted— "I'm not even sure about fishing anymore. I've been working all my life, you know. Think I'll take a little break."

"Money soon runs out. Right? And don't I know it."

"I'm okay for a while." He looks down at his food, even more irritated now at the hint of being lectured.

"Lot of guys around here lost their job at the mine. This town is changing, people moving out, people moving in anticipating Denali's Yosemite-Disney morph."

"Doesn't that always happen? The crowding, the paving of paradise?"

"This is a protected park," she says, restless, sighing with the boredom of the direction in conversation. She tosses her head to the side, demonstrating the body of her lush, black chin-length hair. She slowly caresses together the palms of her hands. "And I'd love to show you more of it."

"I was thinking I should head on back," he says, getting up.

"But I have dessert," she says, screwing her forehead into the appearance of a map. "You're not gonna walk through that fucking door until you get your sweets!" She spanks the tabletop once, stands to clear the dishes.

Ray makes his way around the room, looking at all the objects, afraid of asking any questions, showing too much interest. On a shelf with dust a millimeter thick, there is a small, black glass sculpture of a girl bringing to mind when he was high and fifteen, staring at his black-light poster, Swamp Mirage. It was the silhouette of an hourglass girl, within a tree, who would look to him now like a cross between sixties black power and a Led Zeppelin album cover psychedelic fantasy. He couldn't remember buying it, or who could have given it to him. But he could see it right now in the corner of his room, caught in the dreamy haze of smoke.

"So wha' da ya think of this?" Abbie says, entering with a hot apple pie.

"Wow! Now why didn't I smell that?" he says, rubbing his hands together, then bending his knees like two steps in a dance.

"Maybe it's the incense, maybe it's my perfume," she says, owning off the middle of her chest with her hand. She turns quickly on her heel, returns with a scoop in a mug of warm water, and a pint of vanilla ice cream.

"Hmm, this is righteous," he says, licking his finger, his big, mesmerizingly blue eyes twinkling. The apples and cream melt on his tongue, he closes his eyes, deeply inhales. When he opens, he finds her staring at him as if she were desperately trying to make out his features, wanting to touch their shapes. "Why aren't you having any pie?"

"I'm on a diet," she says, leaving out the diabetes. "Enjoy yourself. And make it good. I'm living vicariously." She leans closer now that she has an excuse. Ray tries his best to get comfortable with it.

"Why do you stay here, Abigail? You're a Northern Californian, and from what I hear, it's just as beautiful." He smacks his tongue, then clears his throat, worrying he might be turning her on. "Those famous drives up the coast, PCH, whatever."

"It's a different kind of beauty here, even more expansive, isolating . . . freeing. There's nothing like this subarctic sky, I've never had a more intense relationship with the dark and the light." She leans back, smoothes the folds in her dress. "I had to kick, you know, the coke and the smack, and then I had this gung-ho feeling, like, like . . . I was going to join the Healy Volunteer Fire Department." Again she spanks the table, and laughs. Ray doesn't join in so, embarrassed, she gets quiet. Ray licks his lower lip of cream.

"And then I went down to Seward. Have you been there?"

"No."

"And I took one of those corny wildlife cruises, and saw the whales, the eagles, I think we even saw a bear, but nothing could compare to when the guide turned off the engine and parked the boat in the middle of the water, so we could watch a glacier melt. I mean the feeling of it, the crash into the ocean like thunder, the silence, the calm that just fills you up. Made me feel like, you know, I could heal all this shit I'd built up inside."

"Yeah, I know." He looks down at the table, then shyly back up at her. "Wow, I'm stuffed right full." He rubs his belly. As if about to give grace, he gently puts both palms on the table, then abruptly gets up. "I should get going now. Thanks for dinner."

"My pleasure," she says, getting up to pull him tightly to her. Her scent is a cinnamon citrus, and though Ray's nose usually takes offense to any kind of perfume, the guesswork at her smell beneath is suddenly intriguing. He swiftly backs away, and she chews her lip.

Ray carefully unrolls the coat to reveal the skull. He chivalrously bows to her. She folds her arms, weakly smiles. She then remembers to wrap up the pie.

"I insist you take this with you. It'll go to waste otherwise. Next time you're the host, right?"

"I've got no kitchen." He raises his hands, balancing in the air the pie and the skull. She shakes her head like that means nothing. He looks at the clock, it's just past nine, and she opens the door to the vivid, extended twilight.

Parked a good distance from her door, Ray walks to his newly rented four-wheel drive, sorely missing the company of men.

At the Denali Outdoor Center, Ray's eyes glaze over with impatience at the guide's obligatory reading of risks he'll be taking in whitewater kayaking. This spiel is delivered with a curt, cocky East Coast angst. Ray assures him he has done this before, and with much talent and confidence, at that. There's a quiet, middle-aged, salt-and-pepper-haired German going solo as well; he looks at the ground during most of the conversation. There are two girls going tandem, and although both of them have swimmer's shoulders, the guide eyes them with suspicion and trepidation. As the jovial driver gets everyone fitted for dry suits, he doesn't laugh as the guide jokes about Ray's size-sixteen boots.

After Ray helps the driver load the kayaks on top of the van, they slap each other five as the guide doubles back for his favorite helmet. The German sits in front of the two girls. Just behind is Ray with his long thighs spread apart for knee-room, his arms sprawled across the top of his seat. The guide prattles on about what to expect, as Ray looks out the window over the shack stores to the forested ridges, then up at the rearview mirror where he spots the driver clocking his irritation at the incessant prickish chatter.

"Where you from?" the driver calls to him.

"Originally?" Ray cocks his head to the side and smiles.

"Okay," the driver says, smiling back like Ray is familiar.

"Born and raised in Michigan, but I've lived in South Florida for the past fifteen years."

"Really. Now I took you for a California surfer. Or some kind of star in extended pose of slumming." He looks at the road then at Ray, with an expression like a wink. Ray rolls his tongue against the roof of his mouth, trying to think of a way to give him shit. But he blows it off. The driver gives up the playful wait. "What do you do?"

"Construction."

"Done a lot of that in the past myself, though I can't say I miss it. *'All I wanna see is assholes and elbows!'*" he calls abruptly in a dumbshit foreman's voice. Ray nods with a forward motion in his neck and chin, as if moving to a backbeat. "I'm from Georgia," the driver continues, "but I've been here longer than I can tell."

"Watch the equipment," the guide says, irritated, as the driver makes a last minute swerve into their destination. The guide nervously runs his fingers through his short, dark, curly hair. He is pale but looks as if the sun might bring out a Mediterranean tone. His bottom and top lashes stick straight out, so close together his eyes appear like sea anemones.

The girls hop out of the truck like five-year-old boys from a family car trip. They jump into the legs of the crackling dry suits, struggling to get the S/M tight neoprene neck over their heads. One grabs the helmets, while the other roughly winds her blunt, thick crop of hair into a ponytail. Ray watches their silent, intimate, choreographed ease, wishing he still had a woman of his own to take care of. The guide stops them from putting the helmets on, so he can further caution them about the speed of a glacial river made of water six hours newborn.

The German has trouble with balance as he gets into one of the inflatable kayaks. Ray turns around to hold it steady for him, then eases on into his own. The German mutters thanks as if to an uncle he always disliked. Ray paddles his way into the center of quiet in the water, which the guide calls the boulevard. He looks up at the driver who makes a peace sign, saluting it from his broad forehead, soldier-style. Ray waves back like a beauty queen on a float. The driver laughs heartily.

"We gotta switch!" one of the girls says to the other. The guide holds his hand up as if he needs to stop everyone from taking off too fast. Ray finally takes a look at them. The one moving to the front of the kayak has a button nose the size of a baby's kiss. The other has eyes that look like the sun is always in them; the freckles on her cheekbones lay splattered there, as if to emphasize that fact. She takes her place in back, to control their direction. She feels Ray watching her, so she meets his gaze head-on.

"Let's go!" the guide says, paddling his classic, tiny sixty-gallon fiberglass in exaggerated demonstration of how easy this all could be if they only watched him. Ray pulls ahead, missing who asked him, but hears the guide bragging of riding his motorcycle from the East to Alaska. If quiet weren't much more important to him just then, he would have asked what kind of bike.

The scenery comes alive on either side of Ray, and he gets that feeling he had as a boy running on the farm for acres until he dropped from exhaustion, the corn crops waving over his head. He would lose himself under them until he was nothing at all.

They hit the speed of the river, now, Ray way in front, the guide calling out the holes that could suck a raft in, swallow the body, regurgitate, and swallow again until the water squelches the belly's last breath. This is what happened last week to the woman on a raft of sixteen—their guide in a foolhardy moment of trust over respect.

"We can relax here, just take it easy. Ladies, okay?" the guide says, paddling backward to them, far from the hole. The freckled one snarls, they don't need him.

The sky is so gray, no sunglasses required, revealing sharply the ridges of the canyon walls, the evergreen pines, and bare rock sometimes stacked straight up. Ray marvels at how clearly he can see water cutting the land, how it makes a path on its own. The river so murky with sediment he can't imagine a fish surviving.

After forty-five minutes of racing the heart and squeezing the palms raw and sore on the paddle, the guide calls ahead that it's snack time. Ray doubles back to the landing.

"A juicy for you, and a juicy for you, and a juicy for you too," the guide says, smiling proudly, the German grabbing one before he can be treated like a preschooler as well. The guide then roughly tosses a granola bar to each, resentful of their attitudes.

Ray stretches his neck, rolls his arms back in their sockets, feels the sharp, cool air in his ears, his helmet now off. The cherry juice is too sweet, but the granola is wedded to peanut butter, inspiring him to lie back in the dirt, fingers clasped to pillow his head.

"You guys are all doing really good," the guide says, hugging his knees, looking at the girls. "So, are you two athletes?"

"We're on the Arizona volleyball team," the button-nosed one says.

"I did crew in college," says the freckled one in her perpetual squint.

"Why didn't you tell me?" the guide asks, leaning now toward them, then turning to check on the German. "You know, I mean no offense to anyone here, but we get a lot of people, foreigners, like Swedes, Germans of course, French, whatever, and usually they come thinking it's some kind of Disneyland ride. Especially the Japanese. You know, we get these little Japanese girls who have been dared to do it, and they're egging each other on, giggling themselves silly, and without fail, they take a spill in this freezing water, risking not only their own lives, but everyone else's, as this does take skill and concentration. This river is not playing games with you."

Ray sits up, tries concentrating on the flow of the water to suppress his slow-building rage. He tells himself he'll just keep his mouth shut, so he can get through the rest of the way as pleasantly as possible.

"What's your name again?" the guide asks the button-nosed one.

"Jess," she says, looking at her friend, then glancing at Ray, as if for defense. The freckled one looks at him too, then at the guide, tennis match style.

"My baby's name is Jessica!" the guide says, smiling ear-to-ear.

"That's not really my name, it's just what adopted me from my school days running track. I'm Hopi, so my real name a lot of people don't get."

"Hopi Indian? You don't look it!"

"And what are *you*?" Ray asks, flaring his nostrils, cocking his head at the guide.

"I'm from Maine," the guide says, grabbing his sack to pull another granola bar to offer to Ray. "The family line is Irish, some English, a little Dutch too."

"Yeah, well you don't look it." Ray stands up, clutching his helmet, walking to his kayak in announcement that break is over. The German sneezes, wipes the snot with the back of his hand, springs to his feet like a puppy. The guide closes up his sack, loudly inhales, then with a slow exhale visually rids himself of whatever bother he'd let in.

The rest of the way is how Ray wanted it. He peacefully tortures himself comparing this Alaskan gray day and the surrounding dark evergreen with that night in Florida, the stark, deep-night blue, the moon lighting the lush neon greens so eerily. The rush of ice water splashes him in the face, snapping him out of it. A grin spreads him warm as he paddles with more strength and speed to meet the ferocity of the current. He even enjoys the guide's native style— circling a rock, sticking the nose of the kayak down in the last hole. The water sucks him in as far as his chest, his back against the rear of the kayak. Stopped by its buoyancy, the guide pops back out vertically, almost airborne.

The driver is waiting for them there at the water boulevard. His worn hands shoved deep down in his bleached-splashed denim pockets, the wind blowing wisps into bangs from his shoulder-length, reddish-brown hair. Ray helps him again in stacking all the equipment. He notices the driver reaches only as far as Ray's shoulders. They exchange names—his is Charlie, which almost suits him.

Later they both happen to arrive a few minutes early at the bar. Ray spots Charlie in the parking lot smoking the end of a fat spliff, so he hops in for a toke. Ray lays his head back on the seat rest, his eyes glazing over with the golden light of the sun breaking through the clouds near eight at night.

"It's a trip, huh," Charlie says, his widely set hazel eyes red but kind and alert. Ray nods his head. "When I first got here, I couldn't sleep the entire summer. I was a walking zombie, so far past tired I may as well have been on meth."

"I know what that's like. Had a few weeks in Florida like that," Ray says, looking at the dashboard.

"Yeah, the heat could do that to me too. Working outside in Georgia in *August*, man. I'd sweat so much during the day, drink so many beers at night, I was so dehydrated I was wired. Then I figured out water and one of these could cure the problem." He holds up the end of the roach and laughs. "This is the kind kind, eh?"

"There's Abigail," Ray says, getting out of the truck. She waves but heads back in through the side door. Ray puts his hands on his hips. "What did I do?"

"You know Abbie well?"

"No, man. She's sure cool."

"She is. She just probably didn't recognize you is all. I get the feeling, you know, she can't see shit," Charlie says, banging his truck door closed.

Together they walk through the side entrance with the happy notion it's a western saloon.

Chapter 6

Sisters from the Lower Forty-Eight

Ruby

At first it is Hawaii at the forefront of Ruby's mind, as Joop suggests. Then Mexico, for how much farther her dollar can stretch. This shifts again to the U.S. for a drive up the southern route from California to New York, because she's never done it. She would need her car for that, and so could forget about the best offer and not sell it. But then this makes her feel too wishy-washy. She'd rather make a commitment to storage, and a change in all of the major areas of her life. Besides, all of the preceding destinations sound too attractive to Hannah, who now wants to accompany her. So a Discovery channel show and a wild hair for adventure switch her sights to Alaska, which is undesirable to her younger sibling. Ruby tries convincing her that her vacation time might be better spent on a relaxing, exotic trip. She reminds her that she's got action, daredeviling, and recharged adrenaline at the top of her list. But Hannah, always resistant to discouragement, packs her bags two weeks thick.

"The men don't seem so randy here," Hannah says, sipping her drink and looking around conspiratorially on their fourth day in Anchorage.

"I kinda knew that. Somebody, can't remember who, maybe a friend of one of the girls at the studio, came here expecting to get laid the minute she stepped off the plane. Never happened."

"Wait. Watch this hot chick walking by us right now, and watch the men," Hannah says, leaning on the table with her elbows spread.

"I know. They're very subtle."

"And the brothers seem like, 'Don't look at me, leave me alone, I came here to forget you exist.'"

"Kinda, huh. But that one at the gym was cool," Ruby says, lowering her voice, hoping for influence.

"Can't believe you dragged me to the *gym*," she says, laying her hand over Ruby's menu, waiting for her to look up into the large exaggerated expression on her face. "And the dreadful boredom of the sporting goods store. We were there all day!" She snaps back into conspiracy tone. "Okay, now watch this chick. A blonde." Her head turns all the way around. "Go on, shake it, honey." She cups her mouth and laughs.

"Hannah. Will you stop? You're so obvious. Will you use your peripheral vision and not your swivel head?"

"She's not paying any attention to me. Look at these guys! They aren't desperate at all!"

"Those two guys over there looked. But do you see how many women are here, Hannah? It's like any city, L.A. even. They can have their pick." She straightens in her chair to crack her back. Because her breasts now jut confidently in her tight black T, the guy at the table diagonally across from theirs notices instantly.

"Wonder if the gay men have the same problem. Some of them have just as disappointed a look on their faces as some of these women," Hannah says. The guy ogling Ruby is behind Hannah's back. "Aren't these women hard?" Hannah presses.

"Will you look at your menu." Ruby giggles, shakes her head.

"So why'd we come, again?"

"Because it's your goal to step foot in every state?" Ruby says, tracing the headings with her finger down to seafood.

"Because *you* want to kill yourself climbing some icy cliff."

"Can I get you something to drink?" The waitress appears, hands on her front apron pockets.

"I think we're ready to order, aren't we?" Ruby says, looking at her sister.

"Go ahead," Hannah says, irritated to change gears, putting her permed-straight hair behind her ears.

"I'll have grilled salmon and—" Ruby begins.

"We don't have salmon," the waitress interrupts impatiently, shifting her weight to the other leg. "We've got halibut, it's good."

Ruby looks at her sister, who looks frantic, studying the menu.

"I'll have a Cobb salad, then," Ruby says, "and a glass of Cabernet."

"I'll have the same." Hannah sighs, snaps closed her menu, hands it to the waitress. She sighs again, slides the catch of her silver chain back in place. Fingers the small heart charm.

Ruby rolls her head backward to crack her neck. She gets a jolt of energy, wishing she could leave her sister sitting here, hop on her board, and skate. Ever since the horrible scene, staying put brings nightmarish images to her head. Nothing shakes the feeling that she is alone, even Hannah's gentle snoring at night, two feet from her single bed.

"D'you know Mom wrote another play?" Hannah asks, now twiddling the tiny diamond stud sparkling the lobe of her perfectly formed ear.

"Did she?"

"I wish she'd do something with it. Those women she meets with once a month do nothing but kill time and her spirit."

"Surprised to hear you say that."

"Why? Don't you know anybody in your world who might have the kind of connections she needs?"

"*My* world? What do I know about theater?"

"Come on, Ruby, you know what I mean. You know so many people in the arts, there's gotta be somebody. Dad's draining her with all these dull city council folks. It's worse than the Urban League, and far, far worse than those nasty academes."

"Surprised to hear this from you of all people."

"Why?" Hannah asks, jerking her head back so far into her neck she makes a small double chin.

"You gotta deal with people like that almost every day."

"That's why I know what I'm saying."

The waitress brings their wine, they clink glasses. Hannah turns around, happens to catch dead in the eye the guy sweet on Ruby. He raises his glass, then his friend turns and does too. Ruby puts her face in her hands, waiting for her sister to quit engaging them.

"What?" Hannah asks, her head to the side. "They're not so bad." Ruby rolls her eyes. "Especially the one with his back to us."

"Not my type."

"What is your type, anyway? I never get it. You are so *all* over the place." She jerks her head quickly, as if shaking crawling skin. She is thinking of Ruby's two women. "And I *never* understood why you didn't stick with Nelson."

"Nelson. His name was enough to get me down," Ruby says, taking another long sip. Hannah bats an imaginary fly.

"Nelson was a fine brother, ambitious and accomplished, and very very charming."

"Nelson *is*, not was, all those things, but he lives in New York!"

"So? You're looking for a change."

"We did so much talking, you know. Talk, talk, talk. I loved it at first, but then the long-distance thing makes everything so fucked up. He's here for a documentary, then he's there for a book, then he's here for a fight, then he's there, three hours ahead and neither of us can remember what the other really said. It just didn't work. No big deal. Wasn't meant to happen." Ruby sighs, exasperated.

"Don't get so excited!"

"I'm not," Ruby says. She almost spills her wine when she looks up to the guy from the table, now approaching theirs.

"Hello," he says. Now behind him is the waitress, irked because she has two full plates in her hand. "Let me get out of your way," he says, adjusting his belt, his posture sad. The busboy brings silverware, crashing like cymbals on the table, just as the waitress sets the food down. Ruby looks dizzy with unease around so many people. Hannah looks like she wants to laugh.

"Hi." She sticks out her hand. "I'm Hannah, this is Ruby."

"I didn't mean to disturb your meal. Bad timing. Just wanted to say hello."

"Well, hello," Hannah says, ignoring her sister, who is dressing her salad.

"Where you girls from?" he asks. Ruby flares her nostrils at the word "girls," feeling like a woman now wanting to look her age.

"L.A.," Hannah says, nodding and looking up as if it hurts her neck.

"L.A., huh. Hollywood. Wow. Mind if I sit down for a minute?" Ruby opens her hands the way Al does at Jeannie when he's irritated.

"Where are you from? And you never said your name, by the way," Hannah says, now dressing her salad but warmly welcoming.

"Born and raised here, actually. And my name's Mike, and that's Bob over there. I thought maybe, if you wanted some tips on the sights, I'd be happy to give them to you. We were going to head over to F Street Station after this and would love if you could join us."

Ruby pushes air through her nose as if blowing out a booger. She finally looks him in the face. His exuberant, protruding forehead is prematurely lined; the dark irises of his eyes blot out most of the whites. His chin so strangely delicate, Ruby imagines his parents to have been mistakenly complimented many times on their baby daughter. If he weren't dressed like he wanted to be taken as an individual, she would assume him to be in a frat.

"So what do you girls do?" Hopefully, he looks at Ruby, then back at Hannah.

"I'm a consultant, and Ruby's an animator. She designs characters for that hit cartoon *Rootown*. You know, Hyena Harry and Pickled Pete?"

"Yeah. Wow. I see them everywhere, T-shirts, lunchboxes, everything. That's cool. Really cool. Cartoons. Yeah. You know, you actually look like a cartoon, and I mean that in the most complimentary way," he says, earnestly looking into Ruby's eyes.

She raises the right corner of her upper lip. Hannah's brow muscle lurches forward.

"I mean you're so tiny and shapely and beautiful, like a brown Betty Boop with all of this big, great hair." He raises his hand to touch it, but she jerks her head back. "I could see you in a comic book, the dynamically gorgeous and cute superhero, you know, slaying men like so many dragons."

"You've got to be kidding me," Ruby says, her mouth a little full of bacon. She looks at Hannah, like get rid of him.

"You look too young to know from Betty Boop," Hannah says, giggling, wanting more inanity.

"My dad was obsessed with her. In fact, it's funny you should be in animation, my dad has all the original Superman comics," he says, looking keen, more willing to press the case.

Ruby suppresses a yawn since her mouth is full of egg and tomato this time. The guy's friend gets up, closes in on the table.

"I'm Bob," he says, shaking Hannah's hand first, clocking Ruby's disinterest.

"Hi, Bob." Ruby then turns to the first guy. "Listen, if Hannah here wants to go to . . . what was it?"

"F Street Station. The food is much better than here, and we can get some drinks."

"Well, if Hannah wants to go, she can, but I'm dead tired."

Hannah looks perfectly miffed at the idea of being ditched.

"No way, I'm going back with you. It's nice to meet you both, but will you excuse us here?" Hannah takes a swig of her wine. They nod and head back toward their table. Ruby watches them squirm with their wallets over the bill. Hannah closes her hands into fists.

"So who cares, Ruby? Come on. I wasn't going anywhere with those fools. Why can't you lighten up just a bit? I mean, even *try* to have some fun. Let's just forget everything. We're on a trip!"

"Did I *ask* you here?"

Hannah freezes in place, looks Ruby straight in the eye, until a little guilt flattens her older sister's face. Hannah turns around, signaling for the waitress. The busboy catches her eye, she asks him for the check. She doesn't touch the rest of her food. And they are silent in the white midsize rental car all the way to the hotel. In the parking lot, Ruby asks her if she has her key, then tells her she's going to the office to check her e-mail. The sky is crinkled with cirrus clouds in the eerie pinkish gray day-for-night. Hannah keeps walking without acknowledging Ruby's sentence.

Ruby smiles at the front desk clerk, who is no more than sixteen. She's gabbing on the phone, Ruby points at the computer, the clerk waves. She logs on, pleasantly surprised that the hotel doesn't charge for computer time. There is mail to RubyFalls@earthlink.net from RochelleX@earthlink.net. Jeannie, still fond of her Rochelle Rosewood days, hangs on to the moniker, her gifts from fans, and her colleague signatures on the walls in her literal hall of fame.

I miss you, Ruby! Hope you're having fun and your sister's not driving you too crazy. How I know they can be. Don't I have too many. And heard from none of them, of course, the bitches from hell. What kind of losers never leave Missouri? All of them! Those little old ladies living in a shoe, ill from the claustrophobia in their heads. Guess who came to see me, though. Henry's daughter, Amy!!! I could not BELIEVE it. She brought me flowers and everything. A month after the fact, but hey. She's got guts.

Courtroom years ago was the last place I'd seen her. She's pregnant with her second child. Spent most of the time talking about her kid, and morning sickness, as if that was something I ever did. She seemed perfectly innocent and sweet, though she had the nerve to tell me about some Rhodesian breeders, as if I don't know any, as if I could even begin to think about something like that. Al still thinks she and her brother had something to do with it. No way, I say. He thinks she has motivations, all the questioning, you know, figures she had to put some good will my way. Get them off the track. But do you remember that guy at your birthday party? The one with the hare lip and the goatee? They brought him in for questioning. I know, 'cause the detective came by to drill me on how I knew him. Fawn's the one who invited him. Anyway, who knows, he was a freak. I can't imagine what he'd have to do with it, though. It doesn't make any sense.

I shouldn't go on about all this shit. Al is driving me crazy, that man is so hard. He picks right now to try and sell the club! Anything to distract him from me, he'll do. That club's been everything up until now, it makes no sense. He's got his eye on some loser restaurant in Studio City. It makes me sick.

Listen, baby, don't forget to go by those mud flats. It's a

beautiful sight. You know what I'm talking about? Reminds
me of this guy Dave I almost fell in love with. He's the one
who took me to Alaska, brought me to the flats. I found it
so beautiful, how the snow melts and brings down the soil
to the water's edge, all the mud just settling there. Spectacular.
And you know that's where all the whorehouses used to be!
And you gotta check out all the fur shops. They're all over
the place, you can get great deals. Coats, gloves. Better yet,
go buy yourself a fur bikini and find some hard, young stud
and fuck his lights out. I think it's so romantic you're there.
I was you in another life. Love you. I keep your little house
empty, should you decide to come back.
　　Big smooch, J.

Ruby massages her forehead, tears stinging her face. The clerk
is still gabbing, so she can lose herself. She begins a letter back to
Jeannie, full of love and appreciation, but then she goes off on the
tangent at hand, so deletes it. She knows she should get back to
her sister instead of sitting here with the intention of ragging on
her.

Upstairs in the two-story hotel, Hannah lies on her stomach,
arms and chin propped on a pillow at the foot of the bed. The TV
is loud, the curtains drawn, the air in the room stifling and tense.
Ruby opens the window, spins around with courage for an apology,
but bumps her toe on Hannah's packed bag.

"You can't deal with anybody, that's your problem," Hannah
says with venom, still looking at the screen.

"Look, I'm sorry. I shouldn't have said that. It's just that you
were pushing me. And you know this trip was my thing." Ruby
stands with her arms folded. Hannah flips from her stomach and
up onto her butt, quick and slick as a gymnast.

"Your 'thing' is right. It's always about you. No wonder you
broke up with Pej. And what was it, really? Did he not jump
through enough hoops?"

"Whatever, Hannah. Let's just leave it 'til the morning."

"And you spent a *fortune* yesterday! Buying all that equipment
just 'cause you tried amateur hour at Joshua Tree. It's beyond rash.

Nothing like taking surf lessons at home the way you did, and borrowing someone's board. I can understand all that, you've always been sporty. But did you notice in that little paper, *Eagle River News* or what was it called? You know, after our hike at the Thunderbird Falls, didn't you see in the obits all the climbing deaths?"

"There were two. *Two* accidents and that's it!"

"And isn't two enough for a tiny town like that? Why don't you spend the rest of the time skating here? Or figure out where to go snowboarding or something."

"It's summer, Hannah, it's June, and it's the best time here to *climb*. And that's what I'm going to do."

When Hannah leaves for L.A. and Ruby checks out of the Anchorage hotel, the only place near Denali not booked far in advance is the beat-up hotel with the restaurant and bar Abbie works in. Doesn't take too long for the two California women to notice one another. Ruby's alone, and Abbie's alone, and together they spar all spurious advances from bored, unemployed men. Since the two weeks of group practice climbs with her yogic, sensitive Colorado-born guide, Ruby comes in for her four-thirty supper near the end of Abbie's shift. First Abbie brings her an empty plate, two packages of cashews from the bar stash, and a glass of bad house Chardonnay. Ruby empties both packages on the plate, picks through to the broken ones, which drives Abbie crazy when she sits down to join her, because she can't see what it is she's doing.

"So tell me what happened with her," Abbie says, opening the restaurant window, lighting up her cigarette.

"Who?" Ruby accidentally bites her tongue instead of the cashew. She touches the blood with her finger.

"Your girlfriend, the one you were telling me about yesterday. The one who looks like Julia Butterfly."

"She didn't really look like Julia Butterfly," Ruby says, moving her neck slightly, slyly, as if to a sexy song. "Before she cut her hair I can remember her being mistaken for her at least twice, but afterward, never. Though her father always called her a treehugger, fittingly enough."

"And so . . ."

"So what?"

"I want to hear about her. You were making me homesick yesterday, going on about her, and I want to be tortured just a little more."

"But I met her in Santa Cruz, my first year in school. We spent only one summer in Berkeley, though she had that stupid little job in Mill Valley. It wasn't very long we were hanging in your neck of the woods."

"But what happened with her? What's her name again?"

"Ireland."

"Ireland, that's right. I remember seeing green when you said her name."

"Her real name is Iris, but she preferred to be called Ireland. Anyway, not much to tell. We met in class, she was very opinionated and glamorous to me. We had a lot of the same tastes and heroes. I ended up at art school in L.A., and she at Berkeley, though she was actually torn between film and studying fish farming at Humboldt. I can't remember now what she actually ended up majoring in. We reconnected years later in L.A. when she got a job with this movie catering company." Ruby looks up at her.

"And what was the problem?"

"She got a little freaky is all."

"Freaky?" Abbie blows her smoke out of the window.

"One night in the car I changed the radio station from some fake and tired Christian singer I was ragging on, and Ireland called me 'Godless,' and that was enough to just cut me to the bone. That was the beginning of all our problems."

"Like what?"

"Besides her going so religious on me?" Ruby leans forward in her seat, her eyes big with the expression that Abbie should just cork it. "She had vengeful fits. Temper tantrums. Chopping her hair off in front of me was one of them. As if that were supposed to hurt me or something."

"And . . ."

"She threw shit. She was jealous. Possessive. Mind games. She was a talker."

"And you don't like talk," Abbie teases.

"It's not that I don't like talk!" Ruby leans forward again in her seat, her arms folded. "I'm hungry, Abbie," she whines, slightly seductive. "Can you see if they've got my dinner ready?"

Abbie pops up to get it.

Chapter 7

Charlie Get Your Gun

Ray

Ray can't break the habit of waking at three A.M. to the intense, glowing, bright blue of the sky. Sometimes he focuses on Abbie's dog skull that sits alone on the blond wood dresser, and he is filled with an unexplained promise of good things to come. Instead of keeping the curtains closed, or laying foil over the windows as so many Alaskans do, he wholeheartedly enjoys the light. So comforting to open his eyes to, after a bout of the sweat-shakes and visions of the swamp.

Today Gary calls with both good news and bad. The bad, that there's a leak in the roof over the garage; the good, that his hearing may be returning to his left ear. Ray was the one who took Gary to the hospital more than a year ago. He was beaten so badly his eardrum was broken. Gary's "brother" live-in lover, Jason, picked the cruelest of times to withdraw his support. He rarely visited him at the hospital, and he implied that Gary deserved it. Ray never forgave him that, but since they are still together, and living in Ray's house, what else could he do but accept it?

He tells Gary to call his old construction boss Kirk to send a guy over to fix the roof. Here in Healy, he takes up the offer from his current landlord—good pay for help clearing the land to build three more cabins. This will mean more than enough money to send Kirk, so Ray won't have to spend the inherited savings on anything more than his pleasure.

Early mornings are all about the ax, chainsaw, stump grinder, and tractor. Late afternoons are spent kayaking with Charlie on the rush of the river. He comes to rely on the fight of clenched fist over paddle with white water, the way the back current drives to meet all his strength, and just in time leaves him to rest from the battle. He appreciates how Charlie always chooses the path of least resistance. How at times the noses of their kayaks might be directly across the river from each other, and while one of them lifts dangerously close to a spill, the other sails smoothly.

Although they usually eat at the restaurant where Abbie works, sometimes Charlie throws meat or fish on the grill. On occasion, they go where Charlie's seasonal girlfriend, Mindy, waitresses at the old folks' more upscale hotel. She charges them for one dinner, or drinks and desserts, when she's served them both the entire works.

Leaving Charlie at the bar, Ray retires by ten, reads three or four pages that send him swiftly to sleep, then he gets up to do it all again. By this time, Ray is familiar with Abbie's fluctuating shifts, and though he doesn't make a point of avoiding her, neither does he make an effort to connect. If Abbie weren't so utterly convinced that Ruby was a lesbian, she wouldn't have suggested so many times that Ray and Charlie should meet them both one evening for drinks. And if Ray and Ruby could have been flies on the wall or partaken in out-of-body experience, they would be stunned at the hairpin turns of their many narrow misses.

"My old man would do it that way," Charlie says in the Healy true-beginning-of-summer heat. He watches Ray brush the steaks with marinade as it sits spitting and smoking on the grill. "And he preferred an audience, you know, like, 'Hey, witness me, your old man, and how good I am to you sorry little piss ants.' And that was as good as it would get. Huntin', killing us some meat, then throwing it on the barbecue or in the oven. Otherwise, he was slappin' us all around."

"Yeah?" Without turning around to look at him, Ray clenches his jaw, lets it go.

"Want some?" Charlie asks, holding up a newly lit joint. His tank top reveals shoulders that are already red.

"Nah thanks, man. I'll take a cigarette though." Ray catches the pack of Camels he's thrown.

"My mom was hard, she'd fight him back. But when she couldn't handle it, which was after five minutes, all four of us would be tryin' to pull him off her. Then he'd start in on one of us."

"Holy shit, man," Ray says, sitting back on a fold-up canvas camping chair. He looks off into the distance at the bodacious length and smooth shapes of the Alaska Range. He then closes his eyes, hoping Charlie will shut up. He takes a deep drag off the cigarette.

"Three boys and a girl. My mom and my sis sure are tough. They would stay in his face, lippin' him off. My brothers and I would steer clear of him most of the time, 'cept when we had to go huntin'. Then when we'd get back home, we'd get in the truck, drive to whatever farm, and go collecting 'shrooms from the cow paddies."

"Yeah." Ray folds his arms, the cigarette dangling from the corner of his mouth. He opens his eyes, looks at Charlie, who's staring blankly at the smoke rising from the grill.

"As the oldest, I sure felt like a punk ass coming home to find Mom in bad shape after whatever deeply fucked up shit I'd missed."

"Yeah." Ray pauses. "Listen dude, I'm sorry but, you got any aspirin here, man? My head's pounding. But I'm probably just hungry," Ray says, getting up.

"Look in the bathroom, there's a plastic bag on the floor," Charlie says, running his fingers through his hair, which looks more red than brown in the sunlight pounding down on them.

Ray bounds through the tiny cabin, grabs the back of his neck for a rough massage, and finds the aspirin exactly where he'd said. He turns on the faucet, makes a cup with his hand, washes the pills down. He splashes water on his face, and wipes his hands on his T-shirt, on his hair, slicking it back, though it is already in a ponytail. He returns outside, raises his brows at Charlie, as if to say, *Look, I'm relieved*, and walks over the dirt to check the meat, put the sliced potatoes and carrots on.

He sits back down, dreading the sure feeling that Charlie will pick up where he left off. He tries sidetracking him instead.

"Do you think you could love Mindy?" Ray asks, clasping his fingers over his knee. "She sure seems to love you."

"I've tried. I wish I could, man. But it ends up being what it is." Charlie shakes his head a little, then smacks his arm, thinking he got a mosquito. "There's some bug dope in there too, man. Do you have on enough?"

"Yeah," Ray says, rolls his head, cracks his neck.

"I always felt like I failed my mom, you know. And maybe that has something to do with it. Mindy's strong like her, and I feel like, what does she need with me? I'll just get in the way. There was this one time, you know, when my mom woke up fed up. Her face so banged up, it was like she finally could recognize it. Like she remembered who she was before they met. My old man was out in the garage, fixing one of his vintage trucks. My brothers and sister had left for school already, but I'd stayed home sick. Maybe I felt like this once I could be there for her. And so she comes into my room, her hands on her hips, and says, 'Charlie, get your gun,' just that, just like that, and so I do. But I was so fucking scared, just *so fucking scared* of what had to happen, and she sees me shaking with it, the rifle in my hand, and she grabs it from me, and charges out. You know I *pissed my pants*, man, at the blast of the sound, and however many seconds it took me to recover from that, by the time I got to the garage, she'd said whatever she said to get him out from under the truck, and she'd shot him in the head."

"*Holy* shit, man," Ray says, his blue eyes huge and watering, not only because he is finally transported back with him, but because he has not blinked.

"But he wasn't dead! She didn't kill him like I wished she had. You know? You know what kind of fucked up feeling that is? And then knowing that if I had had the courage to do it myself, he would be dead."

"Wow man, I'm sorry."

"No," Charlie raises his hand in stop sign. "Things got better after that. You know, after the hospital stay, the recovery, the dropped charges, and all that, my mom went to work—we *all* went to work—and then after a while, he left.

"Wow. Man. Don't know what to say, Charlie," Ray's voice breaks.

"Nothing to be said to all that. But I haven't been shit in any relationship with any woman. You know?"

"Man, my father hit us, but nothing ever we didn't deserve. He kept us in line, taught us right from wrong. But he never touched our mother. And he was much tougher on me, and rightly so, than he was on my sisters. So it's nothing, *nothing* to compare to all that," Ray says, earnestly now, looking him straight in the eyes.

"Dude, *nobody* deserves to be hit, ever. Fuck that shit," Charlie says, shaking his head, getting up to turn over the potatoes and carrots, which are burned.

Not wanting to stand in deep disagreement with him, Ray says nothing, picks up the plate, and moves past Charlie to take off the vegetables. Ravenously, they chow it all down with beer. When Charlie lights up, again Ray refuses, lights a cigarette instead. Charlie looks at him from the side of his wide-set eyes, faded army green in the burnt golden haze of this evening. Ray catches this look, which says, *You're no longer with me; I talked too much.* Ray shakes his head like he heard him, wishing he had the nerve to empty his chest. And if he could truly remember what it was like with his father, before he became a stoner to deaden the pain of being misunderstood, then he would share that with Charlie. Charlie wasn't like Gary, who didn't need words to connect the dots. Gary understands every sigh, grunt, and silence. (Unless he is in a weak moment, worrying over abandonment. With this, Ray doesn't take the full route on his train of thought, as he assumes his loyalty to be ingrained upon everyone he truly befriends. He assumes Gary knows that he would never leave him.) And Gary isn't like a woman—he knows what rage is really all about while women spend unnecessary energy wrongly reacting. Ray nods his head to that, but he is not thinking about everything that Charlie said. If he were, he wouldn't be musing on the tempers of his ex-wives and how they jumped on him for something he'd said. Ray decides in the moment how the best thing he can think of about being gay is how the two men can relate to each other as friends. And though Charlie is right next to him, raw with nerves singing from the exposure, Ray is now coming to the conclusion that there can only be enough real room for one in the heart. Like his father had only for his mother.

Ray believes Charlie is lucky to have Mindy to love him. He looks over at him once—with the slightest bit of disgust for how high he looks in this instance—and thinks, *If I had a woman, kind, trusting, and elegant with self-respect, then I would smother her with the kind of love that neither she nor I could ever forget.*

Of course, Ray does not realize it, but most of his train of thought eventually leads to love, as he can hear nothing else but the drum roll of Ruby's entrance.

Chapter 8

Cars and Bars

Ruby

Muscle-sore and light-headed from the day's new heights climb, Ruby leaves her room in time to arrive downstairs at the bar, eight o'clock sharp. She is wearing new jeans, beat-up brown Australian Blundstone boots, and a tight, faded navy T with GUYS AND DOLLS written in white polka dot letters. She looks around, put off to find that Abbie is not yet there. She spots Ray, whom Abbie had very vaguely described. Since he sits alone, and not with a short, scruffy, redheaded Alaskan-style mountain bum, she's not sure that it's Ray. He looks so long for his chair. Like a commercial, his sun-bleached hair cascades well past his strong shoulders. It is brushed too neatly. His plush mouth is parted, framed with a trim, week-old moustache and beard. Dumbfounded, he is staring at her with huge, serious, opal blue eyes. Ruby doesn't know that Abbie never described her to Ray, and she doesn't assume it. Preferring not to introduce herself, she sits down at the table behind him, her body lit by the sun.

Because she is looking particularly barefaced, young and vulnerable, the waiter cards her when she asks for whiskey neat. She doesn't take this as flirtation, since it's happened often enough when clear lipgloss is her sole particle of makeup. While she shifts her weight in her seat to grab her slim wallet from her back pocket, she doesn't notice Abbie's entrance until Ray stands to hug her hello. Abbie hurriedly introduces them, and Ray steps on Abbie's foot to shake Ruby's hand. He reaches over for his beer and moves it to Ruby's table, sits across from her, puts his elbow on the windowsill. Abbie puts her hand affectionately on the waiter's back as he looks at Ruby's license and says, "Wow."

"'Wow' *what*, Andrew? Haven't you seen Ruby before? She's only been staying here for three weeks," Abbie says, sitting down facing the window. "And she's always gotta sit in the sun, don't you Ruby?" Abbie pulls at the collar of her wrinkled, red thrift-store dress. With a higher wattage smile, Ruby looks up at the waiter. She holds out her hand for him to put back her license.

"Can I see that?" Ray asks, now holding his hand out to Ruby. Her throat dry, her stomach fluttering, she believes the dizzying heat coming over her is just exhaustion from the day, hunger bubbling up under the warmth of the sun.

"Where's Charlie?" Abbie asks, folds her arms, her fingers drumming her flesh.

"Now *that's* a smile. What an angel," Ray says, swooning.

"Come on," Ruby says, looking embarrassedly at Abbie.

"Ruby Falls. Ruby Falls. How did your parents come to name you?"

"My father's name is Nelson Falls." She clears her throat. "And he took my mother, Vera, to Lookout Mountain in Chattanooga, Tennessee. This was early on when they were dating. My father's from east Tennessee, but I've never been there. I heard Ruby Falls is a pretty kitsch place, but it has some kind of meaning for them. They had me ten years later."

"I've been to Ruby Falls," Ray says excitedly. He looks at the license again, then at Ruby. Abbie rolls her eyes, since neither of them is paying attention to her.

"And is it totally kitsch?"

"It's corny, yeah, the amusement park vibe they have going everywhere you look, but it's still beautiful. Who could find anything boring about a waterfall?"

"I've never seen one except for that small one in Thunderbird Falls," Ruby says, looking into his eyes. She feels everything speed up in her chest. His voice, his smell making her weak. It feels wet under her arms, and she is anxious to sneak a sniff.

"That's nothing," Abbie interrupts. "Have you heard of Valdez?"

"Yeah, my instructor said something about it. People climb icicles the size of skyscrapers?" Ruby asks.

"Well you have to go through Thompson Pass to get to Valdez, and it is the most breathtaking sight. And I've been everywhere, seen the Alps in Switzerland, Italy, Austria, but it can't compare to traveling through Thompson Pass to Valdez. And in the summer there are the most awesome waterfalls. You're up at like four thousand feet, looking all the way down to sea level on a clear day."

"Then we should go!" Ray says, looking at Ruby. "And to Ruby Falls too. I've seen a bit of Tennessee, I could show you around. You really should see where your dad comes from, as well as your namesake." He hands the license to Abbie instead of Ruby. Abbie looks at it, pretending she can make anything out, then hands it back to her.

"There's a town called Ruby here in Alaska, by the way. It's not all that far away. And while you're both getting all hot and bothered over namesakes, you should know too that there's an area called Ray Mountains." Abbie runs her hand from her chin to her jaw to the back of her neck and squeezes.

"I didn't know that," Ray says, finally looking at her.

"Yeah. Check out a map," she snaps.

The waiter returns with Ruby's whiskey, she thanks him, irked at herself for feeling so girlishly nervous. She takes a sip and looks at Ray—who hasn't taken his eyes off of her—then at Abbie, who now looks as if she's decided to make the best of it. She orders a glass of red wine from the waiter, who asks everyone if they're hungry. Ray asks for fish 'n' chips, Ruby mutters how she wishes they had salmon on the menu. Ray overzealously agrees. The waiter walks away after Ruby orders the same as Ray.

"So tell us, Abigail, how come we can't find any righteous salmon anywhere?" Ray asks. Ruby wrinkles her nose at the word "righteous."

"You're both food-obsessed?"

"Kinda, huh?" She looks at Ray as if she's always known him. "But Abbie, you must know what it's like for an L.A. girl expecting a good plate of food. All that Northern Cali-delish you grew up on." Her elbow moves closer to Abbie.

"Did either of you try Simon and Seafort's when you were in Anchorage?"

"Yeah," Ruby says in the tone, *So what?*

"Right. Well, what do you expect from a place settled by straight men?" Abbie shrugs her shoulders.

"It's not like Florida cooking is shabby, either. But the point is, how comes we can't find any good *salmon* to eat?" Ray leans toward her too, looking playful.

Abbie shrugs again. "Never thought about it. Probably 'cause it's mostly shipped out. Alaskans catch their own salmon or just get it from a neighbor. No one here comes to a restaurant for it." She vibrates her head a little ghetto-girl style.

"Ahhhhh," Ruby and Ray say in unison.

Abbie rolls her eyes again, excuses herself for the bathroom.

"So Florida, huh?" Ruby looks up at him with her big brown eyes.

"For the last fifteen years," Ray says, taking a sip of his stale beer. He looks up at her, blushes, worrying about his breath.

"That's where people like me get blocked from the vote."

"Ah come on, now. That's long ago and far away. That's all fixed," he says with a playful indignant tone.

"Exactly."

"Come on," he pleads with a boyish expression.

"Bet you're a Republican," she says, cocking her head. Ray smiles sheepishly, looks down at his beer. "Don't tell me you are a Republican," she teases, then her expression goes serious. "You *are* a Republican!"

"Can't we get past it?" he says with his charm smile.

Ruby opens her mouth to say something sassy but doesn't since he seems to be far past the conversation, staring at every detail of her face, then letting her eyes lock his. Abbie returns, clearing her throat overdramatically. Ray stands for the lady. "That was quick," he says to Abbie.

"So where's Charlie? Like I asked you twenty minutes ago," Abbie says with freshly applied red lipstick to match her dress.

"Car trouble. But he'll be here soon. Mindy's picking him up," Ray says, leaning back so the waiter can put down the two baskets of fish 'n' chips. Abbie takes a fry out of Ray's basket, and he looks at her.

"Who's Mindy?" Abbie asks.

"His girlfriend," Ray says, turning around to grab the ketchup from the table he'd left.

"Cars," Abbie sighs. "More trouble than they're worth. Mine has been sitting there for a month. It's easier to catch a ride." She takes a fry from Ruby's basket. Ruby doesn't bat an eye.

"Sure miss mine," Ruby says, eating the fried fish with her fingers. Ray watching like he wants to lick them.

"What did you have?" Ray excitedly asks.

"Baby blue '64 Corvair." She smiles her lazy crooked smile.

"Sweet," he nods.

"Mint."

"Very sweet. Hard top?"

"Convertible. Her name was Dahlia. I got fifteen thousand for her, but if I weren't so eager to sell, I could have gotten much better."

"You sure could. I had a '72 Hemi-Cuda, navy blue, not so mint. Got eleven thousand for it. I could have done better as well, but I guess I was in a hurry too."

"You sold it to move here?"

"No, I sold it for a bike. I've still got my place in South Florida, on the river in Port St. Lucie. It's beautiful there, the water, the boat, my gardens. I'd love to take you there," he says, leaning into her.

"Sounds like you'd love to take her everywhere, Ray," Abbie says, not as bitterly as she meant it.

"That's right," he nods at Abbie, then back at Ruby. His voice ebullient with sincerity, "I don't mean to offend you. But you're the most beautiful woman I've ever seen. *Dreamy*, really." He slowly shakes his head, looking her in the eye. "It's a good thing I wasn't climbing when I first set eyes on you, because I would have died."

Ruby looks at him, then at the table. She clasps her hands in front of her, as if trying to be patient. Abbie is quiet, waiting for her to tell him that she prefers women. Ray swallows and keeps staring at her like he would never take back a single word.

"Everyone done here?" the waiter asks, clearing their fish 'n' chips baskets.

"Oh, I don't think so," Abbie says, her eyes twinkling.

Ray orders another round, just as Luis, Charlie's friend, stops by the table.

"Hey man. Think you can keep all the exotic beauties to yourself?"

"*Exotic?*" Ruby screws together her eyebrows.

Abbie flips her hand at him, pushes up the bridge of her glasses, rolls her eyes. She lights up a cigarette.

"Hey, what's the problem, babes?" he asks, raising his chin at Abbie, cupping his chest as if he had tits.

"You best just keep on walking," Ray says, his nostrils flaring. Charlie strolls up with Mindy, both have bed-hair and afterglow skin. He greets his friend Luis first, who holds up his hands, and walks away. Charlie introduces Mindy to everyone, and kisses Ruby's hand. They pull the two tables together; Ray takes the opportunity to grab a seat next to Ruby.

"So what d'you say to Luis, dude?"

"He's some fucked-up shit."

"He's just drunk, man. He's cool. His brain's a bit frozen from years on this Argentine island, Tierra del Fuego. Sounds like it would be a hot place, but it's close to the Antarctic, man. Then he comes here. He's a little nuts, but he's cool. Wouldn't harm no one."

"Whatever." Ray raises his brow.

"Really, you'd like him. He was a woodcutter, he could relate to what you're doing now."

"Okay, man."

Abbie asks Mindy how long she's been in Healy. She answers three summers, adding that she's left her native Vermont every summer since she was sixteen. Ruby guesses she is about twenty-five at the most, and Charlie more likely forty, but they are closer in age than she thinks.

Since Charlie, Abbie, and Mindy are talking, Ray leans over to whisper. "I don't think you understand. I've never even thought of having children before, until I met you."

Ruby opens her eyes wide as if to say, You *are* crazy.

"Look at me," he says. And she looks until he burns right through her. His eyes are now watery, his expression radiant, as if reborn. "Do you see what I mean?"

Ruby leans over to kiss him. She tickles the roof of his mouth, shines his teeth with her tongue until he gently bites it, then sucks it. As if this first kiss was delivered in too famished a way, they end it sweetly, like babies learning. They look at each other, Ruby touching his ear, his neck, then his chin. She brushes the light brown hair on his forearm. He stays perfectly still, as if she were a wild animal he doesn't want to scare away. He leans over to kiss her again, this time circling the inside of her mouth, but this annoys her and she subtly pulls away. He then softly cups her face and holds it there, as he corrects their tongues' journey, both of them slowly, maddeningly losing all sense of place and time.

"Hey, hey, *hey*!" Charlie says, fanning them with two cocktail napkins. Mindy laughs with her head thrown back, she is lovely.

Ray pulls out his wallet, leaves three twenties, tells Abbie to keep whatever change is left. She gives him a tense smile as he quickly squeezes her hand, then shakes both Charlie's and Mindy's. Ruby is so shy over the dampness in the crotch of her jeans that she can only bend swiftly to kiss Abbie's cheek, then hold up her hand to wave at Charlie and Mindy. But none of them are looking at her, eyeing instead the large pup tent behind the zipper of Ray's jeans.

As they leave the table, Ruby hears Abbie exclaim, "But she's gay!"

"Then Ray just stole your date," Charlie says, and laughs.

Ray walks her to the elevator door, where they hold each other so close, and for so long. He lifts her from the floor, both of them pressing their groins into the other. She lets go first, and with a voice heavy and breathy with lust, tells him that he can call her in the morning. As the doors close, he is still standing there with a look of enchanted disbelief on his face.

Jeannie, the thing about climbing, is the fear. An all encom-passing, smothering feeling. The way I imagine rage to be, something I've never allowed myself to feel. Having always

71

been so even-keeled, I push myself in everyway I can think of, just to feel what it's like to be overpowered. Drugs would be too easy. It has to be real. That feeling like one wrong move, and I could be dead. The panic in losing my breath, the dizzying in my head until I have to take control of it, meet the fear head-on. Using my body, every muscle from my head to my toes. The feeling of running myself ragged with something like this. It's not that feeling of—Climb the mountain because it's there—but rather Climb the mountain because you can.

I met a guy night before last, Ray. He picked me up yesterday and this morning, with packed lunches for my climbs. I haven't fucked him. I know it's only been two days, but we are kissing in cars and bars. He is familiar. At first I thought he reminded me of my friend Joop, because they're similar in type, but then I realized it's much more than that. Because I'm really scared for the first time. Not scared to have sex with him, but scared to ever be without him. And how can I feel that before I've even slept with him?

WHAT'S WRONG WITH ME, JEANNIE? Tell me I haven't met a freak who told me too soon how deeply he's fallen in love with me. For how could he know? How does anyone know that kind of thing when they are simply in heat for each other.

I miss you. I think of you everyday. I've only written a few times because I hate to be so boring with this climbing thing. And now there's a guy. I apologize, in advance, for all you'll have to read from now on. ;-)~

And do keep telling me, blow by blow, everything that's going on with the case. It's my right to hear, and my right to help. I hurt with you. Let me. Lean on me, I'm not that far away. Big kiss to Al. He loves you so. He's just trying to distract you with this restaurant thing. And he knows how you love to cook. No one in this world is a better baker than you. Let him make you into a chef, if you want to. You can do it!!!

Big smooch, Ruby

On the third day, Ruby breaks her climbing schedule to go kayaking with Ray. They go tandem—he sits in back to steer, while she madly but happily eats water, paddling too fast. She grunts, roars with glee every time the icy current chomps at the bottom of the boat, knocking her up in the air. As Ray calls the placement of the holes, and their rhythm back into sync, she inhales loudly through her throat, sticks her tongue way out, pushing out the exhale like a Maori warrior chant.

They grab barbecue to take back to Ray's little cabin. As Ruby sets down the bottle of wine on his nightstand, he spins her around and lifts her to the bed, peeling off her clothes with his hands and teeth. He struggles with the hooks of her bra as if he had never seen such a contraption. She laughs, he holds her down, and with the basest of baritones vibrating from her ear to her belly, talks a nasty, hard but heartcore, opening her all the way up. She puts her nose in his armpits, bites his tiny, tiny nipples, keeps her eyes open as he enters her, studying the proud bristle hairs on his cheeks looming out of their large pores, giving him the appearance of a wolf. They fuck too long for the clutter—which had emptied from her head—not to re-collect in fear of finally giving everything of herself to someone else.

Minutes after he comes he is hard again. He doesn't tell her what the scars and pockmarks are on his hips, until they coo and rest again before the third time. She traces the lines and dips the tool belt made with the Florida water, sweat, and infection. And not before the fifth time when it strikes her that he is the flesh of her unconsummated adolescent sexual fantasia, does she consider saying something to him about the unnatural firmness of her breasts, and the scar arcs on the top of her nipples, as he kisses, licks, eats, and sucks.

Seven hours without darkness is merely a flash in the brain. They eat cold barbecue, he goes out for bottled water. Days that turn into weeks that turn into months of marathon fucking are elusive spots of heaven, flecked with only gashes of bitter jealousies of the other's past. This is no big deal, as gashes heal.

Much later Ruby will be disappointed that she cannot wholly visualize their meeting. She'll imagine it as more dramatic, less comfortable. And there will be nothing to correct her. Even though she will have him right there next to her, his memories cannot be hers. Visions of him licking her asshole, making her come when she menstruates, the sound of his voice telling her he will catch her vomit in his hands, all allow her to think kindly about growing old. How wonderfully lucky she is to have found a man unafraid of all bodily functions. This makes him perfect for any tragic disease or disaster that could befall her, she thinks. And not the worst of it being a coma, because there is always the romantic possibility that he can wake her up out of it.

Chapter 9

Ex-Wives

Ray

Ray had the rain to thank for a week of deliciously extreme and uninterrupted lovemaking, but now to find an excuse to buy more time from George, who has come to see him as a most dependable nephew, or adopted son. They have finished every detail of two cabins, but now George wants to start on the third of six more. Ray had signed on only for three, but he isn't the kind of person who stops feeling responsible after the commitment has been met, or the debt been paid. But neither had Ray planned on meeting the love of his life.

From that first day in bed, none of the feelings, words, or actions that keep pouring from him now will ever surprise him again. For he meant it when he said that he hopes in the next life he gets to be her mother, as he would want to give birth to her, hold her, love her, raise her, watch her grow.

With each day of his heart's new reverie, he tells himself he must give up now on the idea of punishment. He can't quite understand why he had devoted such time and strength into seeking it. As it appeared, he was first immediately rewarded monetarily for his crime over a year ago. And now it seems that he is being blessed emotionally, mentally, physically, and spiritually with this new love, so how can he hang onto the idea that what he'd done was truly wrong?

Right here—as he stares at the curve of her back, the smooth brown skin, the tiny beads of sweat down her spine, her waist, her wide hips, the texture of her shoulder-length hair, spongy and dense like a forest he wants to lose himself in—he gives up on misery. He worships the crease of her inner-elbow, the backs of her knees, the birthmark on her thigh, every crescent, every crevice of her landscape, all the while (for the time being) losing the god of despair.

"Oh shit, here he comes," Ray says, grabbing the wet towel from the floor, tying it around his waist. If sun, work, kayaking, and climbing had sculpted their bodies to a sexy perfection, now fucking with little food makes them look like they could clean up and be cover models for *Outside* magazine. George raps on the door, Ray puts on a sunken tone to his voice and demeanor. Ruby scurries into the bathroom.

"Ready to work today?" George asks, his thumb through the belt loop of his filthy canvas pants, his smile yellowed with carefree hygiene.

"Aagh, George," Ray groans, with his hand over his belly, "I was just gonna try and run the shower over my head to see if I can't lose whatever's been aching me."

"You alright, son?" George scratches his curly salted black hair.

"I thought yesterday maybe it was food poisoning," Ray says, deconstructing his voice into warbled strings of patheticness, "but now the fever is telling me it's something else."

George backs up from the crack of the door. "Well, you just take care of yourself, Ray, and I'll get us started. Get some rest. Maybe Ethel can bring you by some tea later on?"

"No thanks, no George, I'll be fast asleep, I'm sure. Right now I feel as if I could sleep for one hundred years," Ray says, nodding as he closes the door.

Ruby's giggles lightly bounce off the bathroom floor. She rests her butt against the sink.

"Come here," Ray says. He pulls her to the bed, buries his face in her muff, licks her bellybutton, which looks like the inside of a shell, kisses the must beneath her breasts, munches on her perfect ears. She giggles.

"Do you always fall in love this quickly?"

"I've never been in love like this before."

"And this must be the fourth time you've had to say that."

He ignores her. "You have made me aware that sex is the celebration of love . . . and that love is the celebration of life."

"I think you are crazy corny. How come you have all of these perfect things to say? Makes me feel as if you've practiced, or as if you're some kind of sociopath," Ruby winces, as if she knows she is pushing.

"Some day you'll know, like I know, that we were always meant for each other."

"Why didn't you know I was meant for you three wives ago?"

"I'd never met you!"

"What *made* you get married? *Three* times?"

"I was nineteen, the first time. I'd been in Florida for a year. I was lonely, stupid, with school and two jobs. Cynthia lived in the same apartment complex. I thought she was pretty."

"You thought she was 'pretty'? You thought she was *pretty*. And that's why you *married* her?"

"I thought we could have fun together. I didn't know what I was doing, and it was a mess."

"What kind of mess?"

"I don't feel like talking about it."

And so she lets it go until the next day.

"How come you haven't asked me about my old lovers?" Ruby asks.

"I don't want to have to think about anybody else touching you," he says, massaging her feet with shea butter.

"You like hearing about my work, my family, about Caspar and Jeannie, but nothing about my past relationships. It might give you more insight into me, you know."

"You said you don't like 'talk, talk, talk' and how that ruined things with the guy in New York, and how he had the same name as your father."

"That seemed to be all you wanted to hear. You mentioned your third wife, Sonya, as having the same name as your sister. I think it's probably common."

"Yeah? Well, don't give me the psychological bullshit reason."

"People like the ring of a name they've been hearing and saying all their lives. I'm sure it means nothing more than that."

"I didn't marry Sonya because she had the same name as my sister. I married her because we were dating, and she needed a green card, and I agreed to help her. I lied to myself that the sex could lead to love. I had two years of no sex with my second wife, and so Sonya just seemed doubly good to me."

"And why should I believe that this is any more special than that?" Ruby says, sitting up, throwing on a T-shirt.

"This cannot compare to anything in my past. Every relationship is its own separate thing. And I promise you that I've *never* felt anything like this before."

"How do you know that?"

"I have never taken a piss in front of any woman, much less sat on the toilet to take a dump."

"Well you sit on the toilet to piss too," she giggles, "which I've never seen a guy do. But I can't believe you've been married three times and still never *peed* in front of anybody?"

"Never."

"I can't believe that."

"I was a prude," he says in the voice of an uptight old lady. "But now this is really embarrassing."

"What?"

"I have never made any woman come in my mouth before."

"Now that I'll never believe."

"Believe it. I never even liked it before."

"You? You who I can't tear from between my legs? You who will go at it for forty-five minutes a stretch." She cackles.

He takes her face in his hands. "I have never tasted anything in the world more incredible than your pussy, and I never ever will."

It is as if she hasn't heard him. "You who licks up my blood?"

"I never even liked to have sex when somebody was on their period, much less touch them with my mouth!"

"I can't believe this."

"Believe it. I never even used to share a cigarette."

"Well, I don't want your cigarettes," she teases.

"And I've never talked dirty to anyone else before."

"That I will never *ever* believe," she says, laughing.

"I have never let anyone touch my asshole," he says, getting into it now, "and I have never ever licked anyone's asshole. I would eat your shit. I'll lie down right here, go ahead, piss on me."

"Get up," she says, laughing. "Get up." She yanks him by the arms.

"No," he says, pulling her down to him. "Marry me," he says.

"And be your Door Number Four?"

"Are you trying to hurt me?"

"I'm just trying to get all of the truth first. You've asked me to marry you a few times already, and we've just met, Ray. I want to know you. I want to know everything about you."

"By dragging out my past?"

"You still haven't told me about your second wife, Barbara, and why you wanted to adopt her daughter, but haven't spoken to either of them—"

"This is like bringing a *nightmare* back to life."

"It can't have been all that bad."

"Honestly, I want to forget every day I lived before you. I want to imagine I met you when we were three, and I've been trying to get you to realize, all these years, that you were meant for me, and I was meant for you, and it wasn't until early last week that you saw the truth for the first time."

"Okay, maybe we met when *you* were three, but I was six. I'd already met two classes full of personalities and that many more figures of authority, while you were barely out of diapers. What did you know about what was out there? You wouldn't have picked me yet, because you wouldn't have been able to. So I guess we met at just the right time," she says, making two ponytails of his hair to grab him to her mouth.

When Gary calls to check in about the roof, and to confirm that his hearing seems to truly be coming back (he conducts the entire conversation with the phone to his healing left ear with mixed results), Ray begins wishing that Gary wasn't so entwined with his past, and his house, where he'd like to return with Ruby and show her how finely he can shelter, feed, and undress her. He is sorrier still, miserable, when she says how she must return to climbing, make sufficient progress, enough to make herself proud, and that means a climb that will take her away for two weeks, as she will need to camp out. This is unbearable to him, and he tortures himself in his head every day. Things are much worse when they run into her teacher and guide at the deli.

He is a glamorous monk of no more than thirty, six-packed, an unruly mop of black hair, soulful dark eyes, a calm, self-satisfied smile, and a way of looking at Ruby that makes Ray want to kill him. He carries himself as if he's been doing yoga since he was a child. He speaks painfully slow, and it is an agonizing five minutes the three spend in exchange at the deli. Ray works up a cordial goodbye. They walk out the door together, Ray thinking of all the men Ruby could decide would be a better choice for her. He wonders if it had been Charlie who had come onto her first, would she have grabbed and kissed him and gone home with him instead.

If Ruby hadn't gone through the horror of finding her beloved dog murdered, Ray wouldn't have a reason to think again about the idea of being "caught." He felt the full weight of his guilt when Ruby first spotted the dog skull and sobbed for so long during the re-telling, the re-living of it. Naturally, she obsesses on who it is that did it, which begs the question of how she'd feel if she knew what *he* had done. He knows her well enough to assume she might easily understand the reasons he would want to kill, but he doesn't rely on intuition to make that jump and confess. How could he risk losing her? How can he lie to his true love? Did this have to be a catch-22?

And why hasn't he been caught? Because no one gave a fuck about this almost mythically evil scum. The kind of slime who only seconds later might have been picked off by a cop, or even his own mother. Ray had done *everyone* a favor, of that much he felt sure. This does not change the agonizing question of how Ruby feels about justifiable homicide.

Ray might think he is over the idea of being punished, but his nightmares have really been shoved to the back to make room for jealousy and romantic insecurities. He has come to the end of being defined by one event, and is only at the beginning of realization that all is fair in love.

Chapter 10

Jeannie's Past

Ruby

Ruby, I'm so happy for you. Ray Rose. Now that's a lucky kind of name—forget about my bias for Rs. He sounds like he has every reason to make my girl swoon, and no one deserves it more than you. I never got to know Pej, and he seemed intelligent, sophisticated, handsome, classy and all that, but there was something so refined about him, that snobby doesn't begin to describe. He lacked earthiness, like he couldn't stand to ever get dirty, and he lacked the kind of rawness, honesty, I know you've been looking for, and Ray sounds like all of these things, not to mention what a dynamite fuck he must be. You haven't said much about it, but three weeks in bed? What's the reason to ever get up? Money, I suppose. But while you have it, spend it. There is always more. Enjoy yourself.

You know, I didn't mention this before but your friend Joop came around here about three e-mails ago. You said his name in about that many letters back, so I don't know why it slipped my mind to tell you how freaky I thought he was. I found him walking around the backyard, and I would have called the police if you hadn't just mentioned him, and it hadn't all clicked in my mind. If you fucked him, that's one thing, but he was hanging out near your little house, walking around the maze, like a freak. I mean, how dare he do something like that, after everything that's happened! How did he get in? I went running down there, spitting fire, and he stood like stone. Felt like I was Medusa. When he finally spoke, he said he'd come to check on YOUR CAR, and I reminded him that you'd sold it. At that moment both of us knew how full of shit he was. What could he have been doing there? I don't understand it. Obviously you haven't written him as to where you are?

As for Al, I'm never gonna be a chef. Now, I love to bake, and that's a thing of pure pleasure. I could never bake or cook as a profession. No way. Fuck that. I'm a good baker, but cakes and pies at home are enough. Why should I work my ass off at my age? 52 ain't so old, but if I was planning on working at this age, let's face it, I would have never married Henry. I loved him all right, but he was loaded, and he loved me too, and I could never deny that it wasn't a part of the package. And he made me feel like I deserved so much, he really made me look at all the qualities I have to offer, when before, all I'd really respected in myself was my abilities with athletics. ;)~ But no kidding, for a minute I was feeling so high and so full of myself—philanthropic and all that—I could have run against your dad in city council, and I mean it! If it weren't for society so willing to take it all away from me, including my self-respect, I might have done something like that. I loved Henry for taking care of me the way he did, and you know what it was like for me once he died. I don't have to tell you the kind of pain I went through, you were there.

So at this point in my life, I just want to relax. I could think of something silly to occupy my attention from one year to the next, like birdwatching, then needlepoint, then the tuba, but I just don't think so. I enjoy going to lunch, I enjoy my friends, I love baths, I love traveling, I love writing you letters (you know I'm saving all of our correspondence, just because), and I love Al. I got a lot to be thankful for. God knows I came close to losing not only my head but my life—and I don't mean a few months ago, I mean many years past. I've crossed some bad cats' paths, and I've made it without a scratch. And fuck this detective who thinks I brought any of this down on myself. No stone has been unturned, and still he's found nothing. I hurt for Chauncey's folks everyday, and I miss my dogs so much it aches, but what can we do? Where else can we go from here, but onward and upward.

Do you have an idea when you're coming home? I was thinking I'd like to go away for my birthday in October— somewhere like Greece, it would be so magical MYTHICAL if you and your giant gorgeous hunk of a beau could meet us there! What do you say, baby?

Be safe. (To be honest, I was glad Ray's managed to keep you off the glacial cliffs, but I'm not kidding myself. I know you'll be back on the rope again). You're my Stevē McQueen!

Big smooch and hugs, J.

Jeannie, you were right. I just got back from a two and a half week expedition. It was just me and my guide Stu. A couple awful, deadly storms. We called ourselves The Flying Michaels (the rangers require party names for registration). I would have gone with him in a larger group, if I had the nerve to attempt the 20,000 feet—which precious few make anyway—but I didn't want the pressure of having to let down any strangers. I had this realistic goal of the 13,000 summit, which unfortunately we also didn't make.

It's impossible to be alone anyhow, you look up, and all you see ahead are climbers like bugs. It's kinda gross really, campsites are littered with trash and shit. And I mean shit, literally. And before they let you climb, you have to watch this hellish film of all the dead bodies they've recovered, the deformities of frostbite, the ravages of avalanches. It's demonic. Then again, after seeing what I've seen, and going through what you and I went through, mortality—bloody, burned or frostbitten—is not as scary as it is just REAL. Anyway, all of that said, I was thrilled with the feeling of Don't Look Back. If you can bear that kind of violent cold, (it got to −50 below!) throbbing in your membranes (and talk about aching tits, the pressure in my implants felt over-whelming) and you can still make it up with minimal altitude sickness, then your head can't help but come up with all of these lofty mantras to keep you serene. And I was. Partly because I get such a deep rush from the idea of personal best. The challenge was grueling, and I met it. So my head was almost entirely empty of junk. It is definitely what meditation is all about. And I'm not the type who could sit still to do it. Using my body, so extremely like this, leaves space for one thought, and that is to make it through. So I was serene. And I could never deny that this seemingly endless draw of strength must have kept on coming because of what I knew was waiting for me when I got back.

Ray was jittery with fear that he was gonna lose me. Not that I would fall off the rope, or miss my footing. He is crazy jealous of Stu—who looks nothing like his name, but is someone I would never think of sexually, especially after Ray. And Stu did come on to me, in his elevated yogi sort of way, but I know I'm in love now Jeannie. And besides, I got a little angry with Stu, like, I'm PAYING you to guide me up Denali, and I'm sposed to give you a taste too? He's not as sleazy as he sounds, he's actually quite inspiring. At camp he told me the most fascinating stories, I was warm with the listening. He's very illuminated about life. Climbing is like a math problem to solve, and in finding the answer, it is like an affirmation of existence. He doesn't really belong here in Denali in the rat race of all climbs. It seems like he should go back to Colorado, or go live somewhere in the Andes. This in-between seems to be compromising him in some way. And I am more curious about rock climbing, now that I've had this intense christening on ice. Joshua Tree was what had sparked all this in the first place. I'm ready to shed all these layers and equipment, strip it down to tights and chalk.

So that IS SO freaky about Joop. I have no idea what he was doing there! And I'm almost positive I couldn't have ever left the clicker in his car. He's been with me a few times when I've had to punch the code, he must have looked over my shoulder. That's creepy. I'm going to call him. I can't IMAGINE why he would lie like that! That really does bug me out.

84

When you say you've met some bad cats along the way, well, I would figure that, we've probably all crossed the paths of murderers, abusers, and rapists, but has anything triggered in you lately? I mean, the same way that Joop came out of the blue like that, like a freak around the house, has someone come to mind that did something weird like that, which you'd never expect, that might have been hanging on to some warped dream in their head? I know how it's possible to lay down with somebody and not take some part of them with you. I mean, you would have to do that. But that doesn't mean that they haven't taken something from you. Has there been someone like that? Who got inside you, and took something, without you realizing?

I don't mean to get dramatic about it. But it's a raw kind of feeling, being entered so much. Ray can get going five times in a day, he is insatiable! I can be asleep at three a.m. and sometimes he wakes me and he's already inside of me. So not only is my body worn out from climbing, but it's worn—beautiful as it may feel—from the inside as well. And I have this new respect for you, in that way. But I just wondered if anybody ever broke you down, when you were feeling so tender, and they thought they had this part of you, then realized they didn't, and so wanted to get back at you.

Do you know what I mean? Forgive me, Jeannie, because I know you've already thought about all of these kinds of things. But I did sleep with Joop, just once, and it creeped me out that he could lie to you like that, just to hang around, and it reminded me that there must be, for you, hundreds like that.

Know what I mean?

Yes, forget the chef thing. My boss wrote me again about how much he needs me, and I'm crazy to keep him dangling, but I just feel like I'll always be in the same position—under him—if I stick with him forever. I'm really feeling all the possibilities for the first time in my life. You said Henry gave that to you, in some ways, and I think I found all I was looking for in Alaska. Not that I'm staying. I just knew where to go to "find" myself. Greece sounds amazing. I gotta sit down and figure all my pennies, now that I just handed over a huge check to Stu. But I wouldn't want to miss your birthday. I'll see you some kind of way! Love you, Ruby

Ruby lets Ray take off two days to celebrate her return, but she won't let him quit building the cabins altogether, because she isn't quite ready to just pack up and head out. The question of where has too much meaning to her. Wherever they choose would mean a commitment. Ray suggests they head down to Eagle River and go handgliding, and it feels a little forced to her, like trying to keep balls in the air. Ruby keeps her gear at Ray's cabin while, in the spirit of independence, thinking she may go back to the hotel. But this is absurd and will never happen.

"How can you eat nuts in the morning!" Abbie exclaims at the cluttered table in her house. She wears a baby blue, sleeveless cashmere T, chinos, and flipflops. Her black hair has been brushed so much that it flies with static.

"I could eat granola too, or nutbread, but you don't have it," Ruby laughs.

"Four scrambled eggs, three sausage, and you're *still* hungry? I feel like a lousy host!"

"I'm not still hungry, I'm just picking."

"Picking is right, what *are* you doing? It used to drive me crazy at the restaurant, I could never figure it out. Your little four-thirty ritual."

"I'm eating the broken ones first."

"How come?"

"I don't know." Ruby looks up at her, then grabs the whole scoop, shoveling them all into her mouth. She brushes off her hands in three claps. Wipes them on her well-worn blue pinstriped Dickies. Her shoulders and ripped arms shine in her orange tank. "It's probably because my mother allowed me to eat only the broken ones when they were having a party."

"And you kept it up. Your mother building a not-worthy complex."

"Not to me. But, okay . . . you seem to be having a problem with all this. When you first told me about Ray, you mentioned him as this cool guy you were attracted to, but who didn't seem to be in a space for connecting. You wanted me to meet him and his friend, because they were your favorites. I didn't expect to have what happened happen, but it did. But am I sposed to be feeling apologetic?"

Abbie runs in with the pot of tea. "Of course not! I just don't get why you came here and told me about your girlfriends, and then you turn around and snag the one man I find interesting. And you and I click so well too. And I just . . ."

"You told me about your affair with the father and son that dragged on for years, but am I sposed to think that that's *all* you're into? The nastily complicated?"

"No," Abbie says, jiggling her head sassily. She sits down and pours the tea.

"And it's not girl*friends*, it's girlfriend. I had one other fling with a woman, and that was it. The rest have been boyfriends. I broke up with a guy only a few months ago, and we were seeing each other for over a year and a half. The person before that was another man."

"So you're bi, why didn't you say so?"

"Is that something I was sposed to announce? I can't believe what a big deal you're making out of this. It's not cool, Abbie. I don't walk around calling myself anything. I'm just me, and that's it. Take it or leave it."

"Okay," Abbie says, leaning back. "Can I make a peace offering or something? 'Cause I do feel stupid, right now. You know, you're the first person I've really confided in, in a long while. I mean I talk a lot, but not about things that really matter. And I respect you, and I don't want you to walk out the door this morning, thinking you can't deal with me. You know? Because I'd really like to keep up with you. People come and go here, I may be leaving too, but I'll be interested to know how you are, and all that, and I hope you will be interested too."

Ruby bites her bottom lip and shrinks a little in her seat, the way she does when her sister scolds her. Then she springs up again like a flower recovering from too much water. Abbie stands and walks over to the little black glass figurine that Ray had studied. She gives it to Ruby, who twists her mouth a bit, not appreciating the gesture.

"She's sweet, right?"

"Yeah, but I can't, Abbie," Ruby says, shaking her head, trying to hand it back.

"Please take it. It meant something to Ray too, like that skull did. I don't know, just seems like it was meant for you, right?"

"That skull freaked me out 'cause someone shot and killed my dog, they killed all of my landlord's dogs, and they raped and murdered the dogwalker. Her name was Chauncey. She was twenty-two. Lived with her parents. I found them. I found them all. I was the one who came home to . . . all of that."

Abbie's mouth hangs open. They sit there in silence for longer than Ruby is comfortable.

"That's really why I came here. To get away. It was my job too, but my problem with my job is just bullshit compared to all that," Ruby says, now getting riled up.

"But did it ever occur to you that you chose your path? I mean you chose where you wanted to live, with your dog—"

"He wasn't really *my* dog, he was my landlord's, my friend Jeannie's puppy, and he just became my dog." Ruby looks at her lap, clasps her hands, springs her thumbs.

"Okay, so you chose that place to live, you chose that dog, and your landlord as a friend too, and then this happened, and it brought you here to climb, to meet Ray, and go wherever you'll go from here."

Ruby twists her mouth again, noisily scratches her scalp, and sighs. "Okay."

"And have you ever noticed how people choose their deaths?" Abbie places her hands on the table, like a counselor. "How smokers get lung cancer, tightly-wound men get heart attacks . . ."

"You've got to be kidding me."

"My grandmother got Alzheimer's, and before that she was always so detached from the past, from us, from everything."

"Okay, so people choose AIDS? All over the world, victims of chemical warfare set up their psyches for it? All the women with breast cancer create it, and you, I suppose, chose your diabetes."

"Yeah. And with babies, who knows what kind of family debt they're paying."

"So Chauncey chose her own rape and murder? Where do you get this? I don't believe this shit for one fucking minute. Life's a mystery, plain and simple. Maybe we have responsibility in that we can help or hurt one another, but as far as the rest, it's out of our control."

"Well, believe what you believe, and I'll do the same. I'm convinced. You're lucky, my friend. Because you choose so well for yourself. Even your guide seems like some kind of angel in your path, right?"

"You can go pay him some good cash to guide you too. You're thinking yourself into some kind of weird corner. Maybe you need to leave Healy a lot sooner than you were planning."

"Have a little compassion. Most of us don't always know what's healthy. You're glowing with it. I don't have to see it. Your aura is shiny. You'll never find yourself all alienated like I am."

"You want to alienate yourself from yourself—if that's what you're saying—then go on and do it 'til you can't stand it anymore. But I don't know, Abbie. As complimentary as you might be to me, it's also some kind of slap. To everybody. Go somewhere, like home maybe, and get this thing with your eyes all straightened out. How do you know you have the best doctor?" She exhales with little patience. "Do something good for yourself, and the rest will follow." She opens her eyes wide as if her head were about to burst. "God. I'm kinda knocked out here. All the altitude-sickness pills I popped. I'm exhausted and totally out of it. I should get going."

Abbie stands, clutching the glass figurine. "You sound like Ray. That was totally his intonation. He about done with work right now?"

"I don't even know or care what time it is. But I'm heading back."

Abbie hugs her, and tucks the figurine in her back pocket.

"You're so weird," Ruby says, sweetly looking her in the eyes.

91

Abbie kisses her on the nose. She walks her to the door, Ruby then smiles weakly, like *I'll probably never sit with you one-on-one again.* But of course this won't be the case.

Ruby, I've been thinking about it. About what you said. Lying down with some prick who I always saw myself as banging, but had really banged me. But this is the way I had to see it. And normally, I always will. But in this instance, I mean, if I could cut the protective bullshit for a second, think about who might have seen me as fucking him, way back, and wanted to come back and cut me like that, and just found all the babies and Chauncey in the way. Shit. You should see me here, I'm a mess. There were these brother freaks who made a lot of money in the business, and I worked for them for a little while, way back toward the very beginning, when I was a dumb little duckling from Missouri. And I wasn't exactly a victim or anything, you know I knew what I wanted, and to get paid for sex was just exactly what I thought I needed. I mean I really came to love it, but you know all that. Anyway, I was never involved, not emotionally anyway, with either of those freaks. I'd fucked them both, and one of them couldn't care less about me, but the other was a bit possessive. He made it about business—the possessiveness— but I knew it was more than that. And the bigger deal he made of it, the more the other brother got annoyed with every move I made. When I was long gone from them, I'd heard the brother, who was into me, had been killed. ANYBODY could have done it. Including the brother. But, I got a weird note, supposedly from someone else who knew them both. It said how sorry he was to tell me he was dead. I'd already known of course, this world is so infinitesimal. But later when I confronted that person about that note, like, Why the hell would you think I'd really care? that person said he never sent me the note. And I was so creeped out, but I never said anything, because, well, it wasn't such a big deal in the scheme of things. It said nothing threatening whatsoever. It just said, I am so sorry to tell you this. But it was NOT from that person.

So I remember thinking that that brother knew where I was. This was when I lived in the valley. Three houses ago. And everyone always told me I should have dogs, and I never did at that time. I did have a gun for a while, but I got rid of it. Started to freak me out. So I told myself that I was safe, as long as I felt I was safe. I did that thing of imagining a white light all around me, and all that shit. And it does work, when you think to do it as you walk out the door. This could all be nothing. But that brother, those brothers were such freaks. I could imagine him building some case that I deserved to come down. Some people resent you for not killing yourself off with drugs, STD or drink. But I never hated myself into a hole, like quite a few people did. And I could see this brother, deciding so late in the game, to cut me right now. Because he never got me out of his craw.

I told the detective this, and he's following up. Don't know why I didn't think of this before, but what you said about being entered. That concept, I'd forgotten about since way back then. With that freak. Could lead to nothing. But you know, Chauncey's parents had returned my flowers. Maybe some other family member did. And I sent them a note, telling them how I empathize with their pain. And then I guess, like Henry's daughter, they had to come around a bit. I got a nice note from them, that didn't exactly take any blame away from me, but just met me with some kind of sentiment. I understand it. They're justified in their anger, and they made a little step my way. And I hold them in my heart. I have to. Al gets weird about all this. The parents and everything. He hates me even thinking about them, but I understand how he has to keep up this hardness. He thinks he's balancing me, and I suppose maybe he is.

Your description of the climb blew me away. Not exactly pretty. An adventure, for sure, but, I don't know. Are you really thinking of going rock climbing? That's a prettier picture than down jackets, boots, crampons (makes me think of tampons with clamps!) and axes and saws and all that. Way back when you described all the equipment, I gagged. Even *with a yogi hunk. Hell. How could hanging off a glacier compare to a warm bed with a gorgeous, loving man? You can keep your adrenaline going with him. But if not, if you gotta keep challenging yourself like this, why not do it with him? Go to Yosemite, or back to Joshua Tree, and hug the rocks together. Bet he'd jump out a plane with you. Shit. Have I given you too many ideas?*

I'm off to meet Al at the restaurant. He closed escrow. He got the keys.

Remember, if you need a loan for Greece, just ask. I'd make it a Christmas gift, if you let me. Love as ever, J.

Chapter 11

Sins of the Father

Ray

Gary didn't know it was well worth mentioning that after a long and grueling restaurant shift, an irate old woman had come banging at the door looking for Ray. It wasn't until Gary experienced this exceptional wrath that his boyfriend Jason bragged of how he had snarled at this same woman from behind the peephole, twice before that. Jason never opens the door unless it is the postman, and he never finds it in his heart to be bothered with any sour hag's troubles. Still it's not until Gary's day off when now an arrogant but puckered and limp young man rings the bell, and asks for Ray Rose, that Gary thinks to call him about all of this happening.

"Alls I can figure is this must be a subpoena," Gary says, his shoulder cushioning the phone to his one good ear as he turns down the air conditioner Jason has cranked.

"I've got no fucking idea," Ray trails off with a burnt voice. Today it's just as hot in Alaska as in Florida. His throat constricts, his stomach knots, as he thrashes through the slog in his brain.

"He was wearing a nelly plaid shirt and a blazer in this *heat*. Gotta be a sorry little process server, whiny as can be."

"No fucking idea," Ray repeats, feeling doom like a dome over his head.

"Could it have anything to do with your motorcycle accident?"

"Nah, man, that was months and months ago, finished where it started," Ray says, now getting angry. "Asshole that she was, she admitted she ran me off the road. She got out of her car and checked on me. Wasn't a bad spill, the bike barely scratched, and we didn't even exchange numbers. How could it *possibly* be about that?"

"Never know. Maybe this old bitch is her mother, stirring up trouble."

"Impossible."

"Have you been paying the mortgage?"

"House is paid for. All I got are the power bills and the property taxes. You *know* that. How else could I afford for you to live there rent free?"

Gary looks at the phone, then puts it to his bad ear, testing it out. "Don't shoot the messenger, man."

Ray grinds his teeth.

Gary looks at Jason who is clipping his toenails. "Listen, whatever it is, if they can't serve you, they can't do shit." Waiting for a response, Gary throws up one hand.

"Ray?"

"I'm here."

Gary puts the phone back to his good ear, rakes back the impertinent strands from his forehead. "Listen, man, just stay gone and forget about it. I got your back."

"Fuck."

"Ray? I thought I should tell you. But don't worry about it. They can't do shit if they don't know where you are."

Feeling like scales are popping up on his scalp, he scratches his head so hard he cuts the skin. *"Fuck!"*

"Where's Ruby, man?"

"She's inside. I'm a few yards from the cabin where I can get a signal."

"So go inside, man. Calm down. Have a good day, fuhgeddabou' it. 'Kay? And by the way, your dad called."

"Great." He gnashes his teeth again.

"He thought maybe you were back by now. I didn't give him your cell number, but I told him I'd tell you he called. He didn't seem to want anything. 'Just checking in,' he said." Gary plops down on the couch next to Jason, who gathers all his toenails in the crack of a magazine.

"He has my cell number. I'll call him. Talk to you later," Ray says, hanging up before Gary can say goodbye.

Ray lights up a cigarette, walks through the endless thicket of black spruce, a mesh of mosquitoes swarming as if he were bitten fruit. The air is thick with the smell of sap, his skin glistens with sweat. If he were stuffed in upholstery, he couldn't feel any more smothered than right now.

The only thing close to this kind of fear would be the moment his father discovered him in any wrongdoing. His father always seemed so huge to him. Massive and monstrous in his anger. It was never the pain of any flailing that he dreaded, but simply the eyes of a butcher he would see in his father. He would shake with rage, and Ray would feel so very tiny. Sticky, ugly, and brief, like a boil his father could lance.

This was miles from what Ray projected on his own victim that night. Arnie Watson was far from a small, helpless animal, and nearly equal to Ray in strength. And immediately afterward, Ray felt less like a butcher than he felt centered and at one with the power of release. The power of precision. This had nothing to do with coldness and calculation. It was more like being a volcano, finally erupting. And now that he was active, he knew what he was capable of.

After he drove away from the swamp, he didn't feel like running. Instead, he left his fate to the higher laws of the universe. But this did not mean he could sleep at night, particularly those first few weeks. He remained in Florida, and he took the gift of the house— hard to understand as it was, and still is. Now a year and a half later, he has escaped to Alaska, found his true love, and the world is finally catching up to him.

"Ray," Ruby says, as she lightly treads the sticks, leaves, and grass. She looks like a mermaid swimming through the heat. "What's wrong, love?"

He bursts into tears. He thinks because it's the first time she has called him that. But this is not the first time he has cried in front of her. He is a boy-giant in her arms.

"You're getting bored with me, aren't you?" he sniffles, worrying that he might be getting snot in her hair.

"Ray," she says with a mother's tone.

"I promised George," he breaks off, sobbing now.

"What is *wrong?*"

"I promised him I'd help him finish this one last cabin, and then we'd go."

"I'm not in any hurry."

"Yes, you are. Running 'round Fairbanks with Abbie. Next thing I know you'll be off with the monk on some mountain all the way across the world."

"I took Abbie to her eye doctor. I told you that. We weren't running around anywhere. I was cooped up in the office the entire time."

"Don't leave me," he says.

Ruby coos, the sound muffled in his chest. She looks up at him, her arms around his waist. He wipes his nose with the back of his hand. He lifts her up, and carries her back through the woods.

"You pull yourself together so quickly," she giggles.

"I just decided I won't let you leave me," he says, marching like a trophy hunter returning with his prize.

She holds on tighter, buries her face again in his chest.

Around the bend, watering the blooms is George's wife, Ethel. She puts her age-spotted hand like a visor over her ice gray eyes.

"Put her down, you beast!" she calls, and laughs.

Ruby waves, her other arm tightly around his neck. Ray turns toward Ethel and nods, heads for the lovenest.

"Why don't you join us for a little coffee in the morning!" Ethel calls out again.

"Sounds good!" Ray calls back, opening the door to his cabin. He carries her over the threshold, then kicks the door closed.

The room now pungent with the smell of sex, Ruby sits naked on his chest, combs his eyebrows with her finger, traces the arc of his diving scar, which is the size of a thumbnail's indentation. His eyes are closed, he breathes easily for the first time since Gary's call.

"What was all of that about out there?" she asks. His eyes bug open. "All what?"

"All that stuff about me getting bored with you. You were just trying to sidestep. It was definitely more than that." She puts a finger up his nostril, but when he doesn't sniffle or laugh, she awkwardly takes her finger back.

Ray swallows hard, a knife pain like gas in his chest. "I was thinking about my father."

"Is that who you were on the phone with?"

"No, it was Gary." He swallows hard again.

"Are you sure it wasn't one of your ex-wives?"

"I wouldn't lie to you about something like that." A little fresh sweat breaks from his forehead. "I talk to none of them, and I can't imagine ever hearing from any one of them again."

"So why were you thinking of your father if you were just talking to Gary?"

"Gary told me he called."

"So? What's the drama in that?"

"I don't know, I just *hate* the harassment. He waits until the last minute to put his two cents in."

"What's he got to comment on now?"

"My having quit and 'moved' here. It's what he thinks."

"You sure you're just not telling me that you told him you're involved with a black woman?"

"What would be the big deal about that?"

"How should I know if your father's a racist or not?"

"My third wife was black. He's already dealt with it. At this point, he couldn't care less."

"Why didn't you tell me that before?" She crawls off his chest, closes her thighs together, folds her arms over her breasts.

"I told you she was Brazilian because that was the main point— her green card. The fact that she is black has been irrelevant until you brought up all this crap."

"You didn't tell me you had a type, Ray." She grits her teeth.

"I don't have a type! My first wife was tall with short brown hair and a face like Julia Roberts, so every time I see an ad for one of her movies, it makes me sick. My second wife was short and blonde and Jewish, and Sonya was model-size and much darker-skinned than you."

"Oh, so she was 'model-size.' Any other black pussy in your past?"

"Now that's foul. Any other white dick in yours?"

"Fuck you, Ray."

"Well don't speak to me like that. I don't deserve it."

"Why'd you hide Sonya's race from me?"

"I didn't hide it!" He sits up, his face a hot pink.

Ruby grabs her panties on the floor, gets up to find her bra thrown near the bathroom doorway.

"Ever so coy, aren't you Ray? Just keep me guessing, right?" She shakes her head.

Baffled, he looks up at her.

"I need a drink. I need to get out of here," she says, her navy baggy skate pants on now, and Ray's dirty white tank T. His frown uncurls, thinking she meant to wear it, but she doesn't notice it isn't hers, which lies like a kitten with the dust balls under the bed.

She slams the door behind her, waits for him in the car, since he always takes twice as long as her to get ready.

When they get to the bar, it's a little past ten. Ray is exhausted from working all week, Ruby's racial trip, but above all, Gary's news. He is relieved to see that Abbie is sitting with Charlie, though the Argentinean friend, Luis, is also there. Abbie's blunt black hair is caught up high in a ponytail, a light blue ribbon around it. She wears a skimpy pink camisole and walking shorts, like a sexy teenage girl. She has a new medic alert bracelet that Ruby insisted upon. Charlie looks as if he's on his third or fourth beer, his face flushed with a stupid grin. Luis doesn't seem to have been there long. He nods to Ray and Ruby, who kisses Abbie on the cheek.

"Hey, hey," Charlie says, pulling out a chair for Ruby. She smiles and returns the hello. "My long ago kayaking partner, how you be?" He pulls another chair out for Ray.

"A little tired, man, but fine," he says in a tense voice.

"You remember Luis," Charlie puts his hand on Luis' shoulder.

"What's up, man," Ray says. Ruby says hi at the same time.

"It's all good," Luis says, nods to Ruby.

"So I just found out you work on *Rootown*, that's amazing, I *love* those guys!" Charlie says.

"You don't have a TV, man," Ray says, in a short tone. He

turns around to order three beers from the waiter. Ruby looks at him.

"Yeah, but I watch it at Mindy's on Saturday mornings. I used to have a TV before that. I sold it for some cash, got myself off the couch habit, you know." He lifts his chin in the air like a toast.

Abbie lights a cigarette, Ray bums one off her. "This guy never has his own," Abbie says, lighting it for him.

"Tell me 'bout it," Charlie says. "So what's it like, Ruby? To be the proud creator of Hyena Harry and Pickled Pete," his eyes like slits from the beer and weed.

"I didn't create either of them," Ruby clears her throat. "My boss did. I design the incidental characters."

"Like who?"

"Like a lot of the kangaroos, you know, Bobby Roo, Sue Roo . . ." Abbie laughs, Luis does too, Ruby clears her throat again. "And a lot of the guest enemies of the week."

"Funny how Harry and Pete—everyone's favorite—are really the enemies themselves. I mean they came there to take over and rule the kangaroos who just accepted them with open arms. Isn't that something?" Charlie asks, shaking his head with a stupid smile on his face.

"It is a trip. But isn't it always like that?" Ruby says, touching a grain of sugar or salt on the table, and pushing it in a small trail in front of her.

Charlie grins at her, wrinkling his nose with enthusiasm as he shakes his head again. "But you know, wow, that's really great. It's *really* great you have a job like that. I'd love to be able to say I did something as cool as that," he says.

"You and my brother both," Abbie says.

"I didn't know you had a brother," Ray says.

"Yeah well, I rarely talk about him. Maybe it's 'cause he spent most of our childhood trying to think of ways to kill me." Abbie takes a fleck of tobacco from her tongue.

"What?" Ruby asks.

"I never told you that?" Abbie raises her brows; Ruby shakes her head. "I'm surprised I never told you."

"What did he do?" Ray asks.

"We had a brother who died before I was born. He died when he was two, and my brother was six, and by the time I came along—I guess he was almost eight at the time—he couldn't stand the idea of another one."

"What did he do?" Rays asks again.

"He held me under water, tried to lure me off the roof, led my tricycle into traffic . . . Let's see. How did he love me, let me count the ways." She shifts her weight so the waiter can put down Ray and Ruby's beers.

"What did your parents do?"

"My father didn't take it very seriously until some years later when an insurance agent came to the door looking for my brother, who at the age of fourteen, had taken out a policy on my life."

"No *way!*" Ruby says. Luis smirks, looking mildly amused. Ray assumes she is exaggerating, but he's wrong.

"So did he kick his ass?" Ray asks.

"He shook him a little. Pressed him against the wall. It was drama enough for my father's lifetime."

"What do you mean?" Ruby asks.

"I mean my father wrote the book of the stoic." She takes a swig of Ruby's beer, since her club soda is finished. Ray looks at her.

"My father would have tore him up," Ray says, forgetting about Charlie who is looking uncomfortably buzzed and ready to go home. "Anything my sisters did, he'd beat the living shit out of me for it. He saw it as my job to keep tabs on them."

"I hear ya, man," Luis says.

"Though I was the youngest, I was sure protective over them. But if Sadie got caught with the joint, or Sonya fucked up the car, it was *me* who would pay," Ray says, putting out his cigarette.

"You never told me that," Ruby says. Ray nods, and grabs her hand. She finishes off her beer, and burps. She puts her fist over her mouth as if she'd coughed. Ray laughs, squeezes her hand.

"You ever catch your parents having sex, man?" Luis asks, leaning into the table, Charlie blinking slowly, swallowing hard with dry mouth.

"Yes," Ray says, finishing the first beer, starting his second.

"I ask 'cause your father sounds like mine, man. He expected me to watch out for the girls and my mother and all that. Which I did. But one time I came in on them"—he humps his hands together—"and I was as freaked as they were. My mother screamed, but my father froze, like a lizard or something, man, trying to blend in with the bed. He never hit me again after that."

"Oh man," Ray says, really looking at him for the first time. "I didn't actually see them, I just came to the door, and my father came rushing out, shaking, and I mean he was *huge*, his whole body shivering in rage, you know, I'm this little boy of four. He didn't hit me, but if I'd made one wrong move, he sure would have."

"Jesus," Ruby says.

"Same thing happened when he found me and my sister in the tub—we always took baths together up until the time I was five or six—but we were in there playing with her dolls, and I guess I had a hard-on, you know I had no idea what it was, just one of those things, it's not like I was *excited*, but my father came in and hit the roof."

"Wow, Ray, it's a miracle your head is together," Abbie says, half teasing.

"I can say the same for you," Ray says.

"I'll drink to that." Abbie grabs Charlie's beer now. He turns his back to the table, looks around the room.

"Where's Mindy, man?" Ray asks.

Charlie spins back around. "Work." He licks his lips, looks at the floor.

"Can we take you home?"

"I'm fine," he says, looking up at Ray with red eyes. "I was going to take Abbie home."

"I'll take 'em both home," Luis says.

"You sure?" Abbie asks, looking at Luis over the black rim of her glasses, making it clear she'd rather go in his car.

"Yeah," Luis says.

Abbie pulls money out of her purse, Luis stops her hand, pulls his wallet out with the other. She smiles.

"Fuck, man, the light is getting to me all of a sudden, like I haven't lived here for years," Charlie says. Luis gathers the money that he, Ray, and Charlie have put on the table, and gets up to pay the waiter.

"It's Sunday tomorrow. Sleep it off all day, right?" Abbie chuckles.

"Sunday is sweet," Ray says, caressing Ruby's hand lying limp in his.

"Sunday's a cool blue," Ruby says.

"It's that freshwater snorkeling blue. Almost turquoise," Ray says.

"Nah, I see it colder than that," Ruby says.

"You guys must be synesthetics," Abbie says, lighting up another cigarette.

"Sin-us-what?" Ray asks.

"You're perfect for each other." Abbie winks at Ruby, who looks at her with distrust.

"Ready?" Luis asks, holding his hand out to Abbie, who gets up, but trips over one of the chair legs. Luis catches her. Charlie gets up too, leaving Ray to stare at Ruby. He doesn't know at this moment what heavily pulls him, but it's dawning on her—the full weight of the responsibility of living one's life. He leans over to kiss her, and her eyes are wide open as he draws near. So while tasting her beer-stale lips and tongue, he bores into her the look of utter soul commitment.

A week later, Ray and Ruby take that coffee with George and Ethel at their breakfast table. Ray knew that George had been a sociology professor in Vancouver, but he didn't know about the young student wife and the two kids she had for him, and how George had run away from it all for a stint at a college in Minnesota. There he met Ethel, and broke all ties, deciding to lead the kind of life he'd always wanted here in Healy. Ethel wears a noncommittal smile throughout his recounting of the history, but she is cheery enough for her.

"When we got here, ah! It was land of the midnight sun. We were true homesteaders, using the 'honey bucket' before we had plumbing." George winks, Ruby looks at his stained teeth.

"But think of your ass on the honey bucket in winter! Blistering cold, Minnesota was *nothing* compared to this. Night for day, all day, every day."

"Now that's an exaggeration. Farther north is where they get the total darkness," George says, looking at Ethel as if she were a naughty child.

"I'd love to see that," Ruby says, smiling. Ethel shakes her head, puts both hands on her mug like a child saying "mine."

They hear a car climbing the steep graveled road.

"Ah, maybe it's a renter!" George says, standing to peek out the window. An old gold station wagon pulls in near their door. "Do you have a brother, Ruby?" George asks with alarm, as he knees his chair into the table. Ruby shakes her head no in short jerks, looking at George with a face like she smells something stink. Ray takes her wrist, and mirrors his disgust with a bit too much gusto.

George has forgotten that the sign says OFFICE just beneath the window he peeps through, so he is taken aback as the tall young man—who looks nothing like Ruby, but is close enough in skin tone, true enough—proceeds to knock at the door.

"Let him in, for Chrissakes!" Ethel snaps.

"Good morning," he says. His nice summer vest wildly out of place. He glances at Ruby with the slightest tinge of embarrassment. "Is Ray Rose here?"

"That's him," George says. Ray frozen in place.

"Ray Rose?" the gentleman asks, looking him straight in the eye.

"Yes," Ray says, clearing his throat, his chest beginning to pound.

"This is for you," the gentleman says, nods his head to each of them, then turns around to walk out the door.

"Well, I'll be damned," George says slowly and as if to people who don't speak English. "That bastard got you. What did you do?"

Ray swallows, and with glassy eyes stares at Ruby. Sweat rains down his forehead. Because the tension is stifling, Ruby can't stand it; she risks it all and yanks the envelope from him. When she reads that he's been served notice of the hearing contesting the will over the property on Indian River Drive, she takes Ray's hand, thanks George and Ethel for the coffee, and assures them Ray will be back after this all sinks in.

"I'm so sorry, I'm so sorry," Ray bursts into sobs when they are a few yards from George and Ethel's door.

"Don't worry about it, love. We'll figure this all out. There's nothing to be sorry about," she says, her arm around his waist, the other holding the envelope and document.

"Just let me explain, just let me . . ." he can't stop sobbing.

"Explain what? What's the deal with your property? You're being evicted? Or you got this property illegally? What could be so bad? We'll fight this Rachel Sichterman, whoever the fuck she is."

"Rachel Sichterman?" Ray says, now looking like a boy who's been told he can go to the fair after all. He grabs the document to read.

"Who is she?" Ruby asks.

"I don't know! But she must be related to the old man who left me this property."

"*Who* left it to you?"

"This guy Sichterman," he says now with glee. "I found his name on the county records, but the property was left to me anonymously. All I knew was the lawyer's name who handled it."

"You're kidding me, right?" Ruby says, hand on hip. Ray doesn't know she is stunned by the ease she imagines white people to inherit property. He is overjoyed to know this has nothing to do with the murder. He can't jump up and down, and take the chance of further confusing her, but at least he knows now that his confession to her is not so imminent.

Chapter 12

What's It All About, Al?

Ruby

The speck of mistrust grows. Multiplies itself into flakes, first drifting, now whirling. She waits for it to settle into a fine layer of silt. She sees it in the mirror, and on her neck as she examines for hickeys. On the dog's skull, which she feels is Caspar's, that he carefully packs into his torn pleather bag. On his chapped lips that seem sleazy to her as he murmurs the latest of his pillow talk gifts. She knows he can't be telling her the whole truth. His nightmares seem violent. She sits on her suspicions, waiting to blow. During the day-glow nights as he sleeps in guzzled fits of grunts, tussles, and ticks, she becomes the insomniac.

All of this disappears when he is inside her. The silky breadth of her love is staggering. Two weeks with condoms, then four with none must finally wake her to question the soundness of her judgment. He always pulls out in time, but what's to sway the law of accidents? She has never been pregnant. True. No experience in conception, miscarriage, abortion. With the exception of cuddling one toddler cousin, she's never held an infant. What she doesn't know is there will be no dress rehearsals. And it's not that she is infertile. She is one of those women who while thinking about the act can never get pregnant. Regardless, this should be the least of her worries. For she is headed—as they are both headed—toward much more serious trouble.

It's too late for her to get out of it. She's made her choice in love, no matter how much she hangs onto old ideas of her independence and free-spiritedness. She is in it with him for the long haul. She pushes her unease aside to take the next step with Ray—going home with him.

On their way out of town, the rain pours in squalls. They stop by Charlie's place. Mindy greets them at the door. Her smile is magnetic, her face perfectly oval. Her honey and molasses hair is wavy, thick, long, and unkempt. After they stomp their feet of mud on the creaking welcome platform, they follow her into the cabin. Ruby notices how she waddles very slightly with knock-knees.

"My mom sent me figs!" she says. "My absolute favorite. I brought 'em over for Charlie, he should be back any minute. Come sit down and have some with me."

Impatient to see his friend for a last time, Ray sits on the broken-down armchair just in front of the produce crate table. He sniffles, grouchily throws back his wet hair. He looks up at Ruby with a helpless expression. She ignores his pouts, wishes he'd give up on the moot debate that Charlie might have helped lead the process server to his door. Ruby still doesn't understand how essential loyalty is to Ray.

"I keep saying I'm going to send my mom a sample of the famous Alaskan eighty-pound cabbages." Mindy raises her brows with theatrical delight.

"They're incredible, huh. I can't believe my eyes every time I've seen one." Ruby follows her, to offer her help. "If the rain clears by tomorrow, we're going paragliding in Eagle River before we take off from Anchorage for Florida," Ruby says, trying to meet the level of Mindy's cheerfulness, as she cuts six figs in half, puts them on a cardboard paper plate.

"I've gone handgliding before, not here, but in Colorado where I lived for two summers."

"My climbing instructor's from Colorado. Not that I expect you to know him." Ruby smiles bashfully.

"Are you talking about Stu?"

"Yeah," she lights up, ignoring Ray's jealous vibe.

"I know Stu from here. We went out a couple times."

"Really?" Ray says with a snarl.

"He's a very cool guy." Mindy pulls up two camping fold-up chairs for Ruby and her to sit. "Anyway, that sounds like fun, the paragliding. I imagine it's a lot less dangerous. I was pretty scared when I tried it."

"Yeah, well since it's made of pockets, it acts like a parachute, always trying to stay inflated. Brings you down soft," Ray says.

"But you haven't done it," Ruby says.

"I've gone handgliding, but I know what the difference is. You'll like it, baby." Ruby bites into a fig, but Ray passes. "So, when did you say Charlie would be getting back?" Ray asks.

"Any minute. He went to get his pot." She takes a big bite, crunches, looks at Ruby. "I love your hair, you know."

"Thanks," she says, guarded, hoping this doesn't lead to questions about the texture or how regularly she washes it.

"My first love had hair like yours," Mindy says, taking another bite, leaning toward Ruby.

"Really?"

"Not as long as yours, but he used to let me braid it."

"Ray here can braid almost as fast as my mom," Ruby says more comfortably. They sit for a moment listening to the rain pound the roof.

"Wow. You need flippers and fins out there," Mindy says, rapidly blinking. Ruby can see a tiny blue vein over her eyelid. "Hope Charlie's clutch is alright. It's been sticking lately."

The rain plummets, the wind croons.

Ray inhales heavily. "You'd think this was a Florida hurricane coming," he loudly exhales. "So what do you do during the year, Mindy?"

"I'm a first-grade teacher in Vermont. I've been doing it for six years now."

"Oh, I didn't know. My mom was one too. I was in her class. I had to pretend we weren't related and call her Mrs. Rose," Ray says, rubbing his hands together.

"That must have been weird," Mindy says.

"Couldn't have been weirder," Ray says, looking around the cabin, then at Ruby as if asking for permission to make this even more excruciating. "So do you happen to know if a guy came around here asking for me?"

"No, I don't. Why?"

"Well, it's nothing." Ray gets up, puts his hands on his lower back. His T-shirt is wet from his neck to his chest. Ruby gets up too.

Mindy opens the door to the downpour. "Charlie's going to be sorry he missed you. You sure you want to drive in this rain?"

"A little weather's not gonna interfere with my driving," Ray says with his charm smile.

They kiss Mindy goodbye, on her cheek, and make a dash for the car—Ray opening Ruby's door, as he always does, even when she's driving and has the keys.

"That was miserable," he says, turning the ignition, the view from the window like they were inside a car wash.

"Kinda, huh. Sorry you didn't get to say goodbye to him," Ruby says, pinching Ray's earlobe. "You're not mad at him, are you? Why would they ever come looking for you here or at Charlie's work, anyway?"

"I told you, because I charged that first kayak ride."

"So? It was as easy as tracking your cell phone as your credit card. Either way, they were going to find you."

Ray leans over to kiss her, the rain calming down to twists and puffs, as they deepthroat to the smell of damp vinyl.

Jeannie, I'm back in Anchorage at the same hotel. Tomorrow we take a plane to Fort Lauderdale then drive up to Port St. Lucie where Ray lives. He's been served papers for a hearing over some mix-up with the property he inherited, ANONY-MOUSLY. Can you believe it? I'll tell you all about it when we get there.

For the past few days, we were in this little town, Eagle River, where we went paragliding. It is the most incredible feeling. At first my stomach felt like an elevator dropping floors at the speed of light. But once I was way up in the air—weeee, I was flying!!!! I bet you would love it. Anyone can do it. It's like flying a kite only you go up with it ;)~ The whole thing can fit in a backpack and takes like five minutes to set up. Of course you're in a harness and suspended by risers, but you're in a seated position. You lay the wing of the big kite on the ground, and run to make the glider lift up and fly overhead. I chickened out twice before I let myself go. I started to run and it started to lift and it scared the shit out of me. Finally I went with it. It's amazing I saw anything, the amount of tears that just flowed out of me, as we flew. You really feel what an amazing gift it is to be alive. You understand the beauty and the freedom that we actually have. I was a bird. A crying bird. It was unfuckingbeLIEVABLE.

But talk about crying. Tears of joy = Ray. He can cry when he's making love, he can cry when we're talking, he can cry in a moment of silence. He is easily the most sensitive man I've ever met in my life. He likes to comb and braid hair, he likes to paint my nails and toes, he likes to giggle and be silly, he likes to talk about my family. I've learned more about my family—or at least what I think of my family—in the eight weeks that I've known him than I have over my entire life. He pushes that kind of understanding, without pressing. He's at total ease with everything that is "intimacy." Maybe that's because he's been married three times, which bugs me to no end, I'm ashamed to admit. But I realize too that I guess I've always been attracted to men for the degree to which they are female. It goes beyond being in touch with the feminine side. It's much more elemental, more animal than that. And then he is all MAN.

He's got his demons too, that's for sure. He seems to be stuck on remembering his period of adolescent rage. The hormonal thing. However he experienced it, is like a definition to him. He doesn't talk about his mother enough, I think. It's all about the father. But then again, it's so all about the father for so many of us. Eh?

So I called Joop and he totally copped to clocking the code the last time he was with me. He had no explanation. I yelled at him—in a way I've yelled at no one before. He wasn't even that apologetic. He was just dead air. I'm so sorry, Jeannie. I know it's impossible to swear for anyone, but I would never have guessed this of him. Still, it's not like he meant either of us any harm. And he was the one who dropped me off that morning. He couldn't have been more than four blocks away when I found everyone.

I hate that this always has to come up with you and me. We don't deserve it. I hate writing you "that morning." I hate the pain we both have to feel.

Did anything come up with those brothers you mentioned a while back? Did they find anything?

How is Al and the restaurant?! I don't think you mentioned how he's juggling this with the club. He's got a lot on his plate. How are you taking it? Is he still pressuring you to be more a part of the restaurant?

I have your birthday in my head as October 25th. Is that right? Ray is due in court on October 9th, so we're taking this month and a half to find him a lawyer and all that. Are your plans for Greece set yet? It's just around the bend, but now I don't know if I can commit to it until Ray finds the lawyer. I don't know if it will all be settled that day, or if it's possible this will all drag out. This seems to be the raging relative of the man who left him the property. But then you can relate, I know.

I miss you. I really hope I get to see you for your birthday. Ray really wants to go, and he wants to treat. (This man left him a little money as well). But then again, this all depends on the court date.

I'm gonna have my sister send my laptop to Florida. That way I can stay in touch much more frequently. And maybe I can do a little work as well. My boss has offered me the chance to do a little designing from there.

Love you, big hug from your little bird, R.

Ruby, ain't it always a mixed bag? My heart goes out to Ray. Just when he finds love he's got this bullshit to deal with. Well, whoever this fucker of a relative is, they'll find out soon enough the loser they are. You know I didn't even hate Henry's kids when they first dragged me into court. I understood it. How couldn't I? But I gave them a little bit of money, and I didn't have to do that, but they never even thanked me. That's the gaping, oozing sore on my fucking side. When his daughter came over that time, to offer some sympathy over everything that happened, she didn't bring it up. And it grew into a giant zit on her nose that I was dying to stab. I didn't realize it until you brought this up. Before that I was almost forgiving her. And I'll never forgive Henry's son.

All they would have to say is THANK YOU. You know? And I'm not even the common courtesy nut I used to be. Someone letting the door close behind them on you, or some fucker sitting in the KEEP CLEAR section not letting you into the traffic to make your quick turn—used to ruin my day! Now I brush it off. But how can I let go something like what those kids put me through? Henry never liked either of them to begin with. But speaking of fathers, how could I really know what he put them through?

So, no, nothing came of the brothers thing. You know I've found myself watching those cold case crime shows, all those forensic file freakydeaky shows that have Al SO creeped out, he can't stand another minute of it. He really can't. He goes apeshit when he finds me home watching them. But I can't stop. It's a sickness now. I won't stop until they find who did that to my babies.

Al hasn't yet sold the club. I didn't tell you? He's got no buyers. So that makes things much worse. After I got used to the idea that he has a restaurant, I began counting down until he sold the club. Now I'm a bit ambivalent. Because he seems to want some kind of massive drama to boom his big voice over. And it's beginning to hit him in the pocketbook too. I didn't know that until a little while ago. He kept telling me he could handle it. But now he's been talking about needing more investors. You know, I don't really want to go there with him. I could give him a loan, no strings attached, but I don't want to become an "investor" in this business. Do you know he rented a billboard for this restaurant? He rented it on HIGHLAND below Hollywood for this STUDIO CITY restaurant! He won't listen to me.

You know, that club has been good to him. Kept him in

those suits, that car, and that house, that he may just have to sell because of this fucking restaurant! I asked him, What's this all about? And he was livid that I should question his ideas of how to live a better life. But I don't understand what's wrong with the life we have. It's been so fine up until "that morning," as you and I have been calling it. So. This is his way of dealing with grief. I never thought about it before, he never seemed to care much for the dogs, but then again, how is that possible? How can you live with animals, and not miss them when they're gone? Impossible.

Florida is a trip. You're gonna love it, I think. You think you met some characters in Alaska? Just wait 'til you step off the plane onto the Sunshine State!

I miss you, baby. My birthday's on the 27th, but you were very close. And I don't know about Greece yet. This fucking, fucking restaurant. Excuse my ever-fluent French.

Yours forever, Jeannie

"How could you leave without saying goodbye, you bitch," Abbie says first thing when Ruby answers the phone.

"We went by your house that day it was raining, but you weren't there, and you weren't at the restaurant either."

"And you haven't returned my phone call! I was home all day during that storm. It was awful that night, flooding down the street like a river. I was a shut-in, totally depressed."

"I heard it was flooding. But we were in Eagle River by that time."

"And so you just leave this lame message on my machine, like, 'Okay, bye, nice knowing ya'!'"

"Come on, Abbie. I did not."

"Where are you?"

"Anchorage airport. You should see Ray, he's mesmerized by the stuffed bear."

"Isn't it awful?"

"Yeah. And it *towers* over him."

"I can just imagine him, floored by the fact that there's something huger than he is." She exhales, Ruby can tell she's smoking. "Well, where you off to?"

"Florida."

"Knew it. He must be ecstatic. You're gonna marry him, Door Number Four."

"Should have never said that," Ruby says in a low voice, turning her back to Ray.

"He can't hear you."

"Well. I'm surprised we haven't been cut off yet. I've got so little juice."

"Yeah, yeah. Off you go into the sunset. Now what am I gonna do? I guess enroll at the Braille Institute."

"I'm gonna miss you, Abbie. But I should go. Do you wanna talk to Ray?"

"No, no. Tell him goodbye for me. Love to you both. Have a great time. Piss off!"

Ruby looks at the phone, not sure whether Abbie is kidding. Ray turns around from the bear, then gallops back to where Ruby stands. He pulls her into his side, kisses and smells her hair near her temple, his other hand clutching their tickets.

Chapter 13

Up, Up and Away

Ray

Gary makes smothered catfish for the homecoming. Black beans, rice, baked escargot with hush puppies, and sweet potato pudding with raisins for dessert. He has two chilled bottles of Pinot Grigio, one waits in an iced silver bucket. Ruby wants to open the windows, let in the warm, wet air and eat surrounded by the spectacular dark wood details of the dining room, but Jason says he can't live inside without the air-conditioning. Ray leads them all outside to the backyard instead, where Gary resets the table.

Every day Ruby's extraordinary beauty knocks him out anew. And since they have arrived on his stomping grounds, the voltage of her glow is stunning. The impossible—such as infinite optimism and immortality—now feels authentic. He worries even less over the plausible weight of Rachel Sichterman's case. Even as Ruby marvels over the living and dining room columns, the kitchen's mahogany cabinets and marble floor connecting the breakfast area in the turret (the old man was grand in his idea of interiors), Ray does not stress at the thought of losing it. As she graces through the French doors of the master bedroom leading to the balcony, fawns over the view of his butterfly garden, Ray's only sense of attachment is to her. What he doesn't know, or perhaps feels instinctually, is that their luck will fare far better if they get off the property.

"So the dryer's not working or something?" Ray asks, shoveling in the black beans and rice, then nodding toward the clothes hanging off the tree limb.

"Gary has taken to air-drying in the humidity," Jason says, speaking with his fork.

"What?"

"Just kidding. He got caught in the rain yesterday, stripped everything off and just left it there."

Ruby smiles. "That looks about my size." She winks at Gary.

"You two are *totally* the same size, it's the first thing I noticed when you walked through the door," Jason says. "You even have a similar way of holding your head."

"What are you talking about?" Ray asks, cutting into the catfish that tastes like mushrooms.

"Look at 'em," Jason says, Gary blushing.

"How comes you're not touching the escargot, your favorite?" Gary says.

"We had it for lunch, at that place under the bridge with the outside booths that swing," Ray says.

"The Crab Pot," Jason says.

"Yeah. We followed a red hot-air balloon all the way to Boca," Ray continues. "We're going to take one up next week just as soon as I've found me a lawyer."

"How *comes* we're talking about Florida when you just got back from Alaska?" Jason asks.

"I told Gary every little thing about it," he says, looking at Jason then at Gary straight in the eye.

"I love it here," Ruby says, breathing in theatrically.

"Give it a few weeks, then come talk to me," Jason says.

"There's this lawyer, Zev Hogan," Gary interrupts. "You remember Stephanie from the restaurant?"

"Yeah," Ray says, his brows still skewed toward Jason.

"Well he was her ex-husband's lawyer—not for the divorce, but he handled some matters with the ex-husband's property that belonged to him before they were married."

"So she couldn't get her hands on it," Jason says.

"Anyway, they've been dating, and he's a pretty cool guy. Should probably give him a call. I already asked Stephanie."

"Of course," Jason says. "Which doesn't mean 'should' but 'just do it.'"

"Hasn't stopped you from not listening to shit, has it?" Ray says.

"Now, now," Jason says, talking again with the fork. "You've got the house, you've got the girl, and this little case is a flea you can pinch to pulp between your fingers."

"What makes you so sure of that?" Ray asks.

"Statute of limitations. You've had this house for a year and a half, which gave her plenty of time to contest the will."

"You never know," Gary says, pouring more wine in Ray's glass. Ray takes the bottle and pours Ruby more, before he will drink.

"We've looked at a couple places," Gary says. "So far nothing too good."

"No worries," Ray says, raising his glass to the three of them. "You'll find the right thing. Meanwhile, our house is your house." He opens his arms wide as if to hug all of them. Ruby looks at him with googly eyes.

"Just look at 'em," Jason says to Gary. "Ain't new love sickening?"

The clothes unnecessarily embarrass Ray, as Ruby goes through his closet for something appropriate to meet with the attorney. It never mattered to him what he wore to meet with divorce lawyers, but this house seems more and more important to her, so his mind is fixed on keeping it. She has already helped him go through the many boxes (except one buried at the back) to find the papers detailing the property and monies left to him. He doesn't mention to her again that he sure would love to move to California with her, and start clean. She isn't missing L.A. in the least, as far as he can tell, but this life she's beginning with him appears at times to be an escape. What happens when she wakes up ready to go back and face all that is her own? Will that still include him?

His favorite white collarless shirt is on top of the pile of things to go. She's talking to herself, reaching up on tiptoe to pull down the beloved Michigan sweaters of his youth. As he stares at the perfection of her legs, and the birthmark kiss on the back of her right thigh just beneath the delicious round plush of her cheek, he could fall on his knees and praise God. He believes she was made just for him. If he had remembered that she was born three years before him, then he would realize that it was the other way around. Two sweaters fall, bounce off her hair, which is up in a pompom. Ruby catches the third, turns and smiles, screwing up her nose at the navy pattern with snow on the chest. He jumps up from the bed, grabs her, bites the back of her neck. She squirms as he playfully pulls at the zipper of her shorts.

"I wanna finish the job," she squeals, as he lifts her up high and drops her on the bed. He pounces on her, kicking the clothes to the floor.

"Ray, the outfit for tomorrow, watch—" He cuts her off by covering her mouth with his. She pushes him at the ribs; he kisses the crease at the beginning of her underarm. She giggles as if ticklish.

"I heard Jason up here, just a minute ago," she whispers, as he nips and licks her nipple, holding her entire body down with his weight. She tries wriggling from beneath him, he holds her wrists now over her head. "He's going through the linen closet or something, can't you hear him?"

"Shhhhh," Ray says.

"You're the loud one, you shut up," she says, making fists, straining her neck to get up.

"Who cares? He'll be gone in a minute. Besides, we've had to listen to *them*."

Ruby sighs, lets her body go limp.

"I love you," he whispers gravely. She puts her fingers gently on the space between his mouth and cheekbone. "Kiss me," he says, closing his eyes.

In a light blue shirt, khaki pleated pants, and the one nice pair of black shoes he owns, Ray straps on the helmet over his freshly brushed do, a single braid wrapped in a knot at the nape of his neck. Since he insisted Ruby come along at least for the ride, she is wearing Gary's helmet, clutching the black messenger bag Jason has lent them to hold the legal documents. She waits for Ray to get on the bike first, but he is standing there struck at the sight of her.

"Don't be nervous, baby," she says.

"I'm not," he smiles. "I'm just admiring the view."

"Get on, then," she laughs.

He no longer loves the burgundy and silver of his 1200 Yamaha V-Max, since Ruby admired an old orange Kawasaki they passed. She holds on tightly to him as they make the dip from the driveway into the street, and dash down Indian River Drive, through the long canopy of Australian pines and banyan trees.

"We don't need a car, Ray!" she says loudly at the stoplight. "Teach me how to ride your motorcycle!"

"Sure, I'll teach you, but we still need a car for when it rains!" he says, screeching out as the light turns green.

Since they returned the rental they'd kept for a week since their arrival, he still hasn't gotten used to the euphoria he feels every time they take a ride, her small, strong arms wrapped tightly around his waist. The firmness of her breasts pressed against his back as the speed and the wind whips them still closer together. His dick grows. They take US 1 into Stuart, passing Lula's hot dog stand along the way.

"How far are we now from his office?" she asks at the intersection.

"Three minutes."

"Great, drop me off here!"

"Where?" Ray asks, disappointed she won't be going the whole way.

"You just passed it. Drop me off at this corner. I'll be at the coffeehouse just back there."

Ignoring her protest, he makes a U-turn instead, and drops her at the blue and pink door. She takes off her helmet, sniffles, and shakes out her hair; he lifts his up for a kiss good luck. He squeezes her to him before taking off.

At the office building in old downtown Stuart, he walks through two stale beige corridors before reaching yellow caution tape and plastic tarp covering freshly hung drywall. Directly across is the new wood door he's looking for. A male receptionist wryly greets him, and makes him wait on one of two carpeted chairs flanking a small, cheap veneer table of magazines like *Golf* and *Boca Raton*.

Ray turns to look at the painting above his head—what looks to be a wild turkey awkwardly perched on a cypress tree. The receptionist looks up curiously at Ray, his large square head framed by a painting of two shells leaning like lovers against one another. The receptionist's jawbones propel his mouth, which sits in a perfect straight line, so it appears at once to be a grimace and a smile.

"Same artist?" Ray asks, his charm tuning up.

"What?"

"The painting behind you, the one behind me."

"Oh yeah. He's . . . local."

"As in loco?"

"Exactly," the receptionist says. "You have to excuse things around here. We're 'remodeling.'" He makes the quote symbols with his fingers. "It used to be a dentist's office. Did you notice the smell?"

"I didn't. But that doesn't mean much since I can't remember the last time I was in a dentist's office."

The receptionist's flare of his nostrils is barely detectable. "Me either. Can I get you anything? Coffee, water?"

"No, I'm fine." Ray sits back in his chair, picks up one of the magazines, flips through it without looking.

"He'll be with you any minute. He just got off the phone."

"Thanks, man."

Ray's cell rings. "Yeah."

"You in the mood for scallops? I was gonna stop at the store on the way home," Gary says.

"I'm at the lawyer's office, dude."

"Oh. Okay," he hesitates. "Sorry to interrupt. But don't forget to mention Stephanie. They're minutes from the altar," he adds quickly.

"I will, man. And scallops are fine. Later." Ray hangs up. The receptionist looks up at him, his mouth turned up in a more obvious smile. Now that simply hearing Gary's voice has made him nervous, Ray shifts his weight, crosses his legs, looks at the floor.

The buzzer sounds, the receptionist picks up, and tells Ray that Mr. Hogan will see him now.

The lawyer is very young, his hair a longish pageboy, reminding

Ray of a kid who just got a job as a grocery bagboy and was told to cut it. His jacket and pants are ill fitting; Ray swallows hard as he shakes his hand. He looks around the room for graduation seals and plaques, and finds they are plentiful. The lawyer motions for him to sit down in the nice black leather club chair. Ray pulls the papers out of the messenger bag.

"So here's my service of process." Ray leans forward to hand it to him over his desk. "And this Rachel Sichterman is the relative of Bill Sichterman who left me this property on Indian River Drive, along with $349,000 and change, last February. February twentieth is when I received the papers." Ray clears his throat, and hands him those documents as well.

"And what is your relationship to Bill Sichterman?" the lawyer asks without looking up, since he pores over the papers.

"I've never met him. I have no idea who he is. I was left all of this anonymously, as you can see on the documents; his attorneys handled the whole thing. I only found out his name when I looked it up in county records," Ray says with earnestness.

"Have you asked your family if they know him? Is it possible you did something for him as a child or a teenager?" The lawyer looks up at him like a professor waiting for a more amusing excuse for a late paper.

"I spent my childhood in Union City, Michigan. I came to Florida at eighteen. But yes, I asked my father and sisters if they've ever heard of Sichterman, and they haven't."

"What do you do for a living?"

"I'm a carpenter."

"Is it possible you did some work for him but never put it together?" he asks with too much patience.

"I suppose it's possible," Ray says. "But I certainly had never been to this property on Indian River Drive."

"Have you asked your boss?"

"I'm not working right now. I just got back from Alaska. They tracked me down there."

"Well, that would be a good idea," the lawyer says, looking down again at the papers.

"A job?"

"Yes." He looks at him, as if peering over glasses.

"No problem," Ray says tiredly.

"This Rachel Sichterman's case will be based on her proof that she never knew of her relative's death, and whether or not he was of sound mind when he willed his belongings to a perfect stranger. Now you've been there for a year and a half, so time is on your side. She can't have been very close if it took her this long to find out that he died. So, what I'll do is contact Bill Sichterman's attorneys and find out the details of his death, whether they published it, whether and how they tried to contact Ms. Sichterman, and why he came to pick you as his beneficiary. We have a little over a month—which is plenty of time, in fact I'm surprised that the date is this far off—so depending upon what I find out, we'll see how strong your case is. In the meantime, it would be good if you were working."

"Fine. Oh, and speaking of working, I meant to tell you I used to wait tables with Stephanie at Conchy Joe's, years ago. My friend Gary's still there, so he's the one who hooked this up."

"Do you know Stephanie well?" He looks at him now with a touch of fear, as if waiting in the locker room, hoping no one else will show up to gang up on him.

"She's very cool, we had the same shift at least four nights a week."

"Really? Did you know her ex-husband too?" He clasps his hands on his desk like a grown-up.

"Can't say I did, no."

"Well," he says, scooting his chair back to get up, "I'll tell Stephanie you said hello." He shakes Ray's hand from across the desk.

"I'll wait in front at the receptionist's desk while you make copies of the documents, I'd like to keep the originals," Ray says, feeling in charge.

The lawyer tilts his head. "Of course."

"How long have you been doing this, by the way?"

"Three years. And I haven't lost a case. There's going to have to be a first time though." He pulls his pants up at the waist, and buzzes for his assistant.

"Are you saying I don't have a good case?" Ray asks anxiously.

"Not at all. I'm saying I've had an incredible winning streak, and regardless of the particulars of each case, it won't behoove me to remain cocky of my record."

The assistant comes in, she looks as though she could be his mother, though she is dressed nattily, and would never have let him walk out the door looking as he does.

"Will you copy these documents, and give the originals to Mr. Rose, and show him back to the receptionist?" he says curtly, and she nods as if on cue. "I'll call you as soon as I have all the information."

"So what's this going to cost me?"

"My rate is $150 an hour, I'll need a retainer—let's say three thousand to get started."

"Fine."

Ray then turns and follows the tall, stern mother figure out of the door.

When Ray enters the coffeehouse to pick up Ruby, he finds her sitting in a green corduroy loveseat with a guy, his color a gorgeous, deep clove brown, his eyes serious and well-intentioned. She would have done better to knock Ray in the stomach with brass knuckles.

"Ray," she says sweetly, her mouth parted in pleasurable surprise. "This is Lou," who stands up and shakes Ray's hand. "He and his wife own the place," she says, barely containing excitement.

"Hey man," Ray says with unease.

"Welcome," Lou says, gesturing openly with his hands. He walks off to attend behind the counter.

"So, 'Hot Water Music,' huh?" Ray says with his brows skewed.

"What?" Ruby lifts a cheek, revealing the right side of her gums.

"The name of the place," Ray says, jiggling his head like a sassy girlfriend.

"Oh, kinda cool, huh," Ruby says, tightening her knees together. "So, how did it go?"

"He's a kid," Ray says.

"Let's find someone else," Ruby says. "You want a coffee or something?"

"No, I want to get out of here, now." He leans closer to her ear, "I can't stand watching you falling all over some other man's lap."

"*What?*" she snaps.

"First I have to worry about Mindy, then it's every waitress in your face—" he still talks directly in her ear. She moves away in disgust.

"*Mindy?*" she interrupts. "You need to do some checkin' in with yourself, Ray. Don't talk to me like that. I have *never* been more true and devoted in my life. So don't fuck with me. And not here. Because I intend to come back." Ruby gets up, goes to the counter to say goodbye to Lou. His smile is warm, but he is also no one to be messed with. Ray waves in a crippled salute. He follows her out of the door.

"He's married, Ray," Ruby says, strapping on her helmet.

"*Wrong* answer," he says in an evil game show host's voice.

"And *I'm* married." She pats her heart. (Ray would ordinarily let himself melt, but Lou is too dashing, Ruby too free, and way too much of a people-lover.)

"That never stopped anybody," Ray says.

"I am *not* one of your ex-wives, Ray. All of them cheated on you because that's what you were looking for. But you didn't come looking for me, we just happened. Don't you forget it."

"But I *did* come looking for you. I love you with all of my heart and soul—"

"I'm not in the mood now for your corny bullshit," she interrupts.

"Wow. Can't believe you see me like that. But I don't care what you say, I know we were meant for—"

"Then why question my actions?" she interrupts again.

"I just can't stand to see you sitting so cozily with another man. And if that weren't enough, I gotta worry about women too!"

"You're messing up," Ruby snaps, pointing her finger at the seat, stabbing it so hard it must hurt. He gets on the bike, and she gets on the back, holds onto him like the Heimlich maneuver. He doesn't know that the ferocity of his jealousy is motivated by a sense of possessiveness. Anyone moved to murder out of revenge, comes from that same place as well.

As they ride, Ray wonders if Ruby hasn't just jumped on board his true love declarations with nothing else but good faith. What he doesn't understand is that he has done the very same thing, and the only reason it's dissimilar to his past romantic experience is that this time he would eventually succeed in losing himself in someone else.

While he still has the ordinary business to attend to—the guilt over murder, the case over the property—the coming pivotal event will supersede his self-absorption.

Upon reassuring Ruby, Gary, and Jason that the baby attorney Zev Hogan really is the right one to represent him in this case, Ray sets out to follow Zev's advice, dropping in on his old boss at the office. Kirk is happy to see him, and Ray catches him up on what brought him back. Kirk offers that the name Sichterman is vaguely familiar, but he cannot find the name in his records. He says he could have heard that name anywhere, then he changes the subject.

"I saw you with your new girl, the other day," Kirk says, his eyes brightening. "You were on your bike, she was holding on tight." He winks.

Ray smiles. "Her name is Ruby, and I am the luckiest man alive." He closes his eyes.

"So, what is she? Jamaican, Barbadian, *another* Brazilian?"

"Fuck you, Kirk."

"Well?"

"She's American. Californian."

"Wonder if that's worse."

"Man, now why'd I bother to come in here?"

"You missed me, boy. Now come sit in my lap." He opens his arms, laughs, and slaps his knee.

"You little shit. I came to get my job back."

"Somebody's got your job, son," he sighs heavily. "A Conch. He's not bad. Don't understand why anyone would leave the Keys for here, but he has."

"Key West is totally hacked, overrun with buttoned-up morons."

"I'd still rather be there."

"You got any work at all?"

"Nothing more than for a laborer."

"I'll take it."

"We're putting in a floor at the end of next week. Wanna come in then?"

"Absolutely, man."

"I really can't pay you a crew leader salary. Just don't have the budget."

"Got it, Kirk. I'll call you next week," Ray says from the threshold of the door.

When Ray gets home, he finds the breakfast dishes still in the sink, and a note on the counter from Ruby, saying that she and Jason went to Hot Water Music to buy some good coffee, and that after a few errands they would be back by lunchtime.

"Where's everybody?" Gary asks, entering from the back porch door. He puts a grocery bag down on the kitchen island; he wriggles his nose.

"You have the day off, man?"

"Yeah, it's Monday."

"Right. Well, Ruby and Jason went to buy coffee at that new place in Stuart with the hideous blue and pink poles. They left me to clean up this mess."

"Jason left the house?" Gary says, a boggled expression on his face.

"I know."

"And they went all the way to Stuart?"

"It's just as far as town."

"Yeah, but, with Jason they may as well have gone to Texas."

"They'll be back in twenty," Ray says with a hint of irritation, helping him unload the groceries. He softens as Gary reaches up for a high cabinet knob. "So how's your ear, man? I haven't asked you since last you mentioned it. Sorry, man."

"No worries. You got a lot on your plate. It's in and out. But so much better than nothing. Doctor's hopeful."

"So am I." Ray shakes his head, as if shaking off an entire mess.

"Me too. I've actually been having nightmares about it again. I can't figure out why."

Ray's eyes bug open, but he tries to maintain calm. "Well, man. No one's heard hide nor hair from him. I can bet you that motherfucker will never set foot in this state again." Ray's eyes now blaze, and Gary looks alarmed.

"I never asked you, Ray," Gary clears his throat like Ruby does when she's feeling shy. "Did you go and see him that night?" Gary stretches his lips over his teeth.

"No."

Ray walks out the door to take a ride on his bike. He has no intention of tracking Ruby and Jason down, but he meets them two blocks from US 1. He beckons Ruby out of the car, puts her on back, and rides her out to the Boca Raton airport to make an appointment to ride the hot-air balloons. His romantic act is clipped by the fact that there aren't any balloons going up on Monday, so they have to return days later on Saturday, early morning.

There is no wind, and it is so quiet inside of Ray's head, as he holds onto Ruby's hand, that he can hear his heart beating in his chest. He looks up at the balloon, yellow with purple stripes; the basket they stand in hangs from ropes. Ruby looks up at it too, her eyes popping, a girlishly gleeful grin. She bobs her brows up and down like a dirty old man. Ray laughs, and holds her tightly to him. As the balloon climbs higher in the air, Ray makes a silent promise to himself. Happily, he would give his life for her. The world should never be robbed of such a smile.

"Up, up and away!!!" she squeals, her voice sailing off into the calm of his mind.

Chapter 14

Wanda, Wanda

Ruby

Jeannie, I'm just loving it here. And you know I talked to my boss Paul, he said he could still use some of my help, so he's e-mailing me the scripts, and I'm sketching ideas for some of the characters. He got a development deal for another show, and would like my ideas on that too, so it's really kind of exciting.

Ray has gone back to work doing construction for his old boss, as well, so everything is great. The court date is next week, his lawyer seems to think we should be okay. The man who left Ray the property was of sound mind, his attorneys have stated. It turns out this woman is his sister, whom he hadn't seen since they were in their twenties. He wrote specifically in his will that he wanted her to have nothing. There's even an eloquent bit about his desire to experiment with anonymous luck. Seems pretty open and shut to me. While Ray's at work, I've been hanging out and sketching at this little coffeehouse in Stuart, which is two towns south of us here in Port St. Lucie. The owners are this really great couple, Wanda and Lou, who met when Wanda was Lou's high school teacher in Philly. They're the only black people I've met out here (though there are some peeps around) come to think of it, they're the only ones I've met since I've been gone. Lou's a writer—Wanda told me he used to stutter when he was in her class, and he was so shy, but by far the most talented "kid" she ever had. He had Chronic Fatigue Syndrome for

10 years, and he is finally fully recovered. They hooked up around the last year of his illness, and I don't doubt that it was Wanda's full force and cult of personality that helped him come along. Wanda says she's 50, and looks it, but Lou told me she's actually 60. He's 31. I'm finally dropping the little ageist attitude I used to have. I must admit that back then I was relieved that you never had a young boyfriend, or that Henry never left you for an even younger woman, or even that Al has never messed around, for that matter. I don't know how I got this in my head—that people should have similar reference libraries—but Wanda and Lou are changing all that. They're so much in love, and have such a great sense of humor about each other and life in general. We've gone to their house a couple times, they've got a pool and I'm learning how to dive, which I somehow never did. You know I grew up with a pool, and you've seen me swim enough times in yours, but I was always too frightened to attempt diving. I've belly-flopped a bit, and stung the shit out of myself, but I've also been going swimming with Ray in the river, across the street from the house. We take the boat out, and jump in anywhere, it's so romantic.

There has been no daredeviling lately, unless you count a hot air balloon ride, which was such a beautiful, peaceful thing. I just loved it. We get in the ocean, and go boogie-boarding, bodysurfing, but I tend to get all beat up in there too.

Did I mention to you that Ray's best friend Gary lives with us, along with his boyfriend Jason? Jason's been off work for some mysterious disability, he hasn't worked in a couple years. I never pry, but he and I have become very friendly—he has a wicked tongue on him, but he's really quite soft. I like Gary, he and Ray seem to have taken care of each other all this time. A tender thing between men. I love that about Ray. He's so unthreatened by people doing their own thing. And he's so very generous. He gets jealous at times, but I do too, so I excuse it. Sometimes I'm afraid it could all be taken away from me, just like that. I think at times I try and protect myself from getting hurt by nitpicking, creating little problems for distance's sake. Doesn't work, of course. I'm in this for the long haul.

I've been thinking I'm gonna have to get my mind back on money. I've been watching it slip away these past few months. It's cheaper living here—there's no state income tax, no inheritance tax, and property tax is only 1 percent?!—but you sure make a lot less. My father has always hounded me about retirement, so I'm trying to get smart again. My boss and I haven't yet worked out how much he'll be paying me— it's not gonna be full salary—and I know I'll soon have to make some commitments, one way or another. Tell me what the story is for your birthday! If you end up staying home and having a party, maybe I can come for a week or so, have some fun, and take care of business. What did you think of Hannah by the way? She told me she picked up my laptop from the house. I know she comes off the sizing-up type, but she really is a sweetheart.

I forgot to tell you too, I've been learning how to ride Ray's motorcycle. I got my permit already, just have to go back in and take the driving test to get my license! It's fantastic! Already I've dropped Ray off at work and picked him back up a few times. Don't you love it? You should get back into horseback riding. The brain really does need some breeze and a break from all of our tripping.

Big fat hug to you, and lots of love, R.

Ruby, well if you ain't an Aries to the bone. Go, go, go, go, go. Have you no rest? And then getting all that new in-love sex on top of it. You haven't mentioned it lately, but I can't imagine it's still not HOT. You're right about horseback riding. I need SOMETHING. Al is really bringing me down. I curse the day he got this restaurant. This week I did go and have me a little fun and relaxation. I took Fawn out to the desert, Two Bunch Palms, and we had us some mud baths, massages, aromatherapy, and plenty of champagne. It was fabulous. I came back home to Al, grunting about his staff, groaning *about the club—which he is just desperate to unload—and soon enough I was back in bed, watching Forensics Files. I refuse to join in with his shouting matches. And speaking of sex, Al has been having trouble getting it up. At first I excused it as part of the shock with all that happened—since that's when it started—but now I wonder. Funny you should say that Al has never messed around. I've always had that impression too. Even when we weren't so tight, there never seemed to be anyone else. He was just a confirmed bachelor, not so much a playboy. When we met, we really rang each other's bells, and it seemed real. I see no harm in trying viagra. He refuses. It's like I've announced he's old. I'm not saying he is. I'm just saying I'd like to do something about this, and do something about it quick. I'm not ready to go and fuck someone else, but if he leaves me dangling much longer with his hellish attitude about EVERYTHING right now, I just might.*

The more I think about it, the more I realize I need a week in Malibu. Nevermind the best and most available place I know of is my old friend, Jake's—and Al would hit the roof— but maybe this is exactly what he needs too. Maybe he's just too damn sure of me. There's not going to be any party, baby. I just don't have the energy. But any time that you can come back home for a visit, I would be so very happy. Maybe you'd like to come out with me and stay at Jake's? I could teach you a thing or two about diving, myself! E-mail me a picture of Ray, already. I'm dying to see him.

Buckets of love, Jeannie

And though there is no need to worry in this department when it comes to Ray, as Ruby reads about Al's not getting it up, she immediately thinks of last Monday night when she encouraged Jason to surprise Gary with an overnight stay at an oceanside resort hotel. Ruby had gone shopping for a red vinyl mini, hooker see-through heels, a purple boa, and a white lace corset. She found an old Foxy Brown CD, put it in the stereo, and called Ray to ask if he could get a ride home, but to please phone her first before he arrived.

When he walked through the door, she hit the CD player, strutted, bumped and grinded her way toward him, as he stood there with his mouth hanging open. She put his hands on her, then she danced away from him, slowly unpeeling the scant articles of clothing. The music was loud and thumping. She pushed Ray down on the couch, stroking his thigh with her knees, and rubbing her breasts against his face. When she finally put her hands on his cock, he wasn't hard.

She snapped right out of the persona she was so enjoying, and asked him what was wrong. He said it wasn't that she isn't the most incredibly sexy woman on earth, but rather that she could be turned on by being a stripper, and therefore would enjoy letting other men, other women, looking at her. She hit the roof. Having Gary and Jason gone for the night, allowed them to be as loud as they wanted, right in the living room. And that this had to be a yelling match, rather than a wildly nasty delicious and noisy fuck, was typical of human nature, she realizes soon enough.

So no. There is no need to worry about the prowess of her man. And even though they have gone from making love five times a day (in Alaska) to three or even two times a day in Florida, Jeannie had guessed right—the sex couldn't be hotter.

"Let's see what you got there, Missy," Wanda says in her low voice, standing over Ruby's head at the coffeehouse. "What are those, alligators?"

"Crocodiles. This is Mighty Mikey Crock and Billy Bull Crock. They're brothers." Ruby looks up at her and smiles.

"They're pretty sick looking, I like it," Wanda bobs her chin like a car doll. "So the 'toon takes place in Australia?" She sits down across from her.

"Yeah."

"You been there?"

"A few years ago."

"That must have been cool." Wanda lights up a cigarette, blows the smoke through her large and prominent, perfectly round nostrils. "I've always wanted to go to New Zealand too."

"Yeah," Ruby says, still coloring and shading. She stops, picks up the sketch, studies it, nods, and puts it back down. She scratches her head under the yellow bandanna she uses as a hair band.

"Every movie that comes out set in New Zealand, you know, I run out and see it."

"You should go then." Ruby sniffs in, a little sucking sound of snot. She wipes the outer corner of her eye with her palm. Moves the sketch, rests her chin in her elbow, looks Wanda squarely in the face. "Why don't you go?"

"You got allergies, baby girl?"

"No big deal. It's been less than a week."

"It's the bottlebrush trees. Killed me when we first moved here. You notice that thin film on everybody's car?" She shakes her short, tiny dreadlocks, dyed caramel, slick and shiny as worms.

"Guess so. Though Jason's car has sat there for so long, it's plain filthy. Gary washes his car every two minutes."

"Aren't they in the way?"

"Who?"

"Those guys in the house. You two ever get to be alone? Ray's too old for roommates."

"They're looking for a place."

"How long they been looking?"

"Almost two months, I guess."

"Shee-it." She flicks her ash with disgust, her mouth a dollish bow, no matter what she does with it.

"So, why don't you go?"

"Where?"

"To New Zealand, if you've always wanted to."

"I can't just pick up and go wherever I want," she says, pushing one brow down on her heavy Sophia Loren eyelid.

"Why not?"

"I've got this place now," she says in a high singsong.

"Find a manager."

"We don't make enough money for that!" She puts the cigarette out, her arm extending in dancer's pose, spotlighting the emptiness of the place.

"Well put up a GONE FISHING sign and just go."

"Right, little girl. You ever try and support a man who's trying to make his way as a writer, take your *teacher's* savings, move from Philly to Florida, pay *all* the notes, and open up a coffeehouse? *I must be crazy!* How I'm sposed to find the money to go gallivanting after all that?"

"I don't know. If you want something badly enough."

"What I wanted badly was to be with that man, somewhere easy and sunny, where the trash, and the crowds, and the streets, and the sleet, and the grit wasn't burying him, you know? He was so *ill*. It was awful. But now we're here, and it seems like years ago."

Ruby sniffles again and smiles. She pats Wanda's hand. "I gotta go. It's about time to pick up Ray."

"You're a bad biker chick, aren't you now? I saw you when you got here. All that sass as you hopped off your hog." She laughs a big guffaw.

"And tomorrow's court day. If we win, we're gonna celebrate. You should taste Gary's cooking, hmmn! I'll call you, maybe one of you could swing by. Better yet, both of you come late!" Ruby gets up, gathering her things in the same messenger bag that Jason ended up giving her.

"Sure, let me know what happens, girl." She gets up, scoots in the chair, and moves like a lynx back toward the counter.

Ruby has never seen Ray this blitzed and ecstatic before. As he dashes from the dining room to the kitchen and back, he sprint-skips in the air, rolls his hand, and points at whoever happens to be in his way. Ruby imagines the old man, Bill Sichterman, watching over the scene. Jason smirking at the tight, ugly dress on Stephanie—Gary's restaurant colleague—and Zev Hogan, her boyfriend, Ray's and Ruby's knight in shining armor, letting his hair down with each new beer. What Ruby doesn't know is that Bill Sichterman has crossed every one of their paths, minus hers. He has eaten Gary's food at the restaurant, and Stephanie has served it. Jason was once his oldest friend's escort. Before he started the import business, Zev, as a teen, came in with his mother into his furniture store. And Ray was on site when he accompanied a dear client while inspecting her third fixer-upper. This was before he knew he had throat cancer. He was smoking, his ash about to drop on her new floor, when Ray handed him his old soda can to flick it in. This was a trivial event that neither of them could quickly remember even if primed. And Bill Sichterman never knew that the name he landed on in the telephone book was someone he'd actually laid eyes on, and exchanged a few words with.

"Where's Wanda?" Ruby asks Ray.

"Wanda, Wanda, all I hear is Wanda these days." He pinches her cheek. He bends his knees and gives her a little bump with his hips. "Can you believe it, my babe?" He lifts her up and takes her outside.

"I can't believe how shamelessly that Stephanie is flirting with you. Was she like that when you worked together?"

"She is *not*," he says, his eyes wild and red with tequila and beer. His breath heavy in her face, as he carries her.

"Where are you taking me?" She looks to the right, alarmed by the motion-detector light. "You gonna drop me in that pond?"

"Now that rainy season's over, it's almost dried up. You'll soon see the fish flopping on dirt, and frogs that dropped as tadpoles from the sky," he says, still carrying her with a mad glint in his eye.

"Uh-uh!"

"Uh-huh!"

"Are those the toads Jason said people lick the venom from to trip?"

"No, these are frogs, those are toads," he answers sweetly, putting her down in front of the shed door. He searches all his pockets for the key. "Aha!" He shows it to her like a magician.

He pulls open the shed doors, flips on the light with his elbow, and Ruby squeals. He drops the key in the palm of her hand, as she stands frozen, still squealing, at the sight of a lime green vintage Kawasaki.

"Hop on it, baby! It's all yours!" He pulls it out and helps her on. "Take a spin around the yard." His hands are on his hips, he gyrates as she revs up the engine. "Go, baby, go!!"

The loud engine rumbles, everyone pours out of the house to see her riding the backyard lawn in a large, careful circle, still squealing her head off.

Chapter 15

Night for Day

Ray

When Ruby was gone climbing with the yogi letch for those two and a half weeks, it was torture enough for Ray, but now that she's back in L.A. for six days, life is unbearable. She insisted he shouldn't go with her, even though Kirk doesn't have quite enough work for a full week. She is never any good on the phone—long silences, sighs, too many "I knows" and "me toos." Doubt sets in with an aggressive edge. Does she truly love him? Each hour feels prickled with it, every night alone in bed his gut feels torqued.

Things that ordinarily would only annoy him now overwhelm. Like the fact that he finds more galleries of fire ants on the small cliffside at the front few paces of his dock across the street. There is the unmistakable spongy sinking beneath his feet as he steps on them. He swiftly jumps off, anticipating the painful burn and red blisters they leave. Luckily he escapes them this time. Instead of going boating, he runs back to the house to make a list of to-dos before she gets back.

A delicate apprehension comes over him as he sorts the mail and finds a postcard from Abbie. It's a beautiful view of the Alaska Range, but the few words scrawled seem needy. Ruby will naturally want to respond when she returns home. The apprehension is this: Ruby just picks up and goes, and she's likely to do so with anybody. She ran around with Abbie, she runs around with Jason, she runs to Wanda, and now she's run off to Jeannie. Who knows who is waiting in line to see her there in L.A.—the actress she had an affair with (just because they looked alike?!); her boss, Paul, who must be in love with her to give her this much leeway; Joop, the guy she insists is only her "skateboarding pal"; and Pej, who couldn't be over her. Who could ever be over her? He couldn't imagine.

"Divorced again, Goldilocks?" Kirk says as Ray enters the trailer door for his paycheck.

"Ah man, I'm not in the mood," Ray says, hanging his head as if in church.

"Well, this one sure went fast."

"*Ruby*, that's her name, Kirk, learn it. She's been gone for four days, she'll be back in two. I just miss her is all."

"Well. I'll be a slipper in cow dung. The boy's in love." He laughs.

"Suck it, Kirk."

"I didn't believe it was possible. You went through them so fast—or should I say, they went through *you* so fast, there's always a high wind tailing you." He waves his fingers near his temple, bringing the image of a gnome to mind.

"Ooagh." Ray touches his stomach.

"I was gonna ask if you wanna go hit the little ball, but you look like death warmed over. But speaking of pasty, by the way, wha' da ya think of the Conch?"

"Not bad."

"Wha' da ya think the guys think of him?"

"Not bad. Everything seems pretty cool to me."

"Gotta hand it to you. You're no snake in the grass."

"So where's my check, Kirk?"

"Oh yes! Congratulations again, son, on your win."

"You congratulated me already."

"That's why I said 'again.'"

"Haven't I seen you since then?"

"No, I was back in South Carolina, remember? My wife's sister passed."

"Man, I'm sorry. You didn't tell me that."

"Nah. I just told all the boys I'd be out of town. All the sympathy—real or fake—just kinda weighs on ya, you know? Hell, I wasn't close to her, but my wife's in pain."

"I'm sorry, man."

"Yeah. Anyway, son, I'm a bit late on the checks this week, since the job hasn't yet paid, and I spent all the reserve cash on this little trip."

"Wow."

"Yeah, things are tight. You know. Tight for everybody, though. Don't have to tell you that. You're lucky, you know, that house, and all that money."

"All what money?"

"The four hundred g's," Kirk opens his hands as if holding a beach ball.

"You overshot, Kirk. And I don't remember telling you my business, but if you're implying I don't need the money I'm working for, I'll just quit and look for work somewhere else."

"Hey, hey, hey, hold on there, son. You quit, and I took you back, just like that. You're gonna have to be patient with me when I tell you the job hasn't yet paid, and that I'm gonna be late this week with everyone's check. I've been promised the money on Monday, and you will all be the first taken care of."

"See you on Monday, then."

"See you, Goldilocks. And that's a nice crotch rocket your girl-friend's got, by the way. I saw her ride past in town the other day!" he calls after him.

Ray hops on, starts the engine, and screeches out, blowing up dust and Kirk's comment with it. He passes the orange groves, heading for the railroad tracks where he speeds up to take the hill, lifts in flight, braking just in time not to land in the water of Indian River. As much as he loves this little game, he still misses Ruby, achingly, so he heads back to town to go shopping for her. Even though he knows she will be returning with at least two suitcases full of clothes from storage.

He stops first in a Jensen Beach shop that, though tacky, catches his eye with the window's display of a turquoise bikini and matching hip wrap. The salesgirl's hair is dyed a brash red but caught in a single, elegant braid that complements the line of her shoulders. She has on too much mascara, and he notices this since Ruby never wears it at all, still it highlights the deep blue of her eyes. When she asks if he needs help, her voice sounds similar to his oldest sister Sonya, and he wonders if that's just because he might miss her too. She pulls the turquoise bikini from the rack, as he finds a yellow, and now a tan one the hue of cardboard to add to the pile. This last one reminds him of leather and something Ruby would be wearing when he was a caveman and knocked her over the head to drag her into his den.

"Ra-ay." He hears a woman break his name into two syllables with pronounced disbelief in her voice. He doesn't recognize that it's his second wife until he turns around.

"Barbara," he says. He had always called her "Barb" but finds he needs some formality with her now. "What are you doing here in this tourist trap?" He swallows, moves a strand of hair behind his ear.

Barbara looks at the salesgirl with embarrassment, as she rings up the three bikinis and turquoise wrap for Ray. The salesgirl ignores her but looks up at Ray as if she might wink.

"Are you still at the hospital?" he asks.

"I'm at Martin Memorial, now. Six days a week."

"North or South?"

"North."

He nods, looks away, as if imagining the corridors inside. "How's Debra? What grade is she in now?"

"She's fine. She's in fifth going on eleventh, you know. Still a handful."

"Well." Ray takes his credit card back from the salesgirl, signs the receipt, and finally returns his wallet to his back pocket, after missing it twice. He thanks her, grabs the bag, and stands awkwardly in front of his ex-wife. "You must give her a hug for me."

He waits for his cue to walk away.

"How are you doing?" she asks.

"I'm fine. Everything's good. Real good. Still working for Kirk. Um. I'm living in Port St. Lucie—"

"Oh, I think I heard that, actually," she interrupts. "You got a house with Gary?"

"Well, he and Jason are staying with me while he looks for a place. I'm living with my girlfriend now."

"Oh, I see." She looks at the floor. There are more blond highlights than he had remembered. "I thought you'd gotten married again."

Ray blushes, swallows, his Adam's apple bobs. "I did. That didn't last very long." He grabs the bag tighter. "And plenty has happened since. Listen, are you shopping right now? Can I get you a coffee or something? I'm off for the day, and we could go to that place two blocks down and grab a bite, if you're not too busy."

"I have a date tonight. Actually, I'm going away for the weekend, and I ran in here 'cause I thought I could use a new bikini," she nods toward his bag.

"My girlfriend's in L.A. packing up the rest of her things to bring out here, but I couldn't resist." He makes the kind of lipless smile people do when they just want to shove off. He holds the bag even tighter.

"Nice to see you, Ray."

"Yeah, you too, Barb. Take care. Don't forget to hug Debra for me. I really miss her," he says, nodding sincerely, then backs out the door.

As he gets on his bike, all of it comes rushing back to him. The trump card of her kindness—a nurse's kindness—to all types of strangers, any type at all, evil, undeserving, apathetic, or just so-so. Even with a young daughter in the house, she didn't seem to have either a mother bird or bear's protectiveness. He had come home once and found Debra alone with an out-of-town guest. Someone Barbara had met during her late teen travels. A man they really didn't know. It didn't help matters when Barbara got pregnant, had the abortion, and then didn't want to talk about it. Not only did she not want to have his baby, whom he wanted, but neither did she want to discuss it. She didn't want to share the depth of her pain after the abortion. Never *once* did he infer that the baby might not have been his. He did not deserve her silence. Of this he felt strongly. They didn't talk for weeks, and then they didn't talk for months, they just lay in the same bed together. This all added up to two years of their otherwise functioning seven. She was the one who cheated on him first. She was big enough to admit it, and like a business transaction, she was the one to ask for the divorce. She made it clear it was not about this someone else, and implied that her action was meant to define the wedge. They had met an impasse, period. Though she was right, and he knew she was right, he couldn't help but feel she was treacherous. Treacherous shouldn't be the word to fit such a woman—a nurse, a mother, an otherwise fairly honest person—but treacherous is how it felt.

Ray takes Gary's car to the West Palm Beach airport. The steering is so loose he can't believe Gary has avoided an accident. He pines for the time they let you wait at the gate. Standing by the escalator near baggage only reinforces the depression that she really might not be coming back. Leading should be his excitement—and most of him is elated—but the plane is late, he is there early, and she's been gone so long he's afraid she'll somehow be different.

Another flight arrives, the group descends the stairs, and again she is not among them. His chest tightens. He looks down at his nails that are filthy with soil from gardening this morning. He is shocked to have made such an oversight. He's been so conscientious with his hands ever since he met her. Washing, scrubbing beneath the fingernails after work, keeping his hands soft with the shea butter when he massages her back and breasts, which she loves for the scratch of the temperamental itch still alive in the scar tissue from her boob job. Ray never questioned why she did it, and he neither approved nor disapproved, he simply accepted every inch of her. He didn't like knowing that she had the surgery while she was with Pejman. Although she insisted he was against it, it only shows Ray how much influence Pej had. It was with Pejman that she became more conscious of her body's "imperfections." That word made him angry when she said it. But how can a man ever convince a woman he'd never want a single detail about her changed? Ray never truly believed in prayer, but if the day came that he sensed some dissatisfaction in her, he would get on his knees and ask for the guidance to make him an even better lover.

This thought now strikes him as blasphemous, particularly considering the hot water he's in, morally speaking. He laughs at himself, folds his arms, shifting his weight to his heels, his toes kicking up. He catches a woman looking at him strangely, but when he locks her eyes for one split second, she melts with a smile. He nods to her without an ounce of flirtation. When he looks up beyond her head and up the escalator, there is Ruby, tightly grabbing her backpack strap, her wild puff of hair bouncing as she jumps down the first and second steps.

Just when he thinks he might spontaneously combust, she bounds down the escalator, frantically waiting for the man in front of her to get off. As he does, she springs forward, Ray coming toward her, his arms open. Then she stops midstep, dons an exaggerated *think fast* position, and throws her sufficiently heavy backpack. He catches it, his mouth dropped open with glee. She comes running, he bends his knees, letting the backpack fall to the floor, as she jumps spread eagle, her arms flung around his neck. He holds her round bottom, her legs wrapped around his waist; they messily kiss each other's face, eyes, ears, and mouth. He carefully lowers himself, so as not to drop her, and picks up her pack. Like a toddler, her body still clings to him; he walks to the baggage carousel, everyone staring as they pass, as there is plenty to stare at.

"Hmmn, you get an A+ for not looking at that hot babe," Ruby exclaims at the red light, watching a young woman in white skintight pedal pushers cross the intersection.

"Then *you* get an F," Ray says, squinting his eyes at Ruby.

"Fair enough, buster." She smiles wide enough to reveal her gums. The light turns green.

"I can't believe how loose this steering is. He's trying to kill us all," Ray says, shaking his head, driving carefully with both hands like an old man.

"Why didn't you borrow Jason's car?"

"Jason." He shakes his head again.

"What?" Ruby leans over to take the gum from Ray's white T-shirt breast pocket.

"No, that's Nicorette, here's the minty kind." He picks it up from the tray in the dash.

"You're quitting!" She brightens, her body flexed, ready to bounce in the seat.

"Well, now, not quite. I'm fixing to," he says with a mock goofy

Southern accent, making his upper mouth protrude, improvising a bucktooth smile.

"I want you to last, you know. Who else is gonna take care of me when I'm old and gray and falling over?"

"I'm right beside you, baby." He squeezes her hand, then kisses it. "Forever."

"You work your body so hard every day, I can't help but worry about the future."

"Okay." He kisses her hand again. "Shhhh. Okay."

"So. It would be wonderful if you would quit smoking."

"Fine." He pops a piece of Nicorette, enters I-95 going north. "So who all were you seeing in L.A.? Did you look up that actress?"

"Actor."

"She's a woman, isn't she?"

"Yes, but she's an *actor*, not an actress, and no, I didn't see her. Come on, Ray. That was a long time ago."

"What about the other girl, Ireland?"

"I don't even know where she lives. She could be long gone from L.A. for all I know."

"Did you see Pejman?"

"No."

"Joop?"

"No. I told you, the only people I saw were my family, Jeannie, and my boss, Paul."

"He try to convince you to come back?"

"Yes. But he's continuing to let me work from here, so he can try all he wants, I'm not budging. Anyway, this is all so way cool of him."

"Yeah, yeah. *I* know why he's 'way cool' with you."

"Because I'm talented, might that not be the reason?" Ruby says testily.

"What did you do with Jeannie?"

"I told you already, Ray," Ruby says, leaning back in her seat, putting her shades on, though the sun is already yawning down the horizon.

"You hung out with her at some guy's house in Malibu."

"The guy wasn't there, she had the place to herself, I told you."

144

"But she had friends over, I'm sure."

"Yes, she did."

"Any 'hot babes'?"

"I wasn't looking." She shakes her head, folds her arms, staring out the passenger window.

"Did you spend the night?"

"I spent two nights there, Ray. Thought I told you that."

"I thought you told me you were staying at your sister's house the whole time," he says, now getting angry.

"Hannah's seeing this guy now, and I wanted to give her space."

"No wonder you were so quiet with me on the phone," Ray says, stopping too abruptly at the light. Ruby exaggerates the jerk.

"I hate the phone, you know that." She looks up at the sky, thrummed with yarns of clouds. "Besides, Jeannie is going through a hard time. Both times you called, I was a few feet away from her, I couldn't really talk. I told you that."

"You could have called me back."

"Time difference. It never worked out quite right."

"Yeah, as if I were ever sleeping."

"This is becoming a long drive," Ruby sighs. "And all this traffic. Feel like I'm on the 10 in L.A. Ugh."

"Wish they'd put in a carpool lane. Would make a little difference."

"You know," she clears her throat, "while I was there with Jeannie, she was fighting with Al on the phone, and by the time I was leaving, Al was called in for questioning about the murder."

"But he and Jeannie were together that morning."

"I know. It has something to do with Chauncey, though I don't get it. Al was never awake when she got there to walk the dogs—I can't remember him being around, ever. I wouldn't be surprised if they never met. So I don't know what it's about. Jeannie wasn't sure herself, but she's pretty freaked out."

"Speaking of freaked out, the way you handled me on the phone, I swear I really wasn't sure if you'd be coming back," Ray says.

"Baby." She leans over, kisses him on the ear, nips his lobe. She readjusts herself in the seat.

"God, I can't wait to get you home," he says.

She laughs. "You know who I did end up talking to on the phone for a while, though, was Abbie."

"She sent us a postcard too."

"She mentioned that."

"I wonder how old Charlie's doing?"

"She didn't mention Charlie, and I didn't have time to ask. She's really depressed, and that's all we talked about. The light deprivation thing really gets to her, and the days are getting shorter there."

"I know. The postcard says in big letters, 'NIGHT FOR DAY.'"

"Yeah? Anyway, she slept with that guy Luis for a while. It started right after we left. She said it lasted almost two months."

"Huh," he says, not asking but punctuating.

"And her mother came out for a visit in September, right in the middle of it. They hadn't spent time together in years, but her mother's considering divorcing her father, and she came, needing a push. Abbie didn't exactly give it to her. The mother ended up cleaning the house—I'm sure all that dust made her *sick*—and she got rid of a lot of the clutter, had a little roadside sale."

"In Healy?"

"Yeah."

"She said it was kinda nice, actually, all that incredible golden light—or at least that's what she described of September there— but now she can barely get out of bed for work. When she's not working, she doesn't bother."

"That is depressed. She's not drinking, is she?"

"She said she wasn't."

"Did she fall for that Luis?"

"Nah, she said it was just sex. Hey, maybe we could invite her out? Thanksgiving's in a couple weeks."

"You've got to be kidding me."

"Well, why not?"

"Isn't our house full enough?"

Feeling pushed aside by the extent to which Ruby loves people, Ray gets one opening he's been waiting for. Gary and Jason have found a place in Jensen Beach, near the apartment where Ray and

146

Gary used to be neighbors. Their month-to-month lease begins December 1. They have a festive Thanksgiving afternoon of preparation, Ray fighting for equal time and billing in the kitchen with Gary. The meal, although delicious, is a great deal more somber, fraught with silent preoccupation over each of their family holidays past. The next day's leftover celebration is a truly jolly occasion, save the moment when Jason says that Ray and Ruby will have beautiful babies. She gets a very tight look on her face. Ray feels a pump in his stomach, assuming she has realized, right on the spot, that she never wants to have his children. It's not until they are in bed that night when she tells him how offensive is the term "the best of both worlds" as it comes to "mixed" babies. She explains what she finds implicit—that all-white is right and beautiful, but that black is good only when dipped. She goes into a long-winded rant on the absurdity of anyone being pure-blood anything. She loses him partway through as she prattles about geneticists and DNA rendering the concept of race insignificant. All he wonders as she talks is how much could she love him. Why couldn't she focus on the two of them as individuals, and consider the beauty, the life they might create together? What he doesn't know is that she thinks she would if onlookers let her.

Although they have been there a few times before, Ray takes Ruby for her first Florida snorkeling at Bathtub Beach. They hit the high tide, leaving the tub—the shallow water between shore and porous worm reef. The sight of Ruby in the turquoise bikini and fins is as spectacular to him as any of the underwater creatures. Near the stingray, they accidentally clash masks, mesh their bodies, talking to one another with their limbs. He stops Ruby from grabbing onto the reef, lest she stick a finger too far in, teasing out a hungry barracuda.

On the way back home, she casually asks about nude beaches, and he tells her about Blind Creek where he heard the male prostitutes harass all the bathers. If Jason were in the car, they would have gotten into an argument about this. Ray doesn't know that Ruby already misses Jason's challenging opinions to Ray's authority on local flavor. He tells her about the beautiful fallen trunks of Australian pines, becoming sun-bleached driftwood sculptures. And how this beach is near the St. Lucie Nuclear Power Plant, directly in view from their house. Why is it, he asks, getting worked up now, that this plant was so preposterously placed on a storm-prone barrier island? When approaching the cooling towers from either north or south, there are the emergency evacuation sirens, reminding Ray how pathetically tentative life is. He isn't the only one capable of destroying, and destroying en masse, at that.

This last bit Ruby doesn't hear in his mind, but she will get almost the entire story not too far off. She returns conversation to nude beaches, prompting Ray to go on about the nudist colony in hometown Union City, where he and his middle sister Sadie sat smoking and spying. Ruby describes a few of the nude beaches she went to in Sydney, making Ray's temperature go way up high. He doesn't realize that what bothers him most is the fact that he would be embarrassed to go naked in front of strangers, that he would feel inhibited by the scars and pockmarks on his hips left by the tool belt. As Ruby now seems used to the slow cartwheels of his moods, she finally leaves the subject at the side of the road.

Though Ray aims to keep the relationship away from routine, soon enough she is back at her office in the coffeehouse, returning home with stories about Wanda and Lou every day. He's sorry he bought her the bike since he never gets to feel her clinging tightly to him anymore. If he knew what lay ahead, he might enjoy some of his moments of freedom and solitude. Then again, he might disagree with that assumption. For as he has willed himself to be both rewarded and punished, their date with destiny, their moment of eternal, tragic entwining, is inevitable.

Chapter 16

Chauncey Was Always
a Good Girl

Ruby

"So who's on your top ten of authors?" Ruby asks Lou who has come to sit beside her at her usual drawing table.

"Do you read?" he asks, his dimple a lot like Al's fickle one.

"No, not really. I like biographies though," she says brightly.

"Me too. You know, I've found myself writing a short story about a woman who has a very similar essence to yours."

"Really?"

"Yes. She's bold, very adventurous, yet fragile and warm, unsure of her power."

"Is this the character you're describing, or me?"

"Both." He looks at her as if appraising what's between her temples. "I'd love it if you read it. Her name's Sabrina. She doesn't look much like you, she doesn't have the little I know about your history, but you'll recognize her all the same. I'd love to have your opinion."

"My blessing?" She puts her hand at the neck of her yellow tank top.

"Haven't you ever based a cartoon on someone you knew?"

"Yes, but I wouldn't want them to know it!" She laughs.

"Well, okay." He puts both hands up, his light palms deeply lined in the rich dark color of his skin. "If you don't want to read it, I understand." He gets up, his teeth shining down on her a brilliant white.

"How about this? I'll read it when it's published."

"That won't help me, now will it?" He moves his chin into his neck, looks at her from beneath a canopy of brow.

"I don't mind what you do with her. Really." Ruby smiles.

"I always do what is necessary for the truth of any story."

"Okay. So write away!" she says, flashing a higher wattage smile. This she does to ingratiate herself for preferring to be alone at the moment. Pencil back in hand, she nods and Lou returns to the back, busying himself with the leaky faucet in the bathroom.

Instead of drawing, she eyes the computer, gets up, stretching her back, stiff from practicing too many dives off the board of Wanda and Lou's pool. Ray—who supervised each one for safety and form—told her not to overdo it, but she can't help the hurry she's in to physically seize each day. It's her head she's had on hold, never letting much get deeply to her. She has been considering these past eight months since the murders a brain holiday.

She logs onto the computer three tables down from the only other customer in the place. She looks up at the burnt orange wall with small, framed, black-and-white photographs of Philadelphia street scenes, then writes to RochelleX@earthlink.net.

Happy New Year, Jeannie!!! How was your Christmas? I left you two messages, did you get them? Hope you liked the jewelry box. You know it's made of rosewood—couldn't resist—it had both your names on it ;)~

Ray made me a fur bikini. He'd gotten the fur in Alaska and hid his sewing all this time! He did an amazing job, especially for someone who has never done it before. Then he took me out for a boat ride, and gave me a ring, a ruby (of course) to wear on my right ring finger, as a promise to consider hearing him out a year from now when he'll ask me to marry him. As soon as he put it on my finger, I dove right off the boat. A stupid thing to do, considering it could have slipped off my finger and been lost forever in the water. It's a beautiful fit, a gorgeous ring. The stone's a smooth oval set in gold. It scared me, no matter how wonderfully sweet and romantic a gesture it was, and is. I'm just not ready.

You never told me very much about the guy you almost married so many years ago

"Hey, baby girl," Wanda interrupts, her hand on Ruby's shoulder.

"Hey." Ruby turns her head, kisses Wanda's hand, and looks up at her.

"Your man still peeling like a lizard?"

"He's embarrassed to have burned the shit out of himself like that, after working in the sun all day, most every day, doesn't make much sense to him."

"He fell asleep at high noon on that lounge. He's about the longest lobster I've ever seen, and that mop of neon yellow curls. Doesn't he know suntan lotion was invented here? But you sure whipped his butt in the pool. Girl, are you training for the Olympics?"

"Lou did quite a few laps too."

"Can't compare to you."

"Lou's in the back, by the way, last I noticed," Ruby says, grabbing her hair back from her face, to see Wanda better.

"You should lock this hair up, would be gorgeous. Then you wouldn't have to comb that mess every time you get out of the water." Wanda laughs, grabbing Ruby's hair from her with both hands.

"Nah. I like the torture of it, *ev-er-y-day*," she says, closing her throat around the words so she sounds like a horror movie menace. She crinkles her nose, taking her head back from Wanda, who slinks her way toward the counter where another customer waits.

Forgot my train of thought. I'm at the coffeehouse, and Wanda was just right here. So what's going on there? I had such a great time with you hanging out at the beach. I know you were slightly preoccupied with all that was going on with Al, and I want you to know anytime you need to talk, I'm here. Few things are more stressful than starting a business, and considering everything we've gone through at the house, Al's allowed a little slack. He has those angry bursts, I know, but they're not enough for him—I mean he's not properly expressing himself, so everything that needs to come out is still just sitting there ticking. You've been doing the right thing with your little getaways, so remember that. You're taking care of yourself, AND you're taking care of him. As soon as he's able to do a bit of the caretaking again—both of himself, and of you—things will be back on track. I don't feel like that's so long off. Huh?

Call me, or write me so I know there's nothing dreadfully wrong. I was going on and on about myself—to marry or not to marry, and really, I should pinch myself for being lucky enough to have found my guy for life. There, I answered my own question.

Write soon! Love, R.

When Ray brings home a strap-on cock for her to do him with, she breaks out with hysterical laughter. His expression is meek, and he bats his big, blue, piercing eyes, and tells her the only reason he got it is that she whispered all the things she wanted to do to him, and though this was by far the scariest, he didn't want to deny her fulfilling a single desire. She pulls it out of the package, the length of it making him swallow with fear, the color of it reminding her of Eskimo Pie, and she crumbles in laughter again. What's the matter? He asks her, after joining in with giggles that now have her hiccupping. He gets serious again because he's worried he's not turning her on. She hasn't initiated sex one time since he gave her the ring. She reminds him she rarely gets the chance to initiate anything as horny as he always is. This strikes him as a weak excuse, she can tell, but he doesn't press it. He backs his way from the living room as if there were something on his ass he didn't want her to see. She examines her new toy for a while, finally strapping it on. He's in the kitchen, grinding his garden's rosemary and mint in the mortar and pestle, when she pushes him up against the stove. He jiggles, squirms, his shoulder shooting to his ear in an attack of the tickles. Determined now to take it to its goal, she pulls him upstairs to the bathroom for lube. When she's got it in her hand, the look in his eye brings to mind that of a sheep's as he's approached for the shearing of his wool.

Ruby, I should call you with all of this. But I don't have a voice left, from all the crying I've been doing. I don't even know where to begin.

The detective called me and said they were re-questioning everyone who knew Chauncey. He came here re-checking all the facts, how I found her—through her tear-off ad Fawn noticed at Whole Foods—what I knew about her—that she lived with her parents and had gone to community college there in the valley—how she had no boyfriend I knew of, how we rarely saw each other. How I'd given her the driveway gate combination, the dogs would meet her out by the pool-house, and away they would go. I'd leave her check out there for her every Saturday morning. But you know all that. Guess I'm going over it all in my head, for the thousandth time, so it makes any sense. The detective starts asking me about Al— what he thought about Chauncey, anything about her he'd ever said. I told him we'd both been up all of three or four times while she was here, as early as she'd come, that I had pointed her out through the window to Al, and that was it. I remembered later that she'd blocked him in the drive, one morning she was walking the dogs around the neighborhood. It was the rare occasion he had an early meeting. I handled it when she got back, Al was upstairs shitting bricks. Then the detective starts asking me about Al's money troubles, and how long had he been borrowing from me. I got so scared then, Ruby, my jaw just locked up. I kept trying to make it work, you know, I must have looked like I was chewing on some cud, trying to get it out from the back of my throat. Sweat poured. But I wouldn't lie, and I wasn't about to. I told him it was up to about $200,000, but how everyone knows how long it takes to get a new business—especially a restaurant—out of the red the first year. He then showed me a picture of this guy. At this point, I was sure I was going to faint. Prior to this, I'd never had a clue how anyone could. Now I know. I'd never seen this guy in my life. Ever. He must *be about 24, 25, sandy hair, big, nasty, glassy eyes. The type a lot of women might fall for in the dark of a bar. Me, I'd keep the fuck away from him. He asked me if I knew any of the employees at Al's club. I told him I'd met everyone, and was friendly with a couple of the girls. You know that fucker looked me up and down a bit, like, figures.*

Next thing I know, Al doesn't come home that night. No answer on his cell. I go by the restaurant, the shift manager tells me he got a message from Al that he wouldn't be coming in. I go by the club, Andy tells me he hadn't been there either. Andy's looking so freaked out, and I'm crying, getting all hysterical at this point, and he leaves the guard at the door to take me home. He wouldn't say ANYTHING the entire drive. Just let me cry. I'm sure he knew Al had split. If anyone knew shit about Al, it was him.

I didn't sleep that night, and not the next, after the police had come by looking for him. Wasn't until five in the morning the next day, I get a call from Al in jail, needing me to BAIL him out. You know what I did, Ruby? I hung up. It was all coming together in my head. I couldn't believe it, and I got so sick I was on the toilet for hours. I called the detective—and you KNOW there wasn't anybody on earth I wouldn't have rather talked to first, excluding Al. So he told me what happened.

The day he last questioned me, they'd gone to the club with a warrant, searched it up and down, found evidence in Al's office that Chauncey had been there. He didn't tell me what it was—must have been hair or something—and how they'd gone looking for Al and he'd skipped. They tracked him down in IDAHO. Can you believe it? There is SO much I never knew about this man. He confessed right away. He had convinced Chauncey to come try out to be a stripper, she came one afternoon to the club, and they fucked in his office. When she got home to her parents, she was so freaked by what happened, that she called Al and told him she was gonna quit the dogwalking job with me. Both of them knew she was never gonna be a STRIPPER, but the thing about Al is, that if she'd gone through with it, I wouldn't have believed it was

154

Al that dragged her into it. I would have assumed she walked in. She always struck me as that kind of loose cannon. Long overdue for some acting out, but so very good and gentle and loving with animals. Well, Al got scared that she was going to tell me what happened. And why he got THIS SCARED is beyond me. All I can see now is that I was his moneybags. So Al found that glassy-eyed scumbag, paid him to KILL her. Ruby, can you believe this? Can you believe any of this at all? Can you imagine how ripped up I feel inside?

And this monster fucked up the job, needless to say. He was supposed to come in and rob the place too. He wasn't supposed to TOUCH the dogs. So what does he do? He comes in, tries to kill her, and the babies start attacking him. He takes down each one.

The detective said they actually caught him first, and figured out they had Ralph's "blowback" blood on his shirt, as he'd shot all of them but Caspar at pointblank range. Then he raped Chauncey, and killed her.

He started blackmailing Al. Al put the club up for sale, bought the restaurant as a way to distract me from where the money was actually being funneled.

I will never look that man in the face again, as long as I live. He can burn in hell, Ruby. Look what he did just to cover up an afternoon fuck. Do you know what happened today? Chauncey's father left a message on my machine. He said, "MY CHAUNCEY WAS ALWAYS A GOOD GIRL," and then he makes this hideous gurgling sound at the back of his throat, like he was going to spit a big loogie through the telephone wire, and he says, "and now thanks to you, you monster slut, my daughter is dead." Then he hangs up. Ruby, I swear. If I hadn't made it all this way, all this way without destroying myself in any of the usual ways so many girls I know have, I would have done myself in today. I would have done myself in.

I should have called you with this. Fawn's here, asleep on the bed, as I write you at my desk. Thanks to her, I'm alive today. I should have called you weeks ago when this all happened, but I didn't want to mar all the loveliness you've got going in your life.

I'll call soon, I promise. Always, Jeannie

Ruby awakes to a love note left for her on Ray's pillow. Usually she gets up with him, teasing him as he skips the shower and dresses, so he can keep their smell on him all day. But this morning she was so drugged by her nightmares, so stunned by the latest revelation of horror and betrayal, that Ray was only a slice of light in the dream, kissing the bridge of her nose, and closed, flickering eyelids.

She returns a phone message from her boss, though she does this in a haze. She sits back down on the bed, and can't remember what her next step should be. Finally she drags herself downstairs to make green tea. When the kettle whistles and scares her, she suddenly feels intimidated by the nooks and crannies of the backyard. Instead, she takes her cup out on the front porch where she realizes she's never sat alone before. As she opens the door, an egret hurries across the lawn. The faraway scent of bacon hits the thick, wet air, and rival birds chortle up an opera. The neighbor pins a flyer to the street tree in front of her house, then turns around with a sour face when she spots Ruby.

"You haven't happened to see my cat, have you?" the neighbor asks, grasping her loose shirt at her pink, wrinkled neck as if it were cold.

"Sorry, I haven't," Ruby says with a lost but sincere sympathetic tone.

The neighbor bunches her lips, appears to be searching with her tongue for a sliver of food between her front bottom teeth. She walks like a much younger woman up her rose-bushed path, then stops, puts her hands on her hips.

"I can hear your music blasting some afternoons, clear inside my house where I keep all the windows shut to contain the air-conditioning."

Ruby clears her throat, her scalp now prickly with heat. She cannot take any confrontation today. The woman squints, puts her dyed straw, jaw-length hair behind her ears. Finally, Ruby opens her mouth.

"I don't 'blast' my music, and I'm rarely here in the afternoons."

"Well, I didn't say all the time, I said *some* of the time." She walks a little farther up the path, then stops again. "If you see my cat, please let me know. He's been gone for several days. He may wander through your backyard, as I've seen him do."

"I've never seen your cat in our backyard, but if I do I'll let you know," Ruby says, now looking in the other direction, sipping her tea in dismissal.

"My name's Hope, by the way," the neighbor says coldly, brushing off her hips.

"Ruby." She turns toward her, nods once, half her upper lip raised.

"Okay," the neighbor says and waves condescendingly, disappearing behind the palmetto on Ray's property.

Now sorely missing the privacy of her little guesthouse in Laurel Canyon (before all the mayhem), Ruby sips a little more tea, gets up, dusts her butt, and spills on her thin, gray drawstring-waist shorts. She curses to herself. Nothing today is going to go right, she assumes. Her flipflops slap the wood of the porch, she bends to pick up a rubber-banded bundle of solicitor throwaways, goes inside, and slams the door shut.

Chapter 17

Animal Tendencies

Ray

Ray now stands a little beside himself. Ever since Jeannie's news of Al's betrayal, Ruby appears to have found some crawl space in her mind where he can't reach her. She rations her words; her realness, her presence of mind and focus, come in dollops, or not at all. He tries dealing with it in every way he can imagine. Indulging her desires to tie one on, hiring a housekeeper to relieve their weekly half-tilt cleaning sprees, e-mailing her sister, Hannah, to introduce himself and ask for any advice. Al's monstrous behavior has flung Ray to new heights of committed selflessness. To distance himself from guilt, and further foil himself with Al, Ray becomes convinced that nurturing has always been most fundamental to his true nature.

It is now almost two years ago that Ray found Gary, on the other side of their shared wall of the Jensen Beach shack apartments, beaten unrecognizable. He had been raped with a beer bottle, a wrench, as well as Arnie Watson's dick. Ray rushed Gary to emergency; surgery was required to repair the damage to his sphincter. Gary's mother was kept in the dark until this very day, and Jason was nowhere to be found until Gary's third day of recovery in the hospital. If Ray could have forced Gary to press charges against Arnie Watson, he would have. But Gary refused, so what else could he do but pay Arnie a visit? He didn't go there with the intention of killing, but he didn't worry either over all the rage he would most likely unleash.

In Ray's head, both Al and his hired rapist/assassin are like Arnie Watson. Ray's father is the kind of man who would advise

Chauncey's father to kill them both. He taught Ray to guard the lives of his mother and sisters with his own. So rather than judging his own vigilantism as an eye for an eye, Ray sees it as a pure and necessary act of loyalty and devotion.

"Look, over there, baby, is this amazing or what?" Ray says, sitting like a prod in his red nineteen-foot Wellcraft boat, pointing at the pod of dolphins in the distance. He cuts off the engine. The swoosh of the water as it rocks them, the strong, cool breeze in his face, lift the hairs all over his body. Ruby removes her shades, her eyes a beautiful, wet, coconut brown in the glare of the sun.

"I didn't know they ever ventured into the river," she says in hushed tones. Her nipples push up the navy nylon of her short-sleeved shirt.

"They're feeding on the freshwater fish, bass or bluegill. I've come upon them a few times now," Ray whispers too, throws a foot up next to the windshield, rests his chin on his knee. He watches their rhythmic launch into the air, the smooth release into slick arcs of motion. He offers his hand behind him, for her to take. She grabs a finger, her palm cold. "Did I tell you about the time I went swimming with them?" He turns to look at her.

"Yeah, a few times," she says, slowing blinking.

"Let's jump in," he says, getting up, peeling off his faded black, ribbed tank top. The tiny brown, gray, and blond curls on his chest glisten in the light. He pulls her up, his forearm muscles ripple. She tightens her hands in a fist under his grip.

"Come on, baby, let's jump in."

"We'll scare them off, Ray." She shakes her head, closes her eyes as if in trance.

"No we won't, they'll swim right next to us, come on!"

He unzips his shorts, steps out of each leg, revealing Hawaiian flower trunks. Ruby has plopped back down on the red-and-white-striped vinyl seat. He sits next to her, throwing both arms around her neck, kissing her cheekbone with open lips and hot breath.

"I want to dive in with you, my love," he says into her ear. "I want you to wake up. Sometimes it's like you're looking right through me."

She sighs, lines up her front and bottom teeth.

"What?" he asks.

Her jaw tight, she sighs again, her shoulders rock with the boat on the gentle waves. "I know . . ." she breaks off.

"You know *what?*" Ray asks, feeling an eel move around in his gut, twisting its way around his intestines.

"I have been . . ." she clears her throat, "kinda far away. But I can't believe . . ." she trails off again.

Ray puts his hand on his stomach, his mouth dry and sour, he worries he might throw up. "Just say it."

"I *knew* Al. He was someone I saw almost *every day* for a year, and often enough for two years before that," her voice breaks into a low, hoarse scratch. She clears her throat again. Ray's fear switches from the possibility that Ruby might know something about his own crime to the preposterous and paranoid idea that perhaps she slept with Al.

"How is Jeannie supposed to trust any man again? How?"

She frays, her nose twitching like she might sneeze, but instead she starts crying, the tears collecting in a single drop at her chin. Ray licks it and grabs her full into him. Embarrassed by his nausea and suspicion, he takes in the wracking of her body into his until he turns himself over to her completely.

"You're safe with me," he says, stroking her hair with a hand so heavy it molds to the contours of her skull. "I'll never do anything to hurt you, I'll never let anyone hurt you as long as you live."

He can't hear the impossibility of the statement, his heart knitting cello strings, the sound reverberating with the wind and the rocking of the boat, the soft swishing of their shoes on the carpeted floor. The dolphins have made their way back toward the inlet. When the last of her sniffles are short and widely spaced apart, he gets up, turns on the engine and the stereo. Now that it feels like she's finally here with him, giving herself over to him, the adrenaline hits. Antsy but happy, he shifts his weight as he steers, talking over the music to reach where she sits directly behind him. He describes to her in fervent animation the potential of excitement they could have if they learned how to skydive.

* * *

Instead of riding separately as they have ever since he got her the Kawasaki, Ray gets to feel Ruby hold tightly to him on the back of his bike, all the way to Gary and Jason's. Ruby carries inside their housewarming present—it's a painting she found at a garage sale. Neither she nor Ray could have known that it was done by their neighbor Hope, and sold by an ex-friend who didn't appreciate the gaudy aesthetic value.

"What is this, kelp? Seaweed?" Jason asks, holding the square painting away the full length of his arms.

"Must be, huh? And this is the fine mist over it," she says, waving her hand over it, swaying her hips like a game show tart.

"It's obscene," Jason says, his cheek curling with half a devilish grin.

"I know," Ruby nods to an imaginary beat, biting on her bottom lip.

"I mean since when is kelp so sleazy?" He looks at her, arching a single brow. Ray stands behind them both, surveys the room.

"Also looks like some kind of monster in the sky with the stars shining through it." She steps back, cocking her head.

"Did you see this?" Jason calls, heading for the kitchen to Gary, Ruby following, her hands clasped behind her butt. Ray soon joins them, taking in the pungent garlic smell.

"That's pretty wild," Gary says, nodding, showing a bit of tongue at the corner of his mouth. "Did you get our guests something to drink?"

"Right away," Jason says, salutes, clicks his heels, and does a perfect spin. He puts down the painting, opens the fridge, and grabs Ray a beer.

"Nice prep," Ray says, looking over Gary's shoulder at the cutting board. Ruby looks around the kitchen that Jason has done in a garish yellow.

"I think you could put the painting right over there—pick up on the gray corridor and this blast of yellow. You know?" she says, pointing.

From behind the counter, Jason comes with an airplane-service-size bottle of bourbon. He throws it at her.

"Ouch! Right in the yoni!" she whines, Ray missing what happened, as Jason laughs.

"Don't you be treating my woman that way," Ray grunts caveman style. "And you, out of the kitchen." He pushes Gary.

"What are you doing?" Gary says, resisting his shoves.

"I'm gonna do you, like you do me."

"Oh?" Jason mocks a jealous tone.

"Get out." Ray brushes off his hands, Gary now standing at the threshold of the door. Ray returns to the kitchen, pulls bottles of spices from the rack. Jason puts his arm around Gary, whose arms are folded. Ray looks up just as Jason kisses Gary's ear. He is surprised at the relief he feels at their more open affection. Before he was anxious that he might feel threatened.

"So he's taking me skydiving next week," Ruby says, pulling the seal from her tiny bottle.

"He almost convinced me to do that," Gary says, shifting his weight.

"I didn't know this," Jason says, pulling a chair from the breakfast nook, knocking it gently against the back of Gary's knees, so he sits.

"I always thought I'd take the Family of Man trip before I died. You know, tracing the line of our transformation from Africa to Asia to Russia to Arizona to Brazil," Ruby says, shaking her head as if a skydiving accident were a fait accompli.

"Since when are you afraid to die?" Jason asks, pulling out a chair for her too. She falls into it, takes a long swig; Ray looks up at her as he breads the trout.

"Told Ray I knew this guy whose aunt did a Face Your Fears deal that ended with a skydive. She fell to her death, tied to her instructor."

"No *fucking* way," Ruby says, her mouth hanging open.

"Yes *way*," Gary says, making fun of her.

"That is such a one in a million kind of freak thing. Come *on*. All four of us have a much better opportunity of eating it in Gary's car," Ray says.

"Or your bike, dude, you ride like a maniac," Gary says.

"I do not," Ray says, licking his pinkie finger of the carrot sticks cooking in cherry juice.

"Anyway, *I* wouldn't do it," Gary says, looking at Ruby with a mock fatherly expression. "I'm waiting on the hurricane that'll lift me up some gold from this here treasure coast!" He slaps the arm of his chair. Jason exaggerates a posture that says *you're too goofy to be with me.*

Ray warms up the frying pan for the trout, before opening another beer. He cracks his neck, sighs, watching the three of them now laughing over some inanity, and thanks the angels he imagines on his shoulders that Ruby's looking happy again.

His boss Kirk visits the site where Ray is kneeling alone, mixing stucco, having already sheeted the walls with plywood and tarpaper, and hung the wire lath. His palms are more wrinkled than a two-hour soak; just under his right eye is purple, his upper arm scratched.

"You get in a fight, Goldilocks?"

"The drill bit bound, I got too close trying to fix it, then the battery fell out."

"I told you always wear your goggles, son."

"The battery bounced *inside* the goggles." Ray keeps pouring and mixing, irritated to be interrupted from his rhythm.

"Looking like a nasty little shiner." Kirk puts his hands on his hips, pushes some gravel with the toe of his loafers. Ray stands from his crouch, Kirk looks at him from under thin and too shapely eyebrows. "The Conch been by?"

"Haven't seen him. Maybe if you did some work instead of driving around all day you wouldn't need him," Ray says, returning focus to the stucco's consistency.

"I've been thinking of firing him."

"Why?"

"Don't trust him, is all. Never know if my guys have really been by a job or not."

"Well, it's none of my business."

"Don't he ever come and check on you here?"

"Haven't seen him." Ray tightens his bottom lip, picks up the trowel.

Kirk sighs, folds his arms, scans a three-sixty of the property.

"I told those folks they should have cleared out these old scrub oaks, but they didn't listen."

"Why should they?"

"Cheapens the look of the house, obscures the view."

"I disagree," Ray says, now stuccoing over the wire lath.

"Hell, you don't know nothing." He nods, teasing out Ray's attention, but he won't stop working. "So what you got going this weekend?"

"Ruby and I are going to take our first skydiving lesson."

"Boy, I should slap you into next week just in time for you to miss it. She's a pretty little thing, sweet too, why you gonna go and drop her from a plane? You aiming to get rid of yet another one?"

"I'll stomp you back a century if you lump her in one more time with *anybody* else, ever."

"She's a person, ain't she? She's a woman. Or does she have some special status I don't know about?"

"Just shut the fuck up."

"It's the Brazilian I would have pushed out the plane with no parachute."

"God, you fucking piss me off," Ray stops working to point in his face. "If you talk about Ruby, if you so much as even attempt another joke about her, then I'll oblige you with the diet you've been waiting for, and break the fat right off you."

"Where's your sense of humor gone to, boy? You better bite down on that lip, 'fore I knock your eyeteeth to the ground with it."

"I mean what I said, Kirk. Now are you gonna let me finish my work here, or not?"

"Carry on," Kirk says, walking off toward his car. "You oughta be brushing up on those golf clubs, rather than chasing after the dream of some extreme sport, *asshole*," he calls back without turning around. He holds one hand in the other behind his back, intermittently flapping the captured one.

Ray shakes his head, finds the right length for his trowel strokes, but then rudely and abruptly the image of Arnie Watson's red, blistery face appears in front of him. He sees him as plain as the first day he laid eyes on him, staggering onto the job site, another hungover hustler day laborer. The guys tortured Ray—naming

Arnie "Goldilocks' Ugly Twin." Arnie was tall, blond, and thirty-two like Ray was at the time, but the similarities ended there. Arnie said he was from Louisville, Kentucky, though little from his mouth was the truth. He was a farmhand on an orange grove, living in a tent, keeping fuel in the heaters for the crops threatened by the freak season frostbite. When temperatures warmed up again, he found extra work doing construction.

Arnie's first mistake was stealing Ray's leather jacket. Ray knew he did it, and confronted him at the honky-tonk bar next to the dance club in Fort Pierce where Arnie lived, and where Ray had gone to school as well as lived with his first wife, Cynthia. Thanks to his old friends, Ray had gotten into many fights at that bar, and he wasn't about to fall back into pattern for some two-cent redneck bastard.

Ray would never have known Gary was involved with Arnie as well, if they hadn't been sailing in the restaurant manager's boat, and sped right past him. That's when he found out Arnie owed Gary money. This is the way Gary put it, though it was actually extortion. Ray saved this fight with Arnie for after hours on the construction site, and everyone who happened to be around assumed it had to do with Ray's jacket.

A month hadn't gone by since the evening Ray beat Arnie's face into a slightly elasticized version of itself when Arnie paid Gary the fateful visit. From the looks of Gary, gouged, whittled, and bloody on the floor of his own apartment, Ray towered in rage over the rape. Jason had taken off many days before, so Ray had no one to share his grief, rabid and fomenting.

Not a soul was going to miss Arnie Watson. He could have blown out of town the same way he'd blown in—on the cusp of another scaly adventure. But for the first time in his life, he'd splintered even his own sense of limits, bringing a man like Ray to such depth of rage in retaliation, that Arnie could have gotten himself disemboweled. Instead, he was crushed with the kicks of a steel-toe boot. And then fed to the water moccasins, rattlesnakes, and alligators at the swamp.

Ray and Ruby lie kissing on the long, gold corduroy couch. After watching *Willy Wonka and the Chocolate Factory,* her tongue tastes like stale Coca-Cola and popcorn. Ruby had never seen the movie before, and she frowned over the lack of brown faces. Ray was sorry he hadn't noticed that, and still more sorry that she always does.

It is barely eight o'clock; the TV screen is blue with a white numeral 3 in the corner. Ruby playfully wipes off his saliva from her nose. This prompts him to lick her face like a dog. This reminds her of Caspar and eventually makes her cry.

Ray, now traumatized by Arnie's ghost, by Al's heinousness, by Gary's weakness and Ruby's demons, wants to shock and shake her out of it. He'd long ago hidden the dog skull Abbie gave him; he'd tucked away the recurring urges to spill it all out. And now suddenly wanting to prove to her that others have experienced scenes as horrific as the one she did, he waits for the last of her tears to dry up, then recounts the story of Gary and Arnie, up to the point of Ray's vigil at Gary's hospital bedside. He keeps the part about killing Arnie to himself, though it feels so heavenly to begin emptying his chest. He doesn't want to be cruel. He realizes she has enough tales of harshness to last her many years, even though it's not like she'd ever been bombed or lost a loved one in a war. Ray tells himself that as changed as she will always be from witnessing a scene like she did—just as he is from his own hellish experience—it still boils down to the fact that she has lost a beloved dog, and many people, he included, know exactly what that feels like.

Chapter 18

Dive

Ruby

Well, who do you think was invited to receive her Adult Video News Lifetime Achievement Award? Yours truly! (Did I tell you this already?) I went to Vegas last week for the ceremony. I took Fawn, and this guy we met in a bar in Bakersfield. (Can you believe we stopped in Bakersfield? We had to, since Fawn's been having painful periods—they come on time, and then not at all for months. I know she's going through a very early menopause, but since she's only 41, she can't accept it. Can't blame her, I'm 53, and still get mine). Anyway, this boy was a sweet, young, naïve thing—the type whose brothers dragged him out and left him there to see if he'd find the imagination to get into trouble. He said he was 25, but I'd guess 19. We didn't fuck him, if you can believe it, but we partied and we gambled, and had a real good time like I haven't in years.

I put a civil case in motion—I'm suing Al for the restaurant. Not that I want to run it, but I feel like it's mine, like I may as well hire the right people to make something of it. Ruby, you know before all this, if someone had put a gun to my head and asked me if Al truly loved me, I would have said, Yes. How can a person be so wrong about something like that? Some days it feels like somebody's scorching up my insides to a charred quick.

I try not to lie around in it. The award came at such a good time, to get me out of town and keep my mind set on licking it. Fawn thinks I should sell the house, but where would I go? I love this house, and nothing or no one is going to push me out of it. Can you understand that? No one else can, but I know you do.

Thank you, baby, for the calls and the cards. You're a really dear friend, and it means so very much to me. I miss your letters, though, Doll! How are the cartoons coming? How's that big, beautiful man of yours? I have the picture of the two of you in some bar in Alaska on my slideshow screensaver. Can't wait to meet him. Bring him here next time! Big hug and kiss, Jeannie Brave

Ruby begins a letter back, lauding her for the award, her nerve, and resolve to remember the brave in her name. But it reads like a false croon in cheerleader tempo. She promises herself she'll write after the skydiving lesson tomorrow. She turns her gaze from the bay window; Ray is fast asleep in bed, his snores bumping, teeth grinding, in and out of rhythm. He was supposed to work today, but when he called in Kirk didn't need him. Ruby feels pinned into having to change her own workday plans, so they can spend it together. She's not wholly conscious of it, but she's stewing over the fact that Ray's story about Gary and Arnie is rubbing her in a very bad way. She knows there's a hell of a lot more to it than he told her.

She too would have sworn to anybody that Al loved Jeannie. He was tender, sometimes nervous, frustrated to please her. He was a strip club owner, yes, but he dealt with all of it in a very businesslike fashion. He kept his distance from the girls as if allergic. This perception of him certainly called Ruby's judgment into question.

But what neither Ruby nor Jeannie could know is that Al had never cheated on her before this one time with Chauncey. He did not see Jeannie as his "moneybags." And if Chauncey had not blocked him in the drive that morning, he would have never met her face-to-face, and he would never have been angry with her. She had the disposition of a stripper to him, an assumption in her expression that any man was easy to please, that any man could be despicable. A vulnerability in her that also gloated with conceit. He saw the weakness in her, which was her disdain for people; she compensated for that in her exaggerated love for animals. It made him angrier still that she was pale, delicate, thin, and forlorn for some other century when more princesses could exist. It flew out of him, the suggestion that she come in and dance for him. He didn't think that when she actually came, they would never make it out of his office. He rotated off his axis when she appeared at the door with those fragile-looking ankles, the throat so refined, the flanks healthy as a horse. Her raspy voice, and cheeks hot with shame. It was then he wanted to fuck the self-loathing out of her. And the sweat poured, collecting in the dip above her clavicle. When he turned her over he memorized the curves of her vertebrae.

Though a part of him expected it, the looming explosive he smelled—when she called to say she would be quitting—frightened him. He wanted to drive a spike through her heart when she said she just might tell Jeannie. For years he knew of Dave Gardener, the stepson of an old friend. He knew he could do anything for the right price. Al just didn't think he would fuck it up.

"Aagh. I'm driving myself crazy," Ruby snaps at herself. She gets up from the bedroom vanity that serves as her laptop desk, stubbing her toe on the bench. "Shit!" She holds onto her big toe, jumping twice on the other foot, losing her balance. She looks over at Ray, who has stopped snoring but is still deeply asleep, his head now off the pillow, his chin lifted. He looks as if he is listening to an angelic church choir. She wants to kiss him there where his two-week-old beard ends, but doesn't want to wake him.

She goes downstairs in an old gray Kansas City Royals T-shirt she found in Ray's closet. She rolls down the waist of his underwear, pulling the bunching out of her butt. She puts tea on, fighting the hankering to call her sister. She'd rather not bother her with more directionless frustration. What she really needs to do, she thinks to herself, is learn how to meditate.

"Well, look who's here," she says, spotting the neighbor's cat through the turreted breakfast nook window. He is black with cold, hazel eyes, staring back at her, holding his centurion pose. She grabs junk mail for a scratch piece of paper from the island counter pile, and scrawls a quick note. She heads for the living room, jumps into the baggy skate shorts Ray pulled off her the night before. The teakettle screams, she runs to turn off the fire, takes a bowl down from the cabinet, and pours the fat-free milk in. "Sorry," she says to the cat, without looking at him, since Ray's half-and-half would be more delicious.

She walks outside barefoot, carrying the bowl of milk and her note, keeping her distance. It's hot even for a Florida February morning, the grass warm and wet on the bottoms of her feet. She looks back at the cat once, expecting him to follow her to the neighbor's front door where she places the bowl of milk, slides the note through the mailbox slot, and rings the bell. She doesn't wait for her to answer; she trots off on tiptoe, clocking the cat at the side of their front lawn, crouching by the sea grapes, the palmetto hedge hiding the view from the neighbor's door. As Ruby runs up her own front steps, she hears the neighbor calling for the cat, Ruben, which scares her the first time, since she thought she was calling her name.

"Go on," Ruby hisses, flicking her hands at him with limp wrists. As if understanding perfect English, he takes off. "Go on back to the bitch," she mutters to herself, trying the front door, but it's locked. She trots around back, trying not to call any attention, as the last thing she wants to see is the neighbor's face in hers. When she enters the back door, there is Ray, shirtless in unzipped jeans, and standing with a pout, as he grinds coffee for the espresso maker.

"Good morning," she says, snatching a paper towel to wipe the bottom of her feet. "What's the matter?" she comes close to him, runs a finger through the light brown curls of his pubic hair.

"I woke up to an empty bed," he says, exaggerating his pout now, though he means it.

"I couldn't get back to sleep, baby," she says, running her hand now through the back of his hair, standing up on tiptoe again to kiss him on the nape of his neck. He pulls her to him and squeezes, breathing her in.

"What do you say we take the boat out? Dock it at old downtown, have a scrumptious lunch, and walk around a bit," he says, cupping her face in his hands before bending to kiss her and pull with his teeth on her top lip.

"Okay, but I have a couple sketches due, so I do need to get back on the early side and work," she says, subtly pulling away from him.

"Well work here, baby, don't go to the coffeehouse. I want to work in the garden and feel you nearby. 'Kay?"

"Okay," she shrugs.

"Don't be like that. How's that sposed to make me feel?" He pouts again, flaring his nostrils for maximum effect. "Monday is Valentine's Day." He caresses and presses down her knuckles to make them crack. "Wait 'til you see what I've got for you!" he says in a singsong ending on a high note. She pinches his nose, the espresso maker now gurgling and ready.

Ray and Ruby hold hands crossing the street from their house to the dock. When they get to the lift, Ray lets go of her to uncover the boat. He drops her backpack on the cushion, stretches to unhook the wheel. She runs her hand over the front of the tight kinky springs of waves at her widow's peak, realizing her bandanna headband fell off somewhere along the way. She doubles back across the crude long planks of wood, and spots it, bright and yellow, on the cliffside just above the beginning of the dock, below the street. She picks it up, winds it in her hand, then ties it around her head, without really noticing that the bandanna design crawls alive up there, as well as on her hands. When she feels the sting, she doesn't hear what Ray yells to her, as she swiftly unties it and throws the bandanna to the ground. It's only seconds when she feels something like twenty incense ends burning into the flesh of her hairline and forearms. She screams, Ray now running for her, but she hustles past for the edge of the dock. She dives into the river with implausible grace.

Chapter 19

The Glasgow Scale

Ray

Superhuman reflex catapults Ray into the water less than a moment after Ruby dives in. He couldn't be sure that her head would strike the piling at two feet under, but she is unconscious, dead weight. Though his own heart throbs up the back of his throat, seamlessly he lays out her small, baked cinnamon body, slick and wet as a seal, the thin clothes sticking to her as if melted. Pressing just beneath her ribs, swiftly he covers her mouth with his for resuscitation. No space or time for hysteria. He remains on automatic response, breathing out and into her, imagining his energy with the power from the earth's center. Fear gains in decibels and density; he pushes down on her chest. After four rounds and Ray's oblivion to the burn in his lungs and gut, Ruby throws up water, then a hot, dark, golden meal into his mouth, choking him momentarily before he spits it out. Jubilation. The water dripping from his hair onto her face, he talks to her, his tongue dry and disobedient, his voice frayed, as he carefully rolls her onto her side, bringing her out and awake.

Her pupils blot out the beautiful cocoa brown irises; the whites are red, mad with the air, as she holds her eyes wide in confusion. He keeps talking to her, dialing his cell at the same time. With desperate, hurried, and gross detail to the 911 operator, he runs to the boat, grabs a pillow to prop her head. The blood spills across the red and white vinyl, seeping through the foam where there is a hole. With all of that drenched, lush jungle of hair, he can't tell exactly where the wound is.

Ray is crying now but speaking clearly to her, as Ruby opens her mouth to say, "Okay . . . have wishes," then closes her eyes as if hypnotized. Ray gently scoops her shoulders; she abruptly opens her eyes wide again. "You . . . okay . . . wishes . . . ah." Her eyes close, but he can see them work beneath. He calls her name over and over; he gently caresses her face, softly brushing the bumps raised around the hairline where the fire ants bit.

"It's me, okay," she says in more natural rhythm as she touches the back of her head. She looks at her fingers, feels the texture of the blood. Ray keeps talking so as not to lose her again, so as not to be mutilated by his own fear. She blinks rapidly, then normally.

"What is it?" she asks him, looking at the absolute center of his face. Her pupils respond now, closing to the light. "My head, Ray," she says, suddenly sounding like herself. He tells her about the pilings, and how people talk about attacks of the "Now Ants," what it felt like to him the first time he was bit, and how for relief he might have done the same thing by diving in. She listens, breathing in deeply, the exhale revealing her extreme exhaustion.

"Just blown me away . . ." She stops, gasps, sticks out her tongue, her eyes roll up inside her head, then slowly come back to focus. "To cool me off," she says. Ray now looking frantically toward the road, then back at her face. He squeezes her hand.

Finally he hears the siren, hops to his feet, runs down the dock and up to the street, flagging them down. Two pop out; the woman is an EMT, small, quick, and compact as Ruby, the man, a paramedic, red, beefy, mustached, and shaved bald. They race behind Ray with the backboard. When they get to Ruby, he recounts all he said to the operator, as the paramedic tilts her chin, thrusts open her jaw. He locates the wound, applies pressure to the bleeding, and tourniquets. The EMT assists as he checks her vitals. Together they roll her onto the board, ease on the clavicle collar, head blocks, and strap in tight her body and limbs.

Ruby mumbles her name as they lift her up like a sacrifice, her body helpless, appearing lifeless. Ray hears his own breathing speed up, close to hyperventilation. The EMT notices, but he snaps that he's fine. They all rush to the van; Ray insists his way in.

Sound, time crush together, Ray's heart as if in a decompression chamber. He gives in to fate only with regard to the speed and precision of the woman with the tiny head behind the wheel. The siren wails to him from miles away. The knocking sound of the diesel engine mimics a train, echoing the desolation in his head. It seems impossible that the rest of the world could be going on about its business while he rides inside the tick of a bomb, watching his lover's wet clothes being cut off by a stranger.

"Show me your teeth," the paramedic says, leaning over her. The IV hooked up, water bubbles into her arm. Ruby's eyes roll before she bares her teeth in a way that looks as if appraising something ugly.

"Okay, good. Now stick out your tongue for me, Ruby," the paramedic says, showing her how to do it. His mustache is so long, bringing to mind the image of food hanging. His cheeks are the hot, pocked pink of rosacea. Ruby opens her mouth and licks her top lip. The gesture looks sexual to Ray, further messing with his levels of focus, confidence, and courage.

"You're loud," Ruby says, trying to move her head still snug between the blocks. Ray's composure steadily plummeting, he involuntarily interrupts to help her.

"*You* have to calm down," the paramedic says sternly, pointing one finger downward, without turning around. "I don't have to remind you that you're risking her life if you get in my way," he says, now quickly glancing at Ray, after putting the breathing mask on Ruby's face. "This is why we never let loved ones in the van."

He talks louder to Ruby, "Does this feel all right? You feel okay?" Ruby blinks, keeping her eyes closed.

Is it possible, Ray asks himself, to pour forth enough love to purify the world's supply of air for her to breathe? Courage and positivity are both elliptical as he flails about, reaching for them, his innards breaking apart, splintering.

Ray sprints behind the nurses who run Ruby on the wheeled table, he shrieks to her his reassurances, until they stop him, the attending nurses disappearing with Ruby behind the glass doors. Someone redirects him to the triage nurse.

Ray sits with Gary in the waiting room, white and bright with light. The dark green leaves of the hanging plants in unnatural straw baskets appear cruelly placed, like a false sense of hope. On Ray's right lies Ruby's unzipped backpack that Gary fetched from the boat. Earlier, when Ray looked through the pack for her health insurance card, he found her passport too. The idea that she might have considered taking off at any moment, further weakens his faith. Gary tried talking him off this irrelevant tangent. The truth is Ruby always carried her passport on her as proof to herself of her adventurous spirit. Never was she considering escaping Ray; by their second day of meeting, she found it hard to imagine being without him.

Diagonally across the room from Ray and Gary is a son, in his mid-twenties, comforting his mother who stares out stony-eyed. The son's teeth are unusually large for his mouth. With a slight curl, his dyed black hair sticks up from the many times he has run his hand roughly through it. Both of their complexions are yellow with shock.

The doctor appears from behind the doors. He is small, smoky brown, and handsome with raccoon circles around his eyes; his oval spectacles pronounce the effect. His blue surgeon's cap reveals silk jet-black hair shaved close at the temples. Though very businesslike and authoritative, he still looks slightly vulnerable. Ray gets up, tightly holding onto Gary's hand.

"Mr. Rose?" he asks rhetorically; Ray nods in response. "I'm Dr. Ambaji, the neurosurgeon, taking over for Dr. Lennox. First of all, I must tell you that upon arrival we suspected Miss Falls of mild brain injury due to her stable blood pressure and relatively encouraging score of twelve on the Glasgow Coma Scale—"

"Coma?" Ray gasps in interruption; the doctor lifts his hands together as if a quarterback who just said "hut," then he lets them drop gently.

"She was still fairly alert at that point, but as we continue to monitor her in ICU, her condition has not yet stabilized. The CAT scan revealed that there has been some brain swelling, which we have given her mannitol to reduce—"

"What happens if her brain keeps swelling?" Ray interrupts again with pure panic in his voice. He still holds Gary's hand.

"Well the elevated pressure lowers profusion of the blood to the brain, resulting in a lack of blood flow, which could result in heart attack or stroke. So far I haven't found it necessary to place an intracranial pressure monitor inside of her brain, as we may already have the swelling under control. Unfortunately we *have* found that there may be some evidence of a small external blood clot, which I need to get in and take out right away to prevent any further sheering—"

"Sheering?" Ray interrupts, searching the doctor's eyes for some sense of the weight of holding Ruby's life in his hands. He swallows, still searching, shifts his weight.

"The layers of the brain in the setting of impact may 'sheer' against one another, causing tissue trauma. So in order to prevent any additional insult to the brain injury, I need to go in and remove this small clot." The doctor nods once, raising his brows high to elicit agreement.

Ray swallows again, stares at the floor just in front of the doctor's feet. He looks up quickly at Gary, then finally at the doctor. "Okay," Ray says, his voice cracking. The doctor puts his hands in the pockets of his blue scrubs, turns to rush off, leaving Ray standing there to fall apart in Gary's arms. In the twenty minutes it takes for him to pull himself together, Gary then pulls Ruby's cell from the backpack for Ray to call her sister, Hannah.

Now that Gary has left for his dinner shift at the restaurant, Jason sits with Ray, whose head is in hands, elbows resting on spread thighs. Birds of paradise and orchids wrapped in butcher paper stand propped in a dramatic bunch on Ray's right. Jason eats Greek takeout food with a small plastic fork, breaking a single tong in an olive and grape leaf.

"Here's the bugger," Jason says, picking the fork tong out of the feta cheese. "Sure you don't want any? It's delicious. Taste it," he says, holding out a piece of shwarma. Still bent over his lap, Ray doesn't look back at Jason.

"The meat's not very salty at all. I usually hate lamb and beef, but this is incredible. I got a whole other tinful here for you. You really should eat something."

"I can't." Ray tensely scrapes his head with his fingers, puts his head back in his hands.

"You can help Ruby best by being strong. Fit and strong, not tired and strained. She needs you now," Jason says, wiping the corner of his mouth with a small white paper napkin that came from a dispenser. He looks at the grease on it, then crumples it up in his hand, gets up to toss it. He wears new black sneakers and cuffed chinos. He throws his head back before sitting down again.

"She's gonna pull through it, I'm confident of that," Jason continues, flicking muck out from under his pinkie fingernail. He brushes off his pants, the sound making Ray flinch.

"Oh, in the same way you were *so* confident Gary was gonna make it that you stayed *away* from the hospital," Ray hisses, turning back to look at him.

"Yes," Jason hisses back, his full top lip turned up in a sneer. Then he softens, sitting back in the dark magenta, busy-patterned chair, leaning on the hard black armrest. "Gary knew he should have stayed away from him. I met Arnie too, you know. Someone brought him to one of those softball games. First time I see him, he's pointing out a tree struck by lightning—it looked all blasted, burned up, and grim. I remember wishing it were him instead of the tree. God knows he was in the right place for it."

"I don't want to hear this shit," Ray snaps.

"Okay. Change of subject." Jason takes a deep breath in patience. "You know I bought some Mets tickets—a couple night games— make me a little killing with the tourists. No way I'd ever go back to another game myself. And I'm sure as hell not looking forward to all that nightmare traffic. I'm so glad Gary quit those softball Sundays. Used to wear me out just watching. But this one Mets game he dragged me to was even worse. The music exploding in your ears every two minutes between batters, and that *annoying* organist, ugh. Oh, and that centerfield scoreboard—have you been to the stadium?"

"No."

"The Thomas White Stadium?"

"I said *no*." Sharply Ray looks at him.

"Well the scoreboard looks like high school. What a boring, cheap experience. But the tickets weren't cheap. That's how I knew I could make a few bucks this year. The Orioles are in Fort

Lauderdale, the Dodgers are in Vero Beach, the Cardinals are in Jupiter . . ."

"Will you shut the fuck up?"

Jason holds up his hands, Ray doesn't look back at him.

"Are Ruby's parents coming?" Jason asks in a soft voice.

"I spoke to her sister. She and her parents got the first flight out. That should bring them here early morning. Probably get to the hospital about seven."

"You haven't met them before, have you?"

"No."

Ray bites on the soft flesh over his index knuckle. He sniffles and violently wipes the corner of his eye. Jason puts a hand on Ray's shoulder and squeezes. He looks across the room at the mother, whose son isn't there at the moment. But a woman and her teenage daughter have just joined her. The woman hugs the mother, while the teenager stands put, hands in her jean pockets, eyes gaping wide at her. Ray sits up in his seat, gaining Jason's attention and losing the hand from his shoulder. Jason now holds both hands in his lap. Ray grabs Jason's knee, stands up to stretch.

"Maybe I should get a vase from the nurse for these flowers, huh? I wasn't thinking before," Jason says, now getting up too. He walks over to the desk, waiting for someone to appear, then impatiently makes his way back toward the elevator to look on the other side.

Ray paces the room, hating the clean septic smell and the decorative strips of geometric shapes on the wall. He can't help thinking of being in the same place seven years ago in Michigan, because of his mother. How thin she was in the hospital, her skin colorless and transparent, the delicate intricacy of her veins showing the temporary nature of all things. Her hair lay like flat straw with two inches of white at the roots, no longer cared for and teased in a wild auburn bouffant. With an unexplainable cruelty and quickness the leukemia took her. How punctured he felt when he saw the doctor's face. The hot, searing pain of loss she left behind. The aloneness he now so bluntly feels again.

He remembers his father's hands. The thickness, the hugeness of them from manually milking cows as a child. How his father held Ray and Sadie's hands, Sonya standing next to her, how he then held his own face, sobbing in wrenching gulps as they laid his one love to rest. The pinkish red cherry blossoms she loved tied in bunches, and strewn all around the grave.

Ray could go leaping now through the strawberry thickets in Michigan on the farm. Run wild through them, Sadie and Sonya tailing him fast, when they were all less than twelve. Hear the sweet yipping of the tiny one-eyed dog neighbor, Drew, who sometimes accompanied them. Experience a time when nothing ugly, nothing devastating had ever threatened them, a time when mortality had no meaning.

"Now, how's this look?" Jason's voice scares him, as he turns around to see the bouquet beautifully arranged in the vase. "I hated the one the wretched nurse offered, so I went downstairs and bought this decent one."

"Looks nice." Ray gives him a weak smile that swiftly breaks.

"Let's put this over here," Jason says, his voice straining as he bends to put the vase down on an end table near the Levelor-blinded window. "And let's move our stuff over here and admire a different view," he continues, picking up Ruby's backpack. He sits, hits the seat next to him. When Ray doesn't move, Jason turns around to pull up the blinds. "Look here, we can see the night now. We can look out, feeling how smoothly it's all going for Ruby in there, and how soon after recovery you'll be taking her home."

Ray drops into the seat next to Jason. The steely will is going to sneak up on him and surprise him, the moment he lays eyes on Ruby in the hospital bed. He will take the shocking punch and come back standing. He won't cry at the quarter of her hair shaved and bandaged, at the respirator in her mouth, or the feeding tube through her nose. He'll see the IV, the EKG monitor, and the blood pressure armband all working with him to keep her alive. He won't accept the doctor's words that it could be hours, days, or months before she wakes up. He will interrupt him before he can say years. There is *no way* he'll let her go. And just after the nurse makes him leave the room for the remainder of the wee hours of the morning, he will run out to Jason to tell him exactly that.

Chapter 20

Meet the Parents

Ruby

Ruby can hear her mother's voice. Low for a woman, but also tinny when excited or worried. She alternates between long pauses before each sentence and extended run-ons with barely a gasp for breath. This gives her a childlike quality, particularly emphasized when she had braces on her teeth for a year at age sixty. Approaching the eve of senior citizenship status, little about her has changed.

If Ruby could see her mother, standing there in the hospital room keeping as much distance as possible between them, she would know she is wearing a white silk shell inside her tailored navy traveling suit—a linen-cotton blend, creased only at the back vent. Her knee-high pantyhose are in her color, "copper blaze"; her shoes are black low-heeled pumps designed by a woman podiatrist. Her hair is cut short, permed straight, and parted at the side. She wears small gold hoops in her ears, studded with tiny diamonds.

Hannah is speaking in hushed tones, as if in a library. She is completely devoid of makeup; if Ruby could see her younger sister, this would bring back rare glimpses of their girlhood. Under Hannah's eyes the soft skin is swollen to the point where there isn't a single baby line. Her knuckles, joints throb so much from the shock, her pain vibrates. She has an itch at her inner elbow that is an angry red from her scratching in forceful snatches.

Ray is there for only a short time during the family's first brief meeting. Ruby's father is mostly quiet, a dry well at the base of his throat. He stares at the floor just beside Ruby's bed. His loud, black, rectangular-framed glasses are nerdy and stylish, giving him the appearance of an architect rather than a professor-cum-city politician. He is slightly shorter than his wife, who stands five foot eight; he is darker-skinned, more molasses than her golden honey. The girls are their maple mix. Ray safely out of earshot, they talk to each other in suspicious, anxious timbres of despair. Ruby's ear is aware but not conscious of their every word; still none of them thinks to talk to her.

Their desire for her to wake up is irrelevant to Ruby's reality. It's as if she stares into a mirror, studying her features until a hypnotic effect takes place, and she sees beyond the glass, feels from outside her body. A pure separation from identity. So much so that she could become another person, an object, an element. One of the repeating images is her existence as a canoe, drifting downstream without person, paddle, or struggle. She is swift in the water, reaching her destination of the cave with the triangular opening. As she enters, it's only then that she is aware of being cold. The darkness is a mirage until she gets to the other side of the cave to find she is human again. But the humanity is not familiar. It is wholly unrelated to the larger scheme of the mind.

The trauma to her body is outside of her. She leaves her body to mend, or she allows her mind the space and rest to heal. This means that when Jason and Gary go in with Ray, she doesn't recognize their voices. Not at this time. Both of them are attached to a complicated and ugly story she has broken from. And if Ray could possibly be a concern in her head, she would want him broken from their story too. When Jeannie arrives on Day Three of the coma (Ray did not think to call her until after the parents arrived), her voice might belong to one of the nurses for the same reason that she is attached to the horror in Ruby's past.

Besides the thirty minutes Ray thinks to give the family alone with Ruby, he leaves her bedside only when the doctors or nurses make him. He caresses her face, her hands, her arms, her feet; he coos, cries, and squeals encouragement when she twitches, yawns, or raises a brow. Her brain bleats like a sheep, and he hears it. It's as if she is just before REM, approaching consciousness of dreaming, almost aware of being held hostage in a nightmare when the doctor warns Ray about reading into movements that may mean "nothing more than primitive reflex."

But mostly she remains calm in her reverie. This is her long, slow wave, delta sleep. This is her escape from life and death, her long pause before the ultimate choice.

Annoyances, anxiety, and fear are long-gone threats to her peace. She doesn't have to experience anyone else; she doesn't have to witness distress. Though they are in such close proximity to her on that floor, she is oblivious to the other bodies fighting for survival or extinction. She is happily absent from each awkward aura of the various groupings of her familiars in the waiting room.

During those times when he is banished by staff, Ray sits with Hannah and her parents, the latter lacerating him with their eyes, speaking at him in passive combat. There is their near-explosive argument with the doctor, who insists upon the dangers of moving Ruby back to California. There is Wanda reciting from a book she bought on coma, inspiring Ruby's father to whisper in exasperation to Hannah, "Who *is* this woman?" There is Jeannie, already succumbing to the idea of more loss. She falls into the arms of a perfect stranger, Wanda's husband, Lou. Watching, Wanda bites down hard on her lip, struggling to be bigger than the moment.

"Who did this to my child's head?" Ruby's mother, Vera, snaps as she walks into the room on the morning of coma Day Four. Hannah and her father, Nelson, follow her entrance. Her tone hasn't been this aggressive since the fight with the doctor.

"I did," Ray says gently, sitting at Ruby's side, holding her hand bent inward and upward toward her heart. Her hair is in twelve braids, sprawling with life about the pillow. She looks like a beautiful sea creature at rest.

"Well, it looks *awful*," Vera says, angrily yanking open her purse for a comb.

Nelson puts up his hands. "Calm down, Vera."

"She looks like a pickaninny," Vera says, handing the comb to Hannah. "Fix it, will you?"

Ray rolls his chair back, gets up weakly. As if it might slide away, he holds the chair firmly for Hannah. She looks at him quickly with a slight, apologetic expression on her face, but it disappears the minute she begins softly loosing Ruby's braids. She takes desperate care not to touch the bandaged part of her head. Ray stands over her with his arms crossed.

"And you haven't shaved in *days*," Vera says, looking at Ray, crossing her arms too, her heels clicked together. "You look like a wolf. Why don't you go and clean up?"

"I'm okay," Ray says evenly, peacefully, as if in another dimension.

"Did you get any sleep last night?" Ruby's father asks, looking at him as if he were human for the first time.

"I did."

"Ray has a room here at the hospital, Dad," Hannah says, having pulled her own brush out of her bag, stroking her sister's hair down and flat against the pillow.

"How'd you manage that?" Nelson asks, making a stern, puzzled pattern with his forehead.

"Ray's hooked up. His ex-wife works here, isn't that right?" Hannah says in a schoolgirl's tone.

"Ex-*wife?*" Vera asks.

"Yes," Ray says, still standing there, hoping to be able to talk to Ruby again soon. Valentine's Day passed eight hours ago with so much turmoil and rare uninterrupted time to tell her all the ways he will love her for the rest of his life.

"You have an ex-wife?" Vera asks again.

"Yes."

"You heard him, Vera," Nelson says.

"How old are you, anyway?"

"Thirty-three."

She shakes her head, pulls up a chair, and sits, looking up at her husband with resentment that he didn't think to help her.

"You didn't forget the gloss, though," Hannah says looking at Ruby's lips, then combing her brows up with a small leopard-spotted eyebrow brush. "You got it on perfectly." Hannah smiles to Ray in approval.

Vera sighs, softens, not because of the lipgloss, but because she can't sustain aggression. This part of her mother's temperament Ruby relied on as a girl. The eventual flexibility, the seemingly too swift giving-in. Ruby's father passionately disapproved of Ruby's tangential paths to her dubious goals. He hated her choice of UC Santa Cruz, her undeclared major as a freshman, her sophomore choice of psychology, her switch to art school back in Los Angeles after that. He didn't think it was healthy for her to be living so close to her parents. Vera would argue his side only for the first half of conversation, then she would slowly gain a sympathy for Ruby, bordering on humor. At one point she said she could understand the "lack of direction" Ruby had in life. "Ultimately, setting your path toward one thing gives a person tunnel vision," she'd said. "No one could ever accuse you of not taking your sweet time just looking around," and she'd ended that phone conversation with a robust guffaw.

Since Nelson waited a long time in courting Vera at the all-black and well-respected Fisk University in Nashville, he wanted her all to himself once they got married. They spent ten years alone before having Ruby. And though they loved their firstborn with individual intensity, Ruby felt as if her feet were on two logs set at different speeds, adrift.

It is hard enough for Nelson to share Ruby with the doctors, nurses, much less Ray, the coke whore landlord, and all of these Florida strangers. When she was born, he let no one visit her and his wife at home in L.A.'s View Park for an entire month. He was terrified of the *floating* germs. Meanwhile, Vera feared that people thought they couldn't visit because Ruby must have been retarded or deformed.

Vera became obsessed with photographs after that. There was a mailing list of family and friends who got regular documentation of her perfect-limbed growth. Ruby and a poppy, Ruby and the ducky, Ruby on the lawn, Ruby under a palm, Ruby in the tub, and Ruby as a dove. By the age of four, she was allergic to grass, wool, animals, eggs, chocolate, and peanut butter. She broke out with eczema. She got weekly treatments under sunlamps, and Vera went to a psychiatrist who said Ruby's skin problems were a direct result of the difficulties Vera had caused in the marriage.

Vera never liked sex; she found it intrusive, elusive, and messy. She never used it as a power play with her husband, and for the most part he learned to go frequently without. After a while it made sense to him that its main purpose was reproduction and not pleasure. Vera's belief had little to do with her Catholic upbringing; she never found the focal point of her clitoris. Professor Nelson, raised Lutheran but nondenominational by eighteen, had to accept, as he wasn't a terribly determined lover. Hannah was born when Ruby turned six. Once she had someone to share all the attention and paranoia, her skin problems disappeared.

After Hannah, Nelson and Vera discovered travel. The girls had each other, and they had their trusty babysitter, twenty-year-old Anne, down the street in the cul-de-sac. Anne had a six-year-old daughter of her own, Candace, whom Ruby played doctor with.

Hannah developed severe earaches after Nelson and Vera's third long trip, this time to China, but news of her latest infection, just before they would leave, didn't stop them from getting on the plane. Hannah's pediatrician became so familiar with babysitter Anne that he made a successful play for her.

Nelson—as a well-spoken, well-traveled scholar, an African American, tenured history professor at USC—was invited to various functions to speak, leading to a taste for politics. He became used to taking center stage, accustomed to the sound of his own voice booming over audiences well beyond the tender age of twenty-two. Vera was the beautiful, sharply dressed, supportive, educated woman at his side. She wrote plays that, if anyone would read them, certainly a few would find amusing, even intriguing.

Their little girls were obedient and advanced in school: Ruby was athletic and artistic like her mother; Hannah was studious and fastidious like her father. Nelson was the boss of all of his girls, but Vera ruled his world.

Ruby opens her eyes and Vera gasps, then screams. Hannah jumps up; Nelson calls for the doctor, and in runs a nurse. Ray talks to Ruby, tells her how wonderful it is to see the most breathtakingly clear, brown doe eyes in the universe. She continues to stare straight in front of her, without focusing or turning her head. No matter how many times Ray tells her he loves her and encourages her to now move her gaze, her inattention is unwavering. She is still not in their realm.

They can't know that she has gotten to a quickening in her journey where the message says, *Know your death.* The nurse tries calmly explaining that opening her eyes is a natural reflex; this happens on automatic. It is at this point that Jeannie walks in, loosely and gauzily garbed, clutching tightly to her own wrist. Ruby's expression turns into what anyone might describe as a grimace, but she is actually feeling quite peaceful. For how many people get this kind of preview? How many people get to court death while their bodies lie alive and peaceful with their loved ones, their minds continuing at such a state of rest?

Chapter 21

The Special Olympics

Ray

Jeannie and Ray sit alone together at Ruby's bedside. Her eyes are closed but working wildly beneath her lids. Ray has been asking her what she is watching while Jeannie keeps perfectly still.

"Wow, I need a cigarette," Jeannie says finally, running her hand through the center of her ash blonde hair. "You have any?"

"No," Ray says without turning around to look at her. He holds Ruby's hand, stroking the fingers, working to pry them open.

"She looks like she's driving, you know?" Jeannie says in a hoarse voice. Ray says nothing, concentrating on the possibility that he can hear Ruby's thoughts. Jeannie tries stirring up the energy again. "Doesn't it look like she's drag racing down the fucking highway?"

Ray says nothing. He continues stroking her small, tight, tense fingers. Jeannie arches her back, stretching first to the left, then the right. She stares at Ruby for a long moment. She breathes in, then puckers her lips. She whistles a strange tune, soapy and disloyal, making Ray's scalp prickle. After a while, Ruby's eyes stop working beneath her lids, her right thigh, which she usually holds packed, goes loose as if in a hot bath. Ray nods ecstatically, now bobbing his head like a dashboard doll, encouraging Jeannie to come closer with her song. Jeannie gets up, slinks closer to the bed, moving one shoulder and then the other, as if directed in the ultimate show-stopping seduction scene. Ray, not knowing the tune—since Jeannie made it up—begins whistling too, until they degenerate from jazz into the opening of *My Three Sons*.

187

"How the *hell* do you know that one?" Jeannie stops to ask in giddy excitement.

"Do you know it too, baby?" Ray asks Ruby with a psychotic lilt. "Keep whistling, Jean," he snaps tersely. Jeannie picks up the tune midway. Ray does too, but Ruby is back at attention, holding the right side of her body like a board.

"Look at her, shit, she's driving again. Maybe that's good, huh?" Jeannie asks, tilting her head, her hands now on her hips. Her wet, apprehensive eyes, once gold now tawny liquid glass, betray her sheer state of terror. "I mean, sometimes it's good to just gun it, pedal to the metal all the way, right?" She looks at Ray.

"That'll only get you into trouble," Ray says, leaning back with the slightest hint of surrender. "My father could always tell how fast I was driving by how long the bug splats were."

Jeannie laughs a gutbucket, cups both her knees. "I *knew* you were like that," Jeannie says, her nostrils flaring in amusement. "Ruby couldn't have fallen for anyone else but the ultimate Goody Two-shoes. Hell, if my father ever gave a shit where I ever was! You can forget about him caring how long I was gone, and what I was doing. Doubt he ever noticed much difference between any of the five us. Meanwhile, your father's up there examining bug *splats*?" She laughs this time in sweet staccato.

"Hey everybody," Wanda says, sticking her head in the door.

"Hey," Jeannie says, still chuckling, straightening in her chair. Having instantaneously forgotten the last two minutes of conversation, Ray nods vaguely toward Wanda's direction, then strokes Ruby's forehead.

"So what was so funny? I heard you clear down the hall," Wanda asks. Ray motions his chin toward Jeannie.

"I was just laughing at Ray's father measuring the length of the bug splats on his car to tell how fast he was going!" Jeannie says, trying too hard to be familiar.

"That's nothing. Don't let me get in on *my* father. You're lucky if he let you *drive*. My daddy was damned if I could even leave the house. Speaking of which, where are the folks?" She leans forward conspiratorially.

"At lunch," Ray says, still not looking up at her.

"I don't get the feeling Nelson's too fond of me," Jeannie says, making a tight double chin, opening her eyes wide. Wanda flips her hand.

"Have you had the chance to read any of this book?" Wanda asks Ray, putting two short, caramel dreadlocks behind her ear. "I've dog-eared some of the pages you should take a look at." She sits on her white leather-slippered foot.

"I haven't, Wanda," Ray says.

"That's okay, baby, I know you have a lot to deal with." She puts her hand up, her wrists tinkle with thin silver bracelets. She licks her index finger before quickly sifting through the pages. "Oh," she says, sucking in her cheeks as if she tasted something sour. "The first thing I wanted to remember to ask is, do they have her on pain medication?"

"Morphine," Ray says.

"Well, the book says that pain medication can get in the way of her ability to communicate. It's another block to consciousness."

"Hell, she's been through so much, don't you think she needs it?" Jeannie asks horrified.

"If she's too drugged to wake up, how will she ever manage to do it?" Wanda shrugs, then shoots Jeannie a subtly cutting look. "Now, I know, baby, you've been doing some of these things already," she says, looking at Ray, who turns to meet her gaze. His lights turn up a notch, as if Wanda might be the angel messenger. "But what we need to do first, is get in rhythm with her breathing. I'll get on this side of the bed, and we'll just exhale and inhale in rhythm with Ruby. Okay?"

Jeannie gets up from her chair, walks backward, narrowly missing Wanda who is making her way closer to Ruby's bedside.

"I woke up only an hour ago, I'm just gonna go get myself something to eat. The temperature still dropping out there? I've never been to Florida when it was this cold. I packed so wrong," Jeannie says, folding her arms over her breasts.

"Yeah, well, it was hot a couple days ago, we're just entering a little cold snap, that's all," Wanda says with an air of dismissal.

"Bye Ray, see you later," Jeannie says, waving. But since the accident, Ray mostly hears everyone's every other word.

Ray and Wanda bring their faces to either side of Ruby's and begin breathing in perfect unison with her. After seven minutes of this, Ray looks at Wanda, like, *What next?* Wanda keeps breathing, nodding, and looking at Ruby, who's parting her mouth just a bit. Ray gets too excited, as he does with every little change of motion, which is often. Wanda seems to know they're not there yet.

"Talk to her, baby," Wanda says to Ray. She looks down at the book in her lap, then back up at him. "Make sure you speak in rhythm with her breathing. After that, we're gonna work our way down her body, you, touching and pressing, me, humming to her rhythm, and then we'll lift her wrists, while you keep talking to her, then her elbows, then her ankles, one at a time, and so on. Got it? We'll start with the wrists, and we'll just keep going until we get to her feet. Got it?" Ray nods, not really grasping the order but feeling her drift.

"Wanda and I are here, love," Ray says near her ear. "We're happy to know you're dreaming, we want to try and dream with you. Will you let us?"

Wanda keeps breathing, enthusiastically nodding at Ray, her locks bouncing at the top of her head. Ruby raises a brow, twitches her face, then moves her mouth as if suckling a bottle.

"She's done this before," Ray says to Wanda, as if they should already be giving up hope.

"Keep talking, baby," Wanda says. She looks down at the book again. "Actually, we'll end with her head, after the feet. We'll lift her head, and keep breathing, okay? Now keep talking."

But they make it as far as Ruby's elbows before two nurses come in, kick them out to check her vitals, clean her bedding. Before walking out, Wanda tells the nurse that they would like to talk to the doctor about cutting the pain medication.

"You reek, man," Gary says the next afternoon, coma Day Number Six, holding a plastic bag with a Tupperware of food. "Why don't you come to the waiting room with me, have a little bite, and then go home, take a quick shower, and come on back. I'll drive you."

"I'm not leaving this hospital again," Ray says solemnly.

"Don't you think Ruby can smell you? Why should she wake

up to this mess? Look at your hair, man! It's *so* greasy, sticking like that to your peanut head. Do you have a bag, at least, of clean clothes in your room?"

"Everything's dirty."

"Dude, let me take your dirty clothes, bring you back some clean ones. Give me the keys to the house."

Without looking at him, Ray shifts his weight in his chair to get the keys out of his jean pocket. He gives him a set too many.

"Whose are these?"

Ray looks at them, shiny and new in the palm of Gary's hand. "Ruby's Valentine's present."

"A *car!*" Gary says, his sienna brown eyes dancing in the dead neon hospital light. "What kind of car, dude?"

"A hybrid. She'd been talking about them for months."

"Wow, man. You're a good, devoted, adoring husband. She knows it too, and she wants you to take care of yourself." Gary stands there, exaggerating the tilt of his head so that Ray will look at him. "Come on out of this room with me, now. Let's have us a little bite to eat, okay?" Gary holds out his other hand to pull Ray up. Ray doesn't move. Gary turns his head toward the sound of footsteps at the door.

"Oh, hello Mr. and Mrs. Falls," Gary says, bowing his head, gallantly. "Hannah," he nods again.

"Hello," Vera says, entering the room first like a homecoming queen. Nelson, with a defeated expression, says hello as well, but Hannah is as dazed, red-eyed, and otherwordly as Ray.

"I'm trying to get Ray out for a bite here, then take him home and get a shower and some clean clothes."

"Absolutely," Vera says. "And he should shave too."

"I'll make sure of it," Gary says, visibly itching to get out. He seems to do a sidestep dance, the freckles, splattered as they are all over the top half of his face, make him look like a kid.

"One of the nurses thinks he looks like Jesus," Vera says, making more of an effort to be friendly with Gary.

"I can't tell you how many times since I've known him, at least eight or nine, I've heard people say the same thing to him. Gets his boxers in a bunch every time." Gary wriggles his nose.

"He should come downstairs to the chapel with us tomorrow morning," Vera says, Nelson looking at her in shock. Hannah isn't paying any attention, and the two continue to talk about Ray in the third person, as if he weren't there.

In Gary's car, on the way home, Ray's cell phone rings. He looks at it, paralyzed with fear that it may be a member of his family whom he will have to tell the whole story to of his life from last Friday until now. Much worse, it could be the hospital. He picks up.

"Baby, it's Wanda." Ray melts with relief. "Listen. Think of her as meditating. Undisturbed by her own good or bad thoughts. Her mind can't hurt her. She's a nonparticipant, just a bystander to the current workings of her brain." Wanda pauses. Ray is silent. "You got me?"

"Yes," Ray says, as if to his mother, now missing her sorely.

"When she's ready, she'll wake up. Okay, baby? I'm at the coffeehouse if you need me. I know Ruby's phone's got it, but save this number on your cell too. Okay?"

"Okay."

"Lou'll be by the hospital this evening. I'm sending some food with him. Okay, honey, bye."

"Bye," Ray says, tearing up.

"Who was that?" Gary asks, the steering wheel so large in his hands it exaggerates his small size.

"Wanda."

"Wanda's cool," Gary says, staring ahead at the traffic. When he comes to a stoplight, he turns to look at Ray, squeezes his hand. "It's gonna be okay," Gary says, nodding. "It's gonna be fine."

"Yes," Ray says, his voice cracking. He puts his fingernail in his mouth, bites it off, then searches his pocket for a cigarette, but he has none. "But what if it isn't?" Ray asks, turning to him.

"What if it isn't what?"

"What if it isn't okay?"

"Well," Gary says swallowing, looking in the rearview mirror. "Look, Ray, she might wake up and be a bit damaged, you know? There could be something wrong with her speech, or her coordination," his voice cracks. He summons up more courage. "I mean, she could be a cripple, you know, taking her meds, depressed and beat down to hell, waiting to shrivel up and die, but that's just not likely. Because she has you. And she's strong. And so even if she does wake up a cripple or somewhat mentally . . . challenged, she could say, 'Okay, my life was cut up bad, but I'm gonna keep on going.' And she'll go on to compete in the Special Olympics. And you're gonna be right by her side. You're gonna be the one who has to make sure she wins."

At first Ray's eyes bulge in shock, but now he looks at him in utter rage. Who is Gary to believe in the worst? How dare he think for one minute that he would ever give up on her? That he needs any *encouragement* to stay with her? The combustion in his chest is packed so tight, his face inflames with blood, the veins popping in his neck.

"Pull over," Ray snarls.

"But we're almost there," Gary says, looking up and out the window to the shade of the banyan trees, as if they were guards.

"Pull the *fuck* over," Ray snaps.

Gary swerves, Ray jumps out of the car, and starts running. Gary gets out, but then he gets back in the car and follows him. He overtakes him, then hurdles out just in front of the house. Gary pulls out the keys and dangles them, as if holding a treat to try and calm a lion. Ray moves forward at him, and Gary jumps back, puts both hands on his heart with an expression of dumb sincerity. The keys fall to the ground. Ray stands as if poured in stone and hardening quickly. It takes everything in him to self-contain that way. Gary breathes hard, searching his face, trying to figure out what to do.

He doesn't understand, Ray tells himself. He doesn't know what he went through in defense of his self-respect. He had risked his own life, his future, his peace of mind for a friend. But what Ray doesn't realize in this moment is that if he hadn't killed Arnie, he would never have run to Alaska to try and find that peace of mind again. If he hadn't gone, he would have never met Ruby. And Ruby is now his life. This part rings loud like a cathedral bell in his breast. This wakes him up and out of it. Gary picks up the keys, looking up at Ray, feeling his temperature change. Instead of letting out a shrill scream, Ray allows Gary to take him by the elbow and lead him up the sea-graped walkway to the door.

It is not until the wee hours, near three A.M., that Ray can sit with Ruby undisturbed. With the plastic bag of a large slab of shea butter warming in his lap, he tells her how embarrassed he's been to describe how he felt just after she left him the first night they met. How he stood at the hotel elevator, watched the numbers light up until she reached her floor. How his head rippled with bubbles, heat like meteors shooting in his stomach. His balls throbbing in tremors. How he didn't quite make it home, but pulled over at the side of the road just before the hill to the cabin. He unzipped his pants, first catching a few long stray pubic hairs, got himself uncaught, then whipped out his dick. While thinking of soaping her up in the shower, he quickly came right there in the truck all over the front of his jeans.

Ruby's eyes are perfectly still, at rest. Her left side is so relaxed it almost appears dead; her right side is slightly flexed as Ray pulls off her hospital gown to massage her breasts. He concentrates on the scarred arc of her areola, the oil melting on his palms as he strongly works to loosen the tissue beneath with his index and middle fingers. Like a disk he turns her nipple, the full circle cast as dark purple bloom against the small colored lights of the hospital machines. This is the movement she most loves during a massage; this is when she would moan if she were awake. As he continues kneading, now murmuring, he thinks he sees her turn her head less than an inch toward him. He kisses her mouth, but her lips give nothing. He goes on massaging, down from his rounds of the moon to the plush brown skin, feeling the veins, delicate and thin as filament. Her smell rises like baking bread, the nipples now standing stiff and shiny with the butter. Entirely unafraid now of anyone walking in, he tears off her sheets, having yanked down his pants. He messily removes her catheter and plunges in. She is very much alive and pulsating, but no other part of her body seems aware. So when he comes he feels so guilty he reads her grimace as horror of his act, disregarding the fact that her expressions—in all their

194

various muscular alterations—convey sadness, ecstasy, or disgust at most any time.

This doesn't mean he shouldn't try and read her. And it's not like he hasn't made many wrong choices, or never wrongly taken from others. Unaware of having dammed any tears, the amount of the gush overwhelms him. He shakes with it, his nose clogged, his head fizzing, his pants draped around his ankles like that. When the breeze dries his juice to sticky flakes on his thigh, he remembers to carefully wipe her belly off. He redresses and covers her, apologizing for all of his crimes.

"I can't lose you," he says. "I can't be alone," he cries hard again. "I don't want to be on my deathbed, thinking a string of sick shit." He loudly snorts the snot back in, flops down in the chair, now contemptuous of everything in himself.

Ray's ears ring in his own hospital bed a floor below his beloved. His neck muscles crunch into his back. The tendons ache. Inside his head, a hot wind of silence. He doesn't realize it, but all that Wanda keeps telling him about meditation is slowly sinking in. Having hit his threshold of pain, there is no way to come out of it other than with an involuntary kind of prayer. Instead of herding his thoughts under one category of judgment or another, negative or positive, he lets them go. This passing of hypervigilant self-surveillance mode sparks a truer, freer beginning of hope.

Ray keeps Ruby's cell phone fully charged in his room and on him throughout the day so that he can put whoever calls to her ear, to try and wake her. On coma Day Number Nine, he steps lightly off the elevator and into her room just after they've given her a sponge bath. He asks the nurse if she will wait for him before they do that next time. Ruby's phone vibrates in his T-shirt breast pocket, so he answers, and the nurse walks out.

"Hello?"

The caller hangs up. The phone undulates a second time.

"Ruby's phone," Ray says this time.

"May I speak to her?" asks an elegant voice, silky, sleek, indigo, and male.

"Who is this?" snaps Ray.

"It's Pej. Who is this?"

"Pejman," Ray says, pausing for breath. He looks at the floor, watches his jealousy cross it, hairy and large as a tarantula. "I'm Ray, her fiancé. Ruby's had an accident. She's here with me in the hospital, in Florida. She's in a coma, Pejman," he says, his voice cracking with empathy. "Will you say something to her? I'll put the phone against her ear." Not waiting for Pej's response, he just does it. Instantaneously, the right side of her mouth twitches. Awkwardly bending over Ruby and the bed, Ray takes her right hand, tries prying it open to lift it to her ear so that she might hold the phone. The fingers give, her arm flops, the underside of her biceps like jelly, and Ray is overjoyed.

"What are you saying?" Ray excitedly asks Pej before putting the phone back to her ear.

Pej hesitates, still in shock. "I'm just asking her how she is doing." But this is a lie, and as he is returned to her ear, he continues to speak in Farsi (ten words of which she knows), apologizing for not catching up, for never knowing what she wanted, for not having it to give her.

"Keep it up. She has relaxed her hand," Ray says loudly.

"We ran into your ex-wife," Vera says as she and Hannah enter the room. Nelson has gone back to L.A. for a meeting, a forty-eight-hour round-trip.

"Ruby's on the phone," Ray whispers. Hannah, haggard, stares at him. Vera sits down, finite in her faith, nevertheless eager for Ray's inventive attitude to rub off on her. She looks at her daughter, lifeless to her, but responsive in torrents to Ray.

"Who's on the phone?" Hannah asks in a voice raw as a croak.

"Pejman."

"Give it to me," she says, grabbing it from Ruby's hand held by his. She takes the phone outside the door.

"We ran into your ex-wife, Barbara," Vera repeats.

"I heard you the first time," Ray says coldly, looking Vera in the eye, offsetting his frustration with Hannah on her.

"She said you were a good father to her child," Vera says.

"Almost anyone is better than no one at all," Ray says.

"Who is the father?"

"Some fireman, she thinks."

"She *thinks?*" Vera says, laying her jacket on the back of the chair, crossing her legs.

Ray winds his hair in a bun and knots it, the way Ruby taught him. He sighs, strokes her forehead. There is a bit of new acne there, just as he now has on his cheeks.

"She doesn't *know* who the father is?"

"She partied a lot at that time. I didn't know her then. She thinks the father is most likely this fireman she saw briefly." Ray looks at Ruby, massaging her brow with his thumb, sorry that she has to hear any of it.

"What happened with you two? She seems to love you, still."

"Wrong."

"Women know these things."

"You're wrong." Ray looks up at her. "Your daughter is fighting to come back to us. Can't you think of something to say to *her?* I'll leave you alone," Ray says, getting up, looking at her once, still perched in her chair.

Hannah is pacing, still on the phone with Pej. Coming down the hospital corridor is Lou carrying lattes and croissants from his coffeehouse.

"Hey man," Lou says, firmly gripping Ray's shoulder. "This is for you. Please eat something for us all, man. You're wasting away to nothin'." He puts the bag in his hand.

"Thanks, man. Ruby's mom is in there with her. Alone, probably shaking in her boots. Don't know what to do with her. Ruby needs her. You know? And she's on some other planet."

"Hey. I'm watching your six, man," Lou says, pats him on the shoulder, and walks toward Ruby's door.

"Doc," Jeannie says, looking up at him with girl-eyed wonder. "You've come to bust our scene?"

"Not at all, not at all," Dr. Ambaji says with almost an English accent, boyishly blushing, hugging the clipboard to his chest. He recognizes Jeannie, so every time he sees her he is knocked slightly off kilter, and she knows it. He is wearing street clothes with a white doctor's coat hanging over it. He pushes up his spectacles.

Wanda massages Ruby's right foot, while Jeannie massages Ruby's left, and Ray lifts her head, talking to her the whole time. They are breathing in unison.

"You must know something about this yoga breathing, huh, Doc?" Jeannie asks flirtatiously. Wanda glares at her briefly.

"No, I don't, actually," Dr. Ambaji says, stiffening a bit, finally putting on professional posture.

"I think it's encouraging that she breathes from her solar plexus rather than her chest, don't you, Doc?" Jeannie asks. Ray is close to kicking her out of the room, since she is high on coke.

"Well, we continue to be encouraged because her lower brain stem is still functioning, as she can breathe by herself. She coughs, yawns, blinks, and roves her eyes. However, I must remind you that she could continue like this *indefinitely*," he emphasizes this last word, looking over his glasses at them. He clears his throat and lifts his toes.

Ray touches Ruby's throat. He tries blocking out the doctor's presence, creates a tunnel of communication from his head to hers.

"When are you off?" Jeannie asks, taking even more time with her fingers between Ruby's toes. She is wearing a tight new orange velour sweater. She breathes in deeply, turns around with her big leopard eyes to stare him down.

"Soon, actually," Dr. Ambaji says.

Wanda looks at Ray, who returns the look, *Good riddance.*

"Let me take you to dinner, then," Jeannie says, pushing her thumbs into Ruby's arch with expert deftness.

"Well . . ."

"You can't say no, you can only say that it's you that will be taking me since this is your hometown," Jeannie says, turning around to face him again, cradling Ruby's ankle with one hand and brushing her heel off with the other.

"I have two more patients to visit—"

"I'm from Missouri, the Show-me State, so I want you to show it to me," Jeannie interrupts, caressing Ruby's toes.

"Can you meet me at the elevator in twenty minutes?" Dr. Ambaji says, aiming to leave the room before any of them can detect his inner blushing, causing the tiniest of beads of sweat.

"Of course I can," Jeannie says, giggling in rings as she glances warmly at Wanda.

Dr. Ambaji exits quickly, Ray stares Jeannie down.

"Why don't you go freshen up," Ray says with a short tone.

"Okay, I will," Jeannie says breathily. She stands, shakes her head, looks down at Ruby for a moment, then cups her mouth.

If Ray were thinking about the short space of time in which Jeannie lost the dogs she adored, the man she loved, and the friend she counted on, then he would have more patience for her. The fact that she dropped everything, leaving the restaurant in the hands of a doubtfully qualified assistant, should count for something. But he can't think of this now. And Wanda is his backup in justifiable irritation, since Jeannie fell into her husband's arms. Neither of them knows what Ruby sees in Jeannie. Neither does Jeannie know at this time. She is just as lost as everyone else, and no more than anyone else, really.

"Can I get you two anything?" Jeannie asks, folding her arms across her chest. She isn't wearing any eyeliner, her lipstick is chewed off, but her powder foundation seems fresh. She is invigorated without understanding why. The energy among Ray, Wanda, Ruby, and herself still flows through her veins.

"See you later," Wanda says. "Have a good dinner."

"Okay, then. Ray. Please call me," Jeannie says without finishing her sentence. He understands this to mean that he is to report on any change.

"Are you in pain?" Ray asks Ruby, as Jeannie walks out of the room. Wanda watches Ruby's jaw and neck muscles for any sign.

"Do you want to come out?" Ray asks, his voice shaking.

"No, Ray, ask her only when you mean what you're asking," Wanda says, now rubbing Ruby's calf.

"We want to see those beautiful eyes, so very badly," Ray says in a strange singsong, mezzo-soprano then bass. He touches her lids, then the space between them.

"Put your lips on her head, Ray," Wanda says, scooting her chair up to the middle of the bed. "There is fine, but even better on her third eye," she says, gripping his shoulder once, as he gently lays his lips between her eyes.

"Hear me, my love," Ray whispers.

"Just hum right there," Wanda says, taking Ruby's wrist in her hand.

Ray hums, but he moves around as he does it, letting his lips caress her face. Jason walks in with Gary's food from the restaurant. He slows down on tiptoe as he grasps the scene. Ray keeps humming, Wanda presses her wrist while inhaling, then releases the pressure as she breathes out.

"Well," Jason says, putting his food down. He bumps his hip to one side, "Chica-boom, chica-boom," he bumps closer into the bed. Ruby turns her head slightly toward him, Ray feels it and drools.

"Chica-boom, chica-boom, chica-boom, boom, boom," Jason sings, Ruby's cheek twitches.

"Move your hand to her chest, Ray. Now press down," Wanda barks like a coach.

"Keep singing," Ray says to Jason.

"Chica-boom, chica-boom, chica-boom, boom, boom," he says, getting into it now, then he spins, moving his hands over his head, then bringing them down on Ruby's bed. She jerks her head to the side, Ray stops pressing, though afraid to feel much hope as this has happened before.

"Keep pressing, baby!" Wanda says.

"Chica, chica, boom," Jason sings but is interrupted by a loud thrash of a voice. Ray screams, and Wanda stands up, still holding her wrist.

"Oooooh!" Ruby wails. "Oh, goooo-d," she says, though it's not clear if she's saying "God" or "good." Jason now screams too, and the nurses come running toward the sound of pealing laughter and squeals.

Chapter 22

The Square Paintings

Ruby

It was never the physical part of rehab getting her down. When Ray coached her not to try bringing only her left side back to par but to shoot for ambidexterity, she was voraciously up for the challenge. What was hoped of her coordination in three months, she succeeded in half of that time.

She forgave herself the initial disorientation, the extreme nausea on the plane from Florida to L.A. as Ray rushed her to the bathroom to puke. She couldn't give him enough warning twice after that, making a smelly mess of her clothes, but that was all right too. She could live with the hormone treatments for the threat of myxedema, and the ill metallic taste on her tongue. Already the dry swelling of her skin has left with the weight gain and sluggishness. Her constipation lessens, her urination slow but subtly improving. The irregularity of her periods worries her little since she can't remember or keep record of when they are happening.

But these are her primary sources of severe agitation: the short-term memory impairment, the attention, the concentration problems, the utter lack of organizational skills. It is a chore to get dressed. She has to force herself to smile. Politesse and pleasantries are props she'd rather ignore. She can feel her head overload with thought, and she can hear it grind.

"Tell me your soul hasn't been robbed," Hannah says dramatically to Ruby one April day, two months after the accident, back in her little old treehouse on Jeannie's forest-wild land.

"Your soul hasn't been robbed," Ruby says deadpan. Hannah's eyes bug. "Just kidding," Ruby says, but neither of them laughs.

"I think you let Ray do too much for you," Hannah says. Ruby's eyes go vacant. "This is the farthest I've ever seen him from you, and he's barely two yards away, gardening! Doesn't Jeannie *have* gardeners? How'd you let her wrap you up again in her clutches? It makes no sense at all!" Hannah says, not able to control herself.

"Dinner was good last night," Ruby says, running her hand through her hair cut three inches long to better match the lesser growth over the surgical wound.

"'Dinner was good last night.' Are you listening to me?" Hannah says, gently tipping Ruby's chin so she will look her in the eye.

"I don't understand how you guys came to pick this program in Pasadena. It's not like your insurance hasn't been covering everything. It's even cheaper than this High Hopes place in Tustin, of which I hear nothing but good things, so how could it possibly be better? It's not too late to change, Ruby. You haven't had your first day yet, we can still make the switch."

"I like the bottles hanging from the wall," Ruby says, looking up at the ceiling.

"What bottles?" Hannah asks, exasperated.

"The bottles at the restaurant."

"Jeannie's restaurant?"

"Miss Ellie's. See? I remembered the name," Ruby says in something close to excitement.

"Never heard of a Miss Ellie's. Since when is there soul food in Hollywood?" Hannah feels for the catch of her thin gold chain, holds the small diamonded cross in one hand, returning the catch to the back of her perfect neck.

"We had tomato sauce on strings," Ruby says.

"Oh yeah, that's right, Ray mentioned you went to Miccelli's. *Mi-che-lees*. Don't know why you went there, the food is terrible," Hannah says, sticking out her rose petal tongue, making a double chin. "Mi-che-lees," Hannah says again, hoping she'll repeat.

"The lady is nice. I like the colors. They don't hurt my head," Ruby says.

"I was gonna say about these paintings," Hannah says, turning in her chair looking behind her on the walls. "The one over the tub is especially beautiful. It's good to see you creating. I like the smell of oils. Has Mom seen these? I know she'd love to have one, all that white so perfect for their place." Palm over knuckles over the back of her chair, Hannah rests her chin, while still in spinal twist. "What's with all the white, anyway? You let the reds come through just a little bit, but all of these paintings, even the blue and greenish ones—which used to be your favorite colors, by the way—are covered with white. You used to be such a color freak. Your cartoons just *popped*. I like here where you let the red show." Hannah stands up to point at it. "Like this one that seems to be tinted baby pink. They're all square too, I hadn't noticed before."

"The traffic is *ter-ri-ble*," Ruby says puckering, then wiggling her well-formed ears like a clown.

"Yeah," Hannah says, screwing her brows, trying to be patient. "But I was talking about the paintings. Who gave you this beautiful easel?" Hannah touches it lovingly.

"The neighbor," Ruby says.

"Which neighbor?"

"Our neighbor in Florida," Ray says, standing in the now open doorway, bringing in the smell of magnolia, mixing with the oils and turpentine. As he comes closer they get a whiff of his strong funky must, his fingers and pants covered with fresh, dark soil. His arms scratched from bougainvillea.

"'The traffic is *ter-ri-ble*,' he keeps saying," Ruby says, pointing to Ray. She burps, but doesn't think to cover her mouth, or say, "Excuse me." He comes over, puts his arms around her neck, bends over to kiss and munch on her ear.

"We were stuck on Hollywood and . . . what is it near all that skank swank they close off for premieres every day?" Ray says, picking under his nails. Hannah watches, grossing out; Ruby stares at her blankly.

"Highland," Hannah says with slight disgust. She sits back down in her chair.

"'I love this dry air,' he keeps saying." Ruby pushes Ray out of her view of Hannah.

"I do love this air. Feels good on my skin. It's so sticky in Florida, you know, gets to the point where you feel like you're drowning in heat."

"About the neighbor, you were saying," Hannah says, irritated.

"Anyway, about the neighbor—we had this bitchy neighbor named Hope, who had this nasty cat who was always hanging in our backyard. She and Ruby had a tiff over it. But when we came back from the hospital, and she saw me coming and going, packing up things, she asked what had happened. I didn't give her many details, but she ended up telling me about her husband who'd died of a heart attack and had been . . ." Ray clears his throat and sits down on the floor at Ruby's feet. He puts his arm over her thigh. He swallows hard. "Her husband was in a coma for a week. And, well, once he was pronounced brain-dead, she pulled the plug." He breathes in, exhales loudly. "Anyway, she paints, and her grand-kids gave her this French travel easel and paint set long ago, but she'd never used it. So she wrapped it up and left it on our doorstep with a really nice note. She left some canvases too. Four or five of them, they were all square, and Ruby really dug them. So since we've been here, we buy nothing but square canvases."

"There's a cat here too," Ruby says, licking her lips. She bats her eyes theatrically as if there were contacts bothering them.

"Did Dad call you?" Hannah asks Ray.

"He left a message."

"Well I wish you'd call him back. We're all concerned about this program you picked in Pasadena. I couldn't really find all that much about it on the net. How'd you even hear about it?"

"Jeannie's boyfriend—"

"*Jeannie's boyfriend?* Jesus *fucking* Christ," Hannah interrupts, gritting her teeth.

"Now hold on there, just a minute," Ray says, flaring his nostrils.

"Jeannie's boyfriend is a dumbass surfer from Malibu High—"

"He's twenty-two, Hannah, he's long out of high school—" Ray cuts in, and she interrupts him again.

"Okay, a twenty-two-year-old, Malibu band dropout loser little punkass fuck," Hannah says.

"Punkass fuck," Ruby repeats. She tilts her head from side to side, her mouth open, looking mentally challenged. In imitation of

Ray, she loudly cracks her neck. Hannah looks at her in shock, then recovers, still angry with Ray.

"And *this* is who you listen to for Ruby's *life?*" Hannah says, the sound swirl-firing from the back of her throat.

"Let me finish one goddamn word, would you?" Ray snarls, his cheeks flushed almost a sickly orange. "I searched the net for every program across the nation, across the world, for that matter. I came up with a great one in New York, there was even a good one in Florida. There were two in L.A., and that's why we're here, so Ruby could be near all you guys. And then we met Jeannie's boyfriend, who happens to be the son—"

"of a *bitch*," Hannah interjects.

"Look Hannah, if it's anyone who's a bad influence on Ruby, then it's you right now, cursing and carrying on. Particularly while Ruby uses repetition. So either you shut the fuck up, *now*, or you leave, and we pick up on this conversation at another time when you can control yourself," Ray says, standing up, his hand on the doorknob.

"Shut the fuck up," Ruby says, resembling a gargoyle as she flares her nostrils the way she saw Ray did and bugging her eyes like Hannah.

"I can't deal with this right now," Hannah says, standing up, hugging her teeth with her lips. She folds her arms over her chest, looks at the floor beneath the red claw tub. "Ruby," she leans over and kisses her on the cheek. Ruby closes her eyes so Hannah's hair doesn't get in them. "I'll be by tomorrow. Will you call me tonight if you need anything?"

"Ray can call," Ruby says, lets her hand fall on her thigh to make a slapping sound on the nylon of her skate pants. She looks up at Hannah like she doesn't care, but her outward expressions still resemble little of what goes on inside.

Ray lets the door close loudly. He hisses, puts his hands on his hips looking girlishly awkward, his curls lank with sweat so they look like marcel waves.

"I'm not stupid," Ruby says, standing up, her left side held lower though she doesn't limp, she drags.

"I know you're not stupid, my love," Ray says, taking her in his arms.

"Hannah thinks I'm stupid," Ruby says into his chest.

"No she does not," he says, kissing the top of her head, breathing in the lavender scent left from the shampoo he used on her this morning.

"Let's go drive," Ruby says, looking up into his face. She searches his eyes that are so full of love; still she thinks she could be anyone, as she can't be sure who the hell she really is.

Down under the bridge of the Santa Monica Pier, Ruby pushes off the skateboard with her wobbly left leg, her heart palpitating at the sudden dark. She hasn't entered the likeness of a tunnel since the images playing during her coma, so the picture, the feeling, scares her, instead of warming her the way a womb would do, the way her brain had meant it. Ray hasn't skated since he was twelve, so he is slow to help before the fall. She skids on her knee, but it is no big deal, the sturdy cotton and synthetic blend of her pants breaks the burn of the asphalt.

"Get back on," Ruby commands.

"You all right, baby?"

"Get back on," she says, looking mean. She drops the board from high so it bounces on its wheels, and she jumps on as if she's skated her whole life.

"That's my girl, that's my girl," Ray calls out to her way in front of him. "Leave me in the dust!" He laughs, his legs and feet so long on the longboard that all of him looks like a comic book come to life.

Her cheeks smart against the cool, sharp breeze as she makes her way both through and past baby strollers, bladers, walkers, crossers, and sand cutting her speed. Awkward though her stance might be, she finds a delicate balance, a grace in her latent atrophy, a stately, sateen fluidity reflecting the tricky temperament of the ocean. The water appears to be a navy gray against the index card blue of the sky. Her peripheral vision molted, her visuospatial sense a funhouse mirror, the volleyball nets and the sea on opposite sides connect in cursive ceilings over her head.

"This is Venice, baby!" Ray calls out where they can make the choice to join the street vendors, or stay on path winding closer to the water through the sand. "Show it to me!" Ray says, catching up to her, hopping off his board, hoping she will do the same. She lets her board slide off and bang loudly against a garbage can. Ray picks it up, so she grabs his, cuddling it under her arm, as she sees him do hers.

"Ruby!" She hears her name but can't figure where it comes from. "Over here!" She turns her head toward the comedian who poorly imitates her lost look for a crowd of five fast losing interest.

"Fuck you, asshole," Ray says to the mime.

"Hey, how are you?" Joop appears in front of her, looking back first at the comedian, then ecstatically throwing his arms around her neck. Ruby stands there perfectly distant and erect. "You cut your hair," he says, touching the top of her head, patting then grazing with his palm the soft, tight curls springing here and every which way. She looks at him vacantly, and he inches back as if reacting to static cling. Ray moves in, his muzzle protruding like a caveman. "You're finally back! I can't believe it. I'm *never* down here, and now I run into you. Why haven't you called me?" Joop says, maintaining immunity to the red light in Ray's eyes.

Ruby clears her throat, looks back at Ray.

"Jupiter," Ray says, finally recognizing, shaking his head. Joop now looks aghast.

"This is my kin, doll," Ruby says, assuming she is to introduce Ray, as her mother re-rehearsed manners with her since the accident. Joop's face expresses confusion; Ray shakes his head.

"She means 'Ken doll,'" Ray says, squeezing Ruby to him. "You know Jeannie, right? She has this boyfriend she calls her Ken doll." But neither Jeannie's boyfriend nor Ray looks anything like Ken.

"Oh," Joop says, his lower jaw stiff with dismay.

"I had a accident," Ruby says. She nods, her eyes as liquid and hot as bourbon, her demeanor as if she'd drank it. "In Florida, here with Ray," she says.

"A little over two months ago," Ray says. "She's incredible, you wouldn't *believe* all she's come through in such an incredible, incredibly short length of time," he says putting the boards down on the ground. Joop remains in a trance of utter bewilderment. He touches his temple, leans his head back, his thick wheat-colored hair as massive as a wig.

"What kind of accident, Rube?" he asks finally.

"I broke open my head in a *dive*," she says, the last word as if said to the snap of a beatnik.

"She was in a coma for nine days," Ray says, now getting uncomfortable and impatient. Joop backs up a little, bumping into an older woman who is rudely staring at Ruby, then at Ray and Joop and back again. Joop doesn't turn around, so the woman scowls.

"Excuse you," she snarls at Joop, who still won't budge.

"Go back to New York," Ray says. Ruby smiles blankly. "God, I hated season. Fucking New Yorkers bring New York with them to Florida, and I see they bring their hell on here too."

"Yeah," Joop says, without knowing exactly what he agrees with. "I was born here, what do I know?" He shrugs, puts his hands in his pockets.

"I'm not from New York, you prick!" the woman calls back, her sisterly companion grabbing her arm tightly.

"Then she's from Jersey," Ray says, cocking his head to the side, cracking a wicked grin at Joop.

"Hey, nice, *nice*," Joop says in a dramatically sarcastic voice. "Always fun, fun, fun with the tourists in Venice."

Ruby keeps a plastic splash of interest over her face.

"I was gonna say I'm here with my cousins. My dad's side," Joop says, looking at Ruby, as if she should know the depth of his meaning.

"Where are they from?" Ray asks.

"My dad's English, but he died before I turned four. I never really knew him anyway. But my mother doesn't live all that far from here. I guess you'd say she's on the border of here and Culver City."

Ray shrugs.

"You can join us if you'd like," Joop says, looking at Ruby.

"We can't," Ray says. "We're on our way back home."

"Will you call me, Rube?" Joop says, coming closer as if a warmer proximity would get through to her brain. His eyes plead, Ruby looks right into them at her own reflection. Ray represses the urge to bruise his thin, translucent, unblemished skin. "We should go skate." His thumb up, he backs away, beginning to bounce, buoyed by freedom.

"He must have wanted his teeth pushed in, getting that close to you," Ray says reddening.

"Why did you call him a star?"

"A *star?*"

"Who is he?"

"A planet, you mean. Jupiter. Joop. Remember the pictures of you skating with that wispy asshole?"

"Yeah," Ruby says, smiling almost like herself. "He's not asshole."

"Fine, he's not *an* asshole. He's okay."

She walks past the incense vendor, the pungent smoke overpowering her balance.

"You okay?" Ray asks, holding onto her.

"I will be."

"Happy Birthday to you, Happy Birthday to you, Happy Birthday dear Ruby, Happy Birthday to you! And many more!" Jeannie sings a year after the killings, holding a small pumpkin-flavored cake with white icing. Behind her, three waiters and two busboys keen on kissing her ass. It's lunchtime at her restaurant, R & R's in Studio City. The walls are glossy beige with large colorful serial paintings of targets and hearts à la Billy Al Bengston. All tables are filled, the hostess, tall, haughty, and furrowed, has a telephone at her ear.

"So sorry," a waiter says to Ray after pouring the water too hurriedly into his glass. "Just let me get a rag," he says.

"No worries," Ray says, holding up his hand. "I know you're in the weeds, man." He wipes it up himself with the cloth napkin.

"He doesn't know what you mean," Jeannie says, laughing, turning to watch him run off. She licks her thumb of frosting. "This is his first restaurant job. But I was a waitress in my day, I know how to handle the rush." She nods proudly, holds her hand up for Ray to slap five. Her boyfriend, Dean, leans back in a baggy striped T and designer torn jeans. He sips his beer out of a mug, the premature crow's feet pronouncing his narrow Clint Eastwood eyes.

"How'd you ever make the restaurant this popular so quick?" Ray asks, taking the plate Jeannie has just put a piece of cake on, and putting it squarely in front of Ruby, who appears serene or depressed, depending upon the angle.

"These studio folk gotta have somewhere truly delicious and gourmet to eat," Jeannie says, hand on hip before she continues cutting the cake.

"There are plenty decent places to eat over here, babe," her boyfriend Dean says, sassily jiggling his head. He downs the mug to the foam, takes a plate of cake from her hand. She squints her eyes meanly at him, then melts with a young girl's smile.

"Not as good as this one," she says, looking at Ruby for backup, but then Jeannie's face cracks as she remembers Ruby's core now seems apathetic. "Okay, the real reason. I haven't told too many people about this, but they're doing an *E! True Hollywood Story* on me." Dean shakes his head; Ray slacks into half a grin. "The commercials started running yesterday, but people have been crowding in for the past couple weeks. I'm not participating in any way," she says, jerking her head, looking the other direction as if turning away from gore. "And I'm not talking to Fawn anymore when I found out that she is." Jeannie looks at Ruby again, hoping for the slim possibility that she will get the depth of the drama. Ruby turns to look at her, chews on her cake, her expression confounded, as if she can't make out the taste.

"Fawn is a deer," Ruby says.

"She's a cunt as far as I'm concerned," Jeannie says, looking insulted.

"She means that a *fawn is a deer*, not that Fawn is dear," Ray says, opening his eyes wide at Jeannie as if Jeannie were a kinder-gartener. "We're having trouble with homonyms," Ray says, proudly. "But we're gonna get through it."

"Homonyms, wow," Dean says. "A blast from the past. What does it mean again?" Jeannie flips her hand, not wanting to drag out the embarrassment. "No, really, I can't remember these kind of things. Dude, you must be a grammar whiz," Dean says, opening his mouth to purposefully show his clucking tongue.

"Cunt," Ruby says at her plate. Then she looks up. "Malibu High, right?" Ruby says. Dean nods. "I remember," Ruby says, flaring her nostrils, trying to feel accomplished.

"Where did you go again?" he asks.

"Uni High," Ruby says. "My sister Hannah went to Beverly."

"Beverly," Dean says, nodding his head to an imaginary backbeat. "Fuck, I don't know which has the snobbier bitches, Malibu or Beverly, but I can tell you where they're more fine," he says, jiggling his head again with his mouth open for emphasis. He looks Ruby in the eye, igniting Ray's green half.

"I went with Jeannie to your house?" Ruby asks, her expression dry but inside her head working hard to connect the dots.

"That was Jake's house," Jeannie says, getting excited. "You remember that?"

"Yeah," Ruby says nodding. "Yeah," she says softer this time.

"My parents live in Point Dume," Dean says.

"Point Doom, Point Doom," Ruby says, looking haunted.

"You told me about that beach, baby, you love it there. You said you were gonna show me," Ray says.

"Ruby loves Point Dume. I forgot about that," Jeannie says, nodding, looking at Dean.

"Well listen, next time they're out of town, which is often, I'll lend you the keys," Dean says, folding his arms over his washboard belly.

"Only if your parents are cool with it, man," Ray says.

"It's cool, dude. They rather someone was there. Since I moved out of the house they get all frazzed looking for housesitters. Really, man. You'd be doing them a favor."

"That'll be a long-ass haul from there to class in Pasadena," Jeannie says, biting her bottom lip, looking at Ray with discouragement.

"Long ass," Ruby repeats. Dean laughs.

"That's what wheels are for. Who the fuck cares how far it is? Right, man? You need to see the *whole* town. She take you to Silverlake or Echo Park yet?"

"Echo," Ruby says. "Echo," she repeats. "Echo, echo, echo," she singsongs. Ray squeezes her hand.

"So what are you planning on doing tonight for your birthday?" Jeannie asks, finishing up the last of her cake, putting the fork down loudly on her plate. She licks her lips and the top of her front teeth, her tongue rests at the top of her gums for seconds long enough to hold Ruby's eye.

"We're going to Ruby's parents' house for dinner," Ray says.

"Now that sounds like a bore," Dean says, snatching at his balls. "I'll have another beer," he says without looking up at the waiter. "Why don't you go out somewhere?" Dean asks, opening his hand to Ray in a way similar to Al. Ruby notices. "Think of all the places you used to like to go to, Ruby. Would be good for you. You can't be having a swinging good time at the folks' place, can you?"

"You're such a brat," Jeannie says, pushing away from the table to get up.

"Army," Ruby says. Jeannie nods, looks at her blankly, then walks away toward the kitchen, swishing her backside full pendulum.

Ray lovingly caresses Ruby's earlobe, touches the hair at her temple. Dean looks at her with admiration. "Lou was an army brat," Ruby says to her lap. "'Great Santini,' he used to say about his father."

"Who's Lou, birthday girl?" Dean asks, not quite patronizingly but more like a student who volunteers his time at a home. Ray looks ready to pounce on him.

"Lou is Wanda's husband. He talks about interesting things," Ruby says, sitting back in her seat.

"No danger of that happening here," Ray says to Dean.

He holds up his hand, then leans dramatically toward him and Ruby. "Anyone notice who we're really tiptoeing around here? Jeannie could totally *lose* it any minute. Did you know that scumbag's been saying that he was forced into false confession? That he didn't even *know* the guy who did it? The one he *hired* to do the deed?"

"Why did you drop out of the band?" Ruby asks. Dean points his finger at her as if she were a naughty girl.

"Oh, you're good. You're good. You're gonna be out of that place in *no* time," Dean says, snaps his finger, leans back in his seat. "Yeah. Argument over copyright. But I really did write that song, I was suckered into letting him take first credit. So I quit."

Ray yawns, stretches, tries catching the waiter's eye for the check.

"Jeannie tell you I said, 'I don't know him,' or something?" Dean asks, squinching his eyes.

Ruby nods.

"Can we have the check?" Ray asks. Dean's face splits into the You're-a-fool expression.

"This is on Jeannie," Dean says. "You think she'd let you pay?" Ray folds his arms. "I like what you're doing to the garden, dude. You know I cook a little myself, and it's nice having the herbs right there. Heard you have a *mag* place in Florida. Anybody staying there?"

"Renting it out," Ray says. "You ready?" he asks Ruby.

"Too bad, man. I'd say it'd be sweet to trade. You know, Jeannie and I stay out there, and you and Ruby stay in the main house. That'd be cool."

"You couldn't take Jeannie away from this restaurant," Ruby says, looking Dean in the eye.

"And I'd have to say I'd miss the pleasure of watching you swim every morning," Dean says. He breathes in deeply.

"Maybe I'll have to take the pleasure of sticking my foot up your ass," Ray says.

"It's cool. Can't blame a guy for looking. She's a beauty." Dean shakes his head to Ray. "And you've got no worries, my friend, about this place. Dude hanging out on the wave, nuts on a wing, board smacks his skull open. Took fifty metal plates to put his face back together. He had *zero* memory, dude. Zero. Couldn't read a page, couldn't hardly see shit. But my father knew the chick who opened A to Zeal, man. They get government grants as well as private funding since it's a center for research. Chick churns out the folks with their heads screwed back on straight. I'm *telling* you. *All* kinds of people. Not everybody's necessarily paying either, so there's all kinds of people with different backgrounds, different races, whatever. A percentage of every class is on scholarship or donation. It's still ritzy though, dude, don't make mistake."

"I know, we checked it out."

"Zam?" Dean holds up his hand for five. Ray looks at him. "Am I right?"

"Zam," Ruby says, her eyes glassy.

"Dude," Dean says, shaking his head, "you gotta watch her. She drives the men crazy, I'm telling you." Both hands go up in exaggerated surrender. Jeannie returns to the table.

"Jeannie? Dude's over here trying to pick up the check. What do you say to that, babe?"

Jeannie puts her hands on Dean's neck, massages the knots on the back of his head.

"Get on out of here, guys," Jeannie says. "I'll see you at home." She leans to kiss Ruby on the cheek, her face melting into disappointment when Ruby doesn't return it. She looks at Ray like she'll never get used to this change. Dean shakes Ray's reluctant hand.

It's Sunday after six, and the clouds are having a seat behind the mountains. Ray and Ruby leave the main house, the view of the canyon and the city, the big-screen TV, Jeannie and Dean who are sitting on the couch in a daze. Ray doesn't know that he leads Ruby down the path in the same way that Caspar did, particularly that night when the palm reader wanted to walk her home. Ruby doesn't really want Ray to find them another place to live, though he is actively looking. Rehab in Pasadena doesn't start for another week, and all Ruby wants is the time to clean all the slush from her brain.

She sets herself up to paint, she thinks, but Ray has gone behind her in correction of the details. He opens the Grumtine, the linseed oil, helps her into one of her paint-streaked overshirts. She sits at the easel, the square canvas in front of her. There are orderly lines of green and yellow already there, but then they converge into a rubbery form of menace. Ray stands at the door, watching her with concern. She holds the tube of white paint, looks up at him, then flicks her index finger off her nose, their new signal for *I'm okay*. He walks out, and Ruby stares at the canvas. She feels the lines that are dashes, but the dashes are circles. Almost. No, they really are disconnected lines. She puts down the white tube, and picks up the black. She could cover all mistakes with it. The white only fades the color. The black can completely wipe it all up. But what is the problem in the painting? A lack of guidance, a misread of nature, a misunderstanding of the soul? Is it youth or is it age that stands in her way? Is it order or chaos? Has she found an abyss, or does Ray holding onto her keep her from discovering the unknown? Is this the education she was meant for? She never gave herself wholly to anything—not frustration, not depression, not joy, not life. Here in the problem of her square, she searches for form and disobedience. But she can't have both at once. She can't be full in war, she can't be struggling in peace. And now what is *that* annoying sound? She looks at the small silver stepladder sitting next to her. "He thinks of everything," she says out loud, as she picks up her phone which is on top of it.

"Hey!" Abbie says.

"Hello," Ruby says properly. "Who's calling please? Ray is outside gardening."

"It's Abbie!" she squeals like a teen. "I'm not calling for *Ray*. This is *your* phone. Hey girl, how come you ignored like three postcards from me?" she says in California accent.

"I broke open my head in a *dive*," she says.

"I know, but that's no excuse! Right?" Abbie says loudly. Ruby laughs, a milestone after continuously forcing herself to smile. She holds the phone with both hands, trying to cradle it. She gets pink paint all over her nose, ear, and receiver. "You could pick up the phone and call me. You could pick up a pen and write me. Right?"

"Okay, okay. I'll write, I'll write," Ruby says.

"All right."

"I'll write," she repeats flatly.

Abbie laughs again. "Ray told me everything, honey. But listen, everything doesn't have to be so dumbed down for you. You hear me?" Abbie says.

"I hear you."

"This might be in a pickle, but you don't have to eat it. Write down what's in your head. Come on. Describe it, figure out what you're *feeling*. Really. Inertia."

"I can't move sometimes."

"Okay? That's it, right? You're not moving. You're not feeling it. But you are. So write this state down. Okay?"

"I'll write."

"You're around too many blondes. I saw that *E! True Hollywood Story*, by the way. Whoah baby are you ever in the thick of some crazy shit!" Abbie says.

"A lot of blondes," Ruby says.

"Too many blondes, Ruby." Abbie cackles, the sound of her voice reverberating with warmth like tea in the belly on a cold day.

"Got nothing against blonds," Ruby says suddenly.

"Right?" Abbie asks rhetorically, still laughing.

"Ray's a blond," Ruby says. Abbie keeps laughing.

"But seriously. Do you remember Al? Wow. I mean that's *so* scary. *Ruby*. What are you and Ray doing there?" Ruby tightens up.

"I watched it. Just a while ago. But I don't really remember Al. I can't picture him. It's weird what I remember—at times, things from childhood come into sharp focus. But then it's like, water, or something, flooding my head. Too much information, and then I go blank."

"I understand what you're saying. You know, one of my eyes now is totally dead." Abbie pauses for reaction, but Ruby remains silent. "But the other one—you remember taking me to the ophthalmologist's office for the laser treatments?"

"Fairbanks."

"Fairbanks! Yes! And, anyway, the other eye has revitalized. It's compensating, you know, for the dead one. It can see like an eagle."

"'I love watching the hawks riding the thermals,' Ray's always saying."

"Stay with me, Ruby. It can see like an eagle. But since my other eye is dead, I was so depressed, you know. I was in bed for weeks on end. Or I was when it was dark most of the day. Now it's spring, and the light is magnificent. But it's not like that darkness is so far away for me. I was feeling like I deserved to feel like that. To be so low, I must deserve it, you know? Everyone else has that sense of entitlement, to me, it seemed. You know? Something I never had. But now I just want to take up the space I was meant to take up. Right?"

"Take it up, all over the place," Ruby says, wanting to wink at her. She hears Abbie light up a cigarette, and she can smell her brand, different from Ray's.

"I saw this Agnes Martin book, and I thought of you. Calm and order to the storm."

"Did I tell you I was painting?"

"Ray did. He described what the paintings look like. I'm gonna send the book to you. Okay?"

"Good."

"Yes, good. I miss you, you know?" Abbie says.

"Come to L.A.," Ruby says.

"When?"

"Now."

"Fuck it. I may as well, right?"

"Fuck it."

"I'm gonna call you back in a couple days, okay? I'm gonna see what I can arrange."

"Good."

"Bye," Abbie says.

"Bye," Ruby says, and clicks it. She looks at the phone, then can't remember what she was doing, though the painting is right in front of her. Ray bursts back in through the door.

"Holy cow, I found a banana slug. First time I saw one was working on the cabins with George in Healy. Come on out and see it, baby. Hurry before it's totally dark."

"Banana slugs, banana slugs . . . what is that?" Ruby says, reconstructing synapses.

"Come see him. He's beautiful," Ray says, near giggling. He takes her by the hand.

"Abbie just called," Ruby says.

"Oh yeah," he says, giddily pulling her along until they reach the edge of the property.

"That was our mask!" Ruby declares, staring at the long, fat yellow creature tackling his way through the compost of the forest floor, his back untwining in subtly spotted humps. "That was our luck!"

"What do you mean, baby?"

"UC Santa Cruz. We had no football team, no frats or sorori-ties. We had no grades! And that was our name, the Banana Slugs."

"Your mascot," Ray says, bending his knees to look in her eyes.

"Mascot, that's it. An ascot is a tie," she says, nodding, puck-ering her lips as if she might whistle.

"You were some serious treehuggers," Ray says, smiling wide. "Can't imagine a school without grades."

"Ireland," Ruby says.

"I don't want to hear about her," he says, shaking his head, teasing her she thinks.

"Hard to think clearly about anyone else. You're the only one here. You must be lonely."

"Lonely?" Ray says, grabbing both of her shoulders.

"I'm not the same person. I'm all need. How can you stand it?"

"I was born to be with you, born to see you through everything. I love you."

Ruby looks him in the eyes, still trying to find herself, instead of looking into who he is. Still she has the best excuse for self-centeredness. Survival. And she doesn't know yet that there's an even more natural place to hang her hat.

Chapter 23

Ladies of the Canyon

Ray

Jeannie appears at the guesthouse screen as Ray browns the ground turkey meat in onion, garlic, pepper, and paprika. He looks up, waves, surprised to feel a growing appreciation for her. The olive oil softly spits and crackles, calling Ray's attention back to the pan as Ruby, clad in pin-striped overalls and a navy sports bra, throws open the door, gives Jeannie an oblique smile.

"Wow, I never noticed how the passion fruit vine has really taken over that tree out there," Jeannie says, pretty in her tight but simple yellow cotton dress. She holds a proper accordion file holder, and stands there awkwardly in the middle of the small room. Ray's small ass wiggles as he stirs the meat on the fire. Ruby sits on the chair beneath the largest painting—a picture bringing to mind a pigeon's tracks in the snow.

"Did you notice the wisteria down here? It's killing what must have been a Japanese cherry blossom tree; it's near death," Ray says.

"Oh yeah?" Jeannie nods, looks at Ruby who is staring at her.

"Homicidal vine," Ray laughs, then looks at her a bit paranoid. "Well, it's suicidal too, 'cause when that tree dies so will it."

"I've had that wisteria up on the front fence for years. I love how it spills out onto the veranda," Jeannie says.

"The fence is fine, it's just the trees they'll choke out. They could pull down a house."

Jeannie looks at Ruby again, who stares so long her expression appears lurid. "Why's your face so oily, baby?" Jeannie asks.

"Sweating," Ruby says. Protectively, Ray turns to look at her.

"Oh. When she stopped taking those hormones her skin really dried up, so I washed it this morning with that nice scrub you gave me, gave her a clay mask, then used the blue astringent, and the night cream, rather than the day, because it seemed thicker," Ray says, with the confidence of a spa professional.

"I'm sweating," Ruby says.

"Just use the day cream on her in the morning and at night," Jeannie says. "I don't think she needs any more than that." She hugs the folder to her belly, bites the inside of her cheek. "Table looks nice in here," she says, nodding at it.

"Are you hungry? Making tacos," Ray says cheerfully. He wipes his hand on his stained work pants, clangs open a drawer, wrestles around for a can opener.

"Oh, no thanks," she says uncharacteristically shy.

"You and Dean going somewhere tonight?" Ray asks. "If not we'd love to have you both for dinner," he says, now pulling cheddar cheese out of the fridge.

Looking as if she might fall backward, Jeannie makes a hairpin turn with her stacked cork heel. "Oh no, I'm going to the restaurant. Dean's gone every day at the crack of dawn," she says, bug-eyed. "Sometimes he stays out there all evening with his surf buddies."

"Oh yeah?" Ray says, feeling irked with him again. "Wonder when it is he has the chance to watch the view."

"What view?" Jeannie asks.

"Nevermind," he says, flaring his nostrils. He opens up the can of refried beans.

"So how was your first week of class, Ruby?" Jeannie says, clearing her throat before the question.

"Fine," she says curtly.

"So I heard you were supposed to be making lists. Schedules and goals? Is that right?"

"Yes," Ruby says.

"Well, here," Jeannie says, handing her the folder. "It's all of our correspondence while you were in Alaska and Florida." Jeannie licks her lips that look unusually chapped. "Don't know why I didn't think to do this before," she says, her mouth now parted as if breathless. Ray stands on guard, afraid.

"Thank you," Ruby says, pulling out the e-mail printouts. With a sullen expression she begins reading.

"You don't have to look at it now," Jeannie says, but Ruby doesn't pay her any attention. Jeannie's gesture toward Ray appears as if offering herself. "I went and visited Al in jail today." She straightens her dress, then pinches the edge. "He is a reeking, stinking, gaping *hole*," she says, working her tongue as if she tasted it. Ray shakes his head without looking at her, scrapes the beans out of the can into the pot, then worriedly looks back at Ruby. Ruby keeps reading.

"He had the gall to ask me if I still loved him." She pulls on the top of her hair that separates on end like plumage. "He's pleading not guilty to murder," she says so quickly saliva flies. "He's claiming he never knew the vermin. That at first he was blackmailing him over only the affair, and then after, framing him for the murder."

"We know," Ray says, in a high voice. "Bring it down just a bit," he almost whispers, motioning toward Ruby. "She needs calm."

"I'm sorry," Jeannie says. "I just don't know what to do. You know? I feel like I could singe him, char him, cremate him myself."

"Why'd you go see him?" Ray asks, pulling the tortillas wrapped in foil out of the oven. He puts them on the small Formica table he bought this week. It's already set with two plates, silverware, and a single pink rose in a thin patinaed vase.

"I had to," Jeannie says. She exhales, pats hard at the middle of her chest. "Look, let me get out of your way. I just came by to give Ruby the letters. I think it's a good thing for her memory," she says, pulling herself together, approaching Ruby but reluctant to put her hand on her shoulder. Ruby doesn't look up as Jeannie walks out of the house.

"Dinner's ready, love," Ray says, carefully making room on the table for the bowls of lettuce, cheese, and tomatoes. "You want sour cream?"

She looks at him, then her eyes flit from one spot in the room to another in a disconnected fashion.

"Uh-oh," Ray says like a fifties housewife. He takes the e-mails from her, straightens them, and places them in the folder. Ruby looks at him, her composure unraveling. He picks her up swiftly in his arms, carries her through the archway to the dollhouse bedroom, and lays her down.

"Close your eyes," he says to her. "That's it." He wipes her forehead of the tiny beads of sweat.

"I told you," Ruby says, her voice sultry from the strain. "I'm just hot, that's all."

"The letters were too much. Jeannie is too much, we've got to get out of here."

"No," Ruby says, opening her eyes wide. "You don't understand how much this helps me. It's a puzzle. Most of the pieces are missing, but every day I'm here, the picture slowly forms." She swallows. He gently brushes her cheeks, her chin, her neck. Ruby tightens up a bit.

"We can't stay here forever."

"I'm hungry," she says flatly. And he helps her up, even though she clearly doesn't want him to.

Every weekday morning, they make the drive to Pasadena in Jeannie's Range Rover. They take Laurel Canyon Boulevard bumper to bumper up to its highest point on Mulholland, then down into the valley for the 101. From there, a hair-raising fraction of a second in which Ray has to get all the way over for the lane to the 134. Then it's a merciless crawl past the 5 to the 210 freeway. Ray grips the wheel for fifty minutes, pretending not to be queasy with angst.

Ruby's head trauma program, A to Zeal, is off Lake Boulevard on a quaint avenue, typical of Pasadena. It is a craftsman mansion, almost plantation-style, in a business district where oaks line the street. Wraparound porch with a dozen wicker and mission rocking chairs out front, diamond-shaped leaded-glass windows, and impeccably pruned rosebushes surrounding the house. When they pull up, Ray shakes off the perversity of smog and traffic, leading Ruby up the steps, through the doors to the meeting room, and against all rules, coddles her the entire way.

The owner, doctor of research, and head instructor, Graciela

Cortez, flouts the idea of overly compassionate patience and nurturing of the brain injured. Students are allowed only one parent, lover, spouse, or friend caregiver in class, and she warns each session of her twelve students' partners about the dangers of hovering, which only encourages their loves ones to languish under their protection. Graciela is Guatemalan and lives with her husband in Hancock Park. He comes from an old Mexican family who made their money in ranching and oil. Graciela walks briskly, narrow heels clicking into the room at ten A.M. sharp; just behind her in a flurry is her moon-faced and meek assistant, Justine, holding the dreaded red three-ring binder.

Graciela is beautiful at the age of forty-eight. A very low-grade alcoholic, she keeps everything together, despising the idea of excess, even with the wealthy husband, and the appearance of her home and business, which both put on airs. The ritzy affectations would barely exist if it weren't for experiences like opening her own front door to a fourteen-year-old white boy pushing his magazine drive and asking, "Is the lady of the house home?" Being mistaken for the maid, even though her maid is Mexican, is something her psyche cannot take. Lately she has been suffering from the idea of spiritual famine—an offhand remark her husband had made. Barring all this, Graciela is formidable but approachable and cool. Her rehab center has the most consistently stellar success rate, this naturally being of the utmost importance to Ray.

"I've got a current event," the student Bill says in a lethargic tone. He is thin, scrappy, and pale with a wide, square jaw. His two siblings were killed in a car accident that left him brain injured, as well as weighted with responsibility to his young, widowed mother, who sits tentatively next to him.

"I thought we'd talk first about yesterday's incident at the end of class," Graciela says, crossing her legs in an imposing manner, inspiring most of the class to stare.

"Can't we move on?" another student's father says. "What else is there to say? The kid exposed himself, we all know that inappropriate behavior can happen with people in this condition." He puts up his hands, raising his brows as well.

"I'd like the students to speak up," Graciela says.

"I've got a current event," the student Bill repeats. His chest expands but then he retreats into his shell. He stretches his eye muscles in a twitch, the effect as if he were an actor in an old horror film.

"It's Ray's birthday," Ruby blurts out. "Mine was three weeks ago. I'm near the beginning of April, he's near the end," she says, reeling in her imagined gabby self.

"Let's try some order, shall we?" Graciela looks for a moment into each and every face. "Now, Ruby, you shouldn't interrupt, but since it's Ray's birthday, we shall sing. Afterward we'll return to the matter of yesterday, which could have been very disturbing to some of you, and so we will need to talk about it."

She turns to her assistant, Justine, who scans the open page in the binder, then looks up at her boss, terrified of muffling the reminders. Graciela begins to sing "Happy Birthday," and everyone joins in, Ray feeling fallow and helpless. He reaches for Ruby's hand, though she ignores it as she concentrates on maintaining the key.

"And many moooore." Ruby is the only one to sing the last line. Her eyes are closed, trying to pin—like points on a map—every birthday she ever experienced. But this is overly ambitious, impossible, even ridiculous, causing frustration to squash in her head like a vise.

"It's okay, baby," Ray says, getting teary. He can't help attuning himself to her with every moment.

"Ruby, relax. Do you hear me?" Graciela leans forward, talking with an open, clawing hand. "You're just flooding. Breathe deeply." She leans farther. "Are you listening to me?"

Ruby nods, though her body holds the posture of pre-hyperventilation. Ray's arms around her, eyes fraught with despair.

"Let it go. It'll pass. Don't try to fight the ominous feeling that you might be losing. Let go of the judgment, just like that," Graciela says, and she snaps her finger. Her mouth is painted a deep red wine. Her eyes are clear, direct, and empathetic. Justine watches holding onto the binder, biting her lip. Ruby finally looks up at her, her expression depleted, but also as if she doesn't care.

"I've got a current event," Bill says, now raising his hand. Graciela doesn't require this, but when he does this it works with getting his way. He doesn't remember this fact; it is like a profound discovery in human nature each time. Playing into someone else's idea of her power.

"What's your current event, Bill?" Graciela asks, anchoring her body to the chair with a temporary gaze of surrender.

"The daughter," Bill says, in a nonanimated tone. "The fucking daughter."

"What did I say about foul language?" Graciela asks, looking individually into her students' faces.

"'Remember to think about what you are saying,'" says the snowboarder, Lacey, who, after the accident and two spinal taps, is recovering from brain damage due to intracranial pressure. She is in a wheelchair and partnered with her fiancé, who is shaggy and bewildered but resigned to his predicament.

"The daughter who hates her father's wife *so* much," Bill says, glancing at his mother quickly. "So much that she comes in one night with her key, *knowing* her father was out of town, and *then* she stabs the wife." His bottom lip remains between his teeth as if the f sound of "wife" must be held captive.

"Can you believe it?" the same father asks who spoke up about yesterday's incident. His son is quiet every day of class until Graciela forces him to contribute. The father shakes his head, then nods at Justine, the assistant. He is embarrassingly enamored of her, Ray notices.

"The daughter's husband, after finding out what she did, helped her by taking the body to a *tree* shredder," Bill says, still nondynamic but posed as if ready to grab some inner flicker of elation.

"Good," Graciela says, nodding to the progress in his capacity to remember and share. "What did you think about all that, Peter?" Graciela asks the verbose and infatuated father's son. He shakes his head repeatedly, maniacally, like a brat. He glares at her with a look of hatred that incites the protective nature in Ray, who tenses up. Ray doesn't always remember the expressions of the brain injured have little to do with their authentic emotions.

"I think," Ruby says, then clears her throat. "I think the father must have ignored his daughter's problems for too long." She bats her lashes, and chews once on her tongue. Her ravishing maple skin today shines with health rather than overproductive glands.

"She is on medication," Lacey says, both hands on her wheelchair armrests. "What do you expect? I would kill somebody too, if I could." Her fiancé shifts his weight away from her like a first grader who shows the rest of the class he will not catch the cooties.

"I'd like to hear more from some of you guys. You can't let the only two women here speak for you," Graciela says.

"There are more than two women here," Len says, violently pointing at Graciela, then Justine, Bill's mother, the three wives, the two girlfriends, one sister, one aunt, one cousin, one best friend, a committed to philanthropy friend, and a daughter. Then he looks at Ruby and Lacey with the single vertical fold in his forehead, the long dip between his nose and mouth, the fire in his eyes. Ray feels Ruby's relief. Len had been in a coma for eighteen days, with fever and infection. He had cognitive drug cocktails poured through a stomach tube. Ruby aligns herself with him on no true grounds other than he happens to be her choice for being the worse off, which bothers Ray since she is milestones ahead.

"I mean the *students*," Graciela says.

"I'm having trouble with that," Ruby says. "Being a student. I don't remember ever really being a student. I mean, that wasn't me."

"How do you feel about learning here?" Graciela says.

"I feel better. I want to. I just don't have a grip on the past. I can't see clearly. You can't tell me my history. This class can't teach me that."

"Look at the stars tonight, the constellations. You'll see history there. They happened a long time ago. As you look at these stars, and witness the past there before your eyes, you won't feel like you have to have hold of them. You can't do anything about them. You have no choice but to appreciate them and let them be. Do the same with your memory of your life," Graciela says, boring a hole into Ruby with the intensity of her conviction. She wakes up out of it, looks down at Justine's notebook, and her thin, delicate light brown finger resting on the outline of where they are.

"When we take our field trip to the pottery school next week, I want you all to let go of any expectations, of any feelings you might remember having as a child when you made something out of clay. Don't do any throwing to please anybody else but yourself. And even if you aren't successful in pleasing yourself, I want you to sit back in your chair, and just listen to the music we will be playing in the class," Graciela says, looking into each individually glum face of her students. Ray observes his fellow partners/caregivers all looking neglected.

"Starting on Friday, I'm going to have a private conference with every one of you, without your partners, and then I'll talk to your partners afterward."

"No more fucking pegs in the board," Lacey, the snowboarder, says.

"Excuse me," Graciela says, holding up her immaculately manicured hand. "I was talking. Think before you blurt out. Everybody, watch the cursing. Now. I should mention to you, Lacey, that two weeks ago you couldn't even remember that you were inserting pegs in the board every day. It was like a new exercise. Yesterday you were tired of it. Now that's a good thing."

"I don't like the feeling that my IQ is being tested."

"It's not," Graciela says. "This is not the point at all. It's all about coordination and problem solving. Ruby chooses to do the board sometimes with her left hand, and sometimes with her right. All of you do it differently, which is the right way for you." Graciela raises her chin. "Now, the assignment for this evening I want the partners to pay special attention to. I want the *student* to go to the grocery store, buy the five items you have chosen and written on a list, *all by yourself.*"

"I can't do that," Lacey says, holding her hands up, looking down at her chair.

"Stevie can go in with you. And if the grocery store is too complicated, then go to a deli. I just want you to do the shopping on your own, best you can," Graciela says, uncrossing her legs and putting her hands on both knees. Without catching himself, Ray's eyes move from her hands down to her calves, her ankles. Graciela notices. When Ray was sixteen and kicked out by his parents for smoking pot, he slept in a lean-to not far from a thirty-year-old who drove him to Kentucky and fucked him to the wailing banjos under a blanket in the blue grass. When Ray was seventeen, and long since moved back home, he slept with the mother of a classmate he might call his best friend. Even though it was this mother's doing—she'd asked for a massage—it's not like he didn't jump at the chance. Months later, in night school, making up for the time he missed when kicked out, he and that same friend both slept with the teacher, on separate occasions. Ray married Cynthia when he was eighteen and she was thirty-two, and now he and Graciela are the same years apart. If he still claimed old patterns, Graciela would be the perfect partner in lust, as he could tell during the last conference. Still, after the first few blissful months of his relationship with Ruby, he found that it now might be *impossible* to be tempted by anyone. Even though, since the accident, sex is so infrequent with Ruby, and wholly without zest on her part. He continues to have an ever-deepening faith that they will make it back to their erotic heights. He realized that during the coma, whenever his faith waned, Ruby's condition seemed to worsen or complicate, but as he really turned on with his version of prayer, so did her fight to communicate again.

"Class had no order today," Ray says, walking with Ruby down the steep hill of Lookout Mountain Avenue in Laurel Canyon. The street is so narrow that cars can park only on one side, and there is no sidewalk. As he would regardless, Ray walks on the outside, clamping down on her arm whenever a car passes, which is every thirty seconds.

"You're hurting me," Ruby says, perturbed.

"I'm sorry, baby."

"I won't wander into the street."

"I know, I can't help it," he says, smashing berries under his step. He looks up at the tree, then at her face featuring a newly cranky expression. "I'm sorry about the grocery store too."

Ruby says nothing, staring at every fence that meets the curb.

"I just couldn't stand to see you panicking."

"You shouldn't have been watching," Ruby says.

"I'm sorry, I couldn't help but follow you in."

"Let's drop it," she says.

He takes her hand, kisses it as they walk, holds it, rubbing the knuckles.

"Man, this is a disaster waiting to happen. Can't believe the rains didn't take this entire hill down," Ray says, pointing at it. Ruby keeps clocking the fences. "Are you counting or something?"

"No."

"Here they are," Ray says, animated. Two Dalmatians hit the fence and make a ruckus. "Watch them bark and spin," he says, laughing. Ruby doesn't look. "I like the brown spots on the smaller one," he says. Ruby still doesn't turn her head as they pass.

"I'll take the blame in class tomorrow morning," Ray says. "It's all my fault. You could have done it if I'd given you time."

Ruby says nothing.

"Tomorrow, we can try again."

"Tomorrow, *I* can try again," Ruby says in a huff.

"Here comes that dog again. He's so crazy for you," Ray says, putting on a smile, though Ruby doesn't think to.

"We're on the same schedule," the guy says cheerfully. He is short, fiftyish, and balding with bright, devilish eyes that suggest he got his way in business and with women, and that he fancies himself hip. His girlfriend is young, strawberry blonde, and gorgeous when in makeup; she smiles with tolerance.

"What kind of dog is he? Looks part wolf," Ray says, petting him with his left hand. The dog looks up at Ruby, asking her to do the same.

"He is, and Alaskan husky," the guy says.

"What's his name?" Ray asks.

"Blizz," the guy says.

"Liz?"

"No, *she's* Liz, actually," he says, touching her shoulder with propriety. She nods, spreads her smile. "But he's B-Lizz as in 'blizzard,'" the guy says. "I'm Frank, by the way," he offers his hand.

"Ray," he shakes it firmly. "This is Ruby." She nods, takes a step back. The dog sticks his tongue out and pants.

"Are you two into jazz at all?" Frank asks. Ray pushes out his bottom lip, like *not bad*, and nods. Ruby looks at the tip of Frank's nose, which is sunburnt. "You should come check us out at the club tonight. The Catalina Bar and Grill. Me and this here old ugly chick work a mean percussion." He takes his girlfriend's arm and squeezes it. She cackles, startling Ruby.

"You know where it is, right?" Frank says, pointing at Ray and now walking past at the same time.

"Sure do, man," Ray lies, catching up with Ruby, who is taking off already.

"The kids are out of school," she says, walking a little faster to reach the bottom of the hill. Ray grabs onto her arm as she crosses the street to be on the same side as the children. He is baffled by her excitement, since she never seemed to care about kids or even mention a thing about them.

At the fire hydrant, there is a little girl looking anxiously up the hill at her mother who is turning the car around. Ruby notices her shoestrings dragging on the ground, so she bends down to tie them. Surprised, the girl lifts her wrist so as not to touch Ruby's head of short wild hair. Ray notices her Mickey Mouse watch, then searches the girl's face for even a smidgen of gratitude, but there is none. Then he spots the ladybug in Ruby's hair, just as the girl's mother pulls up. As Ruby stands, he delicately places his finger there for the bug to climb on so she can see it. The girl's mother, an assuming but young and not-yet-brittle actress, says thank you to Ruby, as the girl gets in the car. Ruby doesn't even turn around, and neither does Ray, as they look at the ladybug together on his finger, Ray's arm circling Ruby in a grateful embrace. He fights back the tears that Ruby is alive and all his.

When the security gate buzzer sounds, Ruby runs through the hall of the main house, pushes in the button, and bursts out the front door. Ray is right behind her. He is slightly miffed that Abbie can elicit the kind of feeling he hasn't seen in Ruby since the accident.

"Hey, girl!" Abbie calls from the window of her rental car. At first she pulls up to the garage door, then she backs up, jerking herself. "Am I blocking anyone in if I park here?" Ruby makes a visor of her hand, stopping at the end of the walkway. Satisfied to see Abbie's face, she crosses her arms. Ray watches her mood quickly morph from great excitement to blandness.

"Back up just a little more," Ray says, pointing her to the right. "Jeannie's still home."

Abbie gets out of the car, trying to pull her panties out of her butt, though she wears baby blue pedal pushers.

"You sure you're okay to drive?" Ray asks, taking her in his arms for a bear hug. Ruby stands stiffly where she is.

"Didn't Ruby tell you? I can see fine with this eye." She steps back from Ray, points to the left one. "My depth perception's a little off, right? But that's okay." She wrinkles her nose, pushes her hair, now cut in bangs, off her forehead. "Aren't you gonna give me a hug too?" she asks, approaching Ruby. She throws her arms around her neck, Ruby holds her at her waist with a dormant expression.

"Look at you," Abbie says, inches from her face. Ruby's eyes twinkle. "You're my father, totally stoic." She squeezes her hand then lets go. "Oh, I forgot—I've got a couple bags of goodies in the car." She doubles back, but Ray stops her, opens the door, and grabs the pink bags. Ray screws his brows together at the Hustler name.

"You're so *prude*, Ray. I had to fit in here, right?" Abbie says, opening her mouth to show her tongue. Ray gives her a look that says *keep your voice down.*

Chattering the whole way, she follows Ruby through the door. Ray had forgotten how sweetly she sometimes reminds him of his mother.

"Wow, this is *amazing*," she says. "So much more austere than I imagined. Everybody knows how hippydippy Laurel Canyon's sposed to be, like my hood in Marin, right? But inside here feels nothing like it. Though this is very L.A., I guess." Surveying, Abbie stops in the center of the living room, Ray giving her that look again. Ruby stands near the long olive couch, until Abbie suddenly rushes her, pushes her down, then sits on her like a ballast. Abbie laughs hysterically and claps her hands; Ruby pushes her off so that she goes thump on the floor. Abbie keeps laughing. Ray shakes his head.

"What's all this racket?" Jeannie jokes, coming down the stairs with the sweaty sheen of a rigorous workout. She wipes her palms on her gym shorts. "And is this the illustrious Abigail?" Jeannie asks. With a radically charming grin she holds out her hand.

"So good to meet you," Abbie says, blushing. She pushes up her glasses, looks at Ruby, whose expression hasn't changed.

"When'd you get here?" Jeannie asks, pulling the band tighter on her pert little ponytail. Then she puts her hands on her hips, legs apart, ready for drill team.

"Late last night," Abbie says, yanking up the sleeves of her thin, white cotton cardigan. "Flight's longer than I thought. I get *crazy* in that stagnant air of the plane. Thought I might cut myself open with the plastic knife."

"You should have medicated," Jeannie says, cocking her head like she's crazy not to think of it. "Where are you staying?"

"Chateau Marmont. I always wanted to. It's beautiful and *old*, which I love. This morning I hopelessly waited in the lounge for Keanu Reeves, right?"

"Why don't you come stay here, there are *five* empty bedrooms." Jeannie holds up her hand, spreading her fingers for emphasis. "There's just Dean and me, when he's around, that is," Jeannie says, now joining the ladies on the long, plush couch. Ray reclines in the black leather chair. Feeling outnumbered, he plays piano on the armrest.

"Jean and Dean," Abbie giggles, then girlishly covers her mouth. "I love being so close to the Sunset Strip, you know? All the shops, oh my God, on the way here, just at the beginning of Sunset Plaza Drive, I could have died staring at those Herve Leger dresses in the window. I pulled over, not far enough, 'cause people were honking."

"I know. Wicked," Jeannie says in a British accent, then flips her hand. "So come on, it would be fun. Ruby would love it, wouldn't you?" Jeannie says, turning toward her but afraid to focus, as if her face were grotesquely burned. Ruby renders something close to a loving gaze at Abbie. Ray sits, the toes of his work boots fondling each other. He looks at them from beneath heavy brows. He can't stand his own impatience and possessiveness.

"Oh, I don't know, that's so kind of you, but I hate putting anybody out," Abbie says, smoothing out the couch as if she'd ruffled it. Jeannie squints her eyes at her, Ray now feeling protective of Abigail, but what he doesn't know is that Jeannie is sizing her up as a personal assistant.

"Can I get you something to drink? We've probably still got some coffee on," Jeannie says, heading for the kitchen. "Would you like some?" she calls from there.

"No thank you, I had breakfast a little while ago. Did you all feel that tremor this morning?" Abbie says with a serious expression. She squeezes Ruby's knee.

"Yes, I did," Ruby says.

"I was thinking, great, first day I get to L.A. the building's gonna crumble down on top of me. Very fitting."

"It could happen in Alaska," Ray says.

"Or at home, where I'm going after this, by the way," Abbie says, proudly smiling.

"You don't get earthquakes in Florida, only sinkholes, but they can swallow a whole house. Of course there are the hurricanes. You can't escape what Mother Nature's got in store."

"That's right," Jeannie says, making a little fun of Ray, he shoots a look that gives her a little shit back. She sighs, holding on tightly to the glass of water in her hand. She had popped two Advils in the kitchen. She quickly massages her own forehead. "I gotta get over to the restaurant soon. Abbie, it was nice to meet you," she nods, sticks her nose under her armpit. "I'm heading for the shower." She adorably scrunches up her nose, shrugs, kicks up one leg behind her like a dancer, then takes off.

"She's much prettier in real life," Abbie whispers to Ruby, then looks at Ray, waiting for agreement.

"I wouldn't know, I've only seen her in real life."

"But you saw the *E! True Hollywood Story*," Abbie says dramatically, then laughs in silly trickles.

"After the fact," Ray says, getting up. "Would you keep it down, Abigail?"

Ruby gets up too.

"I want to show you where I live," Ruby says, Ray watching her and feeling hurt that she said "I" instead of "we."

She walks without looking to see if they're following. Ray grabs the bags, looks at Abbie, waiting to see how bad off she thinks Ruby is.

"There's an ebb and flow to everything," Abbie says. "As you might say, Ray." She nods to him like an officer to a lieutenant.

All the way down the path, Abbie coos at the forest and the gardens Ray has started. At the front door, Ruby thinks to use her key, which is something she has forgotten to do ever since the accident. Ray leans over her shoulder to tell her how proud he is of her, and she bites her bottom lip without acknowledging him. He still can't get used to her embarrassment when he calls out her every new accomplishment.

"I'll have to get used to this new glib Ruby," Abbie says, knocking her chin. "I rather like it. Right? I always wanted the courage to be rude," she laughs. "And you never wrote me, you bitch," she says.

"You bitch," Ruby says to her, sitting down at the little table.

"Look what I brought for you, bitch," Abbie says. There is the sound of the toilet flushing, then Ray reappears. She pulls out two art books from the bag and a stack of comic books. "There's nothing from Hustler for you, in here," she teasingly swings her head on her neck side-to-side. "But this is the Agnes Martin book I was telling you about," Abbie says, putting it in her lap. Ruby opens the pages, slowly goes through them; Abbie watches her, then looks at the painting on the walls around them.

"And now, here's one with all the black stars—Chris Ofili, Fred Wilson, Kara Walker—"

"I love Kara Walker," Ruby interrupts, taking the book to flip through for the silhouettes. "Brilliant."

"You remember her?"

"Yeah. *Yeah*," Ruby says, looking up at Abbie, then back at the page.

"You're doing some beautiful work here, girl," Abbie says, nodding slowly now. She seems to have forgotten that Ray is watching, he's consciously made himself invisible. "I feel almost silly having brought these," she says, patting the comic books. "You've gone in such a totally different direction."

"Let me see," Ruby says, hungrily. Ray doesn't take his eyes off her.

"My brother sent me these, okay? I'd told him all about you, and because he worships your entire world, he got so excited, he said he'd send a stack of stuff for you to have. And he *did*. First time I've talked to him in what seems like years, okay? This is the one who was always trying to kill me. So you've brought me and my brother back together, right?"

"*Martha Washington Goes to War*," Ruby reads the cover of the first graphic novel. She stares at the fierce brown face, the "flesh-colored" Band-Aid on her forehead, the machine gun in her hand. The peace sign in her ear.

"Of course he sent a black superhero," Abbie says shyly. "And here's the *Silver Surfer*," Abbie says, covering up the other, "a few *Love and Rockets*, which are so classic." Ruby puts Martha back on the top of the stack.

"You know that saying, 'Lose a son, gain a daughter,' or however it goes? That's totally my brother. He's forgotten about all of us, though his wife checks in with my mom every once in a while. How can men be so consumed by their sexuality? Tell us, Ray," Abbie says, folding her arms.

"Don't know what you're talking about," Ray says, sitting on the floor, resting his back against the tub.

"Admit it. Sex rules your world. Well, when was the last time you talked to your family?" Abbie asks, gloating to put him on the spot.

"Um," Ray says, his voice shaky. "Let me see." He looks at the floor, chews on his bottom lip.

"Just as I thought," she says, holding up a finger. "Ruby, you gotta see that this man checks in every once in a while with his people," she says in her best stern, manly voice.

"Fuck you," Ruby says, then pops Abbie's thigh.

"Fuck *you*," Abbie says, pops her back.

"Don't mess with this good man," Ruby says, looking up at him. Ray gets teary, not only over the sentiment but also over the fact that she goes from childlike to astute more swiftly, more frequently. "Think of what a lonely business this has been. I'm a one-way need street," Ruby says, frowning though she doesn't mean to.

"You get better every day, it's incredible," Ray says, sniffling.

"That's why I'm here, right? To witness the speed, and toughen you both up," Abbie says, getting up to her feet and stretching. Ray playfully rolls his eyes. "What you got in these cupboards? I got a *mean* sweet tooth," she says, winking.

"Which reminds me," Ray says, following her, "I got you some near-beer."

"Ugh," she says.

"It's Bucklers. Try it. I'm getting into it myself."

"*Why* when you don't have to?"

"I just want to watch myself now," he says, pursing his lips again. He flips off the cap. Abbie takes a swig, wipes her mouth with the back of her hand, and opens the cupboard. A moth flies out.

"Eeeew," she says, stepping back. Ruby looks up with a blank stare again.

"What's so nasty about a moth?" Ray asks, digging around until two others fly out. "Uh-oh," he says, opening up the flour. He makes a slurping sound, as if he'd watched someone get sliced. "Just what I thought."

"EEEEE-ewww, you're *infested!!!*" Abbie squeals. Ray quickly folds up the flour full of mealy moths and throws it in the garbage. He then begins the long and tedious job of opening all the items, sorry to find them writhing in most every unsealed product. "And I thought *I* kept a messy house," Abbie laughs, stepping back to sit next to Ruby. Ray holds up his middle finger.

Nagging at Ray are Abbie's words about men and family. This would be the farthest worry in mind if he knew that the teeth of his victim, Arnie Watson, just turned up in the swamp. Too intimidated to call his dad, he calls his oldest sister, Sonya, whom he hasn't spoken to in well over a year.

"Rinky Ba-Ba! How are you?" she says too loudly into the phone when she hears his voice. Ray puts an inch between his ear and the receiver.

"I'm fine, So. How are you? How are the kids?"

"We're all right," she says, trying to make little of a lot more.

"What's wrong?"

"Nothing, Ba-Ba. So I hear from Sadie that you were in Alaska, and you're divorced now, and . . ."

"Yeah. That was a blip."

"I know what you mean, baby."

"But, I've been involved with this woman, Ruby. I'm in love, Sonya. I'm so in love. Like never ever before. You know?"

"I'm so happy for you. You sound like you mean it."

"It's been almost a year that we've been together. She doesn't want to get married yet, which I totally respect, but this is the one. This is really the one I want to spend the rest of my life with."

"I am happy for you, Ray. I really am. That's why I feel like a heel telling you I'm getting a divorce now too."

"No," he says thoughtfully.

"Yes. It's time. You know, the kids are almost out of the house, and we've been holding onto nothing, really."

"What's he done to you?" Ray asks, getting excited.

"Nothing! Really. It's totally amicable. We just haven't had a marriage in years, is all. And it's better to do something about that while there's still time to get on with your life, you know?"

"I always thought it was so hard for us, all three of us, to find anything to measure up to what Mom and Dad had," Ray says, sounding like a little boy.

"Mom? She was *miserable*," Sonya says, exhaling loudly into the phone.

"What do you mean?"

"Well, sure she loved Dad, but she was exhausted. I mean, it wasn't like he was the easiest person on earth, and then she had us, and she had the farm, and she had work, and, I just don't think she was satisfied as a woman."

"It was hard at times, yeah, but they were so in love. Come on, So!"

"You're not listening to me," she says in a singsong. "Look. I don't want to burst your bubble or anything. But that's what ate her up alive. You know, she was having an affair on Dad. You didn't realize that, 'cause you were a baby. But I saw the fireworks. I felt it, you can be sure of that."

Ray's jaw drops open.

"Oh yeah. I shouldn't even tell you who it was. But my point is, you always had this kind of fifties picture-perfect image of everything, especially of all of us, and I never got it. You know? But you're such a dreamer. I love you, little brother. I really hope you found the one this time. It's hell wasting away with somebody you know is not the one after a while. That's what Mom was doing. She loved Dad when she married him, but she didn't have that passion for him after that."

"Passion?"

"*Passion*," Sonya says, getting firm.

"I had no idea. No *idea*," Ray says, not having blinked for longer than he realizes.

Ray finishes up the conversation without telling her everything that has happened during these past intense months, and though it is a myriad of turbulent thoughts shuffling all logic in his head, he still feels relieved to have connected with her, and to hear the proof in the sound of his own voice, his undying love for Ruby.

When he leaves the guesthouse he finds Ruby and Abbie in the pool. Abbie moved into the main house the day before, and already she looks like she's lived here forever.

"This is so *macabre*," Abbie says, stopping in the middle of her breaststroke in the shallow of the pool, where Ruby wades in her turquoise bikini. Abbie looks up at Ray, nodding to her own comment. Wet and without her glasses, she could be mistaken for a teen. Ruby's body is too curved and voluptuous to be taken for the same.

Ray shakes his head at Abbie, like *don't remind her.*

"It's not, though," Ruby says, lying on her back to float. Ray peels off his clothes to get in, afraid that she might panic. "I don't remember everything that happened, it's true. Just fragments. When I heard you ask Ray about the skull, I could see Caspar, like I couldn't see him before. The actual photographs brought back nothing. For some reason. I get flashes, but they are so abstract. They are like paintings. And I try to capture them. It doesn't work, but it feels good to try. I like being here for the images. Pieces of my past."

"What about your parents' house?" Abbie asks, her arms stretched out over the water.

"Same thing. But it's not a challenge. When I'm with my sister, my past *feels* clear, even if it isn't. But she's so frustrated at the sight of me. My parents are too, that's why I could never take any of them as a partner at rehab. Jeannie is frustrated too, but at least she knows how to get around it. Hannah can't take it."

"That makes sense."

"Sometimes the paintings seem ugly to me. Or too simple. I'm beginning to crave depth. Complexity."

"You should come with me up north. We should do the drive together, right? Santa Barbara, San Simeon, Big Sur, Carmel, San Francisco, Marin, hell, we could keep on going. Stop in the redwood forest, hug some trees! Go buy us a little winery in Mendocino; you could write hit graphic novels while I run the business 'til we're ready to retire."

"She's got graduation yet," Ray says. "And you're not taking her out of my sight," he says, crouching in the shallow end instead of doing the laps he needs to.

"Would you want to, Ruby?"

"Yes."

"When are you leaving, Abbie?" Ray asks.

"I could wait for her graduation."

"That's in *three* months," Ray says, getting worked up. "You planning on using Jeannie that long?"

"Are you?"

"No, I'm planning to get us the fuck out of here. I haven't been able to get a job while Ruby's in class, but I can the minute it's over, and Ruby feels ready."

"I'm feeling ready, now, Ray. Ready for you to do what you want," she says, flipping onto her feet from her back. She nods at him, he takes her in his arms and kisses her on the mouth. She seems to want to return it, but then she pulls away, as if entrapped. Abbie swims to the deep end. Ray looks Ruby in the eye, a surge of fear in his chest. This is the first time he's felt, since the accident, that she's coming back into her own, but that this new self just may not include him.

Chapter 24

Graciela's Graduate

Ruby

Up until this point, Ruby couldn't know or overly concern herself with the fact that Ray has been hinting at a dire need for the company of men. She listens with interest to his reminiscences of job site games with the guys; she laughs at their practical jokes like nailing the sawhorses down to the concrete just to piss someone off. She can feel how Ray is saturated with Abbie's saccharine antics; she agrees that Jeannie navigates for control, using posh gifts and the ace of her grief. He seems more than slighted by Ruby's partiality to both women, and she consciously turns her attention to him, as he has so selflessly done for her. Ray exists as he did as a boy on the farm, entirely victim of girl power, and Ruby can finally see it.

Abbie has indeed become Jeannie's assistant. This, at least, has waylaid the Northern California trip. Ruby's interest in it, anyway, has dwindled. She has taken to the tactile. Presently, all of her paintings slope or indent with scrawling illegible madness, unless they dip in orderly craters like anthills. When they are dry, she prods, flicks, or caresses them. At the end of the day, they evoke little she intended.

Always encouraging, Ray works to give her the impression he finds these creations intriguing. His effort is now tangible to her, marking a giant step forward from the self-centeredness necessary to recovery. More and more aware of how others need to grapple with their own problems, in September, a mere seven months after the accident, Ruby steps out of the vacuum.

"Put that on speaker phone," Ruby commands Ray, when he mentions he's calling Kirk to ask if he can use his name as a job reference.

"Why?"

"I want to know your world again," she says proudly.

"Very well," he smiles. She sits down at the kitchen table, eyes soft with a strange and sudden euphoria. She puts her chin and cheek in hand.

"Kirk."

"Ray?"

"What kind of time you wasting over there in that pisshole?" The rhythm of his speech slows down for swagger. Ray winks at her. "You still trailing after Mr. Key West?"

"Nah, the Conch is gone. Fired his ass. Got this greenhorn working for me now. The idiot doesn't know shit," Kirk says.

"Another sorry situation."

"How are things with you, son? You still in L.A.?"

"Things are good. Ruby's graduating next week from her rehabilitation program. She's pretty much fully recovered. She's *amazing*." He stands near Ruby, strokes her hair. ("Fully recovered" strikes Ruby as impossible, and it is.)

"That's great to hear, kid. Hope you long gave up on the idea of jumping out of a plane. You thinking of coming back?"

"Nah, man. I'm applying for this job as a ranch overseer in Ojai, that's about an hour, hour and a half from here."

"And so what, you think I could endorse a sorry ass like you?" Kirk says.

"Not only endorse, but get on your knees and choke on it," Ray says. Ruby looks up at him, mouths the last three words.

"On a ranch?"

"That's right."

"And so what? You gonna spend all your time hooking come-alongs and running fence rows?"

"Since my sister won't be there to crash the fence and let me take the fall, I don't reckon they'll be of much concern."

"I see, so the better part of your day will be sucking stallion dick."

241

"Just me and your dad." Ruby makes an O with her mouth.

"So who'll be calling?"

"Don't know yet. There are two jobs I got my eye on. One's closer to town in the San Gabriel Valley, a live-in carpenter/handyman situation."

"How have your renters turned out?"

"Still paying. Far as I know, the house is still standing. Probably gonna arrange soon to ship the bikes and the car out here."

"So you're serious about old La-La, eh? You always were a big dip, bet you fit right in," he laughs heartily.

"Fuck you, Kirk."

Well son, I gotta jump. Give my best to Ruby. Congratulations. Don't think about the reference, kid. Just give 'em my number."

"Thanks a lot, Kirk. I appreciate it."

"Take care, son."

"You too." Ray hits the button, breathes a heavy sigh. He looks at the floor, his eyes wide with inner distraction, when Ruby clears her throat. He turns to look at her with a warm smile, works his fingers into her scalp.

"You always talk to your boss like that?" Ruby asks.

"That's nothing."

"I couldn't imagine ever talking to Paul like that, after all he's done for me."

"Well, where is The Great Paul now?"

"What was he supposed to do? Keep my position open all the while I was goo-goo ga-ga?"

"You're an incredible talent. He's lucky to have you."

"I don't know if I can draw anymore, Ray."

"You can, you just keep at it."

"That's just it. I'm not 'at it.'"

"Then maybe you will be, or maybe you won't, if you don't want to. I don't want you worrying about all that right now," he says, cupping her small face in his large hand. What she doesn't know is that Ray purposefully kept her boss Paul at a distance. He didn't allow him to visit, afraid of pressuring Ruby at the thought of not measuring up.

"Graciela would flip," Ruby says suddenly.

"At what?"

"The way you talk to your boss, Ray," Ruby giggles goofily, and he squeezes her to him, so much so that she feels smothered in his chest.

"Well Graciela's not our concern for too much longer," he says.

Ruby pulls away from him, and he stands to stretch. Distracted again, he stares at the table. She looks up at him, objectifying him for the first time since the accident. She begins experiencing a pure lust. She stares at his hips, fetishizing the bones and the way they protrude, imagining them rocking into her. Ray snaps out of his fog, feeling the heat emanate from her. She senses his fear of making any assumptions; he shyly touches the line of her jaw, looking into her face. She wants to tell him not to worry about her needs. He kisses her. She puts her hand on his ass, attempts to probe the hole from outside his loose jeans. As desperate as he's become, this one move eclipses all since the dive. His head goes back and he moans, hoping this is the new harbinger of all great sex to come. Ruby's fingers explore him but when he tries to reciprocate, she grabs his wrists to keep them still. He obeys her as she takes him in her mouth, coldly expert in its need for control, and when he comes she laps it up like milk.

Through the open window, the piercing, nagging sound of a Chihuahua's bark comes closer, whipping Ruby from the mood as quickly as it took over. She wipes the side of her face, stands up as if hearing her name during roll call. Dean's outlaw eyes and winsome manner appear at the screen door.

"Boo," he says, deadpan, then smiles slyly from one side.

"Go *a-way*," Ray enunciates loudly, zipping up his jeans.

"Come in," Ruby contradicts. Ray couldn't be more annoyed, bordering rage. Dean walks in, jangling keys, and the Chihuahua follows. Looking up at Ray, it won't stop barking.

"This is Eartha," Dean says, his hand open, gesturing at the dog. "This is the only kind of entrance she makes." He puts the keys in the pocket of his D&G cargo shorts. His slip-on sandals, also designer, reveal a Mexican sun and eagle rising from his foot to his ankle.

"This is the kind of dog that chased me across a park when I was a kid," Ruby says.

"See? You're fully loaded," Dean teases. "What'd I tell you about that chick?"

"Graciela," Ruby corrects. "And *you're* the one who's loaded."

"Right on," he points at her. "My old man calls her Gracie. And speaking of the old man, he has a conference in *Tahiti*, poor prick, and Moms is going with. They're actually in Australia right now. Brisbane, I think," he says, hands on hips, watching the dog who is still barking. "Cool *out*, Junior," he says. Ray rolls his eyes, rather than breaking Dean's neck. "Did I mention she's a junior? My folks buried her mother, Eartha Sr., last year."

Ray folds his arms, and grunts. Ruby smiles, feeling calm and familiar with a lot of things.

"You notice the mold and mildew on the step, dude?" Dean lifts his toes. Now at the sink, Ray ignores him. Supposedly he washes dishes, but banging them seems to be more like it.

"It's a beautiful green," Ruby says.

"Now you would see it that way." He cocks back his head and looks at her warmly with his tight eyes.

"You should bleach the step, dude. Don't you think?"

Ray still doesn't turn around. Finally the dog stops barking.

"Thank you, Eartha." He puts his hands together in prayer and bows.

"Now that the dog has shut up, maybe the owner will too?" Ray turns to look at Dean with a tough expression betraying more playfulness than anything else.

"The man's phobic," he says, pointing his thumb at Ray. "Now, Rube, this is what he needs." He dangles the keys in front of her. "Happy graduation. It's yours for three weeks." He puts the keys in her hand, closes it around them, kisses her soft, brown fist.

"What's this? A new car?" Ruby jokes.

"Not so mag, but a few weeks at the beach, and without this little bitch, I might add." He gestures at Eartha who barks once at him, then sticks out her tiny tongue. "I've been there partying for the past week, but Jeannie needs me now. You know the hearing is in a few days."

"I know," Ruby says. "There couldn't be more happening."

"Well, there could. I got a new band," he says, owning off his chest with his hands.

"Good for you," Ruby says, imitating someone, she's not sure who, but it is her mother.

"We practice downtown at the Brewery where dude has a killer loft. When we tried at the folks' place, too many complaints. I used to not give a shit, but why fight the fuckers when you've got a better space no-how?" He claps once. "You got any paper, doll?"

Ruby's head pivots on her neck in such a way suggesting she can't recall what was triggered. It is Al, who always called her "Doll." Also, she used to play with paper dolls as a girl—one of her few traditionally feminine pastimes.

"Here's some right here," Dean says, ignoring her confusion, grabbing Ray's carpenter pencil. "'Kay, dude, the house is on Heathercliff Road, main drag of Point Dume, the light at the shopping center off PCH. It's almost to the end, before the beach. *Killer* view. Got it?" He hands the pencil to Ray and grins, daring him not to like him.

"Come on Junior," he says, nodding to the dog once, then grabbing his balls. "We're outta here." And Dean slams the door behind him.

It's a long drive to Graciela's in Hancock Park from the beach where Ruby and Ray have stayed in glorious seclusion for the past couple days. Making a wrong turn through crowded, cluttered Larchmont Village (which is like a plate that shifted from Pasadena), Ray lets the expletives rip. Ruby points out one of the many fussy, dainty shops where they might stop for a gift for Graciela, but Ray hits his forehead.

"You don't want to, then?" Ruby asks.

"I should have thought of it before," Ray growls.

"*I* should have thought of it," Ruby says. "Where's our manners?"

"Where are *our* manners? That's what I'm saying," Ray says, double-parking, waiting for a car to leave the precious space. "And I know how you hate being late."

Ruby, never having been one to dawdle, is still relatively slow to choose, due to injury. She knows Ray feels the pressure since her mind tends to smash in on her when they're not on time. One minute short of brusque, Ray pulls her into a chocolate store where she rediscovers the scintillating rush of the natural fruit of the cacao tree.

"Any time now," Ray says, as Ruby leans over the case. Her hands are now clammy with frustration that she can't move fast enough. Ray looks at her, softens with an empathetic glint in his eye. She tries to pull herself together so she doesn't have to see him scared. She tells herself she is in no danger of flooding, no maddening, overwhelming crush of thought. So she picks a box of truffles, and feeling every grain of the asphalt through the thin soles of her ballet slippers, they dash through traffic across the street to grab a bottle of wine, Ruby leaving the decision to Ray.

It is an ostentatious three-story brick house, the hedges lit with festive white Christmas lights and red balloons at the exquisitely carved mahogany door. Justine, the assistant, happens to be in the gold leaf vestibule when they ring, so it is her kind, vulnerable, and childlike face that greets them.

"Ruby, you look so pretty in a dress!" she exclaims, gleefully.

"Thank you, so do you," Ruby says, a bit like an automaton. Justine always wears a dress.

"Wow," Ray says, as they follow her through the long corridor.

"I know, these paintings are incredible, aren't they?" Justine asks, pointing at her favorite. "Bobby, Graciela's husband, has been collecting Colombian art, and all of these paintings, if you notice, show the missionaries in the act of converting the native people," Justine says, raising her brows. "Incredible, aren't they, Ruby?"

"I like this one. I like the state of ruin it's in," Ruby says, getting close enough to the paint to resemble a very old man trying to read a caption.

They follow Justine into the grand living room, and as in the dining room, there is an imposing Irish crystal chandelier. The walls are a rustic green with inset moments of antique Mexican carvings and figurines. A few of the students are inside, but most everyone else is outside in the warm L.A. September evening. Not all are ready to finish the program, so the moods are most definitely uneven.

Graciela doesn't always throw graduation parties at her house, but every once in a while she takes a shine to a particular class. In royal blue, she stands near the pool, talking to the caterer with an antagonized expression. When she spots Ruby and Ray approaching, her face smoothes with welcome.

"Hello, hello," she says, ingratiating herself as if she were the guest.

"This is for you," Ruby says, handing her the box of chocolates and bottle of wine.

"Thank you so much, that's very thoughtful of you," she says, now holding the neck of the bottle in a manner of overt control. "Did you see your parents yet?"

"Well, thank *you*, for everything, and no, we haven't seen them," Ruby says, her eyes wide. She feels Ray tense up.

"It's been my pleasure, really, you don't know what a privilege it is to witness such tremendous progress," Graciela says, smiling without showing her teeth. "Your parents are just around the corner, by the way, out here at a table. I hope you're hungry."

"We are," Ray says.

"And I hope you're very proud of yourself, Ruby," Graciela says.

"I am," she nods, biting the soft flesh inside her bottom lip.

"Do you have any immediate plans?"

"We're staying at the beach right now, but I may be getting a job as a ranch overseer in Ojai. Ruby can paint there, and she's become interested in graphic novels, so she may move in that direction."

"Ruby can speak for herself, right Ruby?"

Ruby nods and swallows. She feels a little anger rising in her, not for Ray, but for something she can't put her finger on.

"So, Ojai? That's where the wonderful potter Beatrice Wood lived before she died," Graciela says, turning to Ruby. "I had the pleasure of meeting her. She used to keep her studio open for visitors. The place was managed by this very inviting, distinguished gentleman, Singh, who was supposed to be her friend. I would have sworn he was her lover. If not, they had an incredible friendship."

"It's possible," Ray says.

"She lived to be a hundred and five! My husband's grandmother almost made it. Did you meet Bobby, by the way?"

"Not yet," Ray says.

"I expect he'll outlast me," she laughs. "We live in harmony, even though the Mexicans stole the Yucatán from us Guatemalans." She makes a sassy face. "I'm at this point way out of step, but my brothers still speak Quechua, the ancient Inca language. And they write poetry. Bobby and I tease each other over whose history is richer."

Ray watches her with an awkward expression; Ruby is fascinated for a moment, but then it passes.

"But why go on about such things?" She senses her, and touches Ruby's arm. "We're constantly at war, the universe is accelerating, and we don't even know if we'll be here tomorrow morning," she shrugs, purses her deeply red painted lips. "Ah, here he is," she says, her body readying for a half embrace. Wearing stilettos, she is taller than her husband, who wears boots with an incognito two-and-a-half-inch heel.

"I'm Bobby," he says, holding his hand out to Ray, who takes it firmly.

"This is Ray, Ruby's fiancé. Ruby is my star pupil," she says in proud, hushed tones.

"I am?" She blushes girlishly, after being taken aback at the word "fiancé." She never remembered saying she would marry Ray. She takes Bobby's warm hand.

"She made it from A to Zeal in leaps and bounds," Graciela says in a bombastic voice.

"Beautiful Ruby. Pleasure to meet you." He bows. He seems like the type who might give a kid life lessons while watching the plays in football. But they have no kids, and he only follows baseball. "I met your parents a little earlier," he says, gesturing toward the vast, sprawling, sparkling green lawn lit by lamps and the near-full moon. Ruby feels suddenly like her parents could be lost somewhere.

"Velma and . . ."

"*Vera*," Ruby corrects.

"That's right, Vera, and, and"—he puts his finger up, so as not to be interrupted or corrected—"Nelson, right?" Ruby nods. "And your sister, she looks just like you, only with long, silky hair," he says. Ruby squints and scrunches up her nose as if smelling something stink. "Yours will grow back. Don't worry. All the girls in Graciela's program are always worrying about their hair." He laughs thickly like a rogue.

"My hair is growing back. I always wear it like this," Ruby says with a sting.

"So," he says, cheerily trying to recover what he assumes to be her embarrassment. "Coincidentally enough, your father and I served on the same board. Only it wasn't at the same time. So we *almost* crossed paths, and then we did, thanks to you, tonight," he says brightly and with charm. He scratches behind his ear with his index finger. He turns to Graciela, asks her in Spanish if she'd like anything, she shakes her head no. "Can I get you two anything? Something to drink? There's plenty to eat in the gazebo. I'm sure your parents would like to catch up with you." He clasps his hands together like a sultan ready to command any delight for his guests. "If you'll excuse me." He turns on his heel like a soldier. Ruby cocks her head, watching him as he walks off.

"Take my hand, Ruby," Graciela says, babying her for the first time since class began. Ray follows, greeting both the students he likes and dislikes; their families he ignores. Feeling clumsy even in her flat balletlike slippers and soft, flowing, plain burgundy dress, Ruby holds onto Graciela, wishing to have that same power of being enthralled with oneself.

"Ruby!" Her father stands up as they approach the table. He gives his daughter a hug while radiating respect and adoration for their host. He wears a double-breasted navy blazer with gold buttons, dark pants, and a thin black turtleneck sweater, though the day was dry and hot, the evening sultry. "Congratulations, Pumpkin," he says beaming.

"I haven't heard that in years," Hannah blurts out jealously, then looks up at Graciela as if she'd given herself away. She isn't paying attention, since from across the lawn Justine exaggerates a laugh with the student whose father leers salaciously at her. Graciela moves on to nip it in the bud.

"Will you all excuse me?" she turns to ask, already three feet away. Nelson stands again for the lady, just as he was in the act of sitting back down.

Vera squeezes her daughter's hand, while Ray heads for the buffet table to get two plates of food.

"How is it going?" Hannah asks Ruby. "The ceremony this morning was beautiful, by the way."

"You left early," Ruby says.

"No, I didn't. I had to rush to a meeting right afterward, but I didn't miss the ceremony. We hugged and kissed, remember?"

"Is there any chocolate here?"

"Sure, baby, there's all kinds of chocolate on the dessert table," Nelson says, patting his full stomach.

"Ray and I brought Graciela some chocolate. Guess that is the last thing she needs. Some wine too," Ruby says, swallowing, looking at each of them with a worried look. "Red."

"What's the matter now?" Vera asks. "I think you need a break from your landlord and that Abbie girl. Don't know *where* they're coming from," Vera rolls her eyes. She is elegant in a simple black dress, high at the neck, a single strand of topaz beads. Her short hair perfectly coiffed.

"Abbie's encouraging my drawing, Mom," Ruby says flatly. "Anyway, we're at the beach. Graciela mentioned this old potter who lives in Ojai where Ray and I might be moving to."

"Ojai?" Nelson screws his brows together. "We only see you every couple weeks as it is, why would you move that far away? What's there besides still another golf course?"

Ray returns in time to answer. "It's only an hour and a half away, and it's a beautiful ranch that needs an overseer. Ruby can relax there and work on her drawing. There's a lake close by."

"The old potter lived with this man named Sing," she says. "I'd like a name like that," she says.

"Singh is an Indian beer," Hannah says.

"I don't know about that doctor," Vera says, conspiratorially.

"Dr. Ambaji?" Hannah asks.

"You never know with Indians and Negroes."

"Koreans either," Hannah adds.

"Negroes?" Ruby asks. Ray looks at Hannah and Vera with disbelief. Nelson diplomatically clears his throat.

"I wonder how hard he tried. Sometimes, I wonder, sweetheart, if you would have had all this work cut out for you had he done his job," Vera says. Ruby gets a sickened feeling in the center of her chest.

"Ruby's life was never in his hands, *Vera*. Her life is in hers. I believe he did his best, and still none of this matters. Here she is, on the occasion of her graduation, living proof of a miracle." Ray lifts his beer for a toast.

"I wholeheartedly agree," Nelson says, clinking the bottle with his glass. Hannah looks at her food, then picks up her glass, quickly hitting both once. Ruby, without acknowledging any of them, sips her wine. She then nibbles on the chocolate, avoiding her food, thinking about how both her mother and her sister can be so bad for her at times.

"This pork is righteous," Ray says, not bothering anymore with polite and proper forkfuls. He looks over at Ruby, scoots himself closer to her, and picks up her fork.

"Don't you dare feed her here, Ray," Hannah says meanly. "Not today. I can't stand when you do that."

"Graciela's hair looks like it might have been relaxed," Vera says, trying to change the subject.

"I don't think so," Hannah says in hushed tones.

"Who's the girl following her around everywhere?"

"That's Justine, her assistant," Ray says.

"Is she Filipino?" Vera asks.

"Yes, Mom," Hannah says.

"What kind of name is Justine for a Filipino?"

"Vera," Nelson says in his checking tone. Ruby sighs loudly.

"How do you know she's Filipino? She could be Indian too, or Hawaiian or something," Vera ignores them both.

"Not likely," Hannah says.

"Ah, Los Angeles. What a wonderful, global salmagundi of a city, a *wealth* of cultures," Nelson says, leaning back, wiping the corner of his mouth with a napkin.

"Yes, but all of them segregated," Vera says, sipping her wine.

"I'll have to agree with both of you," Hannah says, then hiccups.

"Well, there's nothing segregated about this gathering," Nelson says, looking at Vera as if he has hit the gavel.

Ray closes his eyes, and Ruby watches the balls move underneath the lids. She pulls out the stomach of her dress, pinches at the puffed sleeves, then sits straight in her chair like a princess. "There's no place like home," she leans over and whispers to Ray, and joyfully clicks her heels. She can tell he wants to lift her up, take her back to the beach right now, midmeal, midconversation, but instead he stifles the love, stacking from the pit of his groin to the tip of his throat. She touches the sides of his head as if anticipating the butterflies escaping from his ears.

On the morning of the hearing, the drive from the beach to Laurel Canyon—PCH to Sunset Boulevard—is mercifully not so bad. As they pull in through the gate, they see the stretch limo waiting in front, Ray wishes aloud that Jeannie had thought to have it pick them up. Once inside, on the couch in front of the TV they find Jeannie, fully dressed in a vintage Halston tailored tan ultrasuede suit, with matching tan-and-black pumps.

"I love Al Roker. He makes me feel so good in the morning," Jeannie says, drinking a Diet Pepsi, now that her gin fizz is finished. A lit cigarette with frost pink lipstick prints looks like candy in the ashtray. "Come here, baby," Jeannie says to Ruby in a groggy voice. "Give me a hug and a kiss." Ruby obliges her, plops down next to her, lets her squeeze her hand, bend back the fingers, try to crack the knuckles.

"Ouch," Ruby says.

"I'm sorry. You don't like that? I do it whenever I'm nervous."

"I'm not nervous."

"Good, that makes one of us."

"I like the suit," Ruby says, taking her hand back but patting Jeannie once on the knee, at the hemline.

"It was Henry's favorite," Jeannie says, turning down the sound now that it's the local weather and traffic report. "I figured I'd wear it for good luck. Make sure that scumbag goes to the slaughterhouse," she says, chugging back the rest of her soda. "You look nice too, baby," Jeannie says, making a mushing sound with her tongue. Ray is eyeing her, trying to figure out what she's on, which is Valium. Ruby, so used to the subtle mood changes in Jeannie—who is never quite out of hand with any drug—finds her fairly good and normal.

"Where's Abbie?" Ray asks.

"Still getting ready, as usual," Jeannie says, licking her top front teeth. "Would you bring me another soda!" she yells to Dean, who's in the kitchen in the new housekeeper's way. He enters the room in conservative slacks Jeannie bought for him, and a designer bowling shirt. He has the soda can next to his face like a commercial. He grits his teeth, makes a silly face at Jeannie and Ruby.

"Check out Ruby in a dress!" Dean says. She is wearing a black linen shift over an embroidered white slip that shows in back—one of the dresses Pej gave her for her birthday last year. "You're *rav*, baby," he says, bobbing his head, handing the can to Jeannie without looking. He then heads for the sliding glass door, lets in Eartha who runs on her squat little legs, barking until her eyes appear to pop out of their sockets at Ray. He bends down to pet her head, pulls on her perked ears.

"That dog's driving me mad," Jeannie shakes her head. "I never got little dogs, did you?" she asks Ray; he shakes his head as if it throbbed. "Ah, *here* you are, Miss Princess," Jeannie says irritatedly to Abbie as she walks in. "*Finally*, what does it take, huh?"

"The water pressure's down in my bathroom," Abbie says, almost whining.

"Then call a plumber to fix it! But in the meantime, just scoot down the hall and take a shower in any of the other four!" Jeannie gets up, smooths her skirt down the sides. She pats her forehead like a faint old lady. "Are we ready, everybody?" The dog patters over to her, and she gently pushes her away with her foot.

Ruby and Ray walk ahead for fresh air. A strong breeze left over from the violent, hot Santa Ana winds the night before. Branches and eucalyptus leaves are scattered all over the property. They wait out front near the limo, where the driver reads the paper inside, the music fairly loud. Still, it takes Jeannie, Dean, and Abbie a while to join them.

"I never thought Abbie would kiss ass like this," Ray says to Ruby low enough for no one else to hear. "I'd never dreamed she'd stick around for this shit."

"You're disappointed," Ruby says, compassion oozing in her voice.

"Well, yeah."

"Don't be."

"If it were that simple."

"Don't set up any expectations for anybody," she says.

"Easier said than done."

"I've done it for myself."

"If you had no expectations you couldn't be where you are," Ray says softly.

"If I knocked myself for not meeting the goals I actually wanted, I'd be a depressed and angry mess. So it only makes sense I keep it just as low for everyone else. You can't be let down."

"I wouldn't be here if Jeannie didn't care so much about you," Ray says.

"We go way back," Ruby says, imitating her mother.

Abbie and Dean, so familiar by now they walk together as if two halves of a whole. They approach Ruby and Ray from the walkway, Dean kicking the acorn caps of the eucalyptus.

"How's the beach, guys?" Dean asks, hitting both pockets to make sure he has his phone.

"Man, it's heaven," Ray says in surrender.

"Wha' d'I tell ya?" he singsongs, pointing at him with his thumb, as the other one goes up too. Ruby giggles. "The CD's in your purse now, isn't it, Jean?" he calls behind him, as she closes the front door, stress marking her forehead and the corners of her mouth.

"Don't call me that," she snaps. "Al called me that."

"You never said shit before," Dean says, getting truly freaked by her tone. He grabs her wrist, tries to look into her eyes, but she snatches her arm away. "You got every reason to be all frazzed this morning, 'kay? Baby?"

Young, tall, and curmudgeonly, the driver steps out of the limo and puts on a face of service. Fancying himself more intelligent than the lot of them, he opens the door for Jeannie, everyone piling in after. Ray helps Ruby get to her seat, though in the moment he actually hampers her ease and confidence. Dean opens Jeannie's purse for the CD he wanted, reaches over Abbie to play it. Abbie brushes off her brown pleated skirt, checks Jeannie's mood, making sure she doesn't want anything. If Ruby still operated in her pre-accident universe, Abbie's new position as well as the purpose of this journey would both be unsettling.

"Pop the champagne, baby," Jeannie says to Dean. Coming too loud from the stereo are twangy vocals and guitar, but a seductive and unusual backbeat. Dean pours Ruby and Jeannie a glass, but Abbie and Ray abstain. When Jeannie lights up her fifth cigarette for the morning, Ray and Abbie both bum one off her. Dean fires up a roach.

"Did you bring the breath mints?" Jeannie asks him anxiously, like a mother.

"They're in your purse," Dean says. "I'd like to toast, everybody." He raises his glass. "First to my new band, that's what we're listening to right now, The Beefeaters." He nods, clinks Jeannie's and Ruby's glasses. Abbie laughs.

"I still think that name sucks," Abbie says.

"Secondly, I'd like to toast Jeannie, who's a brave woman." He flares his nostrils proudly to know he can do public speaking just as well as his father. "A woman who's going to do a *fine* testimony today in that courtroom." Dean abruptly downs the glass and takes another toke. "Abbie, just you wait and see on that name," his voice squeezing down on the words, holding the exhale, he lifts his brows at her.

"Well, this is a superb breakfast before a hearing," Jeannie says, blowing her smoke to the side.

"A *preliminary* hearing," Dean reminds her.

"Turn that down a little, will you, baby?" She looks at Dean. "So what's this I hear about moving to San Gabriel Valley, Ray?"

"Oh," he looks at Ruby, who licks the sweet bubbles from her lips. "We met this guy in Ruby's class, the father of a student, actually. And he knew about this job in the San Gabriel Valley. There was another one in Ojai, but it looks like I might be getting this one."

"San Gabriel Valley?" Dean says, squinting his narrow eyes, holding the joint out to Ray, but he refuses. "What the fuck is in San Gabriel Valley?"

"An honest day's work," Ray says, glaring at him.

"Come do honest days for me at the restaurant," Jeannie says brightly. "Lord knows I could use your help. Got a bunch of nouveau hip dumb ducklings."

"You went for the look, didn't you baby?" Dean cocks his head to the side at her. She gives his cheek a soft fake slap.

Ray shakes his head with a thin smile.

"You'll make great tips," she takes a higher octave on the last word.

"I can't, Jeannie. I prefer working outside. I love building, I love creating something with the sun in my face," Ray says. With his beard and hair tied back in a neat bun, he looks like a young Berkeley professor.

"Well, I hear that," Dean says, nodding. Jeannie shrugs, looks at Ruby like she's slipping from her fingers. Ruby looks back at her blankly, but not because of the accident. She is trying not to feel any fear of remembering the bloody event.

Abbie rolls down the windows, airing out the haze of smoke. They ride mostly in silence, with small interruptions from Dean, all the way downtown. They get through the metal detectors and arguments over which way their courtroom is. When they get to the right one, they're informed of the late start and the change in order of Jeannie's time on the witness stand. So her testimony won't be tainted, Jeannie isn't allowed inside. Dean walks her up and down the halls, gabbing, making her laugh, waking her from the Valium, psyching her up all the way with his special blend of lover's flattery. Ruby, Ray, and Abbie enter the courtroom to listen, Ruby's face candid with interest. Focused on the stenographer and then the judge taking notes, Ruby is unaware of Ray's internal rage building in insufferable increments at the sight of Al's head. When Ruby fixates on the back of Al's full dyed dark mop of hair, she recognizes the way he scratches at his scalp in quick snatches of frustration. His neck is still thick but vulnerable the way it sits on a roll at the top of his sky blue collar.

If Ray had his way, Ruby would never be here, and she knows that. But she insists upon meeting this part of her past that made her run away. And though she'll never remember the day of the dive, as most head injury patients don't or can't, she'll continue to be pulled by nuances she can pick and choose to reconstruct.

Al's club manager, Andy, almost trips on the step as he takes the stand. His black hair clasps at his face, he shakes it back quickly, like a twitch. Though he is no older than Ruby, he looks twice her age, drained by the predicament his ex-boss has dragged him into. His cheeks are flushed a berry pink, though his skin is very pale; his voice shakes as he states his name and spells it. He knows a little more than he lets on, this much Ray can tell and whispers to Ruby. But she doesn't care, rooting neither for Jeannie nor the truth. She watches life as it happens. She is convinced that when she fully participated, physically and intellectually, she was punished with the accident. After a couple years of relearning the power of emotion, she will overcome this fear and superstition.

Andy admits that he met Chauncey the day she came to dance for Al. He insists he saw, heard, and knew nothing about them having sexual intercourse. This is true, and he wouldn't have cared to know about it, anyway. He maintains claim of his ex-boss's stability, reliability, and fine character, "particularly for this business." He says he did not note when she left, though he remembers not seeing her car in the lot a couple hours after they met. He remembers to squeeze in how "carried away" Al always was about Jeannie. When they show him the photo of Al's hit man, he says twice that he never saw that face before. The defense attorney's cross-examination is swift to reaffirm all the positive points Andy was able to bring up.

Jeannie is exactly the opposite of him as a witness. She is confident, cocky, very unsympathetic. Her language grows from flamboyant to churlish, though she naturally considers the prosecutor her comrade. She is resistant to his leads back to respectability. She says she is sure that Al took her away that weekend to Palm Springs, the very weekend he knew Ruby would be away, to give his hit man free rein over her property. With the defense attorney, she appears overly accusatory and too sure of his guilt, begging the question of what she was ever doing with Al. The defense attorney asks what drugs she was on the morning of the murder, and she puts her hand up as if to block the flash of a paparazzi. The judge orders her to answer; she says contrary to popular opinion, her only vice is an occasional A.M. Bloody Mary. When he repeats the question, she said she had one when she found out her babies were killed and that Chauncey, her dogwalker, was naked and dead in her pool.

When the judge adjourns court for lunch, Jeannie is informed that she will not be called back either today or tomorrow for the end of this preliminary hearing, which is only to determine whether they have enough evidence to prosecute Al for murder. The attorneys had long ago decided it would not be prudent to put Ruby on the stand, due to the condition of her memory. As they leave, squabbling over what restaurant and ending up at Mon Kee's in Chinatown, Jeannie narrowly misses a bad run-in with Chauncey's parents. Not Ruby or the rest of Jeannie's entourage can know that later they will miss Al's emotional interjection that after nine months in jail, he now has colon cancer.

Friends of Dean are already at the house, splashing in the scene of the crime—Jeannie having planned a Day-One-Down party. Pretending to be panthers, Ruby and Ray skip the labyrinth to their little house by leaping over the maze delineated with ivy. Ray needs more shorts to take back to the beach, but before they can leave, Ruby preens in the mirror for the first time since the accident. This inspires a drawing Ray must sit through, while listening to the distant noise of the party. Two hours and four portraits later (one of Ray and three of herself), they make their way back up the path, Ray's head turning against his will at the sight of faces he recognizes.

"Since when does Jeannie hang with rock stars?" Ray asks Ruby in full annoyance of the spectacle. She shrugs and smiles. Jeannie is in the silver bikini she wears in Ruby's favorite photo; they missed her grand, drunken entrance. Dean wears the same bowling shirt from this morning, now open, over his swim trunks. Making fun, he snaps his finger at a topless girl in the pool, teasing her into a messy flip while everyone laughs.

Having trouble backing out and maneuvering onto the street, Ray honks at valets and arriving guests who jump out of their cars with no regard to order. At the bottom of Sunset Plaza Drive, Ray huffing and puffing, Ruby takes the wheel for her first long drive to the blissful ease of the beach. It is bright orange and violet sunset as they pull in the carport of the stark white, swank, and modern house. They have spent every evening down the cliff of the rocky, narrow stretch of beach, lying in the sand in each other's arms. Ray doesn't know how Ruby plays at love as if it were a movie— a French film she was sure would end in tragedy. She doesn't know this is where she gets her awful assumptions, even as devotion stares her straight on. She doesn't know that the coolness, the remoteness she always hated in her mother is now the quality becoming her.

So Ruby plays with wall-to-wall sex in the borrowed mansion of another life. If only she could step back into her skin, feel the body's functions again, without fear or terror. If only she could relearn the powerful lessons of weightlessness during her period of lost worldly consciousness. This evening at the beach house, Ray comes four times, and Ruby believes she does too. But as Ray enters the bathroom, lights a cigarette, talking to her while he sits on the pot, she leaves the theater of romance, staring out at the sea, reimagining her death rather than embracing the sounds, the smells, the tastes of her life.

Chapter 25

Time

Ray

"Gary," Ray says, happy to hear his voice after a month. "I was just thinking about you. I left a couple messages. Did you get them? Where you calling from? Your mother okay?"

"She's fine. She scared me for a couple weeks there, but she's suddenly so fit that she's picked up and moved into a phase four in Boynton Beach," he answers, his tone still tense.

"She's a strong one!" Ray says, full of pep.

"Well she exaggerated her condition, and she always has. She gets me all wound up, and then *poof*, her troubles are over. She's already hooked up with a guy on the senior volunteer service patrol. Some kind of gung-ho blue-haired home front security. She wants to do it too. It's not love, it's adventure."

"Good for her."

"So I'm in a phone booth. Ray, I'm terrified. They found Arnie's teeth in a swamp. Turns out he was wanted for armed robbery in New Jersey, and there was another charge of assault with a deadly weapon in Georgia."

Ray makes a choking sound.

"Ray?" Gary exhales from his nose in a manner that sounds like he's crying. But he isn't yet. "Instead of any kind of closure, you know, my nightmares have come back."

Ray might be doubled over from the pain in his stomach, if it weren't for Ruby drawing in the other room of their newly rented cozy cottage, nestled in the lush and woodsy Sierra Madre Canyon in the San Gabriel Mountains.

Gary clears his throat. "Jason's stopped blaming me. But he still thinks I had a thing with him. But *you* know I never did. You knew, Ray, you knew it wasn't my fault," Gary's voice cracks. "It was never my fault." He covers his mouth, and the beginning of his crying sounds like wheezing.

Ray can still say nothing. In fast-feed motion, he retraces his steps on that February night three years ago, his head pounding.

"Ray? Are you there?"

"Here."

"I . . ." Gary gulps. "I've never told you how much your friendship means to me, man. You've done things for me no other friend would, no one in my own family would even consider and . . ." his voice trails off in a wisp.

"I gotta go, Gary," Ray says, shaking. He holds the phone so hard he hits a number key, piercing Gary's trick eardrum.

"They won't find out, they'll never find out, *I promise you*, man. God is on your side," Gary says just as Ray abruptly hangs up on him.

What neither of them know is that not only did they find two molars, but they found Arnie's coccyx bone as well. Both the New Jersey and Ringgold, Georgia police consider it a closed case, but there's a Fort Pierce rookie who'd like to test her mettle with the simpatico in forensics.

Every siren he hears rolls a boulder over in his gut. Each night he has the recurring dream: The police come to handcuff him while Ruby watches in the window, perfectly framed, totally emotionless. If anything, she appears to be relieved.

Never does he ponder, during this entire period of maximum edginess, the criminal minions who walk free after murder. Neither does he think of the opposite—the many innocent suffering unjustly in prison. There's more logic, more order than chaos in Ray's head. He knows that sludge and scum help maintain a well-functioning septic tank; subterranean termites will take the soil all the way up with them to eat wood on the fifteenth floor. Respecting the laws of nature, he waits for the system to come down on him.

Because the neighbor is an ex-criminal—comparatively trivial though his crimes may be—Ray declines three invitations for a drink from the ex-pot dealer and his girlfriend who carves and paints gourds, hanging them with palm fronds. Upon the fourth invitation, Ray accepts, beaten down by his own threshold for rudeness. Ruby always wanted to go, being bored by the middle management insurance guy across the cobblestone-walled street, a gentle soul who had kindly invited them to his New Year's get-together, which they actually attended, insulting Jeannie. On the opposite side of the ex-pot dealer is the law firm computer supervisor who hired Ray to build a library. This supervisor lives alone with his eight-year-old son who speaks to him in such degrading tones Ray found he could no longer look either of them in the face.

Ray and Ruby arrive at the iron gate, carved and painted like calla lilies. She carries a bag of avocados from their backyard. (She wanted to bring a handful of wild daisies as well, but Ray thought this was much more than their neighbors could ever deserve.)

"So how's that hybrid treating you?" the pot dealer says, after greeting them and closing the oak and stained-glass door. He adjusts both sides of his wire-rim glasses as if they were new.

"G-reat!" Ruby says like Tony the Tiger.

"I see you sometimes on your bikes too. I had a bike in Maui, man. How I miss those days," he says, shaking his head.

"I'm sorry, man, but you know I've forgotten your name," Ray says, as Ruby hands the dealer the grocery bag. Slightly confused, he looks at it in his arms.

"Earl, and this is Narine," he says, now opening the bag and holding it out to his girlfriend, though she lays on the couch covered with colorful afghans, blue light playing on her black hair and long, pointed face.

"Hi," she says, then looks back at the TV.

"Ah, avocados, freaky! Thanks much, guys, very freaky of you." He smiles warmly, looking as if he wants to hug them. Ray looks at Ruby, not sure if they speak his language. "My buddy John is over here in the kitchen," Earl says, leading them through the living room of hanging, painted gourds, one of which hits Ray in the head.

"Nice deck, man," Ray says looking through the slider doors. "The curved lines are really nice. Beautiful work."

"Yeah, thanks, brother. I know you do some beautiful work yourself," Earl says, stopping in his tracks in a wide-open stance. He nods, then puts his hand on his forehead as if he remembered something, but he's really just appreciating the view of the new hot tub. Ruby walks past him into the kitchen; Ray follows quickly as if she could catch a virus if he weren't there to protect her.

"Hey man," the buddy, John, says, a roll of flesh pushing the T-shirt up and out over his jeans. Ray shakes his hand and introduces Ruby.

"And this is Rascal," Earl says, pointing out the small, white Himalayan cat who sits on the window ledge near the yellow Mexican-tiled bar counter. Ruby pets his head. "Be careful. Never know with him what kind of mood he's giving."

Ray gets behind her, softly takes her hand from the cat, and kisses her fingers, one by one.

"Man, I backed over my fucking cat," John says, shaking his head, opening the fridge for a soda. He turns around quickly as if to scare them all. "So I had to shoot the motherfucker." He opens his eyes wide at them, then laughs maniacally. Ray looks at Ruby protectively, she gives him her *you're smothering me* expression.

"Though he's serious, please ignore the jarhead, man," Earl says, lovingly putting the avocados into a large orange Fiesta Ware bowl.

"My father was a jarhead, dude," Ray says, looking at Earl, pointing at John. "But this guy gives them a bad name."

"I didn't know that," Ruby says, snapping her head around to look at him.

"When'd your old man serve?" Earl asks.

"Two years after college, in the sixties. Did his time, then got the fuck out," Ray says, shrugs his shoulders at Ruby.

"I was in the fucking Gulf, man, Desert Storm," John says, putting his soda down, rubbing his stomach like a Buddha. "Ask me, and I'll fucking tell you," he says, cocking his head from side to side, then laughing maniacally. He pats Earl hard on the back. Earl looks delicate as he tries to recover his stance.

"What can I get you to drink?" Earl says.

"Wine for me, please," Ruby says, now wandering off to the bookshelf.

"So where were y'all living before this?" Earl asks, pouring Ruby a glass of wine. Ray takes it and hands it to her.

"We were only a few streets over and down from here; one of four bungalows on the same property. Then this house opened up, so we grabbed it. Much more privacy."

Earl pulls some Doritos down from the cupboard and rips them open. He pushes his glasses up his nose. "Over by the dam, you mean?"

"Not quite, a little west of there."

"Oh, I know exactly where you're talking about. You had some tweakers living next to you then." Earl chuckles, shaking his head.

"Man, tell me about it," Ray says, exhaling loudly.

"How long were you there?"

"Only a month or so, couldn't take much more than that. We were in Laurel Canyon before."

"Laurel Canyon," Earl says nodding, offering Ray a beer, which he refuses but takes a soda instead. "You know, I always thought that this here is a much more beautiful canyon with none of those modern monstrosities you got over there," Earl says. "And none of that Holly'*tude*, neither," he says, shaking his head.

"I agree, man," Ray says.

"But you know, here in Sierra Madre's where they used to dump bodies in the seventies, man. And back in the thirties they were dropping here with TB."

"There's quite a body count in Laurel Canyon," Ruby calls to them flatly.

"Yeah, I guess you're right. But you get more love here, you know? More intimate vibe," Earl says.

"I think I like it over there better," Ruby says, shrugs, and pulls down a book.

Ray's jaw drops a bit, she'd said the opposite thing when they moved here.

Earl's girlfriend Narine enters the kitchen. "I whisked this little lady out of Glendale," he says. She gives him a jaded smile as he smacks her butt in the white short shorts; there is ample space between her thighs.

"Cop almost gave us a ticket for skateboarding over there, man," Ray says, sitting down on a cobalt blue barstool.

"See what I mean? Place is whack," Earl says. "Too many bad vibes." He shakes his head as if he had the willies. "You two skate?"

"She's more of the skater."

"All *right*. Freaky," he nods and smiles.

Narine grabs a beer from the fridge, spots Ruby pulling down one of her many Jim Thompson novels, so she brightens up, hustling over to join her.

"You like him?" she asks Ruby.

"A friend of mine in Florida had a few of these," Ruby says, thinking of Lou. "Him too," she points with the book at the Sam Shepard stories. Narine nods, scrutinizing Ruby as if she were a specimen. She slugs down her beer.

"Y'all came from fucking Florida?" John asks.

"Ruby's from here, I'm from Michigan, but we lived in Florida for a while," Ray says.

"This fucking transvestite today, man, said she was from Florida, tried to pick up on me. Fucking chicks with dicks, man, they'll get you into trouble every time," John says, opening his eyes wide, laughing maniacally again. Ray sighs wearily. "I mean, who the *fuck* would want a chick with a dick, man?"

"Fortune 500 assholes and you," Earl says, holding up his beer and laughs. Narine shakes her head, feels up one of the dream-catchers hanging near the bookshelf. Ruby reads a few lines and looks at Narine. She smiles, a bottom front tooth tilting insolently.

Ray downs his soda. "Well, thanks for the drink, man. We best be going, got a family thing to go to." Ruby looks at him with one brow screwed.

"So soon, man? You just got here, brother," Earl says, opening his arms. His friend John chomps on the Doritos.

"Fuck, man, dude's shaking 'round the *killer*," John says, curling his arm with rolled fists as if in a Mr. Universe contest. *"The killer, the killer, the killer,"* he says, working himself up in the poses, his eyes red, his voice deep and raspy.

Ray grabs Ruby's hand, she defiantly looks back at her hosts.

"My brother kicked some ass yesterday in school," Narine says suddenly, following them to the door. "Gonna end up no good, like this one," she gestures backward with her head.

Ruby stops in her tracks; Ray wonders why she lately takes interest in stories of fistfights. "Where's your brother?"

"He's in Glendale with my folks," Narine says, Earl at her side now, but the buddy John stays in the kitchen.

"These Armenians," Earl says, squeezing her to him. "You know they can't get along with anybody," Earl says, his laugh like a scratch in a CD.

"Fuck you," Narine says, pushing away from him. "It was nice meeting you," she says, waving to Ray and Ruby, then she walks off barefoot, her thighs and legs so long and thin, the cheeks won't show in the short shorts.

"Next time we'll have you for supper. Give you a proper feeding, okay?" Earl says, opening the door.

"I miss Florida," Ruby says as they climb the steps back to their own door.

"Do you really remember it?"

"I remember the wet air on my face. I remember nice friend-ship."

"Hmph," Ray says with the sitcom corn of a guy who stops reading the paper to consider what his lady says.

"Why'd you say you prefer Laurel Canyon to here?"

"Because I did in the moment." She looks up at him with her big brown eyes, then enters the house.

"And why were you so interested in her brother's fight?"

"Because my man used to be a fighter, remember?" She knocks him under the chin, and he squints at her, not sure of what she's saying.

He decides right then and there that the house on Indian River Drive should go up for sale, but he is not going to mention it. Just after the accident, the regret seared him at the thought of ever uttering Arnie and Gary's rape to Ruby. He couldn't help feeling like some-thing shattered inside her—the strength of her self-knowledge, the trust she had in her experience of all that was Ray.

266

If he sells the house, they can take the money, forget all about Florida, and rebuild their lives in California. He can put that much more distance between himself and his past. He doesn't know that the car, which held Arnie's body in the trunk, had been scrapped for parts. And Arnie never had a car—the farm managers assumed he took off on them, leaving little behind, since he was in trouble with the law. Ray could get down on his knees for the fact that Gary never reported the rape. Besides the fight on the construction site—which was one of a few for Arnie—there was little linking Ray to his murder, as the Fort Pierce rookie and her forensics pal soon find.

Ray walks in soot-filthy and late from a demolition job in Monrovia. He finds Ruby sitting up in bed, her back against the headboard, her open sketchbook on the floor. She is eating potato chips, watching *Cold Crimes*. There is a message on the machine from the owner of the ranch in Ojai; Ray asks her why she didn't pick up the phone. She says she was too involved with her drawings that are just beginning to tell a story. He asks why she didn't tell him about the message, she answers that she forgot. He says he hopes she will always be honest about where she does or doesn't want to live with him, she answers that it doesn't matter to her as long as she's with him. Though he imagines his smell is unbearable, he still sits down on the bed and looks at her with deep gratitude. She returns his gaze with the full warmth of her eyes.

He never knows exactly how to kiss her. Sometimes she gives her mouth freely, other times he has to work to find it, and still she might not give it to him, even while she lets him move inside her. This is one of those times where his tongue seeks its way from a belly of loss he cannot explain. He licks at her, sucks on her, bites and chews with an intensity of grief she seems to fill herself with. There is no blocking one another or hiding from each other on this bed, as she slides off from him the pants, thick with dirt and stink. He raises his arms above his head, and she lifts his shirt, pulling the hairs around his nipple with her teeth.

As they lie there, the come momentarily gluing them together, the TV still on with some other forensics files show, Ray blurts out, "I killed Gary's rapist, you know."

"Yes, I know," Ruby says, swallowing, then she closes her eyes as she rolls away from him. Ray runs to the bathroom to throw up, then he sobs over the toilet. He is thinking that if she had any mercy, she would come and comfort him. He doesn't know that she feels she just did, and so lies on the bed and waits for him to finish. By the time he returns from the bathroom, now also reeking, she doesn't ask for the details, so Ray keeps it to himself for another time, years from now.

Bill Sichterman's will said: "As I have chosen a life free of exploitation by familial obligation, a life neither restricted nor oppressed by charitable, political, or religious organizations, I have been free to experiment with the anonymous chain of reaction, the most superb and glorious of gods, Luck. Therefore I hereby will my property and monies to Ray Rose, whom I most happily have no blood or business connection to whatsoever."

Karma may have something to do with it, Ray figures. But self-determinism even more. Ray now considers that he may have already paid for his crime with Ruby's accident, though what it is that *she* might be paying for, he can't fathom. Maybe she believed that freedom and love were heavily taxed.

On the ranch in Ojai, Ray hears that if he walks out the door each day saying he is happy, eventually he will be. And it is Ruby who thinks they should take that skydiving lesson on the second anniversary of her accident.

"I love to watch the hawks riding the thermals," Ray says on the way to their appointment.

"I know," Ruby says. "You've said it many times before."

"I used to take my glider, remote control, and up they'd go with the buzzards who ride the thermals. You know what thermals are, right?"

"Hot bubbles of air," Ruby says, slowly blinking, licking her lips and looking out the window. He doesn't know she's thinking about speed and rush and adrenaline, imagining herself on her motorcycle, riding off a cliff, wondering what the moment would feel like just as the wheels leave the dirt.

"They'd go up like fifteen hundred feet, ride around the edge, start circling, flying with the buzzards. And those gliders are so quiet, they don't faze them."

Ruby nods, looking out the window. When he finally asks what she's thinking, she says she is visualizing herself on the plane with the parachute on her back.

Freefalling just before he pulls the cord, he fully understands the idea of a joyful suicide. Then just as quickly the moment is over. Ruby is higher in the sky, descending from the smoke of clouds in dizzying speed. He frantically calls for her to pull, and she does it screaming and laughing. He had misunderstood the madness in her face, which appeared as if she had jumped to escape a fire. Now the parachutes abruptly lift them in an awkward aerial dance, Ruby talking with her hands in a hula.

When they hit the ground safely, Ray becomes convinced there is a point of revelation, a complete realization of who you are. This must be when you reach nirvana, he thinks. His next step is to agree that this happens alone. But for the time being, he'll go on believing that he can do this with Ruby, and only with Ruby, and she won't let on that she knows any different.

Chapter 26

A Graphic Novel

Ruby

God, how I was missing you, Ruby. I kept wondering where you were. I was feeling like you were lost to me, until I realized you were lost to yourself, and needed to find your way back. I always thought the coma was when you were doing all the seeking, you know? I had impossibly expected you to come into some kind of exalted, enlightened place when you woke up, like a guru. But instead you were a struggling mortal, like the rest of us, trying to deal with the accident. And it's taken all this time, two years, and why wouldn't it?

But I recognize you now. And it's so damn MARVELOUS. You're happy and you're glowing. You should be proud of that book, it's something. I was never into comic books before, but this is really something. You got a very important thing out of your system, it seems to me. Ojai really must be the place. Though I don't imagine you guys there much longer, I think you need your own roots. I think it's good Ray sold the Florida house—I can't imagine the memories would be all that great for either of you, after what happened. But I hope you buy something soon, Ray needs to be working for himself. Anybody can see that. He's a talented, industrious, loving, incredible man. It gives me hope, just knowing men like him actually exist.

Dean's still in the picture. I know I didn't bring him up for the visit, but it's all so back and forth. I mean, who am I kidding? He's a BABY! He's been really sweet, and it's been really hot, and considering he's in a band, he still falls on this *side of responsible and committed. But I know the day will come when a chick his age will turn his head and lead him with her ticking clock straight into matrimony.*

Don't get married, Ruby! You guys are so perfect just the way you are. Why not stay lovers forever? If it ain't broke, don't fix it, that's what I'd say.

Have you heard from Abbie, at all? She's changed her cell number, and I called Marin County, but her mother doesn't seem to know where she is. You and Abbie and Dean are the only native Californians I know, I realized. And all three of you are the only ones who have ever really been very real with me. Makes me wonder how you see me. Have I been a good friend? I mean, am I full of shit in any way at all? If so, please tell me. I swear all I care about these days, is being a better person.

Al—may he rot in hell—is still trying to appeal the decision. If he hadn't gotten life, I would have gone over the edge, I'm sure of it. I was heading for it. The restaurant wasn't me, it was him, and so the right thing for me to do was to sell it. I'm not concerned that I have no pet project right now. I'm not all about Dean, I'm not all about some business, or some hobby, I'm just . . . alert. You know? I'm ready. I wake up everyday grateful that I'm awake.

I bought four copies of your book and sent one to each of my sisters, the little bitches. They need to open up their minds. They'll take one look at the first page and shit in their pants, but I know that curiosity will get the better of them, after a while, and they can't help but be inspired. In some little way. You don't know how much people like you in this world, really help give us the beautiful examination we need. Maybe that's what I oughta do! Maybe I should become an art patron, eh? Can you see me hobnobbing with all of those lunching, brunching, bitchy Beverly Hills wives? Not.

Come down and visit me soon! Love you, my little chicka-roo, J.

Jeannie, we just got back from Florida. We cleared everything out of the house before it closed. Hope—the one who gave me the easel and all those square canvases—still lives next door, so I brought pictures of my old paintings for her to see, and I gave her a copy of the book. It was a special goodbye. Who ever likes farewells? But this was really intense as we discovered a meaningful connection. There's something about her work that I really respond to, and there's something in me that she seems to recognize. Before I knew her I'd actually bought one of her paintings at a garage sale for Jason and Gary, and we didn't figure this out until this meeting, until I saw her work everywhere in the house. I plan on keeping in touch with her. She's almost 70 years old, and truly doesn't look much more than in her late fifties—if you don't look at her neck. She's fit; she's got a great attitude, particularly for a widow who was so in love with her husband. I can't imagine living without Ray, and though I can't see doing myself in if he goes first, I also can't imagine going on.

We stayed with Wanda and Lou while we were there, and they gave me the nicest little 39th birthday party. Jason and Gary came, and everybody was feeling so festive. Jason and I started singing that Vegas-y tune that he and I made up—the one that woke me up out of the coma—and we were so great together, this dance we did made it seem as if we were separated at birth. I got to feeling so high for the inhibition that had nothing to do with my impairment (as I've become very reacquainted with ego, my own and others), that it inspired another impromptu dive. Fully dressed, I got up on the diving board and with precision, I plunged in. I had to do it, so I wouldn't still have this overwhelming block to get over. Ray turned blue, but everyone else clapped, and I felt so damn happy, so FREE again.

While we sat through Al's trial I asked myself why I ever ran away from my problems. Because it was like an affirmation of a turning point in my life, to sit through it all, every detail, and go through the horror again. Had I stayed, I would have never lost the facility and ease with my brain. I took my health, my talent, my compassion for others, all for granted—and then all of those things I lost, and had to rebuild, had to work to attain. I could have died in that accident, I could have died on the operating table. I might have never woken up. But then, I also could have been dead had Joop dropped me off an hour earlier that Saturday morning. So, if I hadn't run away from my problems, I would never have gone to Alaska, and I would have never met Ray. Maybe there's a price you have to pay for following your heart. Maybe true love doesn't come without losing a chunk of your spirit. Or maybe you have to learn how not to look at yourself in pieces, rather than an indivisible whole. I don't know.

I did hear from Abbie the other day. She's going to call you. She was up north with her mom for a while, but then she returned to L.A. She said she's feeling very Southern Californian, shiny, happy in the warmth of the sunshine, and intolerant of the northern Cali superiority. (Though she does believe life is "deeper" up there). She's living in Echo Park and working part-time at the UCLA Hammer museum. She's trying to figure out what kind of business she could start for herself—her father said he'd back her. But I should let her tell you all this, I know she really does want to catch up with you. (I think she had the impression you were pissed off at her. She really was glad to hear that you asked about her).

You're right about life on someone else's ranch. We've just about come to the end of the rope, and Ray's been working his ass off. Still it's really been good for me, for that period of writing the book. Ray's now looking into working in the desert—all that development that's going on in the Yucca Valley area. Somebody wants him to build their home in Pioneertown. You'll have to come visit us again, wherever we end up. My sister was just here, a little after you left. You should have seen her on the horses. She just might have a life change as well. My parents, of course, forget about it. They don't understand me, nor do they understand any of this.

Give Dean a hug for me. I think of him fondly. His folks' house was so important for us. We needed some kind of neutral space to rediscover each other sexually. I needed it anyway. Initially, that was another huge loss with the accident. But we *got it back! ;)~ (You're right, I'm not going to marry him. Considering my ego, rather than thinking of myself as his fourth wife, I'd much rather remain his only lover). Don't play Dean too cheap, he just might surprise you in the end. After a few more years of growing up. I've got a feeling about him. Go on, indulge yourself on emotional whims! Don't hold back. Life is so ever fucking proverbially short.*

Love you, Ruby

Ruby bases her graphic novel, *Parable of the Avenger*, on Ray's adventures. It is first in a trilogy titled The Subordinates. The murder is changed from a passionate, justifiable act of revenge to one of a crazed mercenary plagued with patriotic zeal. She does not intend it as a work of irony or sincerity. She means it solely as a work of someone else's truth. Her drawings, like her old creations for *Rootown*, are childishly glossy but eerie with shadow and color that seem to morph with omen.

"It's not Dostoevsky," Abbie says to her, turning the last page of the graphic novel in Ruby and Ray's new house in the desert.

"No, it's a comic book. But I worked my ass off like it is," Ruby says.

"Okay, I see that, right?" Abbie says, smashing her lips together as if blotting lipstick. She stares at Ruby, whose hair seems to be grabbing at the walls of the saunalike room. Abbie takes a long, cool drink of her lemon blossom ice tea. She clears her throat the way Ruby normally does. "Don't you believe in air-conditioning?"

"I can turn on the fan."

"What's *it* gonna do?" Abbie says, looking above their head.

Ruby gets up, turns on the wall switch. She gently rubs her pelvis, then touches the side of her neck.

"So don't you think you should write your own story? I mean with a protagonist closer to the likes of you? Certainly enough has happened to inspire it, right?" Abbie asks, pulling with her fingers a nibble from the zucchini banana nut muffin Ruby baked.

"I already have it in mind. *The Penitent's Cycle.*"

"Now that's a dread-filled title!" Abbie exclaims, wiggling her head sassily. "Here you are in the baking hot comfort of your dream home in the very inaptly named town, Snow Creek. And you're making a living, once again, at something you love, even after overcoming near tragedy. I'd say regret or sin is in none of the above, but maybe there is a cycle somewhere." She sticks out her pink tongue.

"I'm thinking it will start with the waterfall we hiked to this morning."

"You were named after a waterfall, weren't you? I remember all that namesake fuss you and Ray went on and on about the night you met."

"Yeah," Ruby says, her smile breaking since she can't remember that night. "It's the reason we chose this area—a hidden waterfall in the desert? Couldn't believe it when we saw it. Seems so impossible and yet there it is. A flight of fantasy, like any good comic. Her name's Mary, and she'll be born of the waterfall, and her struggles will be human, and heroic."

"Good and corny. What about race? You didn't deal with it much, if at all, in the first one," Abbie says, now eyeing the corner with the globe on the pedestal, spotting the dog skull she hadn't noticed before.

"Because he didn't have to deal with race, he was on top of it all! But with her, they'll be throwing it at her, all right, but she won't oblige them by wallowing in it."

"That doesn't remind you of Caspar anymore?" Abbie points with her index knuckle, in the shape of a hook, at the dog skull in the corner.

"Yeah, it does. Now that's the point. I'm so glad you gave it to Ray."

"Jeannie told me a lot about him. How he was a rescued pup. Didn't have the ridge or the perfect tail or bite. How he'd been kept confined by some sicko."

"Yeah," Ruby says, nodding. In the glare of the sun, she squints her eyes, sparkling, liquid, and dark as root beer, the lashes thick with curl.

"It's funny Jeannie let him get away with a name that didn't begin with an *R*."

"Yeah, well, there was Tug too. She named them all," Ruby says.

"I know. But I would have spelled it with a *K*—I don't believe in the legend of that Hauser boy, anyway."

"And if you did, you'd figure out the way he brought the situation upon himself."

At once Abbie winks, clicks her tongue, and points at Ruby, who relaxes back in her seat.

"So, no wandering eyes for either of you?" Abbie asks, now taking a big bite of the muffin, then rubbing her fingers together, flicking away the crumbs.

"Nope," Ruby says, imitating her father.

"No hot chicks in the neighborhood?" Abbie cocks her head, wipes the corner of her mouth. Ruby presents her middle finger. "So why do you have all those cut-out babes from magazines over your drawing table?"

"Don't talk with your mouth full."

Abbie chews dramatically, then swallows just as much so. "Why do you have all those babes hanging over your drawing table?" she enunciates.

"Why do you think? There are men there too! I use them as models for the drawings. Duh." Ruby flares her nostrils for emphasis.

"You never did that before," she says in a teasing tone.

"I wasn't doing graphic novel drawings before, now was I?"

"No. All the same, there's more than *four* pictures of the same girl," Abbie points at Ruby again. "Is that the actress you were involved with?"

"No, you'd recognize her," Ruby says in a bored tone, because she can't really recall any of her past lovers, although she does remember the girl who told her she could never truly love herself if she'd never gone down on a woman. Ruby didn't sleep with that girl, but she remembers naïvely taking on the challenge.

"So who *is* the girl all over the wall?"

"She's my waterfall Mary's body double!" Ruby answers loudly.

"Okay, I give up. So your playing days are over," Abbie says, putting up her hands.

"When did you ever know me to *play?*"

"I didn't. I'm just saying, okay, so you're really married."

"We're not married."

"You know what I mean," Abbie says, trying to put her chin on her collarbone.

"You're so weird," Ruby says, shaking her head.

Abbie licks her lips, looks at her lap, then deviously puckers. Fraught with purpose, she looks up at Ruby. "Did you ever have sex with Jeannie?"

"No!" Ruby snaps too loudly, and as if blighted by blasphemy.

"Why not? I did." Abbie pushes up the nose of her glasses, folds her arms.

"Don't tell me about it," Ruby says, looking disturbed. "Does Dean know about it?" her voice cracks.

"He should, he was there."

"Don't tell me any more," Ruby says, sticking her fingers in her ears.

"It was the night of the Day-One-Down party—"

"La, la-la, la, la-la," Ruby says, squeezing her eyes shut, rotating her head. Abbie grabs her hands.

"Okay, okay! Subject change, right?"

Ruby opens her eyes slowly, theatrically, taking the time finally to behold Abbie's face. Abbie giggles.

"You and Ray are prudes at heart!"

"You think you're so wild," Ruby says, now folding her arms too.

"And so where are all these infamous desert meth freaks?"

"Haven't met one yet. We happened to fill our quota in the Sierra Madre Canyon, though."

"It's so quiet here."

"It was quiet there too. It's just that first place, the bungalows we were in, there were some strange people around. Once we moved, the cottage was nice."

"I thought Ray was building houses around here. All of a sudden, he's making furniture. And where's he selling?"

"Ray's got a little savings, and the book did just fine. We can afford for him to do what he's been wanting to all this time. His work is amazing, isn't it?"

"Of course," Abbie says. "He's a talented guy. It's just a tough business. I'm still trying to figure out what I'm going to get into. And it's sure high time now that I'm pushing thirty-one."

"He'll sell. Someone's already commissioned a rocking chair. It'll come together, I know it."

"Okay. I agree, right?" Abbie turns her head to the side and looks her straight on with her one good eye. "Are you pregnant?"

"Where the hell did *that* come from?" Ruby says, her mouth dropping open.

"I don't know. You're ever so slightly rounder, you're drinking a lot of water, you're moody, a bit on the slow side, I mean, I could actually keep up with you on that hike. You seem a little tired—" Abbie sticks out a finger for every point.

"Bullshit!" Ruby interrupts. "Jeannie told you, don't lie to me," she says, narrowing her eyes.

"Okay, she did."

"I can't *believe* her." Ruby grits her teeth, though she is not as put out as all that.

"Well, why didn't you tell me?"

"Because I'm worried about it. We didn't plan the baby at all, it was a total and complete surprise. Out of the blue. I always thought I was infertile, so a year ago we stopped with the birth control. I've never had an accident in my life. And then I never ever imagined having my first child at forty," she sighs heavily. "*Anything* can go wrong."

"I think you've already had your portion of that. Don't worry, be happy! I'm so excited for you! You should have told me yourself, you *bitch*. Right?" Abbie says, smiling so widely she slips a few tears.

Ray walks in, a tool belt hanging loosely, sexily on his hips. In a messy ponytail, his gold hair hasn't been combed in days, the curls near locked. His forearms, forehead, and strong cheekbones are brown with sun. He smells like toast and pungent must. Abbie quickly wipes away her tears, recovers ready to sass.

"Congratulations, you beautiful kept man, you!" Abbie exclaims.

"And when was it you said you were leaving again?" Ray says, looking at his watch.

"Come on! We should be celebrating, right?" Abbie pounds the table, gets up on tiptoe to hug him. When he lets her go, she throws her arms around Ruby's neck. She is still sitting, so from behind Abbie kisses the side of her head, where the trauma used to center. "I was just kidding, by the way, about sleeping with Jeannie and Dean," she whispers.

Ruby gasps like an old man about to have cardiac arrest. "You are *so* sick! That was so not funny," she says, patting her chest and looking up at Ray.

"What?" he asks, getting concerned.

"Prude, prude, prude, prude, prude!" Abbie says in the na-na tune.

Ray feeds her peaches most days of the pregnancy because Ruby's aunt said it made her cousin come out sweet. He shaves her pubic hair so she doesn't have to look at the grays in the mirror, which she can't see anyway for her belly.

No one, least of all Ruby's mother, prepares her for the lapses into emotional overdrive. She yells at telephone solicitors, she sobs after nice trivial exchanges with strangers at the store. When she draws, she can't concentrate or stay awake long enough for a movie. She watches Ray with the saws in his workshop, and sometimes hysterically worries aloud that he will get hurt. Coming out of the coma took away her original sense of self, now pregnancy returns her to the feeling of being hijacked.

The baby arrives five weeks premature, C-section. But Arnold Falls-Rose makes it through. (He actually remains healthy for the rest of his life, though he will die in New York at the age of sixty-eight in a taxicab accident.) Troubled by the intense pain and ache of blocked milk ducts due to the boob job, Ruby is distraught that she can't breastfeed, but Ray reassures her with an endless source of nurturing strength. Arnold is so tiny she's afraid to take her eye away; she becomes so anxious that Ray does most of the holding, bathing, burping, and diaper changing. After a while, she is convinced that Arnold prefers getting the bottle from Ray, which finally brings her up to the challenge of proving she's the mother.

Gary and Jason come to visit when he's well into his second

month and Ruby's well out of the danger of a postpartum depression. One night in the rocking chair, Jason falls asleep securely holding the baby in the crook of his neck, and from this bond he becomes so attached to little Arnold that he later obsessively sends gifts when there is no occasion for it. For a while he remains as freaked as Gary that they could have given the baby such a name. Since his middle name is Ray, Jason and Gary call him Baby Ray, (though he ends up going as Arnie well past his teens).

When adding a box of twelve-month outgrown baby clothes to the attic, Ruby discovers a box of Ray's old letters. There are sexy cards from his third wife, unopened divorce proceedings from the second, though nothing to find of the first. As she keeps digging, she feels a dread so deep it could move her bowels. There are many letters with photographs from internet lonely hearts he'd courted. He was an equal opportunity dater, not a single girl is remotely alike. She checks and rechecks the dates; all envelopes are stamped after the period of his second divorce. Because she'd had no jealous horror with him since her immediate imaginings during the first months they were together, the letters static through her with electric current.

The baby sleeps soundly as she rages in his workroom—Ray pink with shock until he numbs with an almost arrogant relief that now not a single secret exists. And as she can't believe he even kept the letters, he tells her he now knows why he did. There is nothing unknown between them. Though he is never one to sit too long at the computer, after the discovery of this past, Ruby no longer trusts him. This is too bad, because never again (since the sharp post pain of the second divorce) did a chat room ever tempt him.

Ruby realizes the place jealousy always had with them—in spite of her free spirit, she needs to feel his longing to possess her. For this revs her up to spark long periods of hot sex.

By the time Arnold is two, Ruby completes the second graphic novel, which makes some money for them, though a third less than the first. No longer busting his ass on construction, an artful and skilled craftsman on his own good time, Ray is just as fulfilled by being as much of a mommy as a daddy. Arnold is a dream child—

restful, cheerful, quick, and reasonably obedient. Ruby soon slips into the traditionally spoiled role of sole woman in the house. But there is never a question of which two are the lovers.

Raising a son, Ruby assumes his experiences might bring back her childhood into keener focus. But watching her sister Hannah with him—so natural she appears to make a better mother—at times she doesn't recognize either of them. Arnold's observations, his wanderings on the lunar landscape of the desert, inspire Ruby's vivid chameleon dreams. She is a different person every night, male or female, young or old. She doesn't remember that before Alaska her dreams featured speed and height—climbing, rising, flying. During the coma, and the canoe she became, descent was the perpetual swim into the self. Any marvels Arnold illuminates, all the stunts and field goals he achieves, intensify her night visions of others, rather than that of her own history.

She pulls out the skateboard and goes for long rides alone. She feels again the lovely hold of balance, and the freedom of speed. She realizes what no longer captures her attention—the obsessive need for self-analysis. To be called Mama or Babe is no compromise to her identity, small facets that they are. And they can't compare to the trap of ego, which she wants to let go altogether.

This is the base of her desire, to create or to love without worrying for the returns. She doesn't have the longing as she did before Ray, but her spirit still craves the key to all mystery. How to question when there is no resolution? She doesn't remember as a kid her relief that there were no definite answers (as in mathematics) to the most important things. By the time Arnold is five, she moves closer to the realization that everything she wants, she already has. This feeling of loss and low self-worth—due to the previous facility of her brain—vanishes with this revelation.

Each day that Ruby walks out of the door, she remembers to claim happiness. It is like meditation, but she would never call it that. Ray does too, as he is the one who first heard of the practice. And as they negotiate on contentment's terms, they learn joy.

A Note on the Author

Lisa Teasley is a native of Los Angeles, where she currently lives and works as a writer and fine artist. Her debut collection of stories, *Glow in the Dark*, won the 2002 Gold Pen Award and the Pacificus Foundation Award. Her home on the Web is www.lisateasley.com.